THE LONE TEXAN

**Center Point
Large Print**

Also by Jodi Thomas
and available from Center Point Large Print:

Rewriting Monday
Tall, Dark, and Texan
Twisted Creek
Texas Princess

**This Large Print Book carries the
Seal of Approval of N.A.V.H.**

THE LONE TEXAN

JODI THOMAS

CENTER POINT PUBLISHING
THORNDIKE, MAINE

This Center Point Large Print edition
is published in the year 2010 by arrangement with
The Berkley Publishing Group,
a member of Penguin Group (USA) Inc.

The text of this Large Print edition is unabridged.
In other aspects, this book may vary
from the original edition.
Printed in the United States of America
on permanent paper.
Set in 16-point Times New Roman type.

ISBN: 978-1-60285-670-7

Library of Congress Cataloging-in-Publication Data

Thomas, Jodi.
  The lone Texan / Jodi Thomas. -- Center point large print ed.
    p. cm.
  ISBN 978-1-60285-670-7 (lib. bdg : alk. paper)
  1. Widows--Fiction. 2. Texas--Fiction. 3. Large type books. I. Title.
  PS3570.H5643L66 2010
  813'.54--dc22
2009042870

PROLOGUE

Whispering Mountain Ranch
September 12, 1859

LATE SUMMER STILL HUNG WARM IN THE night, even though a few of the leaves on the live oaks along the hills had begun to change. Drummond Roak walked silently down the hallway of the McMurray ranch house toward the main study, where all records and correspondence were stored.

He knew he didn't need to be quiet. The family was in town at the fall school welcome, and Martha, the housekeeper, had retired before dark to her cottage over by the pond. Drum had seen her light go out and knew that, as always, Martha went to bed with the sun.

Smiling, he thought of all the years he'd moved through the rooms of this house, sometimes by invitation, sometimes out of curiosity, and once in a while out of need to check on Sage. He'd been here so often, he thought of this place as home.

The McMurrays would be surprised to learn that the night they'd first caught him on their land, he hadn't been stealing horses but books. Books he couldn't read. Teagen, the head of the clan, would never have caught him if Drum hadn't been afraid the books he carried would be ruined if he jumped into the water. He'd hidden them in the brush by the river and faced Teagen.

Even as a boy Drum had loved the McMurray horses, craved their books, and longed for their sister. All three were perfectly good reasons to kill him by McMurray standards.

At six foot one, he no longer fit through the thin study windows, so about the time he turned seventeen, he'd chosen to come in through the mud room off the kitchen. On a ranch as protected by hills and rivers as any fort by a hundred troops, no one had ever thought to put a lock on the door.

Moving past Sage's old room, he forced himself not to look in. When the only sister of the McMurray men left to go back East to medical school, the wives had changed her room into a sewing area.

He hated the change. He wanted it to be as it was, looking like she might walk in at any moment. She'd been gone three years, six months, and a few days, as long as he was counting. The ache for her had never changed. She was his one dream, his one passion, his one goal.

He smiled. That kind of obsession would probably get him locked away if anyone knew about it. A man at the beginning of his twenties doesn't carry one woman in his heart; he collects as many garters as he can. Mooning over Sage was about as practical as planning a trip to Mars.

Only for Drum, there was no one else he wanted and only one dream he'd fight for.

Moving to the study, he crossed to the desk and leafed through the letters from Sage. Thanks to scouting for investors in the North and helping Texas Rangers with trouble on the border, it had been almost a year since he last visited Whispering Mountain. He'd told himself it was because she wasn't here, but he knew he had finishing to do. When she did come back, he wanted to be the kind of man she needed—the kind of man she'd want. Making a living with his gun was the only way he knew. If he kept saving, he'd have enough for a start soon.

Drum moved back through the house to the cellar, where no lantern light would be seen. As he crossed the kitchen, he picked up Martha's cookie jar and a jug of milk. With all the kids in this house, no one would miss a few ginger cookies. He set his feast up on a crate in the root cellar and began to read Sage's letters.

She'd completed medical school. He grinned. He'd finished school also, but not the kind with books and assignments. For him, it had been bullets and wars. The pay had been unbelievable and so had the risk.

He flipped to the next letter, all about her work at Massachusetts General Hospital, in the heart of Boston, with a wonderful doctor named Lander. He found himself sensing what wasn't there more than the lines she wrote. She was busy, challenged, sometimes exhausted, but she wasn't happy.

Drum was proud of her. She'd had the makings of a doctor before she left; she just didn't have the confidence. She was building that belief in herself, but she talked of no joy, no fun, no adventure.

I haven't ridden in months. I miss it terribly. The snow came and went, and I never had time to walk in it. In Boston the stars don't shine as bright as they do at home.

"It's time she came back," he said as he finished off the milk.

The last letter held the plans for a house and a one-page note. He almost tore the paper in his grip when he read, "I'm coming home."

He glanced at the date. August 4. She was already on her way. Hell, in less than two weeks she'd land in Galveston.

Drum stood, folding the letters. With luck, he'd be there to meet her.

Retracing his steps, he left the empty milk jug beside the washtub and the empty cookie jar where he'd found it, slipped out the back door, and climbed on his horse.

Patting Satan's neck, he whispered, "Let's go get her, boy. Let's go get Sage."

He could almost feel her in his arms. This time, when they met, she wouldn't think of him as a kid three years younger. This time he'd be the man she needed.

CHAPTER 1

Galveston, Texas
September 24, 1859

Storm clouds rolled like the murky waves against the Galveston shore as the dilapidated *Mollie Bea* docked from New Orleans. Passengers shuffled among cargo, fighting to disembark before rain drenched them all.

Sage McMurray Lander walked down the rickety gangplank and stepped onto Texas soil for the first time in almost four years. She'd left barely twenty, full of dreams and plans. She returned educated, widowed, and so homesick she almost jumped from the boat and swam the last mile.

Closing her eyes, she took a deep breath of the warm, humid air and relaxed for the first time in months. Home. She was finally home. Unlike most people on the dock, she was born in this untamed land. Texas ran wild in her blood, and no matter how far she traveled, it drew her back like a jealous lover.

"This is it?" Her traveling companion, Bonnie Faye Pierce, said from behind Sage. "This is Texas? You got to be pulling my leg, Doc. This can't be the place you've been bragging about ever since I met you."

Sage smiled up at the bone-thin woman who'd

hesitated to follow her from Boston. If Bonnie had anywhere else to go, she wouldn't have left the city. She'd inherited an old two-story house from her parents that she hated and a black cat named Bullet that she loved. The thirty-year-old considered herself too homely for the marriage market and swore she'd remain single rather than settle for the few half-wits who'd asked her out. Her youth had been spent taking care of aging parents who left what little money they had to her brother with a request that he take care of his sister. He'd ignored their request, leaving Bonnie to have to find employment.

Sage had met the tall nurse during a flu epidemic two years ago at Massachusetts General Hospital. Bonnie Faye had just signed on as a nurse in a free clinic. The minute she spotted Sage, she claimed that her calling in life was to serve as Sage's nurse. From that day on, she called Sage Doc, as if there were no other doctor in her world. Bonnie's schooling was minimal, her energy endless, and her loyalty total.

Sage realized that a trained nurse, especially one who would work with a woman doctor, might be impossible to find in Texas. Convincing her to come hadn't been easy. Talking her into staying might be harder still. To Bonnie, the West was a fictional place men wrote about in adventure novels.

"This is just the coast. It gets better," Sage

promised. Rows of cotton bales stacked ready to load and pens full of half-wild cattle weren't much of a first look at her beloved Texas. "Wait until you see my home, Whispering Mountain." They moved through the anthill of people and products being delivered and being shipped out.

"Well, I hope there's more to see, or I might just swim back, Doc. This place looks like hell must on a cloudy day and smells worse than New Orleans, and I thought that would be impossible." Bonnie batted at flies with her long, thin hand as she leaned sideways to compensate for the two bags she carried, one for her personal things and one with her black cat inside.

Sage lifted her own worn carpetbag and maneuvered along the dock. Horses were corralled a hundred yards inland. Pigs and chickens were boxed in wooden crates probably being readied to load on the ship for the return trip. A dozen odors, all bad, floated on the gray, stagnant air like invisible smoke trails.

"Some say Galveston has half a million people." Sage tried to paint a positive picture. "They've even got a store that sells nothing but jewelry."

"That *Some* who counted must have included pigs and chickens."

A drunk, half a head shorter than Bonnie, bumped into her, almost knocking her bag from her fist.

The nurse awkwardly danced around him and

widened her stance. "And a few in Some's count could be considered half-pig." She frowned at the man trying to stumble down the narrow walk and wrinkled her nose. "And half-horse, from the smell of him." Bonnie stared up at the brooding sky. "Lord, make it rain before that man can find shelter."

Sage grinned. She'd made the right decision to talk Bonnie into coming along. The woman was stronger than most men and as fine a nurse as any Boston hospital ever produced. And, best of all, she tolerated no dirt. A patient, bleeding and near death, would be lovingly cared for until he was out of danger; then he'd be scrubbed clean.

They reached the sandy boardwalk and dodged traffic as they worked their way toward town and the hotel. She could have hired a cart, but a walk after being trapped on a boat sounded good.

Sage promised herself as soon as she had a bath, she'd put away her widow's black and slip into the same riding clothes she'd worn when she left Texas. Only four months had passed since Barret had died, but four months seemed long enough to mourn a man she'd been married to for only four weeks, a man who'd never once said he loved her, not even on their wedding day. In the months she'd worn black for him, Sage realized she'd admired Barret Lander but never loved him.

At the market, they moved beyond the stores and offices packed together in long rows of storefronts. While Sage searched for the name of the hotel her brother wrote he'd booked for them, Bonnie set her bundle down and watched the street. Galveston spread like a tapestry of cultures and colors before her, a place where civilization and the frontier met. There were men in fine suits and uniforms, traders in fur, and cowboys with wide hats and guns strapped across their chests.

Bonnie smiled. "I can't tell if there is a sample of every kind of man about or if this is just where the scraps got left off."

"A little of both." Sage laughed.

Carts, wagons, coaches, and half-broken horses maneuvered down the road, and every single one seemed to be trying to get around the others.

"This is true chaos." Bonnie set her cat down to push her tiny round glasses farther up her Roman nose. "Half these people need to go home and come back tomorrow."

When she put her fist on her hip, a broad-shouldered cowhand, carrying a fifty-pound bag of grain on his shoulder, bumped into her. He swung around, knocking a burly man into the street as he tried to apologize to Bonnie.

She stood, like a turnstile, in everyone's way, as she stared at the fellow in chaps and boots who towered almost a head taller than her.

"Pardon me, miss." The cowhand smiled down at her as if a six-foot woman were nothing unusual.

Bonnie remained speechless. This sudden contact with the locals seemed too much for her ordered world.

Laughing, Sage realized Bonnie would never speak to the man, no matter how long he stood in the middle of the street apologizing. Between shyness and being raised by overbearing parents, the old maid was destined never to talk, much less flirt, with any male.

Sage looked past Bonnie and the cowboy and spotted the hotel directly across the street. It was so new, the whitewash didn't look dry. Her protective older brothers would, of course, have found the best place they could to welcome her home. It wouldn't matter to them that she was a doctor or a widow; to them all she'd ever be was their kid sister.

A dog's yelp drew her attention to the husky man who'd landed in the muddy street. Anger wrinkled his reddened face, and he kicked again at a stray mutt beside him. He marched back toward the spot where Bonnie now stood. He took one look at the cowboy with the huge bag on his shoulder still trying to apologize and decided to kick the dog running in the street instead of picking a fight he couldn't win.

The animal took the second blow and limped a foot away, whimpering.

The man wasn't finished. He swung back his leg to plant another blow.

Sage reacted before she thought. Her bag slammed into the stout troublemaker at the same moment his foot reached the wounded dog. The man fell backward against the boardwalk, and the dog rolled farther into the street.

She jumped to snatch the animal back and too late realized she'd stepped directly into the path of a team of galloping horses.

Sage scooped up the pup and closed her eyes, bracing for the blow to come.

Bonnie's and her screams blended, but neither had time to move.

Like a swift wind, something or someone brushed against Sage and lifted her off the ground a second before impact.

Feeling suspended between life and death, Sage didn't dare breathe. Maybe that's how it is when you die, she thought. Maybe the angel of death grabs you a split second before you feel the pain.

But she could feel the dog in her arms. She could feel something strong and warm locked around her waist. A second later, she was plopped down on the walk out of harm's way.

"Damn it, Sage!" a furious voice thundered. "You about killed yourself over a stray dog."

Sage cringed. Recognizing the voice, she opened one eye. "Roak?"

The man before her was filthy from his dusty hat to his mud-covered boots. If Satan hired wranglers, this trail duster would get the job. He was tall, dark, and the kind of lean that's molded from solid muscle.

"Roak?" she whispered again. After almost four years there was no mistaking the wildness of Drummond Roak. His stormy gray eyes glared at her as if he was considering murdering her for almost getting herself killed. The lean boy's face she remembered seemed chiseled in strong, hard lines now. Just as she'd suspected, he'd grown up mean and heartless, probably tossing women aside in every settlement from here to the Oklahoma Territory.

She opened her other eye. "It is you, isn't it?" None of the boy she'd known remained. This man before her almost frightened her.

He pulled off his hat and shoved midnight hair out of his eyes. "Of course it's me, damn it. Teagen told me you'd be in this week. I had to ride like hell to get here, and what do I see . . ." He swallowed hard as if choking down curses by the dozen. "I have half a mind to turn you over my knee and whip some sense into you. You must have left your brain back at that college you went to."

"Stop swearing at me!"

"Stop yelling at me!"

From behind him, Bonnie pushed her way through the gathering crowd. She stood almost eye-to-eye with Drummond Roak. "Who is this man, Dr. Lander? He can't talk to you like this. I won't stand for it." There was no doubt Bonnie thought she could straighten him out with a few words.

Sage almost laughed. Bonnie saw herself as not only nurse but bodyguard. As far as Sage knew, the nurse had never met anyone who didn't bend to what the hospital called her "sergeant tone." Sage had seen entire waiting rooms grow silent at her order, but Nurse Bonnie Faye had never encountered Drummond Roak.

He turned toward the nurse before spitting his words out. "Who am I? Who in the hell are you?"

Sage faced them both, her anger blending with embarrassment as a crowd gathered. "He's a dirty, foulmouthed kid named Drummond Roak," she answered before Bonnie could defend herself, "who has been driving me mad since he was no more than half-grown. I thought I would have at least a few months' peace before I ran into him again." Sage glared at Roak as if she were six feet tall and not barely over five, but to Bonnie she said, "I don't need protection from this man. I only need distance." She shoved the rock-hard wall of his chest one last time for good measure as though she believed she could budge him.

"I just saved your life, Sage!" Drum shouted. "The least you could do is thank me before you start insulting me."

"Stop yelling at me." She poked him with her finger as if it were a saber.

"Stop calling me a kid." He shoved her hand away, but it swung back.

She had to admit there was little of the boy she'd

known standing before her. She was three years older than he was, but he'd never acknowledged the difference that made between them. He'd stolen a kiss from her when he'd been fifteen and always told her that someday she'd be his. Looking at him now, she realized how ridiculous his dream had been. In the years since her brother Teagen had caught him sneaking onto their ranch, from his dress Drum hadn't changed much from the dirty, wild kid raised in an outlaw camp. He looked like he belonged back in the lawless wilderness he'd come from.

Bonnie finally found her voice. "You're Drummond? The Drum that the doctor has told everyone about for years? The boy who tried to fight her big brother, a man twice your age and size? The kid who can swim the Guadalupe River to climb onto their ranch at Whispering Mountain? The Drum who fought with them against invaders and swore he'd die with the McMurrays if need be?"

"Who are you, lady?" Drum asked. "How do you know about me?"

"I'm Bonnie Faye Pierce, Dr. Lander's assistant." Bonnie stood tall. "You got to be Drum Roak. She said you had the gray eyes of a wolf."

Sage wished she could take back every word she'd ever said about Texas. She'd thought the stories on cold winter nights at the hospital were harmless. Everyone seemed to think they were just adventures in fiction. Now, Bonnie was staring at Roak as if he were a hero from a novel come to life.

He lowered his voice and frowned. "Who is Dr. Lander?"

Sage knew it was time to mention what she'd left out of her letters to her brothers. She only wished she were telling them first and not Roak. "I married five months ago. My name is Lander now."

His stormy eyes flashed for a moment with something that might have been pain. "You're married?" he said. He straightened and added, "You're Dr. Lander?" All emotion suddenly was gone from his voice.

"Widowed," she answered.

Eyes that had drunk in the wonder and sadness of the world when he'd been younger showed no sign of feeling anything now, and Sage realized that standing before her was a stranger she didn't know at all.

The dog moved in her arms. She said in the level tone of a professional, "We need to move someplace where I can have a look at this animal."

Roak stood stone still, and she knew if she wanted his help, she'd have to ask.

Biting her lip, she said, "Drum, will you see us safely across the street?"

He nodded, silently accepting her tacit apology. He reached for her bag and would have lifted both of Bonnie's as well, but the nurse grabbed the carrying cage. "I'll handle Bullet."

Roak raised an eyebrow but didn't comment.

They dodged their way across the street and into the alley beside the hotel.

"You can see to the dog in the washroom out back," Drum said over his shoulder. "I'll drop your bags at the front desk and tell them you'll be by later to pick them up along with the key." He reached for the cat, but Bonnie was not willing to hand her pet over to a stranger, even if she had heard stories about his bravery.

Roak seemed to understand, for he nodded. "Then I'll be on my way, Dr. Lander. Miss Pierce."

Sage wanted to yell at him a little longer, but the whimpering dog in her arms demanded her attention. After taking a few steps toward the back entrance, Sage looked over her shoulder belatedly to thank him, but Drummond was already gone. Apparently he wanted no more of her than she wanted of him.

CHAPTER 2

Drummond Roak dropped the luggage at the desk and stormed out. Over the years he'd thought of a hundred things he'd say to Sage McMurray if he ever saw her again. He'd even thought of a few things he wouldn't mind doing.

That had all changed. Nothing today had gone like he'd planned. Much as he wanted to blame her, he knew the fault lay with him. He'd been so frightened when he saw her about to be hurt that he boiled over in anger, and she'd answered in kind.

Part of him wanted to grab her and say simply that it was about time she came back. He'd waited for her. Dear God, how he'd waited for her.

Time may have passed, but she was never far from his thoughts. He could have filled an entire book with the dreaming he'd had of her. Apparently, he was never even a footnote in her life.

Sage would be far too busy with the mutt to worry about her own comfort, so he'd ordered her a bath and tea sent to her room once she arrived. Evidently she was still picking up strays. Drum figured he was probably only one of hundreds.

Crossing the street again, he retrieved his horse and headed for the first bathhouse he could find. He hadn't expected to see her five minutes after he hit town. He'd thought he would at least have time to clean up and shave.

He swore under his breath. It had been years, and she still looked at him as if he were the scrawny, wild kid they'd tied in their barn when they caught him on their land. He'd proven his worth to her family a dozen times over the years, but that hadn't changed a thing in her eyes.

Drum tossed four bits on the table at the bath-house door. "Hot water, lots of it, and whiskey."

The old man behind the table nodded and pointed to the third door. Half door really, for a foot at both the top and bottom had been sawed off. The bottom was left open so the bathwater could run out and the top so that the owner could know what was going on in his establishment. The old guy looked like he allowed pretty much everything, but he'd want a price for anything more than a bath.

Drum slammed the flimsy door closed and dropped his saddlebags on the bench. He pulled out his fine tailored black shirt and pants and the leather vest he'd planned to be wearing when he saw Sage. He had a new hat with a silver band hanging on a peg at the Ranger station a few blocks away. She wouldn't have thought him a kid if she'd seen him dressed up.

He stripped off his filthy trail clothes and slid into a tin tub of lukewarm water. Part of him knew it didn't matter what he wore; she'd never think of him as her equal.

Before he could relax, the old man kicked the door back and added two steaming buckets of water to the tub, filling it completely. "You paid for soap and a towel. We'll settle up on the whiskey when you leave." He marked the level of the bottle before setting it next to the tub.

Drum leaned back and closed his eyes, letting the heat settle around him. He never should have come to Galveston. He should have stayed half a state away from Sage. He'd asked for trouble and, as usual, he'd found it. No matter what he did, she'd never see him as anything but worthless. He had more important things to do than come here to be insulted.

A smile lifted the corner of his mouth. No one else in Texas would have the nerve to insult him but Sage.

"You want me to wash your back?" A woman's voice jarred him from his thoughts. A round head covered in orange curls popped just above the door.

Normally, he would have said no, but today, he nodded once.

A stout woman in her thirties squeezed along the side of the tub. She had soap in one hand and a scrub brush in the other. She smiled and began her work. Within seconds, the front of her blouse was soaking wet, showing her wares, and her washing had become stroking.

When her hand dipped beneath the water, Drum pushed her away gently. "Thanks for the scrub, but I can do the rest."

She winked. "Are you sure? I don't mind. With a man built like you, it would be a pleasure."

He reached across to the coins lying next to his guns and tossed her one. "Thanks for the offer, but no thanks."

She looked disappointed.

Drum dropped his head into the water. When he raised it again, she was gone.

He grinned, wondering how much of her desire

was spurred by the need of money. Leaning back in the water, he took a long drink of whiskey and tried to imagine Sage offering to wash his back.

Not likely.

He knew he was wild. How could he not be? He would have had better parenting if he'd been raised by wolves. His mother never even attempted to tell him which one of the bandits who lived in the hole of a town where he was born had been his father. She'd lifted her skirt so often for the price of a drink that most of the time she was so drunk she didn't remember having a child and never thought of caring for one. Other boys had mates; his first memories were of fighting the stray dogs in the camp for food.

Drum let the past he usually kept tucked away flow through his mind: the time he'd been five and had been beaten because he couldn't hold the target still so the drunks in the camp could fire, winter months when he'd hidden in the wood by the fire for warmth, cleaning up his mother when she threw up on herself.

He hadn't even cried when she'd died. He hadn't cared. He'd thought women were useless creatures. Or at least he had until he'd stumbled onto the McMurray Ranch.

Teagen McMurray had caught him trespassing and tied him up for the sheriff. But while he'd waited in the barn, he'd seen a way of life unlike anything he'd ever known. The McMurray men were strong and hard, but they protected and cherished their women, and the women, right down to the housekeeper, cared for others, even him.

Drum had been wiry thin and not fully grown, but they'd fed him and put blankets over him to keep him warm. Sage had doctored his wounds as if it mattered to her whether he lived or died. To this day, he could still remember the feel of her gentle fingers on his skin.

He took another drink, ignoring the burn of the liquor. He'd never seen anyone as beautiful as Sage McMurray. At fifteen he'd fallen hard for her in those few days, and no matter what she did or how much she despised him, nothing changed his mind. He'd asked her to wait for him to grow up so he could be her man, and she'd laughed at him.

He poured another drink, realizing she was probably still laughing at him.

Now she was back in Texas about the time he'd forgotten how many times she'd pushed even his friendship away. She'd married someone else, just like he'd feared she would. She'd never given a moment's thought to waiting for him.

Drum stared at the ceiling. Hell, she'd probably come back to Texas just to remind him how there would never be anything between them.

"Roak!" Like a cannon shot, a booming voice filled the outer room. "You in there?" The door flew open so hard it hit the wall, rattling the entire building.

"What did I get," Roak complained, "a swinging door on this bath?"

Captain Turner Harmon walked in as if he'd been invited. He was tall, with a barrel chest and a good salting of silver hair. His sun-wrinkled face made him seem ageless and indestructible.

The big man didn't bother to close the door. "I thought I'd find you here. I saw that devil of a black horse you ride. There's not another one like him in the state. I figure if Satan's tied up in front of this dump, you can't be far."

Drum glared at the head of the Texas Rangers. "I'm not here. Every time I see you, I wrestle with Death and his brothers. Get out, Harmon. I'm taking a bath."

Apparently Captain Harmon was deaf, for he showed no sign of being offended. "You look clean enough. Get dressed, Roak. I need you and that lightning gun of yours."

Roak lifted the whiskey bottle as casually as if they were simply having a drink. "And I've got plans in town tonight."

"Meet me out front. You've got five minutes," the big man ordered. "Your plans can wait. We've got a real problem, son."

The half-empty whiskey bottle hit the door just as the captain stepped out.

Turner's laughter echoed through the bathhouse. "I'll take that as a 'Yes, sir.'"

"Take it any way you like," Roak shouted back.

"I'll pay for the bottle while you dress." Turner's words lowered to be deadly serious. "Lives depend on you tonight, Drummond. You've no time to waste."

Drum stepped out of the tub and grabbed a towel. He wanted to go back to Sage all cleaned up, but she'd probably only insult him again. Maybe, after talking to her for ten minutes, it was already time to put some space between them. At this rate, they'd spend most of their lives avoiding one another.

He pulled clean trail clothes from his saddlebags and shoved his fine duds back inside. When it came right down to it, risking his life fighting beside the Rangers was probably safer than trying to get Sage to go to dinner with him. He might as well go fight and worry about her destroying him later. Maybe, if he got lucky, he'd manage to get himself killed before he caught up with her again.

Strapping on his holster, he shoved his dripping hair back and could think of nothing but her. He'd find Sage later, and he'd say a few of the things he'd thought about saying to her if he had to hold her at gunpoint to do it. Turner wouldn't have come after him if it wasn't something important. The captain was right; Sage could wait a few more days.

As he walked out of the bathhouse, he thought of her in black. Maybe he should give her time to mourn before he did what he'd thought of doing since the first time he'd seen her. He had told her that night in the barn that he would make her his woman someday, and the years hadn't changed his mind.

Now the biggest problem he faced seemed to be changing hers.

CHAPTER 3

THE PATTERSON GRAND HOTEL STOOD LIKE a castle between smaller, duller hotels and storefronts. Sage couldn't believe she was smuggling a stray dog up to the third floor of one of Galveston's best, but there was no helping what had to be done.

The poor animal was too weak to take care of himself, and someone would only shoot him if they saw him hobbling down the street. She'd never doctored anything but humans and horses, but she guessed the dog had a few broken ribs. He'd whimpered until she'd bandaged him. His filthy black coat looked even dirtier with the white cotton wrapped around his thin body.

When she'd left him with Bonnie and circled around to the front desk to pick up her key, she'd been surprised that Drum had ordered a bath and tea to be sent up as soon as she arrived.

The clerk apologized that there would be a delay, saying the girls would be free soon and could take care of it.

Sage slipped back to the back stairs where

Bonnie waited with the dog wrapped inside a sheet. "We have to hurry."

"Can we get arrested for this?" Bonnie whispered as she lifted her side of the makeshift litter in one hand and her cat cage in the other. Awkwardly, she started up the stairs. "Because I've heard what they do to women in jail, and I'm guessing it would be double bad in Texas."

"No," Sage answered, then whispered, "at least I don't think so. Besides, I've got a brother in Austin who is the best lawyer in the state. Travis would get us off."

Bonnie paused to catch her breath. "Meaning no disrespect, Doc. I've heard you talk about your brothers for years, and I know they're fine men, but they can't walk on water. My guess is, if you keep looking for trouble, you'll finally find a problem they can't get you out of."

Sage laughed. "Wait'll you meet them. Not one man in the state stands as their equal."

Bonnie frowned. "That'll make it mighty hard for you to find another husband."

"I'm not looking," Sage answered. "Not now. Not ever again."

They made it to their room and bumped their way inside. Bonnie lowered her end of the sheet first. "I don't see what we're going to do with this dog up here. Now we'll have to smuggle up food, and I'm not cleaning up after a mutt." She lifted the cat carrier. "I'm keeping Bullet in here. I don't even want to think about what harm he'd do to that dog if he got out."

"It's just for tonight. Tomorrow morning, I'll find someone to take care of him. Maybe the livery will let him stay there for a few days until he's better."

Bonnie didn't look convinced. "I'll go ask for a cup of milk and a few pieces of bread. If he eats that, he'll probably live. I don't think doctoring a dog is much different than treating a man. If he eats, he's mending." She set the cage down just inside the first bedroom.

Sage nodded and knelt to check the animal while Bonnie left on her mission. The bony mutt licked her hand and pushed his head against her palm. She wondered if he had once belonged to someone who'd taken care of him and for some reason he now found himself alone. Folks heading west and north usually took their dogs, but maybe his owners had given up homesteading and boarded a boat back East. If so, they might have no use for a dog.

In the stillness of the newly painted room she relaxed for the first time since she'd left Boston.

A breeze ruffled the curtains, offering slices of sunlight blinking across her. The air smelled different in Texas, she thought. She didn't know how or why she believed it, but she could feel a freshness, a wildness, a wonder of the land all around her. Or maybe *she* was just different here. She belonged here. No one looked at her strangely as soon as she spoke. No one frowned at her dreams.

Texas was as wild as she knew her heart to be, but right now that heart was bound in black. She wished she could go back to when she was eighteen and believed in love, but she'd realized months ago that the only passion she'd ever know would be for her work. She wouldn't be a man's possession, like most wives were, and no man she'd ever met, besides Barret, had treated her as an equal.

If she wanted to be independent, she'd live her life alone. She was a fine doctor, and that would have to be enough.

The tiny gold band on her left hand flickered in the light. Barret had been her teacher in both years of medical school. He'd been one of the few who hadn't laughed at her desire to practice medicine. After the bad luck she'd had with men in her teens, she'd decided to accept his offer of marriage, even though he was fifteen years older than she. Barret was a brilliant man, the best doctor she'd ever seen, but his body had never been strong. He'd told her once that no one expected him to live beyond five or six. When he did, they pampered and protected him. The weak heart inside a frail body housed a determined mind. She'd admired him from the day they'd met.

A single tear slid down her face. She'd known from the beginning that there would be nothing romantic between them. He'd kissed her hands the night they'd married and promised not his love but that he'd make her a great doctor. It seemed he knew his time was running out, and he wanted to pass on as much knowledge as he could.

"Knowledge in medicine is expanding like an exploding star," he'd told her. "And you, Sage, will be part of that new age." He hadn't added that he planned to be at her side. They both knew he would not.

Sage shoved the tear aside, wishing she'd only wanted what he offered, but she'd wanted more. A week after they married, she found him asleep in a bed in the hospital storage room. She crawled in beside him and wrapped her arms around him. All she'd wanted to do was sleep next to her husband. That surely hadn't been too much to ask.

But Barret had gently pushed her hands away and moved off the bed. "Sleep now," he'd whispered. "I need to make rounds." She heard the familiar coughs rack his body as he moved away.

She thought he would come back when he finished, but he hadn't. To her knowledge he never slept in the storage room bed again. He never slept with her. He was the kindest man she'd ever known, but he couldn't bring himself to love her. The legacy of his talent was all he had to give her.

When he finally gave up the role of doctor and became a patient, she'd asked him why he'd married her, and he had whispered simply that he was so sorry, but he didn't want to die alone. She understood then and stayed beside his bed until the end. He'd made her a doctor, and she'd made sure he wasn't by himself when death knocked, but she'd never truly been his wife.

A widow without being a wife is doubly lost.

The sun slipped behind a cloud as though the day outside her window was reflecting her mood. Sage straightened her spine. Melancholy was not a cloak that fit her shoulders. She would not wear it well or long.

A knock rattled the thin door, making Sage jump. Bonnie wouldn't have knocked on the door to their suite, and anyone else would not be happy to find a dog in the best room of the hotel.

Sage wrapped the mutt in the sheet and carefully carried him into the second of the two bedrooms, not wanting the two animals in sight of one another. All she'd seen the black cat do was sleep, but it would be her luck that Bullet would decide to wake, just to pester the dog while he was feeling bad.

The dog didn't move when she laid him in the sun by the window. "Stay," she whispered as another knock sounded. "Please, stay."

The animal put his head on his paw and closed his eyes as if content to do as she asked.

Rushing through the sitting room, she pulled the door wide, already planning how fast she would get rid of whoever it was.

The blood froze in her veins as she stared at the man before her. "Barret?" She tried to breathe as panic rose. In the dimly lit hallway, her husband stood before her.

"No, miss. No." The man waved his hand as if he could take her fear away. "I'm not your Barret come back from the dead. I'm not him."

Sage tried to breathe. Of course he wasn't Barret. She'd buried him back in Boston, and she didn't believe in ghosts. She'd washed his cold body and dressed him in a fine wool suit. She'd walked beside his casket all the way to the cemetery so he wouldn't be alone. Then she'd placed him in the ground beside his mother and father and stood watching as the undertaker covered the coffin with six feet of dirt.

"I'm Shelley, miss. Shelley Darnell Lander," the man in shadow announced. "Barret was my brother."

Sage took his offered hand, noticing the softness of his skin. Barret's hands had been rough and often cracked from constant washing, not smooth. She examined the man standing before her. He wore a tan suit, wrinkled and stained at the cuffs. Barret changed into clean clothes sometimes three or four times a day. He didn't believe in walking into a new patient's room with the blood of another on him.

"Mr. Shelley Lander," she managed as she tried to think of the few times Barret had mentioned his brother. Worthless, he'd called Shelley. Worthless as warts on a leopard. Apparently all the Lander family strived to mold meaningful lives, except Barret's older brother, who embarrassed them all by wasting his life in saloons.

The replica of her dead husband strolled past her and into the seating room as if he'd been invited. "I tried to catch you before you left the ship. I wanted to explain why I'd missed the funeral and offer my protection on your journey home."

Sage left the door wide open and followed him to the settee. "I don't need protection," she said, thinking of the derringer tucked in the folds of her traveling skirt. Since she'd been involved in a stage robbery years ago, Sage made sure all her petticoats and skirts had a pocket big enough to conceal a weapon. "I thank you for your kindness." She tried to think of something to say. "And I'm very sorry for the loss of your brother."

As she studied him in the light, she was amazed at how different the two men were. He was a muddy water reflection of her husband. Barret's eyes had sparkled with intelligence; Shelley's were dishwater blue. Barret's movements were driven with purpose. Shelley swayed as he walked, as if he couldn't quite make up his mind about which direction to take.

He waved his hand, offering her a seat on her couch before taking his place as if he were the one entertaining. "Lovely suite, my dear." He looked slightly embarrassed. "I hope you don't mind me calling you dear. I feel as if I already know you for, after all, you were married to my brother."

Sage had never been one to tolerate fools, but she hesitated, telling herself that though she may have lost her teacher and husband, the poor man before her had lost his brother. In the years she'd known Barret, to her knowledge, Shelley had never visited, but the two must have been close as children.

"I didn't know of his death in time to come to the funeral. He wrote me that he was ill, but I'd had a dozen similar letters over the years." Shelley looked like he might cry. "This time I ignored the letter. I could have done little even if I'd rushed to his side, but I'll never forgive myself for not being there for you, you poor, poor child."

"I managed," Sage answered. She had ignored the "my dear," but the "poor child" was laying it on a little too thick. "How did you find me?"

He seemed surprised at the direct question. If he'd expected to find a weeping widow, he'd come to the wrong place.

"I have a friend in Boston who posts me now and then. I've been in Galveston for almost a year now, so when I heard about my brother's death and that his widow would be returning to Texas, I began to check the logs of each passenger list coming. My place of business is very near where the ships dock. I knew there would be a good chance you'd be passing through this harbor, and

I wanted to be here to offer you my shoulder. My brother might have tried to forget I existed, but I make a point to do my duty."

Sage wasn't sure she wanted any part of the man before her. Something in his manner told her he wasn't quite the respectable businessman in town, and he didn't look strong enough to be able to work for a living. He fit more into the down-on-his-luck-gambler category or worse, one of the men who posed as investors and sold free land to immigrants.

She decided to play along. If he was mourning Barret, she owed him a bit of comfort. "Would you like some tea, Mr. Lander? I asked for some to be sent up when I arrived."

He smiled. "Oh, call me Shelley, dear. We are family, you know."

She could almost see him settling in like a hen on a full nest.

He leaned back, relaxing. "I'd love some tea."

Bonnie banged her way through the door with a jug of milk and a half loaf of bread about the time a maid arrived with the tea tray. The tall nurse took a look around the room as if she thought she might be in the wrong place. When her gaze rested on Sage, the doctor shook her head slightly.

Shelley didn't fool the nurse for longer than a blink. "You look like Dr. Lander," she said. "So I'm guessing you're a relative."

Sage shifted her gaze back and forth from the

milk to the bedroom door, hoping Bonnie would take the hint.

Shelley stood and bowed. "I'm Barret's brother, and you are right, I've come to pay my respects to his widow. And you, madam, must be my poor brother's widow's traveling companion."

"No, sir. I'm her nurse."

Shelley dropped back on the couch with a look of horror. He grabbed Sage's hand. "Oh, you poor, poor child; you're ill."

Sage frowned. There it was again, the *poor child* label. "No." She pulled her hand away. "I'm a doctor, like your brother, and Miss Pierce is my nurse. She works for me."

Shelley looked like he might argue but instead wisely kept his mouth closed for once.

Bonnie sidestepped toward the bedroom as the maid set up the tea. "Well," she said a bit too loudly, "you two enjoy your tea and visit. I'll just take my snack"—she lifted the jug and bread— "into the bedroom."

Shelley watched her go, huffed twice, and returned to his seat. "Odd creature," he said as he began pouring tea with hands that didn't look like they'd been washed in a week.

The place is thick with them, Sage thought.

As she watched the man eat all the finger sand- wiches, she fought the urge to ask him how he made a living. As far as she knew, Barret's people were educated but relatively poor. As a doctor, her husband had worked more days for free than for payment. He would have had little money to send to a worthless brother. The gentleman bred in Shelley was tarnished as well as his manners.

Sage leaned back on a pillow and waited to see if he'd prove himself a fool.

Shelley liked to talk, even if he didn't have much to say. He rattled on about the history of Galveston as if he were a native Texan. Finally, with all the tea gone, he decided it was time for him to leave.

"I know that you'll be needing someone to advise you, and I want to offer my services. You're very young, and women have no mind for business, so if you'll allow me, I'll be your guide through the stormy seas to come."

"Thank you," Sage said, not bothering to tell him that she'd been handling her own affairs since she turned eighteen and began to share equally in the profits of the ranch.

Shelley walked to the door, then turned back to her with a sad expression on his face as though he dreaded having to tell her something. "One thing, my dear sister. I know you think you have lots of money from my brother's estate. I'm sure he left you well provided for, but I must begin my duty by asking if you think it wise to book such expensive accommodations. I could find you more reasonable lodging for a third the price."

Sage considered saying that she'd paid for his brother's funeral, but she couldn't be so unkind.

"Thank you, Mr. Lander. I'll give it some thought."

She closed the door before he could think of more advice and leaned against it for good measure.

Bonnie stepped from the bedroom, making no pretense that she hadn't been listening. "Odd duck, don't you think?"

Sage laughed. "I do. Maybe we can manage to stay out of his way for the next few days. Once we get supplies and I take care of some banking, we'll be on our way to Whispering Mountain, and Mr. Shelley Lander will have no idea where we've gone. It's a big state. He'll have to find his tea somewhere else."

"Sad, really," Bonnie whispered. "Him living and the good Dr. Lander dying. Maybe it's true what they say that the good die young."

The memory of her first love, a tall, handsome Texas Ranger who'd been killed, came flooding back in painful waves. "Yes. Very sad."

CHAPTER 4

DRUMMOND LISTENED AS THE RANGERS went over the plan one more time in detail. He didn't really need to know everything. He just had to know who to shoot.

"We'll meet back here in half an hour," Captain Harmon said. "I want all men sober and ready to ride. Have weapons fully loaded and fresh horses saddled. We'll ride hard through the night."

A half-grown kid stood between the desk and the stove. Fear and worry blended among the streaks of tears on his cheeks. The captain put his arm on the boy's shoulder and told him he had to eat and drink something, or he'd never make the ride with them. The boy nodded and dropped on the chair behind the desk, but he didn't seem to notice the food before him. He stared at the men in the room, searching each one's face as if looking for one who might save his family.

The Rangers collected their gear. Not one spoke to Drum. He wasn't one of them; he never had been. They respected him, spoke to him when they had to, but not one invited him to join them. He was an outsider they sometimes needed. He signed on for the same dangerous missions they did. He risked his life, like each one of them, but not one would mourn him if he didn't come back alive.

Drum told himself he didn't care. Friends had never been a luxury he could afford. Words like *family* or *friend* or *loved ones* were not part of his world. He'd do this job and be paid well if he lived. Then he'd go on with his life the only way he knew how: alone.

After the captain dismissed them, Drum slipped through the back alleys of Galveston unnoticed. If he only had a half hour left in town, he didn't want to waste it. The moon sliced between the buildings, leaving most of the alley in total darkness. He didn't slow; he knew his way well in the shadows and moved without a sound.

Within minutes, he'd stepped out onto the roof of the Patterson Grand Hotel and swung along the ledge to Sage's room. He knew where she'd be: the best room in the place. Not because she'd asked for it but because her brothers would have demanded it.

All the lamps were out, but there was enough moonlight to guide him through the window to the only third-floor room that faced the gulf. He stepped into what looked like a little living area. Trunks and scattered clothes lay atop most of the furniture.

Drum swore he could smell Sage in the air: the hint of honeysuckle she used in her hair, the lavender soap. He crossed the room, the rug muffling any sound.

The tall woman who'd been traveling with Sage slept in the first bedroom. He could see the top of her head with hair twisted into rag knots. Her clothes were neatly organized in rows on the other bed in the room. A huge black cat slept on one pile.

Drum silently moved on. A washroom came next, with porcelain glowing in the light and ladies' underthings hanging on thin strings crisscrossing the room.

He walked on down the hallway. The door to Sage's room was open only a crack, but he could see her asleep.

Moving silently closer, he drank in the sight of her like a man dying of thirst. She wore the same kind of white nightgown he'd seen her wear when she was eighteen. It buttoned all the way to her throat and had puffy sleeves that covered her as completely as a nun's habit. Her hair was braided in one long braid resting over her shoulder. As always, she slept soundly and at peace.

He grinned, remembering how she used to sleep with her hair free and wild all over her pillow. After he'd met her, he'd returned from time to time to Whispering Mountain just to check on her. He told himself it was just to see her, to make sure that the girl who'd let him outrun the law when he'd been fifteen was still safe. In truth, he risked his life just to stand near and watch her sleep. If her brothers had caught him, they would probably have taken turns killing him. But it had been worth it. Sage looked like an angel when she slept.

In those years, when he felt like he fought against all the world, those few moments watching her sleep were the only calm he'd known.

Drum fought the urge to touch her now. She'd always been a sound sleeper. Would she wake if he just brushed her cheek?

When she'd left for Boston he'd still been a boy; but he was a man now, and Drum knew touching her cheek would never be enough. He leaned over Sage and kissed her softly on the lips.

She moaned as if talking in a dream.

Smiling, he kissed her again, this time letting his mouth explore the curve of her lips.

She opened her mouth and sighed. Every muscle in his body fought to pull her up to him. "Someday," he whispered in promise. "Someday we'll finish this kiss." He'd made up his mind a long time ago that they'd go slow, drinking in passion a drop at a time, so they'd never get their fill. He planned to still be making love to her when both their hair had turned gray and their grandchildren were sleeping upstairs. He didn't want to own her, or take her, or have her, he wanted to be with her so completely that one of them couldn't fall asleep at night without touching the other.

He frowned. It wasn't easy telling a woman how he felt about her when she was busy yelling at him.

A movement in the corner caught his attention.

When he stepped away, the dog she'd saved slowly stood from his bed in the corner. Drum knelt and patted the mutt. "Take care of her until I get back," he whispered to the dog.

He crossed the little room and slipped out the same window he'd entered. For a few minutes his mind was at peace. Sage was close. He knew he meant nothing to her, but it didn't matter. His thoughts were on her as he saddled up with the half dozen Rangers and rode out along the shoreline. For once, he didn't feel the loneliness of the ride. He had the taste of Sage on his lips, and for the first time in a long time, he wasn't cold as stone.

They rode until almost dawn before anyone said a word. Drum knew they were close when Captain Harmon pulled his huge bay up beside him.

"Work in as close as you can, son," he whispered to Drum. "You have to take out both the leaders, or we'll have a full war on our hands. There aren't enough Rangers within riding distance to fight all the raiders if they get pissing mad and have someone to direct them in a fight. Our only hope is to take out Franky Bellows and the man they all call Scar, then hope the others aren't smart enough to organize before we have them rounded up and tied down."

Drum nodded. Captain Turner Harmon was a law-abiding man; he wouldn't order a man to shoot someone if there weren't other lives at stake. Drum had enough details about each man that there would be no question who his targets were.

Turner hesitated. "If the other border raiders fight, there's a chance you'll be caught in the crossfire. I'm hoping the hostages will huddle down, but if we hit them as the sun comes up, the boys won't be able to tell you from the raiders."

"I know." Drum had been in this situation before. The Rangers needed a good shot to start the battle—a very good shot—but if he were close enough to shoot the leader in the middle of his men, he'd be among the raiders when they started to run. "Don't worry about it, Cap." Drum grinned at the captain. "Just take care of my horse. I don't much like the idea of having to walk back to Galveston."

"I've got to make sure the boy stays well out of the fight. Holding your horse should keep him busy." The captain nodded and moved on to the other men.

Ten minutes later, the sky was about to color when Roak slipped silently around one of the outbuildings and climbed into the rafters of a lean-to. He had a clear view of the run-down settlement. The homestead looked more dugout than ranch house. A few small sheds, maybe slave quarters for a dozen men, maybe smokehouses, and the skeleton of a barn still smoldering from the raid that probably happened less than twenty-four hours ago.

He pulled his weapons, checked his loads more from habit than need, and waited.

The place reminded him of a few camps he'd stayed in when he'd been little. His mother traveled with outlaws. He'd been born in one of the camps, though she'd never said where. She'd had several miscarriages and stillbirths after him. He'd often wondered if the babies had died or if she just hadn't bothered to wake them up at birth. She couldn't take care of herself or him, much less another child.

A boy of about four or five opened the door to the dugout and walked across the shadows to the well. For a moment, the place looked peaceful in the dawn, except there were too many horses and saddles in the makeshift barn, too many still-smoking campfires around for a family. Bloated remains of a cow lay thirty feet away. Drum smelled whiskey in the air along with urine. If any family lived here, they were long gone or dead by now.

If the raid happened yesterday, the men would probably round up anything of value along with the stock and head south within a few hours. If the Rangers hadn't ridden all night, there was a strong possibility they wouldn't have caught up with the raiding party before the border.

Two men stepped out the doorway. One, slightly shorter than the first, half dragged a woman behind him. He wore gun belts across his chest with pearl-handled guns strapped into holsters. As he walked, he favored his left leg. "Franky." Drum silently checked off traits from a list and leveled his rifle.

The two outlaws walked toward his hiding place, both looking around as if they were seeking somewhere to talk. The pair stopped at the corner of the lean-to. Drum could see the crescent scar on the taller man's cheek: the final piece of identification.

Scar lit a cigar while the other pawed at the woman's blouse as if he were playing with a mouse. She made weak efforts to push his hands away, but she looked barely strong enough to stand.

"I say we kill her now," the one with the cigar

growled as he pulled his handgun and pointed it toward her. "All she keeps doing is crying. The only men getting any sleep are the ones smart enough to bed down under the trees."

The other swore and shoved her to her knees between them. "She's the only thing we got to bargain with if that husband of hers comes back. Our orders are to kill Lloyd and his sons. I don't think she matters to the job."

"Her husband ain't coming back." The first man poked the woman with the barrel of his gun and laughed as she tried to move away. "He's probably glad to be rid of her. Noisy bother."

"No." The shorter one slapped the woman to the ground with the back of his hand and put his foot on her back. "He might come in shooting if he thought she was dead, but if he thinks she's alive, he might try to bargain. And when he does, he's a dead man."

The other shook his head. "He'd be here by now if he was coming. Shoot her and be done with it. Then I'll shoot the boy, and we'll go after Lloyd and the other brat. They couldn't have gotten far."

His partner pulled her up by her hair. "Yell!" he demanded. "Yell so that man of yours knows he needs to come get you."

She shook her head, refusing.

He had to hit her hard twice with the side of his gun before she screamed, her voice hoarse with exhaustion and panic. Her cry echoed through the still dawn. One of the men wrapped in a blanket a hundred yards away yelled for someone to shut her up.

Even in the pale light, Drum could see her eyes were swollen and black, and her face was covered in dried blood. He wondered how many times in the past twelve hours the men had forced her outside and made her scream. She didn't look like she could take many more beatings. He didn't even want to think what might have happened to her inside the dugout.

When the short raider called Franky dropped her to the ground with a hard kick, Drum pulled the trigger, putting a bullet through the man's skull. A heartbeat later, he fired his pistol, sending the second man crumpling in a dead gurgle of pain. The gun in the raider's hand fired more from reflex than defense.

The dawn was silent, then he heard the woman whimpering as she crawled away from the blood pooling in the dirt and into the shadow of the lean-to.

He knew he should stay put—those were his orders—but he couldn't. Drum dropped from the rafters and lifted the woman out of the dirt. She feebly tried to fight him as he carried her back to the shadows of the lean-to.

"I've got to get you out of sight," he whispered. "You'll be safe soon. Until then, I'm here to help."

She nodded once in understanding as he

lowered her into an empty water trough and tossed two saddle blankets across it for cover.

Men pulling on their guns exploded from the cabin; Roak slipped back up into the rafters. The men around dying campfires scrambled out in their long johns, strapping on their gun belts as they stood.

He watched the gang run around like headless chickens. They examined the dead bodies and shouted guesses as to what must have happened. Before anyone could take charge, the Rangers were on top of them. A half dozen men rode in hard with bullets flying and war yells like they were a hundred strong and not outnumbered.

When the firing stopped, half of the outlaws were dead, and the other half looked like they wished they were. One Ranger had been grazed in the leg.

Roak lowered himself from the rafters again. He pulled the saddle blankets off the trough and lifted the woman out. "It's over," he said as he carried her into the yard. "No one is going to hurt you again. The Rangers are here."

The youth he'd seen at the Ranger station ran up to him, but when he saw the woman's face, he seemed afraid to come closer. "Ma?" he whispered, as if he wasn't sure of her identity.

"She'll be all right," Captain Harmon said almost convincingly enough to be believed. "Your ma will be fine."

The other kid Drum had seen getting water ran out of the cabin. He would have run to the woman, but his big brother stopped him.

"Where's your pa?" Drum asked the older brother.

The kid shook his head. "He told me to ride for the Rangers. I started, but when I heard fire, I doubled back. My father was shooting at one of the raiders from the trees. He killed the man, but my father took a bullet in the stomach. It took him some time to die, but he never made a sound. I covered him with brush so no one would find his body."

Drum heard the hint of an English accent in the older boy's words, but there was no time to ask questions.

Captain Harmon gave orders to round up the outlaws and tie them to their horses. He'd been a Ranger for ten years and had hardened too much to offer the boys comfort. Times were harsh in this land. Words couldn't change that fact, he often said.

Drum didn't have to ask about what to do with the woman. Turner Harmon wouldn't know the answer. It wasn't his problem. If she'd been dead, they would have buried her, but his worry was getting the raiders to justice, not caring for the injured. He needed all his Rangers to move the prisoners.

Drum turned to the older boy. "You got family near? Or friends?"

51

The kid shook his head. "That's the reason we picked this place. No one for miles and miles."

"You got a wagon?"

He nodded.

"Then hitch it up." Roak looked at the younger brother. "You go get all the blankets and any canteens of water you can round up. I'll ride with you to Galveston and see if we can't get your mother some care. I know a doctor staying at the Patterson Hotel who might be able to help."

Both boys seemed grateful to have something to do. They followed orders. Within minutes, the wagon was ready. Roak lowered the woman in among the blankets as the boys climbed in. The youngest carried a huge family Bible.

When he swung into his saddle, Turner said, "We can't wait on her, Roak. She'd be safer here than alone out on the road."

He hadn't said the words, but Roak knew the captain thought she was already dead.

"I'll ride with them," Roak answered.

Captain Harmon shook his head, then turned and ordered the Rangers to mount up.

Drum tied his horse, Satan, to the back, knowing the wagon would never keep up, but he'd do the best he could. He handed the youngest boy his bandanna. "Keep this wet and covering her face. Maybe it'll help some. Give her water any time she'll take it."

One by one, the Rangers passed him without a

word. He had a feeling they thought he was a fool. The woman had two small sons. Busted up like she was, even if she lived, her life would be one step above hell. It almost seemed kinder to let her die.

As the last man passed, he slowed and handed his canteen to Roak. "You might be needing this," the young Ranger said. "It's water laced with a bit of whiskey."

Drum took the canteen. "I'll get the canteen back to you, Daniel."

Daniel Torry nodded once and spurred his horse forward.

CHAPTER 5

SAGE SPENT THE DAY SHOPPING FOR CLOTHES she'd need when she returned to Whispering Mountain. Galveston, the second largest city in Texas, seemed made for such a day with endless shops, food vendors on every street corner, and the sun shining so bright everything sparkled. She found herself wishing the sunbeams could reach deep down to her heart.

She'd left, a girl wanting to change the world, and returned, a widow knowing she could change nothing. The heavy veil of sorrow she'd been surrounded in for months seemed to lift only a fraction now and then.

The trousers and plaid cotton shirts she'd stored away for her return didn't seem right somehow.

That young, adventurous crusader was gone. She bought tailored split riding skirts and fine, lace-trimmed blouses, careful to pick blues and browns, no black. She also bought boots and jackets made for warmth not fashion. Her life was twisting again, and all she felt she could do was circle with the current.

Bonnie, who had trouble finding anything to fit, walked with her. She bought little, but she ordered a few dresses that looked more like uniforms than proper dresses. She said that she might be going into the wilderness, but that was no excuse for not being a professional. She also ordered a dozen heavy cotton aprons for herself. In one store she let Sage buy her another traveling suit. The first one she'd worn since they left Boston was of such fine material it still looked new. The second suit was of hardier material still, made for their fall journey to Sage's family ranch.

By late afternoon, they stopped to eat supper on the wide porch of the hotel. Bonnie disappeared to check on her cat, while Sage relaxed into the sounds of an evening in Galveston: people rushing home, music pouring out of saloons, children laughing.

When Bonnie returned, Sage asked, "Are our stowaways all right?"

Bonnie nodded. "That mutt seems happy to just stay in the corner of your room and sleep. Bullet, however, is used to the run of the place. She's not too happy about having to stay in my room."

They ordered, and as they had almost every night, Bonnie questioned her about what it would be like when they got to Whispering Mountain. The plans to change a house the family owned in town into a doctor's office made the nurse's eyes sparkle. She'd told Sage of the huge old home her parents left her. Everything was rotting from neglect. Bonnie had only been able to earn enough to feed and clothe herself. She'd admitted to Sage once that if the house had been worth anything, her older brother would have tried harder to take it from her when their parents died.

Halfway through her meat pie, Bonnie interrupted her thoughts. "You still haven't done anything about that dog."

Sage sighed. "I smuggled him out for a walk early this morning, and he did his business."

"That's not what I mean. You were going to find him a place to stay."

Sage hadn't even tried. "I'll work on it tomorrow."

Bonnie didn't look like she believed the promise. "Speaking of dogs, I haven't seen that brother of your departed husband."

As if her words conjured up the man, Shelley Darnell Lander stepped onto the porch. He'd shaved and brushed his clothes today, but there was still something about him that made Sage uncomfortable. He wanted something more than to help; that was plain.

"Evening, ladies." He bowed low. "I was hoping to have the pleasure of buying you two dinner, but I see you've already ordered."

He pulled up a chair and ordered a whiskey from the passing waiter. "I guess you heard the Rangers just brought in a band of raiders who may have been the gang giving the homesteads to the south a hell of a time. They ride in fast and hard, taking as much of the ranchers' herd as they can stampede out."

"No." Bonnie's eyes widened. "Raiders?"

The nurse had an I-don't-know-if-I-can-deal-with-this look on her face.

Shelley moved in closer. "Word is this last raid was personal. They weren't just after the cattle; they wanted the man and his family dead."

"They came to kill?" Bonnie's breath squeaked in and out.

"Not just rob and kill him but wipe him and his off the land."

Sage leaned back in her chair. Stories like this reminded her of the time she and her brothers had found trouble. Every time, the fear of losing one of her brothers was far greater than losing her own life.

Bonnie stared at Shelley. "How close was the ranch these raiders hit?"

"A day's ride, maybe less." He patted the nurse's hand. "But don't you ladies worry none. I'll stay close and protect you. In fact, if you have any valu-ables or money, you might want me to put them away in my safe while you're here. I have a place down by the docks. My office is as guarded as a bank. I've got a safe shipped all the way from Chicago that no one will ever break into."

"We have little," Sage lied, "but we thank you for the offer."

Shelley cut her a glance then smiled, and she swore she could hear him thinking that he knew it wouldn't be that easy to separate the little widow from her inheritance. "Of course," he said out loud. "You are safe at the hotel. However, if you venture out, please send for me. The streets are safe enough, but the docks are not. I can't tell you the number of times I've been robbed, and I run a respectable house."

Sage was about to ask exactly where and what his place of business was, when a broad-shouldered cowboy stepped up to her table. He was dusty and didn't look like he belonged on the gingerbread-trimmed porch of the Grand, but the circle star on his chest demanded respect.

"Miss," he said as he removed his hat. "I beg your pardon, but do you know where I can find a doctor staying here? The man at the desk said he saw you carrying in a medical bag, so you might know. It's real important that I find the doc."

Sage stood. "I'm a doctor."

To his credit, the Ranger took the information in stride. "Do you know a man named Drummond Roak?"

"Is he hurt?" She fought down the vision of him hurt and dying. She'd spent more than one night worrying about the wild kid killing himself. The fact that she still cared about him surprised her.

"No, miss, but he's coming in with a wagon carrying a woman who has been beat up bad by the raiders. He said if there was anybody who could help the lady it would be the doc at the Grand Hotel. I figured I'd help a little by letting you know they're coming."

Bonnie stood, ready for action.

Shelley pushed his way between them. "There's a misunderstanding, I'm afraid, sir," he said to the cowboy. "This little lady was married to my brother. He was a well-known—"

No one, including Sage, had time to listen to Shelley's rambling.

"We'll have everything ready." Sage moved toward the hotel doors and noticed that both Bonnie and the Ranger fell into step beside her. "Will you let us know when he pulls up?"

"Yes, miss."

She glanced back over her shoulder as she stepped inside. "It's *Doctor,* Ranger. Dr. McMurray." Without much thought, she'd dropped Barret's name and returned to her own.

"It's Daniel, Doc. Daniel Torry."

"Now look here," Shelley's voice came from somewhere behind them. "You can't ask a lady to see to—"

Sage barely noticed Shelley running to catch up as she stormed the front desk. "I'll need a room on the first floor to care for an injured woman and water put on to boil."

The clerk, who'd been listening, nodded. "You can use the office."

She turned to Bonnie. "I'll need—"

The nurse was already halfway up the stairs. "I'm on it. Bag, aprons, and bandages. If you get the room, I can have it ready within ten minutes."

Sage stood for a moment as everyone rushed to follow orders. Barret used to call her the little general in skirts when emergencies came into the hospital. She'd thought she'd left that all behind, but it seemed to have followed her to Texas.

An hour later, half the hotel staff and all the guests were in the lobby as Drum carried in the patient wrapped in so many blankets no one could see her. Daniel Torry directed him to the first room on the right and then stood guard so no one else could enter.

Drum nodded toward Sage as he moved in. "She's been quiet for a long while. I don't know if that's good or bad. I pushed the team as much as I dared. Some of the blood on her belongs to the guy who did this to her."

Sage helped lower the woman onto a table and began to slowly fold back the quilts. "How bad off is the guy who beat her? I can see him next."

59

"Pretty bad," Roak said as he moved out of the way. "I shot him through the head from five feet away. If you want to see him, you'll have to wait until I scoop up his brains."

Bonnie's squeak was the only sound in the room. Roak looked totally serious, but Sage had a feeling his last words were his idea of a joke.

Sage folded back the last quilt and felt bile rise as she stared down at her new patient covered in blood.

Roak lowered his hat and backed a few feet toward the door. He'd done all he could.

"We'll take over from here." Sage squared her shoulders and stepped closer to the table. She gently checked the woman's pulse, then moved her fingers over the head wounds to make sure the skull wasn't fractured.

Bonnie cut away the clothes now stiff with dried blood as Sage searched along the woman's body, analyzing what had to be cared for first. The doctor that Barret had made her into by all those years working beside him served her well now.

She glanced back at Drum leaning next to the door. "Thanks for getting her here alive. She's in bad shape, really bad, but she'd have had no chance without you."

Drum didn't move. He might have stood longer watching, but Daniel pulled him backward through the door.

"Come on Roak," Sage heard the Ranger say. "I'll buy you a drink."

"I don't need a drink," Drum answered.

"Then I'll drink them both." The Ranger closed the door.

CHAPTER 6

SAGE AND BONNIE BEGAN THEIR WORK. THE woman must have passed out with the pain, but she kept fighting, kept breathing. She had broken ribs along her left side, three broken fingers, and deep cuts on both her arms as if someone had carved on her for fun. She had what looked like burns on both her palms and a long, thin gash across the top of one breast deep enough to still be bleeding and get infected. Bruises were too many to count, but the worst were on her face. Both her eyes had swollen shut, and there was a good chance her broken nose would never heal straight.

Bonnie washed away the blood as Sage moved from wound to wound. "I'm not a violent person," the nurse whispered, "but I wish Roak hadn't killed whoever did this so I could kill him myself."

"Her chances don't look good, but we'll do the best we can," Sage added. "We'll have our hands full keeping fever and infection down, even after we set the bones. I fear one of her ribs has punctured a lung. Out on a farm, with no skilled care, she wouldn't have had much of a chance. He did the right thing."

"Maybe this Drummond Roak isn't as worthless as you take him for?" Bonnie mumbled as if to herself.

"I know he's probably a good man. More than once he helped my family when we were in a fight, but that doesn't make him less of a pest. He used to do things, say things, just to drive me crazy." She didn't add that once he'd won a kiss from her in a bet. He'd been nervous and untrained, but that kiss had haunted her dreams more than once over the years.

Before the conversation could continue, Sage asked, "Hand me that splint for her finger, then thread up another needle. I want every wound cleaned and closed."

Bonnie followed orders but whispered, "Her breathing is so shallow. The odds aren't with us."

"We have to try." Barret's words drifted through her thoughts. He used to say, "Even if the odds are a hundred to one, we'll save the one."

Sage worked fast, trusting in her skill. Bonnie had been by her side long enough to almost read her mind. The woman on the table whimpered a few times. Once she cried out for her husband then, crying softly, begged him not to come.

An hour passed, then two. Drum leaned his head in when the hotel housekeeper brought fresh water.

"How is she?" His gray eyes were filled with concern.

"We're working on her face now. Using cold compresses to take a little of the swelling down." Sage stepped to the door and stood close to him as she whispered, "All the flesh wounds will heal if there is no infection. I'm not so sure about the broken ribs. The dark bruising bothers me. I fear one break may have done some damage to her lung."

He leaned so close she could feel his breath when he asked, "Can her boys see her? They both think she's dead and we're not telling them. I can't get them to eat or sleep."

"I don't know, she looks pretty bad."

Drum frowned. "She couldn't look worse than she did all day, and they took turns washing away oozing blood."

He had a point. "All right." Sage nodded. "Tell them they can come in for a minute."

She turned back to her patient, making sure she was covered. In truth, the woman looked far better than when Drum brought her in. She was clean, her cuts bandaged. Bonnie had even taken the time to run a comb through her hair.

The two sons, looking exhausted, moved slowly into the room. They stood three feet away and stared in horror as if they didn't know the woman on the table. Sage closed her eyes, feeling their pain. She could deal with cuts and breaks and illness, but when the human heart broke, she had no idea how to mend it.

Bonnie looked up at the thin brothers and met their stares. She cleared her throat. "She's all bruised, boys, but she's a fighter. I didn't get a chance to introduce myself to her when she was awake. Could one of you tell me her name?"

"Margaret, but my father called her Meg," the older boy said as if remembering his manners. "My mother's named Meg Smith, and I'm Will and this is Andy Smith."

Bonnie smiled as she changed the cold rag pressed against their mother's face. "I'm Nurse Pierce, and the lady by the door is Dr. McMurray."

Neither looked like they believed the nurse. "She's a doc?" the smaller boy whispered to his brother.

Will nodded. "I think she is. The Ranger called her one, and Dad says you can trust a Ranger with the truth."

They both looked toward Drum and waited for him to nod before they both seemed to believe.

Bonnie pulled out the woman's one hand that was bandaged but had no broken fingers. "You know, boys, you might hurt her if you touched her face, but I bet she'd love it if you took her hand for a minute. Your mother is very brave. As brave as any soldier I've ever seen, but even the brave need a little comfort now and then."

The older boy moved closer and took his mother's hand. He held it gently, then bent and kissed it lightly. When he straightened, he tossed his hair out of his face and didn't try to rub away his tears. The second boy did the same, holding her hand as gallantly as a knight of old.

Sage smiled at the way Bonnie had with people. She wasn't a woman anyone noticed, really, until they saw her heart.

"Now, boys," Bonnie continued, "your mother is going to need you two when she's back on her feet, so I think you'd better go get some food in the hotel café and then find a place to sleep. We'll call you as soon as she wakes."

Sage met Drum's gaze. "Take them up to our rooms. We'll both stay down here with their mother tonight."

Drum nodded and motioned for them to follow him.

"Aren't you going to ask which room?"

"Nope," he answered just before he closed the door.

Sage frowned. She wasn't even going to ask how he knew. She had a feeling she wouldn't like the answer. Moving the lamp close, she said to Bonnie, "Let's get her settled and as comfortable as we can, then we can take turns sitting up with her."

Two hours later, Sage felt the low back pain of exhaustion. Meg was sleeping. It was time to let her rest and heal.

"The boys should be asleep by now," she said to Bonnie. "I think I'll go upstairs and wash up, then I'll take the first shift, and you can sleep."

Bonnie nodded. "Take your time."

Sage pulled off her apron and slipped from the room. Part of her wanted to curl at the bottom of the stairs and sleep a few minutes before she made the climb, but the need to wash away the smell of blood drove her to take one step after the other.

As she'd thought, the rooms of her suite were dark. The boys had taken the two small beds in Bonnie's room. Bonnie's cat was sleeping beside little Andy, and to her surprise, the mutt lay at the foot of Will's bed.

Drum rested with his long legs over the arm of the settee like some giant forced to sleep in a dwarf's bed. She couldn't help but smile. He'd ridden all night to save the family and then pushed hard to get Meg back for care. He deserved sleep.

She moved closer and studied his face in the moonlight. Bonnie had been right. He was handsome, but even in sleep there was something about him that drew her and warned her to stay away at the same time. He wore his gun low as though he had regular occasion to use it. His clothes were worn and dark as if he dressed to move unnoticed among people and through the night. There was danger about him she would have found fascinating when she'd been younger, but now she realized she'd put adventure aside.

Slipping past him, she crossed to the washroom. After pouring water into a basin, she stripped down to her satin underclothes. Before marriage, she'd always worn cotton next to her skin, but a few days before her wedding she'd decided to replace all her camisoles with silk and satin, wickedly choosing cream and black instead of all white.

Sage stared at her reflection. She'd wasted her money. Her purchases had gone not only unnoticed but unseen.

Slowly, taking care not to miss a spot, she washed. When she finished, she slipped into one of her old shirts and a worn pair of trousers that she'd pulled from a trunk. Whoever delivered the trunk to the hotel must have ordered all her things washed. She could smell a hint of soap and the sunshine air they must have dried in.

The clothes felt strange somehow, as if last worn when she was a hundred years younger. Some might say twenty-three was still young, but Sage had experienced too many days lately when she'd sworn she could see herself aging in the mirror: long days studying in medical school, endless hours of work learning to be a doctor, longer hours practicing beside her husband who never allowed her to slip or leave a single detail undone, and then the later months watching him die without being able to help him.

She was old, she realized, not in years but in life.

The door creaked open. She saw Drummond leaning against the frame. His hair was a mess, his eyes still half asleep. "You all right?" he asked.

"I'm ancient," she whispered. "I don't even remember the girl I was when I last wore these clothes."

"You look about the same to me." He took the time to study her from toe to top. "I remember when I saw you in those trousers. It was dark in the barn, and your brother had been trying his best to pound some sense into me. I thought you were a boy until I got a look at the way you filled out that shirt."

"You shouldn't be looking at my shirt. It's not something any gentleman would do."

"I'm not a gentleman, Sage, but I doubt any man would fail to notice that beneath those clothes, which you probably inherited from one of your brothers, is a woman's body." The corner of his mouth lifted. "The kind of body made for passion, I suspect."

Sage stepped to move past him, thinking of Barret and how he never touched her. "You're wrong," she said simply.

He followed her into the shadows of the sitting room. "About what?"

The darkness made it easier to tell the truth. "About any man noticing me."

He moved behind her and placed a light grip on her upper arms. The warmth of him brushed against her back.

She could have pushed away, his fingers rested

gently, but she didn't. She wasn't afraid of him, she never had been, and it was time he knew. Words of anger formed, but she held them in. Drum wasn't to blame for the way it had been between her and Barret. No one was, she told herself. She'd loved a man who hadn't loved her, at least not in the way she'd wanted him to . . . needed him to.

"I'll ask again," he said so close she could feel his words. "Are you all right, Sage?"

Just once she wanted to lean into the warmth of a man. She'd had to be strong for so long. She'd had to be alone. It couldn't be a crime just to feel for one minute.

As if he read her mind, he pulled her to him, folding his arms around her, pulling her back against the wall of his chest.

Sage knew she should step away. This man wasn't the right one to turn to. But his arms felt so good that she thought she'd stay if only for a moment. The darkness made the intimacy seem more dream than real.

"I'm fine," she lied as his hands moved along her arms, gently brushing away the hours of tension. "I'm just tired."

His fingers trailed slowly down her back then molded along her sides.

She leaned her head against his shoulder and felt the warmth of him blanket her. All the months of hell she'd just passed through drifted over her, and tears she'd never allowed flowed.

When she began to shake, he turned her within his arms.

He didn't say a word; he just held her and let her cry softly. Her brothers would have thought her ill if they'd seen her like this. Her husband would have thought her weak. But Drum, the man who probably understood her less than any man she knew, seemed to understand.

He held her as if there were nothing more important in his life than giving her comfort.

Finally, she raised her head and straightened. "I'm sorry. I'm fine really."

He wiped the last tear off her cheek. "You're more than fine. You're perfect."

When she backed away, he let her go, his hand lingering as long as he could on the small of her back. When they reached the door, she turned around and faced him once more. "I'm not perfect. I didn't cry when my husband died, and now I cry for no reason. Something is cold inside of me, maybe dead. Stay as far away from me as you can, Drum. I'm not perfect; I'm like a plague. Every man I've ever cared about, from the first one I kissed to my husband, has died."

Drum opened his mouth to argue but remained silent as they both heard the tapping of feet hurrying up the stairs just beyond the door.

Bonnie pushed into the room, almost stumbling into them both.

"Doc," Bonnie whispered, "you got to come quick. Meg's awake."

She glanced past Sage to Drum. "And she's asking for you, Mr. Roak."

Sage's last thought before rushing down the stairs was that Bonnie had called Drum Mr. Roak. He'd earned respect in everyone's eyes tonight, even hers.

CHAPTER 7

DRUM REACHED THE BEATEN WOMAN FIRST. He kept the shock from his face as he looked down at her. The bruising looked far darker, turning half her face a smoky red. The other half looked muddy-water blue, but one of her eyes had opened only enough for him to tell she studied him. Raising her bandaged hand, she touched him as if making sure that he was flesh.

"You're Roak, the one who saved me?" she whispered.

"I was there. I brought you in for care."

"You killed the men who were torturing me?"

Drum nodded. He saw no reason to lie. She was there. She knew what he did, but it bothered him to talk about it.

"My boys?" she whispered, an edge of panic in her voice.

"They're both safe," Drum answered. "They're upstairs asleep."

"Good." She seemed to relax. "Would you tell me if my Lloyd is dead?"

Drum knew she trusted him to tell her the truth, and he didn't lie. "Your son Will said he hid his father in the brush so the raiders wouldn't know." Drum wished Sage would move from the shadows and talk to the woman. He didn't have much to tell her that wasn't bad. "Your boy kept his senses about him. If they'd thought your man was dead, they might have killed you and the little one."

"He was right. That was the only reason I was kept alive. They were hoping my screams would make Lloyd come in. But he wouldn't have. We knew almost from the first that they were there to kill us."

Finally Sage moved to Drum's side. She didn't touch him, but she was close enough that he would have known she was there even if his eyes were closed.

"You need to rest, Meg." Sage straightened the blanket over her patient. "You'll have more time to talk to Roak tomorrow."

"No." She gripped his hand. "I have to tell you something." Her words were muffled by the swollen jaw and lips, but he could hear the desperation in her tone.

"I'm listening," he answered, holding the bandaged hand without closing his fingers.

"Meg?" Sage tried again just as gently.

"I'll rest," the woman promised. "But first I have to talk to Roak alone."

Sage hesitated, then said, "All right." Without another word, she motioned Bonnie to follow her out of the room.

When the door closed, Roak leaned closer to Meg. "Tell me now."

Her swollen eyes were only open a slit, but he knew she was taking in his worth. "The two men you killed were not the leaders."

He'd already figured that out and planned to tell the captain when he had time. "I know. I heard them talk of a boss. Someone else must be planning the raids."

She patted his hand. "It wasn't a raid. They came after us. They came to kill all the males. I just got in the way."

He nodded slowly, trying to understand. He'd already wondered why one ranch was all that had been hit. He figured it must be the first, and others were between the Smith place and the border. Usually raiders came in and hit several fast and hard, sometimes only stealing cattle in the night, and by morning they'd be miles away. They didn't stay around long enough to sleep or to torture folks.

Meg continued, "They didn't come to rob. They wanted my husband and my sons. They were planning to make it look like a raid so that no one, including the Rangers, would ask too many questions. They talked openly about their plan because they knew they'd be leaving me and Andy dead within hours."

He thought he heard a refinement in her voice, almost an English accent blanketed in a slight southern drawl. "But . . ."

"They wanted it to cover up the murder of us all." She cried out softly as if the effort to talk was hard.

"But why?" Drum asked.

She leaned her head to the side against a pillow. "Why?"

Her voice was so weak he could barely hear her. "When the man who wants us dead finds out the boys are still alive, he'll send more men to kill them. He won't stop. He'll never stop until the bloodline is wiped off the earth."

Roak didn't understand why, but he believed the woman. "What can I do?"

"Keep my boys safe," she whispered, out of breath and energy. "Keep them safe."

"I promise."

She nodded once and curled around the pillow at her side, like a child going to sleep.

He tried to ask more. He even called her name, but she didn't answer. Her bruised cheek rested against the lace pillow, and he wondered if she'd been beautiful, for even battered, she had a delicacy about her.

Sage stepped back into the room when he called and checked on her patient. Drum stood back, wishing he knew more about why someone would hate a family so much that he wanted them all dead. It couldn't have been for money; the Smith family barely had enough to run the farm. Hate could run deep, but Drum doubted it could run deep enough to kill two little boys for something their father had done.

"She's gone," Sage said calmly as if the woman had simply left the room.

Drum backed to the door and watched Bonnie and Sage pull the sheet over Meg's face and straighten it as carefully as a mother straightens her daughter's wedding veil. He couldn't watch any longer; he stormed from the room and didn't stop until he made it to the cool darkness at the corner of the wide porch.

The town was quiet with few lamps still lit. The cloudy day had settled over the streets, and rain hung in the air as if debating falling. When this storm came, it would be a bull. Roak hoped he'd be somewhere dry to wait it out, only the way his luck was running, he'd probably be hit by the lightning.

He took a deep breath. One good thing, in this kind of night, this kind of darkness, he felt safe. When he'd been a boy, nowhere in the outlaw camps had ever been safe but the shadows. He'd learned early to disappear at nightfall, when the drinking started, and never sleep where anyone could find him.

He moved farther into the moonless night, thinking of the woman who'd just died. She hadn't said a word about her own life; she'd worried about her boys.

Swearing softly, he realized she had a right to worry. If they had no kin, the boys would be on the streets before her body was in the ground. Only, he'd asked what he could do to help, and with her last breath she'd told him. He had to keep them safe, and doing so would probably get him killed.

Drum smiled. For as long as he could remember, he'd been making a list of what would kill him. At first it had been all the animals and half humans in camp. Once he'd started to roam, Apache in the area made several additions to the list when he kept stealing their game. Then, of course, there were the McMurray men, Sage's big brothers. Teagen, the oldest, swore once that Drum was worse than any of the plagues of Israel. Tobin, the youngest brother, had given him the meanest McMurray horse on their ranch in payment for a favor. He'd been so sure Drum would kill himself on the horse that he'd slipped a double eagle inside the saddlebag to help pay for Drum's funeral.

And Travis, the middle brother . . . Drum drew in a deep breath. Travis had found him a job. Correction: the most dangerous job in Texas. Drum had made that death wish by showing off one night to Travis and his Ranger buddies. He not only was fast with a gun and accurate but, thanks to good night vision, he was as good in almost total blackness as he was in daylight.

He outshot them all that night, and now they paid him well for doing what none of them dared.

Lighting a thin cigar, he leaned against the railing and got back to the problem at hand. How was he going to keep the Smith boys safe, when he could barely manage to keep himself alive most of the time? He knew nothing about taking care of kids. The only role models he'd ever had on how to be a man were the McMurray brothers, and they occasionally took turns arguing over which one of them got to shoot him.

Even in the darkness, with his head full of worry, he sensed Sage was near before he heard her footsteps behind him. He waited without turning around until she halted next to him.

For a moment she didn't speak, she just stood beside him, then she asked, "What did Meg need so desperately to tell you?"

"That her boys are in danger. Great danger. She wanted me to get them somewhere safe."

"Relatives?"

"I asked. Both boys said they had none. They'd only been out here for a year, and before that, they were in Virginia for a while. Will said they kept to themselves. The boys couldn't name their nearest neighbor."

Sage brushed his side as she folded her arms. "Do you think there *is* someone trying to kill them?"

"Yes," he said, wishing he didn't. If he could

convince himself they were in no real danger, maybe he could find someone to take them in and walk away. But Drum made a point of never lying to himself.

She twisted and leaned against the railing. "I hate losing someone. Sometimes I feel like I'm playing a game, doing the best I can, and I still can't win. The angel of death seems to hold an extra ace."

Drum knew she was talking more to herself than to him. He tossed his cigar and put his arm around her shoulder. "You did the best you could." She felt so right, close like this. He had to fight the urge to crush her to him.

When she didn't comment, he tugged her away from the railing and kissed the top of her head. She had no idea how long he'd waited for her to come back. She'd probably laugh if he told her about how he dreamed of going up to Boston and seeing her. Sage was the one dream he let himself believe in.

Without giving it much thought, he leaned down and kissed her gently, a soft hello kiss with a promise.

For a moment she didn't react. When she did, she pushed hard. "What do you think you are doing?"

"Kissing you." He frowned. "We've done it before. I thought you'd recognize it. It happens when two people touch lips."

She stomped halfway across the porch, then

turned back to him. "There for a minute I forgot how infuriating you can be. It's been almost four years since I've seen you, Drummond Roak, and, if you ask me, that's not half long enough. I'm a widow in mourning. I'm older than you. I'm . . ." He was making her crazy. She couldn't even think, but she knew the list was long. "Men don't just go around kissing women when they feel like it."

"Sage, we need to talk about this . . ." He had no intention of stopping, so to his way of thinking, she might as well settle into the idea.

"No. We need to talk about the boys, and that's all. This . . ." She waved her hand at the space between them. "This, you and me that you seem to think exists has never been more than a boyish infatuation on your part."

"I'm not a boy." He was getting real tired of having to remind her. He'd been a man since she left. "I'm man enough to be your man," he said in a low tone.

"No," she answered. "Never, Drum."

He watched her walk back into the hotel without another word. He told himself the gun on his hip had more to do with why she didn't want him than his age, but he couldn't be sure. The night he'd first seen her, she'd been crying because her first love, a young Ranger, had been killed. She'd sworn then that she'd never marry a man who lived with a gun within arm's length of him. She'd fallen for a preacher who proved to be an idiot before she

79

married him, and she'd evidently fallen for a doctor who'd died on her right after the wedding.

Drum figured she'd been unlucky in love enough to be marked as trouble by most, but that didn't matter to him. In his mind, she was already his woman.

If I had a heart, he thought, that woman would not only break it, she'd stomp on it and set it on fire. There must be something wrong with me, Drum decided as he followed her inside. Shooting his toes off one at a time couldn't be any less painful than trying to court Sage McMurray.

CHAPTER 8

DRUM MADE IT THREE STEPS INTO HER SITting room before Sage demanded, "What do you think you're doing here?"

He didn't back down. "I'm doing what I swore I'd do. I'm making sure the boys are safe." He almost added that he liked the way her gown clung to her, but he knew she wouldn't appreciate his compliment.

Bonnie walked out of the washroom with her hair in rag knots. Without her glasses, she had to squint to see him. "Evening, Mr. Roak. I left you an extra blanket in case it gets cold on the settee."

"Thank you kindly, but I think I'll try the floor." Drum smiled at the nurse. If possible, she was even plainer without her glasses than with them.

"Sleeping on that thing is like trying to sleep in a four-foot canoe."

Bonnie giggled.

Sage looked at her friend as if she'd lost her mind. She'd never heard Bonnie giggle, not once in two years. "Good night," she managed as she turned back into her room. Let the man sleep out in the sitting room if he wanted to. She'd be sharing her bed with Bonnie so the boys could have the other room.

The nurse followed her in and closed the door. "I feel so much safer knowing Mr. Roak is just outside."

"He's not outside," Sage corrected. "He's inside, and if you think that is safer, remind me to introduce you to a few wild animals."

Bonnie didn't get Sage's point. "Why?"

"Because that's what he is: a wild animal. He may look like a man, but trust me, there's the blood of a wolf in him."

Bonnie laughed. "I don't think we have to worry about Mr. Roak biting anyone."

Sage crawled into bed and muttered, "I wouldn't be too sure."

She wanted to ask Bonnie why she kept calling him Mr. Roak, but she was too tired to think. All she wanted to do was sleep.

For several minutes the sounds beyond her door kept her awake. Drum moved around and made no attempt to walk softly. Probably just to irritate her, she thought. She heard him look in on the boys and cross to the door, double-checking the lock. Then she guessed he moved to the window, because she thought she heard the rattle of shutters.

All was quiet for a while. Bonnie's slow breathing from the other side of the bed had almost lulled Sage to sleep when she thought she saw a shadow walk the ledge outside her open window.

She didn't move. They were on the third floor. No one would dare step outside or try to stand on the ledge.

Then she smelled the faint odor of a cigar.

The lean shadow crossed again, then sat on the windowsill, half in and half out of her world. He propped his foot against one side of the frame and leaned his head back against the other. The tiny glow of his cigar moved across the midnight.

She watched him through her lashes and wondered who Drummond Roak was truly guarding, her or the boys. He slept so little she couldn't help but wonder if he trusted the night or if he were constantly on guard against the unknown hidden in the shadows.

The thought crossed her mind that this wasn't the first time he'd watched her sleep. That was impossible, of course. She'd been away, and before that, she lived in a busy house full of people on a ranch that was a fortress.

Yet she couldn't shake the feeling. If she hadn't been so tired, she would have crawled out of her warm bed and given him a piece of her mind. In fact, while she was at it, she'd tell him to stop smoking those cigars. But telling Drummond off would have to wait for another time. She needed rest.

Closing her eyes, she relaxed and drifted into sleep, knowing that he was there and despite what she'd said to Bonnie, believing that she was safe.

Once, turning in her sleep, she opened her eyes and saw that the windowsill was empty. Tiny little plops of rain tapped on the wood where Drum had sat. The damp air had also washed away the hint of cigar smoke. She wondered if she'd only dreamed that he'd been at her window.

For the first time in months, she slept the rest of the night through without waking. There'd been no rounds to make, no husband to check in on, just the peace of a gentle rain.

The sun was bright when she shook sleep from her head. Sage brushed her hair out of her eyes, pulled on her robe, and poked her head out the bedroom door. Bonnie was the only one there, fully dressed and looking like she'd been up for some time.

"Morning," Sage said, feeling a little foolish.

"Morning." Bonnie looked up from her mending. "Mr. Roak took the boys and that dumb dog out for breakfast. He told me not to wake you, but the man is having coffee brought up every fifteen minutes so it'll be hot when you do get up." She

83

looked miserable. "So far I've managed to drink most of it. No sense it going to waste."

Sage shook her head slightly, hoping the pieces would fall into place. Since when did Drum have any say over her sleeping habits . . . or her dog?

Bonnie stood and put the mending she'd been working on in her trunk. "He asked me if we'd be ready to leave by tomorrow. He's decided to take the boys to Whispering Mountain, so he'll be riding along with us."

"When was he planning to ask me?"

Sage answered the door and thanked the maid for the coffee. When she turned back to Bonnie, she continued, "You can tell him—"

Bonnie rushed past the maid. "You'll have to tell him yourself. I need to be out back for a while."

She was gone before Sage could argue.

After pacing around the room for several minutes, Sage decided leaving tomorrow would rush her, but she could make it. Drum was right about getting the boys to safety, even if she wasn't sure she believed that someone was plotting to kill them. The hotel clerk had promised to make the arrangements for Meg's graveside service. Sage had asked that he buy two plots so that her husband's body could lie next to her. The Rangers were sending men out with a map the oldest boy had drawn. Will had wanted to go with them, but all agreed it would be safer if he disappeared with Roak as soon as possible.

Sage began her list. The funeral, supplies for five for the trip, clothes for the boys.

She tapped the pencil several times against the paper before adding, "Say good-bye to Barret's brother." She really didn't care if she ever saw the man again, but she supposed it was the right thing to do.

Bonnie came back into the room, her cheeks flushed from climbing two flights of stairs.

"Will you go with me to see Shelley Lander?" Sage asked her.

"One of the bellmen told me he runs a gaming house down on the docks. How about we just send him a letter?"

Sage shook her head. "No, he's Barret's only living relative. I owe him a visit."

"We could invite him here."

"Not if we plan to get packed by dawn tomorrow. Yesterday when he visited, I thought he'd never leave." Sage wanted to add that he'd also had his bar bill put on her account. "We can go after the funeral service."

"All right, but I got a feeling we haven't seen the last of that man. How about we swear not to tell him where your ranch is?"

"Sounds like a good idea." Sage twisted her hair from the braid and began combing it out with her fingers.

It had been years since she'd worn her straight hair down, but somehow the action made her feel a bit like the girl she'd been growing up. Now that Drum had set a time to leave, she found herself in a hurry to see Whispering Mountain again. Her parents, Andrew and Autumn, had married at eighteen and settled the slice of land between two rivers with a cluster of hills guarding their back. Teagen told her once that their Irish father and Apache mother had been happy and safe on the land until Andrew left to fight for Texas independence. He'd died at Goliad, and she'd followed him a few months later, after giving birth. Sage never knew them, but when she was home, she swore she could feel their love around her.

"Doc?" Bonnie broke into her thoughts. "Do you think we'll be safe on the road between here and there?"

"Yes," Sage answered as she added rifles to her list of needed supplies.

A herd of footsteps pounded up the steps. Sage wasn't surprised when Drum opened the door and entered without knocking.

"Morning." He smiled as he lowered saddlebags by the door.

Sage's smile was for the boys. "I understand we're leaving tomorrow at first light." She faced the oldest, Will. "Is that all right with you?"

Andy played with the dog but, at seven, Will was old enough to be consulted. "Do you need to go back to the farm to get anything?"

Will shook his head. "We got the Bible. That's all

86

we need. Mr. Roak explained to us about our mother dying. He said she was real sorry to leave us, but she's with our father now, so Andy and I will have to take care of each other."

Andy looked up from petting the dog. "Mr. Roak said he knows a place where we'll be safe from those bad men. We voted at breakfast and decided we would go with him."

Sage faced Roak. "You seemed to have set all the plans."

"Not quite," he answered. "I figured we could head toward Whispering Mountain as soon as possible. If we get out before dawn tomorrow, no one will see the boys leave with you. On the road we can talk about where they can stay. I thought Mrs. Dickerson, in town, might take them in for a while if Teagen's not at the ranch. Since she was widowed again last year, she could probably use the help, and there seems no better home than with a schoolteacher."

Sage realized she had something in common with the old schoolteacher. Mrs. Dickerson was a wise choice. She loved children, and she lived close enough to Sage's brother Teagen to run to him for help if trouble came.

"First light tomorrow," she agreed as she pulled shipping receipts from her bag and handed them to Roak. "If you'll see that my equipment is loaded, I'll buy supplies for the trip and make sure the boys have what they need."

He raised an eyebrow. "How much equipment?"

"A wagonload. Teagen probably left a wagon and two teams of horses at the livery. I told him I'd like a buggy if possible for Bonnie and the luggage. She's never traveled by wagon across open country."

Roak frowned. "Sounds like a caravan. I'll hire a few drivers."

"I can drive our wagon." Will straightened, obviously not missing a word.

Roak nodded. "Good. We can load most of the supplies for the trip on your wagon." He smiled at the boy. "You'll be a big help on this trip. I can use another man along the trail."

Sage started to the bedroom to dress, but Roak's words stopped her. "I'll meet you back here at sundown. Be ready."

She whirled. "Maybe we should get something straight, Drummond. You are not in charge of me or responsible for any of my belongings. I agree we should work together to leave as soon as possible and travel together for safety, but no one elected you the trail boss."

He nodded once. "Fair enough." All the anger left his tone when he added in a low voice, "I'm surprised even one man got his rope around you, Sage."

She resented the comment. "Once and never again."

CHAPTER 9

SAGE AND BONNIE WALKED WITH THE BOYS to their mother's grave for a prayer. They knew of no minister, but Bonnie had managed to find a few wildflowers for the boys to carry. The young Ranger, Daniel Torry, met them at the opening to the cemetery. He tied his horse at the gate and pulled a Bible out of his saddlebag.

"I know the words to read," Daniel whispered when they started across to the newly dug grave. "When I was half grown, I thought my calling would be to preach. I'm as much of a preacher as any of the others you'll find around here."

"That would be nice," Sage said, thinking that she'd heard them enough lately to know them by heart. The boys walked ahead with Bonnie toward the open grave. Daniel and Sage followed.

She thought of asking if Drummond was coming, but she knew the answer.

Daniel seemed to read her mind. "Roak can't make it. He's tied up at the docks. He—"

Sage saved Daniel from further lying. "He doesn't do funerals."

Daniel nodded. "That's about it. A lot of the men are that way. I guess they feel close enough to the grave in everyday living. They don't want to stand over one."

"And you?" she asked.

Daniel grinned. "I'm the son of a preacher, miss. A funeral or wedding didn't much matter to us kids. It meant we'd eat good that night." He straightened and stepped into place, looking every bit the preacher, except for the gun strapped to his hip.

Seven-year-old Will stood like a little soldier at the foot of his mother's grave, not allowing one tear to fall. Andy, at four, didn't understand. He asked when she would be coming back from heaven. When Sage explained that she was never coming back, he cried until Bonnie told him that their father went with her so she wouldn't be alone, and they left Will and him here so they'd both have company too. Andy stopped crying then, as if her words had made sense to him.

Sage gave the boys all the time they needed at the grave, but when they left, she knew they'd all have to hurry through the rest of the day doing everything on their list. Daniel left them at the gate. He swung up on his horse, tipped his hat to the ladies, and shoved the Bible back in his saddle-bag next to a half-empty bottle of whiskey. "I'll be at the Ranger station if you need me, miss."

Sage glanced back to make sure the boys couldn't hear, then asked, "Doesn't what you do now, killing outlaws, conflict with the preaching? Shouldn't God be the judge?"

Daniel smiled. "Way I look at it, I'm just seeing that they can plead their case face-to-face." He winked at her.

Sage smiled. The others joined them.

She directed the boys toward the shops and noticed only Will looked back at the cemetery. He was old enough to remember all that had happened for the rest of his life. For Andy, she hoped it would only be something he was told about.

Hours later, loaded down with supplies and clothing for the journey, they returned to the hotel room to find Captain Harmon waiting for them.

Sage liked the man. Her brother Travis knew him well and trusted him. She smiled at him, thinking of years ago when she'd fallen for a young man with a badge. They'd both been young enough to promise forever, but he'd died before her eighteenth birthday. Now she couldn't help but wonder: if Michael Saddler had lived, would he look as weathered as the captain by now?

"Sage," Harmon said slowly, as if it were an endearment. "How are you, honey? I'm powerful sorry about you losing your husband."

She set her bags down and hugged him lightly. "I'm fine, Captain, and you don't look a day's worth of different than when I last saw you."

He grinned. "I see you learned to lie up there in the big city."

"I learned lots up there," she said with a laugh, "but it's good to be back."

Sage introduced the captain to Bonnie and the boys. Will and Andy paid their respects then vanished to go wash up.

The nurse seemed nervous as she always did around men who weren't wounded or ill. She excused herself, saying she had to go down and order food for the boys before they started gnawing on the furniture.

Sage waited until the nurse's footsteps died away. She knew the captain wasn't here on a social call. She didn't have to wait long.

Harmon glanced at the washroom door and said in a low voice, "I need to talk to Will and Andy alone before you take them to safety. They might know something that could help us catch whoever ordered their parents killed. Do you think I could have some time now?"

"Of course." She picked up her doctor bag. "Bonnie and I have to say good-bye to someone, and I'd just as soon the boys not go with us. Then I need to stop by the alchemist counter and refill a few of my bottles. Would thirty minutes be enough time? I think I can be finished by then."

Harmon nodded. "If you're not back in half an hour, I'll take them over to the Ranger station and keep them there until you pick them up."

She didn't have to tell him not to let them out of his sight. He'd seen their mother. He knew as much as she did the danger they were in. She'd also noticed several times during the day that a man with the look of a Ranger was close, watching over them. Roak and the captain would probably deny it, but Sage bet there hadn't been a minute that the boys were without a guard today. Even Daniel at the cemetery was probably acting under orders.

Sage met Bonnie halfway down the stairs.

"We in for the night?" Bonnie asked. "I got a meal coming up directly."

"One more thing on my list. I have to say that good-bye to Barret's brother, but I could go—"

"Don't even think it," Bonnie answered. "I'm going with you. Knowing Shelley Lander, he's living in a snake den. We'll be in and out and back home before sunset. In fact, I suggest that as soon as we catch sight of the man, we both wave and yell our farewells from a distance."

"I'll settle on five minutes." Sage hurried down the stairs. This was the one errand she didn't want to do, but she owed it to Barret. She'd wrapped her husband's pocket watch in one of his handkerchiefs to give to Shelley. One memory of his brother.

They followed the directions given by the clerk: third boardwalk off the first dock, a green building with Chinese lanterns hanging from each corner.

From the distance of the shoreline the place looked festive. Sage shook the sand out of her shoe and told herself this wouldn't be so bad. Few were on the dock at this time of day. The workers had gone home to their supper, and the gamblers hadn't come out to play yet.

From twenty feet, the building looked neglected,

and the boards rattled beneath her step. The lanterns were in shreds, the paint peeling. Someone inside with no skill was banging on a piano. The music pulsed through the late-afternoon air in jerky rhythm. Nothing about the place welcomed them.

Bonnie moved closer as they walked an uneven little bridge to the green house built on stilts. At high tide people used boats to dock on one side. The wind whipped in from the gulf, battering the building, which seemed to squeak and rattle in protest. The tide was rolling in with each wave, and the dock swayed from the force of the water.

Sage noticed a small boat bucking the waves toward the side dock. There were six men inside, all dressed with more the look of wranglers than sailors. All wore guns strapped around their waists, and several rifles poked out of the boat. Maybe they were guards delivering liquor or men from the bank picking up money. She could believe liquor coming in under guard more than that much money going out. Shelley didn't seem flush enough to have to send his deposits in.

"The doorman said it's a gaming house, and we'd better be out of here long before dark." Bonnie shortened her steps as if to slow their progress.

"No problem. I'm beginning to think your idea of sending him a letter was a good plan."

They reached the porch and knocked twice

before the door opened. A thick man little more than Sage's height, with his sleeves rolled up well past his elbows, answered. He looked puzzled then frowned at them as if they were two jellyfish that had flopped in on a wave.

Sage straightened, wishing she'd thought to pull her gun from the folds of her petticoat and put it in her purse. "We'd like to see Mr. Shelley Lander, please."

The man stood as if he'd replaced the door. "State your business, and I'll see if he's in."

"I'm Sage McMurray, and my business is private."

He raised a bushy eyebrow. "Well, I'm Tony, and no one gets to the boss—"

Sage's patience ended. "I'm Dr. Lander, and my business is none of your concern." She took a step toward the man as if she fully intended to push him out of her way.

Tony hesitated, then stepped back with a curse. "It's bad for business having you two standing around out here. You've got five minutes, lady."

Bonnie passed the man, towering over him by a head. "That's four more than we'll need." With a smile, she whispered, "Don't mess with the doc, or you'll be looking up at your own headstone."

Sage forged ahead. "What business?" she said under her breath.

Tony had to scramble to keep up with the women.

They all moved inside to a small foyer, which split off into several hallways. Tony took the first one on the right and motioned for them to follow. The entire place smelled of cigar smoke, damp dirt, and whiskey.

The first room they passed had several tables inside, but only three men sat near the back, playing cards. From the look of them, they'd been there for days. Empty bottles littered around their table, and a ring of smoke hung over their heads as thick as a storm cloud.

Sage noticed not one of the gamblers even lifted his eyes to watch their passing.

The second room looked more like a saloon. Here the piano played, but no one seemed to be listening. Several men, sailors mostly, drank and talked while two bored barmaids refilled their glasses. Sage couldn't tell if they were the start of tonight's party or the leftovers from last night.

Bonnie tugged on her arm with a sudden jerk. "Look," she whispered, "there's the guy who ran into me on the walk the day we arrived." She raised her nose as if looking down into the bottom of her glasses. "I thought he looked like a nice man; just shows you how looks can be wrong."

Sage spotted the tall cowboy near the back of the bar. He had a drink next to him, but he wasn't paying it any attention. Instead, he stared out a long, slanted window that looked like it opened into a big room. She couldn't see much, but the sounds of coins being shuffled along with cards drifted from the open window.

"In here, Doctor Miss." Tony pointed toward an open door that looked like it led to an office.

When Bonnie moved to follow, he stopped her with a muscular arm. "One at a time. It's the boss's rules."

Bonnie looked at Sage in near panic.

Sage hesitated. "I'll leave the door open. Shout if you need me. I'll only be a minute."

Bonnie nodded once. "Stand where I can see you."

"I will." Sage forced herself to step into the office.

At one time the place might have been considered nicely furnished, but it, like the building, hadn't weathered well. The couches were tattered, the drapes so old only dust and mildew kept them up, and the carpet was worn to the boards in several spots. French doors opened behind Shelley's desk, and she saw that he could look out into a large gaming room with tables for cards and dice. The place was almost empty.

Shelley moved from behind his desk, tugging on his coat as he came. "Welcome," he said, smiling. "I'm delighted you've thought about my offer and have decided to change your mind. I'll be happy to show you my safe, my dear. Several travelers trust their valuables with me."

Sage didn't move. "Thank you, Shelley, but I

97

haven't time. I only came to bring you this." She tugged the handkerchief from her bag and handed him Barret's watch. "I think your brother would have wanted you to have this."

He unfolded the cloth and stared down at the gift. Big tears bubbled in his eyes.

Sage fought to keep from moving backward, not wanting the man to hug her, even if he was almost a relative. Barret had loved that watch. He'd said his parents gave it to him when he finished school. It was probably the most valuable thing he owned. She only hoped Shelley would treasure it also. Her husband had never mentioned what he wanted her to do with it, but since it bore the Lander name engraved on the back, she thought Shelley should have it.

The clank of a bell sounded from somewhere deep in the house, and shouts of alarm came from the dealers in the main room. The rush of men scrambling seemed to rattle through the house like giant mice running in the attic.

Pocketing the watch, he rushed toward the French doors, trying to see any sign of trouble through the thin lace curtains. "Tony!" he yelled in the direction of the hallway, "get down there and settle everyone down. Tell the newcomers docking that they'll have to come through the front door if they want to get in."

Shelley watched the room below, forgetting that Sage was even in the room as he muttered through the house rules. "No entry in the back, only an exit. Don't want the prospective suckers bumping into the broke drunks leaving."

Shelley reached in his desk drawer for a pistol. He paused for a moment, fighting to control the anger in his face. "I didn't realize you were still here, my dear. Please stay back while I deal with a slight problem." He slowly opened one of the doors behind his desk and leaned out only a few inches.

"What the hell is going on!" he yelled and opened the door wider, revealing what looked like an empty room.

A moment later, shots rang out in rapid fire. Sage jolted backward.

Shelley seemed to straighten in slow motion, closing what was left of the shattered French door. Then he turned toward her and hit the ground, clutching his shoulder. A high-pitched scream of pain filled the office.

Sage ran to him and knelt by his side. Blood bubbled from a hole high on his arm. She clawed his hand away to see the wound as he swore.

"Bonnie!" she shouted as more shots rang out. "Bonnie!"

Shelley screamed again that he was dying and she had to help him.

Sage tugged the jacket open and tore the shirt off his shoulder. Blood covered the wound, but when she blotted it, she saw no entry point. The bullet had only grazed him, ripping flesh in a two-inch groove across the top of his arm.

"You're all right, Shelley. It's only a flesh wound. You're all right." She knew black powder could still poison the blood, but if she got the wound cleaned and let it bleed, it would heal fast.

The man seemed intent on playing a grand death scene. "Help me," he cried. "It appears I will follow my brother to the grave."

"Bonnie!" Sage cried again. When she moved to go get the nurse, Shelley's hand grabbed her wrist and begged her not to leave a dying man.

She'd been so occupied with Shelley, Sage hadn't noticed what was going on in the room beyond the French doors. The six men she'd seen in the boat a few minutes before were moving through the room toward her, their rifles pointed and ready to fire. A few of the dealers who hadn't moved fast enough at the sound of the bell were now dead on the floor between the gaming tables.

She managed to stand as two of the robbers crashed through the doors. "Get up, Lander," one yelled. "If I'd wanted you dead, you would be."

They pushed past Sage and jerked Shelley to his feet. One man pointed the barrel of the rifle against his throat, while the other one said calmly, "We want you breathing so you can open the safe. If you cooperate, we'll leave you alive to make more money so we can rob you again one day. If you don't cooperate, we'll kill you and your little lady friend right here and torch the place. That grand safe of yours will sink in the gulf of no further use to us or you."

"I'm not his lady friend," Sage said before she thought to stay quiet. "I'm a doctor, and this man needs medical attention."

They both looked at her as if she were completely mad. And she was more mad than frightened. Shelley, no matter how much of an idiot, was her patient, and these robbers were interfering with her care.

The one with the gun against Shelley asked, "Is that true? Is this little woman a doctor?"

Shelley was too frightened to think of anything but himself. "Yes, it's true, and she's trying to keep me from dying. I've got a weak heart. I could go any second."

"Then open the safe fast," the other man yelled as he kicked Shelley hard enough to push him to his knees.

Shelley followed orders, whining and swearing with every move.

As soon as the safe's door swung out, the man with the gun hit Shelley over the head hard with the butt of his gun. "That'll help you forget about dying." He laughed.

Sage dropped down by Shelley's body. Now the poor man had two wounds she'd have to deal with. As soon as he woke, he'd not only complain about being robbed, he'd probably think he was dying of brain damage as well.

One of the men shoved all the cash in the safe into an old leather saddlebag.

"Got it," he said as he stood. "Wave for the boys to shoot up the place and let's get out of here."

The second man turned to the shattered French doors, waved, and turned back. His black eyes looked straight at Sage. "You're really a doctor?"

"Yes," she said as shots rang out.

"Then you're coming with us." His black eyes danced. "Grab her bag, and let's get out of here."

The other man agreed and, before Sage could fight, they'd each grabbed one of her arms and started back through the shambles of what was left of the gaming room. She almost called for Bonnie, then stopped, suddenly hoping the nurse was still hiding in the shadows of the darkened hallway. Maybe she'd even managed to run free to get help.

When Drum heard of this, he'd kill them all, if the Rangers didn't find them first. She wasn't just some woman in port they were kidnapping, she was Sage McMurray. These two-bit crooks had no idea of the hell they were pulling down upon them.

Sage kicked and screamed and tried to bite her kidnappers, but neither seemed to notice as they shoved her out the back door onto a rain-slippery dock. One held her while the other tied her hands behind her and added another rope at about knee level around her skirts, then they tossed her in the boat with the bag of money. As she drew in air to scream, one of them strapped a gag around her mouth.

"Hush up, little doc," came a low whisper from behind her. "We ain't gonna hurt you. We're just gonna keep you."

Wiggling and kicking at everything and everyone crowded into the boat, Sage barely saw the oar rise above her head. A moment later she watched it fall, and all went black.

Her last thought was that she wasn't going to make it back to the hotel before dark.

CHAPTER 10

BONNIE HEARD THE SOUND OF THE BELL and shouts. She took a step toward the office and Sage.

Tony's thick arm blocked her way. "Not so fast," he muttered. "The boss is real big on rules."

"Something's wrong." She started to explain why she had to go to Sage.

Angry shouts exploded and echoed through the room and down the hallway.

"No," the man whispered. "The bell means trouble in the big room. Mr. Shelley will handle it."

Shots sounded close enough to have hit the study. Bonnie stretched her neck to see into the room.

"Gunfire," she said as if the stout man beside

her might not know what the sound meant.

He pushed her backward down the hall, knocking off her glasses when he rushed into the study to investigate.

Bonnie steadied herself and prepared to barge her way past the man just as a hand slapped around her mouth and another about her waist, pulling her backward.

"Quiet," someone said from behind her. "Or you'll end up in the middle of a robbery."

She thought of trying to fight but realized the body against her back was taller than her. She twisted enough to see his hat and knew it had to be the cowboy. He'd come to her aid.

"We got to get out of here, or we're liable to be dead."

"No," she struggled. "I'm not going anywhere without the doc."

The cowboy appeared deaf. He locked one arm around her and lifted her up against his side. In what seemed like very few steps, he was out the door and halfway down the dock. With no pause, he dropped off the pier into the fading light of a golden sunset. His arm still held Bonnie so tightly she couldn't breathe. Landing in the soft, damp sand, he whistled, and a horse bumped against them from the shadows beneath the dock.

"Easy boy, easy," he whispered as he grabbed the reins with his free hand. "How about taking the little lady for a ride?"

"No," she protested as gunfire went wild inside the gaming house. "I'm not going anywhere."

He lifted her up onto his horse and swung up behind her in one fluid movement. Before she could build a grand scream, he tapped the mount, and they were at full gallop. In panic, Bonnie stopped yelling and hung on for dear life. She'd only been on a horse a few times in childhood and never a thundering beast like this one.

She was too scared to cry, too near panic to think. All she could do was hold on as the damp air streamed past.

They rode away from the lights of town into the night so dark she couldn't make out a single landmark. Rain fell, but she hardly noticed. The cowboy slowed enough to pull his coat over her shoulders. She rested her head against his chest, needing the warmth of his body. They rode on along a road she couldn't see but he seemed to know well. She could feel as well as hear his heart pounding, and it calmed her enough that she could think.

"You have to let me go," she said with enough force that it sounded almost like an order. "You can't kidnap me. You can't. I can't go with you. I've a responsibility to the doctor."

"I saved your life, lady," he said against her ear. "That doctor is probably already dead."

"No."

He tugged her closer. "I'm sorry. But I'd say it's an even bet that she's dead."

"No," Bonnie whispered. "She can't be."

This cowboy could never understand that she'd had no one on earth when she found Sage. She couldn't even think about losing her. Some people needed wealth or power or love. All Bonnie Faye ever wanted or needed was a reason, one reason why she was put on this earth. Sage gave her that reason. "The doc's not dead."

"You got a look at those men shooting up the place. They'll probably kill everyone in that hell-hole before they leave."

She shook her head. "No! You're wrong. You don't know that. I didn't see anything. They'll let me go."

"They'll kill you," he said flatly.

Bonnie fisted his shirt in her hand. "You can't be sure."

"I know. I'm sure," he said holding her tight. "I know, because I was one of them."

CHAPTER 11

ROAK LOADED THE LAST OF SAGE'S MEDICAL equipment and headed back to the hotel. He had one quick stop to make at the Ranger station before grabbing a few hours' sleep then setting off at dawn. He wanted to check with the captain to see if there was any word of relatives who might be claiming the boys or leads about who killed their father and mother.

He'd be glad to get out of Galveston. The dull

rain this time of year made him feel cold down to the bone. He decided to order a bath at the hotel after everyone else had bedded down for the night. He knew he wouldn't sleep soundly until they were on Whispering Mountain property.

Stepping into the station, Roak's senses heightened at the stillness. This time of night, Rangers usually checked in to pass the evening over coffee. He'd hung around in the shadows a few times to listen to the stories the old guys told of trouble in the early days, when Texas was little more than a settlement of three hundred. In a strange way, the tales gave him a sense of the history of the place.

He hadn't been born when Houston and his men won independence from Mexico, but the battles were in his blood, a part of him as they were everyone who grew up on Lone Star soil. He wasn't around when the Alamo fell or the men were shot at Goliad, but a few of the Rangers still yelled the battle cries of "Remember the Alamo" when they rode in, fighting.

Roak made it through the main office with one wall lined with rifles and the other with shelves of coffee mugs. He was well into the bunk area before he heard a sound. A dog's yelp and a cat's hiss. Then, the laughter of a child.

Drum's tired muscles relaxed. Nothing could be too bad if the boys were laughing.

"Look, Mr. Roak," Andy shouted. "Bullet's trying to box Mutt."

Turning full into the room, he spotted Daniel Torry playing checkers with Andy Smith. Will was curled up on one of the bunks, trying to read a book Sage bought him. All three were watching Bonnie's cat and Mutt fighting out round one.

"My money's on the cat." Daniel laughed. "That dog's been pestering her all afternoon."

"Anything else going on?" Roak kept his voice low, conversational.

Daniel did the same. "There was some trouble down at one of the lowlife poker houses on the dock. A robbery turned murder. The captain and everyone else hanging around decided to go have a look." Daniel leaned back in his chair. "I decided beating this little fellow at checkers was far more fun than going sloshing through the rain and mud."

"You drew the short straw?"

Daniel smiled. "Something like that."

Drum sat down on an empty chair. "Any idea where the ladies are?" If the boys were here, they had to be out somewhere.

"Captain said they had an errand to run before dark. Must have got to talking. They said something about visiting the doctor's brother-in-law."

Roak leaned forward on the edge of his chair. "Happen to catch his name?"

Daniel shook his head. "Might have been the fellow with them when I met them at the hotel the night we brought the boys' mother in. I think he said his name was Shelley something."

Standing slowly, Roak asked, "It wouldn't have been Shelley Lander, a lowlife who passes himself off as a gentleman from time to time. Wears a light-colored suit that doesn't look like it's been cleaned in years. Hair combed back like he thinks he's a peacock."

Daniel nodded and met Roak's stare. They didn't have to say more. They were both thinking the same thing: Shelley Lander owned a gambling place down by the docks.

"Go," Daniel whispered. "I'll watch these two until you get back."

Roak didn't have to ask the Ranger to swear; he had his word. Drum grabbed his new hat from the peg and was through the office to his horse before he let out a breath. He rode straight to the coastline, where he knew Shelley Lander's place stood far out on a neglected dock.

He tied Satan to a pole and almost knocked men down as he ran. The place was in chaos.

Drum pushed his way through the front door and down the hall. The first room he came to had four bodies. Only one looked like he'd had time to pull his weapon from leather. The rest were still holding their cards when they fell.

He moved to the next room. A sailor and a barmaid were dead.

Drum rushed to the third room, an office. Shelley Lander lay on a ratty couch, holding a towel against his head. Blood stained his shirt along his shoulder.

"I need medical attention," he whined. "I've told all of you everything I know; now you've got to find me a real doctor."

Captain Harmon stood in front of the gambler. "You haven't told us what happened to Sage McMurray and her companion."

Drum moved in to listen.

"I don't know. Ask Tony. He let them in. I'd only had time to say hello to Sage when the firing started, and I didn't even see the nurse. Tony would know if that beanpole of a woman was with her."

"Tony's dead," Harmon answered. "Looks like he made it to the big room just about the time a bullet went through his forehead."

"Oh, God!" Shelley yelled. "This is more than I can take. First they clean out my safe, and next they kill the only good bodyguard I've ever hired. They took everything. Everything. Not just my money but all the stuff I was keeping for people."

"Not an answer to my question," Harmon muttered. "Where are the women, Shelley? I don't care about the safe."

Shelley ignored the questioning and started bemoaning his fate. Drum's gaze met the captain's. He knew Cap. He wouldn't have long to wait.

Harmon raised his hand and hit Shelley hard across the face with the flat of his palm.

"What are you doing?" Shelley screamed. "You

can't hit me! I'm the one who's been robbed. I'm wounded."

The captain straightened. "You're right. I shouldn't have hit you, Mr. Lander. I need an answer to my question, and you're the only one around alive who can comment. What happened to Sage McMurray and her friend?"

Shelley snorted. "Forget about her. I'm the one who will be dead when all the people who trusted me with their valuables find out I've let them be stolen. They won't consider that I had no choice but to open the safe. No. They'll blame me."

Drum moved in front of Shelley, knowing the order would come.

Sure enough, the captain turned and said calmly, "Shoot the man, Roak. If he doesn't know what happened to Sage, he's of no use to us."

"What?" Shelley's eyes widened as he stared at Roak's weapon sliding free of leather. "You're going to shoot me because I don't know what happened to the twit?"

The captain turned as if he were leaving. "Don't worry, Shelley, Roak here is my best shot. He can put the bullet through your ear so you'll still look good laid out on the board in front of the undertaker. If you're one more casualty of this robbery, no one will blame you for opening the safe."

Harmon raised his eyebrows. "Which reminds me. Why *are* you still alive, Shelley, when all your men are dead?"

"They must have thought I was dead," he said far too quickly for it to be the truth.

"You know who they are, don't you?" Harmon looked like he was piecing a puzzle together. "It makes no sense you're left alive."

"No." He shook his head. "No. I never saw any of them before."

Drum grabbed the man's hair and held his head still as he shoved the barrel of his handgun against Lander's ear. "I'm only asking once, Shelley. Who took the women?"

Tears ran down the man's frightened face. "I only saw one woman. Sage. I didn't see any other woman, I swear. If they took Sage, she'll be on her way to a place called Skull Alley." Shelley's wild eyes glared at Roak. "You'd be better off thinking her dead than thinking of her there. It doesn't matter who they take in; no one except outlaws ever comes out of that place."

Drum shoved the man's head so hard he tumbled back on the couch with a thud. Shelley cried out in pain, but no one was listening.

The captain blocked Roak's path. "You know where this hideout is?"

"I know. It's a long dangerous hideout west of here. You'll never find the opening to the alley unless you've been there. Once in, the canyon walls hem you in for miles," Drum answered as he holstered his gun. "I'm going, but don't try to follow me. They have enough guards that they could pick

Rangers off one at a time. They wouldn't even have to fire, just send a few rocks over. Once you're in, if you make it past the guards and rattlesnakes, the settlement is full of men who kill for sport."

The captain frowned. "Her brothers will all three come after her. There's nothing I could do to stop any one of them."

"Tell them I'll bring her out," Drum said. "Alone. It's the only way. If they tried to go in firing, they'd die."

Shelley laughed as if he knew a secret joke. "No one's ever come out of there."

Drum stepped around Harmon and said over his shoulder, "He's wrong, Cap. I made it out once, and I can do it again."

CHAPTER 12

BONNIE AWOKE WHEN THE COWBOY LIFTED her down from his horse. She felt as if every bone in her body had been broken and put back together backward. She wasn't sure she could have stood if he'd set her on her feet.

She'd cried and fretted for what seemed like hours, then she'd done the unthinkable when in danger: she'd fallen asleep. Here she was, convinced she could survive in this barbaric place, and what does she do the first time she's tested? She sleeps.

The cowboy carried her through a low door and

into a dark little house that was smaller than the hotel room back in Galveston.

"You'll be safe here," he said as he lowered her to her feet.

"Safe!" she said, trying not to wobble. "I was safe back in Boston. I was even safe in Galveston. How can you possibly think I could be safe out here in the middle of nowhere with a man whose name I don't even know?" She was getting wound up, and once she was wound, she would steam for a while. "I'm out here in the wilderness with all kinds of things outside that door just waiting to kill me or eat me. And inside seems no better. How am I safe in here with a man who'll probably ravish me or kill me at any moment?"

She drew in a breath to continue, when he stopped her with a short question.

"Which do you want first?"

"What?"

He squatted and lit the fireplace. It was well after sunup, but the rain at the open door made it seem like night. "I said, which do you want first, the ravishing, or the killing?"

Straw caught twigs aflame. The fire flickered. Bonnie stood frozen, her back to the fireplace. Her worst fear was about to be realized. The constant harping of her mother to stay away from all men had been right.

Never in her life had Bonnie Faye ever been speechless. Until now.

The giant stood and stared down at her. "I vote for the ravishing. I've never done it with a woman I thought could take my weight before." A grin grew slowly across a face that hadn't seen a razor in a week.

Bonnie Faye did a second thing she'd never done before: she fainted.

CHAPTER 13

BY DAWN SAGE HAD KICKED, SHOVED, AND bitten so many times that they covered her head with a burlap bag that smelled of potatoes and tied her onto her horse both at the horn and thigh level with belts. She could make out daybreak and knew they were traveling west. As the hours passed, she tried to rest as much as she could, knowing that night would be her best time to escape. She'd need all her energy then.

For almost four years she'd been up North in what most call civilization. She hadn't needed her survival skills. Her life hadn't depended on constant vigilance. Only, now she was back where her life might depend on what she observed and knowing the right time to act. Though her eyes were midnight blue and sunshine streaked her brown hair, Apache blood ran in her veins. Her mother's people had thrived on this land for generations, and she felt those ancestors near as the hours passed and her senses honed. She thought of nothing but breaking free.

The men talked among themselves. Slowly she pieced together facts. Four voices. Two of the six who'd helped row her away from Shelley's place were either silent, or they'd disappeared somewhere during the night. The others didn't seem to be celebrating their bounty. She got the feeling they were hired men doing a job, and that job wasn't over until the bag of contents from the safe was delivered.

She might not have sight, but she knew enough to describe each. One she called Big Hands, because when he'd lifted her, his hands circled her waist. His voice, mostly orders, came from in front of her.

Another man she thought of as Frog. His voice was low and raw as if overused. He smelled unwashed. Sage was glad he rode behind her, downwind of her. He didn't seem to like having her along, but he did whatever Big Hands told him to do.

The third man she guessed was thin and wiry. He paced when they were stopped and circled round the others when they rode. She guessed that he must be of a small build, maybe so small he couldn't have lifted her up into the saddle. His words came quick, and usually when he passed beside her, he'd warn her not to fall asleep. Twice when she'd thought she heard other travelers near, he'd whispered that he'd put a bullet in her back if she so much as sneezed. After that, she thought of him as Sneezy.

The last, she hadn't decided what to call, for he spoke little and kept his distance. Mostly, she heard the other three talking to him, and from that she knew, he was having trouble handling his horse.

They followed no road or even a trail, which was probably wise, since they were surely being followed by now. Several times during the night Big Hands ordered everyone to pull up until he decided on a direction in the dark.

Each time they stopped, Frog released her bound hands from the saddle horn and lifted her down. When he pulled off the bag, she tried to hold her breath until she was a few feet away from the smelly man. He'd mumble a few swear words, then loop a rope over her neck. "I ain't losing you in the dark," he'd say as he pulled it tight, "but you can walk around a little if you want."

Sage dug her heel into the soft, wet ground, hoping the print wouldn't be washed away in the drizzling rain.

When Big Hands told everyone to mount, Frog tugged on the rope, pulling her back to her horse. Each time he lifted her up, he remembered to tie her legs down. Sneezy circled by twice and asked if he could hold the rope when they stopped, but Frog told him that it was his job.

Despite Frog's smell, Sage was glad he didn't pass her off to Sneezy.

One thing she found strange. To the man, none

touched her more than was necessary. They hadn't even checked her to make sure she wasn't carrying a weapon. To them she seemed to be no more than something they were transporting.

After several hours of riding in daylight, Frog pulled the bag off her head again and offered her water and an inch of dried meat to chew on. He tugged off her gag but didn't appear to have even heard her questions. He had a hard face and eyes dulled from seeing too much of life.

When she demanded that she have a moment of privacy, he tied a noose around her neck before freeing her hands. After pulling the noose tight, he moved to the other side of a tree. Her allotment of privacy lasted as long as she could function without breath, for the knot was too tight to budge.

She thought of reaching for her gun tucked in the folds of her petticoats, but the pistol only had one shot. Even if she was lucky and killed Frog, there were still three others, who looked like they'd kill her without blinking.

Sage decided to bide her time so that when she shot, she'd have a good chance of escape.

Quickly, she went back to Frog, and he loosened the noose just enough for her to breathe while he retied her hands.

"Don't fight it, miss," he said as he led her to her horse with the noose still snug around her neck. "It'll go easier for you if you don't fight so much."

"I don't want to go with you," she whispered

back just in case her kicking and screaming earlier hadn't convinced him.

He tugged the noose off and replaced it with the sack. "It don't matter what you want. We don't care. You're going into hell with the rest of us, and there ain't nothing you can do about it."

He lifted her onto the horse and tied her legs tight to the saddle. "Country gets rougher from here on out. Don't want you falling off."

Big Hands' voice came from in front of her. "If you behave yourself, we'll take the sack off tonight. No one to see or hear you out here."

CHAPTER 14

BONNIE AWOKE TO THE SMELL OF STEW. THE air around her was warm and dry, but the tapping rain still sounded above her. She took a deep breath. Fresh beef stew boiling in a pot not far away. Smiling a moment before opening her eyes, her thoughts drifted as if trying to remember a home that had almost been real. A place where she used to imagine she lived when she was young. As soon as the adult in her reminded her there never had been such a home, she realized where she was. Not in a dream. Not safe.

Her hand shot up to her breasts, her throat.

Her dress was gone; only her cotton underwear remained.

She knew it. She'd been ravished. Some man she

didn't know had taken her, used her for his pleasure, stolen her virginity . . . and she'd missed the whole thing.

That only left being killed. She'd probably be dead as soon as he finished his meal.

"Hungry?" a male voice said.

Bonnie twisted until she could see him half a room away at a table set for two.

"Do I get a meal before you kill me?"

"Might as well. I'll have to toss the stew anyway. Cooked more than I can eat."

Bonnie started to get up, then realized she had no clothes. She tugged a thin blanket around her shoulders. "You took my clothes."

"One," he said as he ate, "they were wet. And, two, I figured it'd keep you inside if you don't have any dress to run away in. You'll be warm enough in all those underthings."

"Oh," she said as if he made sense. She was caged with a madman. Silently she added clothes thief to his list of ravisher, killer, and robber.

There was nothing practical to do but eat, and Bonnie prided herself in always being practical.

She tiptoed over to the table and sat across from him. "Did you . . ." She didn't even know how to ask what he might have done to her.

"No," he said, pushing the pot close to her. "I figured I'd eat first."

Carefully spooning one serving, she lied, "I'm not afraid of you."

"I guessed that," he lied back.

She felt like they were having a picnic in the middle of a great battle. She should be screaming and running around and fighting to save herself, but all she did was take a bite.

"This is good," she said after her bowl was half empty, and he hadn't attacked her.

"Thanks," he answered, still staring at her. "I learned to cook as a kid hiring out with a railroad crew."

She looked everywhere but at him. She didn't want to talk to the man who was going to use her and murder her.

The cabin was small but clean and orderly. Not the place she'd think of as a stage for killing and torturing. She also noticed that the chairs were a few inches taller than most and the table higher. He was a man who liked things that fit his body. Gulping, she realized he considered her one of them.

He stood and collected two cups and a bottle from the one shelf above the pump. He poured her an inch of something from a bottle. "Drink this. It'll take the chill off." He added another inch. "At your size, you'll probably need more."

For the thousandth time in her life, she wished she was shorter. Everyone knew the perfect height for a woman was five feet two. If she'd been nine or ten inches shorter, he probably wouldn't have even noticed her in the hallway.

After downing the drink, she coughed.

The stranger handed her water, then moved to a chipped washtub to wash his hands. She studied him. He was very tall but well proportioned for his frame. His hair, sun-bleached and too long, looked like he'd cut it himself with a dull knife. There were wrinkles around his eyes, making him seem hard. She'd guess him in his late thirties and wondered if he'd spent all his life alone, for there was nothing in the house that hinted of a woman or any family. She also noticed no books or paper. Though the table had two chairs, only one rocker sat by the fireplace. A workbench nearby was covered with harnesses he must have been working on.

The door was closed, but the bolt lay against the wall. If she ran, she might make it outside, but where would she go? Even if she found a horse, she didn't know how to saddle one or have any idea which way would take her back to Galveston. A bear or some other wild animal would probably have her as his midnight snack.

"You can't keep me here," she said as calmly as she could manage.

He didn't answer.

Bonnie stood and moved closer to him. "And you can't kill me, so get that out of your head. You've got to let me go. Right now."

His long arm swung out and caught her waist with a sudden movement that threw her off guard. He pulled her hard against him with one tug. "Stop talking, lady. Both our lives depend on you staying right here with me."

He pulled her back to the bed and tied her arm tight to one side. He covered her with the thin blanket, then he tugged off his boots and shirt. He carefully placed his shirt over the back of one of the chairs, throwing the bed in shadows. Then he lay down on the other side of her, locking his fingers around her free arm in a grip that said he had no plans of letting go.

Somewhere in the night, she heard horses coming fast. In a few minutes she'd be rescued. There was no need to struggle.

"Don't move." He shoved her hair away from her face. "And don't say anything. Not one word."

He was so close, she could feel his warm breath. The weight of his arm rested just below her breasts like an iron bar holding her down.

"Do you understand, lady? Not one word, or you're dead."

The horses were getting closer. She nodded, knowing she only had seconds to endure.

He must have known it too, but his reaction surprised her. Instead of running to bolt the door, he rolled over on top of her and kissed her hard, full on the mouth.

She struggled beneath him, feeling every part of his body move against her as his tongue went deep into her mouth, taking the taste of her with him.

He pulled back and stared down at her as if seeing something that displeased him, then he cupped her jaw in his big hand and held her still as he kissed her again with all the force of a man starving.

The power of him, the weight of him, the savage kiss, all warmed her body and fired her cheeks.

Her heart felt as if it were thundering faster than the hooves coming. She stopped the useless struggling and accepted his kiss. His whole body seemed to read her reaction. In a split second, his assault softened and turned tender.

He pulled away to study her, then smiled down at her as if he now liked what he saw. "I'm going to kiss you whether you're willing or not, but I'd prefer it this way." He lowered and brushed her lips.

She opened her mouth to object to his advance just as his lips touched hers again.

She didn't move, more surprised by the gentleness than by the assault. This was a kiss as she'd always imagined a kiss could be, bold and tender. She couldn't have fought if her life had been the price. He made no attempt to brace his weight but rested over her as he drank her in. She shifted slightly, matching the feel of him, until they were both comfortable. She accepted his kiss.

The cowboy smiled down at her, then brushed her cheek and touched her lips with his fingertips. "Delicious," he whispered. "Just as I knew you'd be the first time I saw you. I knew you'd taste like heaven and feel right beneath me." When his mouth covered hers, he seemed to be searching, trying to please her, not take.

Never in her life had she been kissed like this. In childhood she'd always been too tall for boys her age, but a few times at school, when no one was watching, older boys had pulled her into corners and tried to kiss her or feel her body. Their touches had bruised and hurt. She'd had no one to run to, no one to tell, but by the time they tried again, she'd learned to fight with words, threats directed at their weakness.

Only this time there were no words. This man wasn't a boy. And, she realized, he wasn't taking; he was giving.

The door slammed against the wall as it popped open. He pulled his mouth from hers.

"Get out!" he yelled as two men stormed in, dripping from head to toe and swearing at the weather.

Bonnie tried to pull her senses together enough to think. All she had to do was tell these strangers she was a prisoner and she'd be saved.

"I said get out, Sol, and take your no-good friend with you." The cowboy rose slowly like a bear protecting his kill. He shoved the straps of her camisole off her shoulder as he pulled away, making her appear naked beneath the blanket.

For a second their gazes met, and she saw fear in his sad eyes as if he were sorry for what he'd had to do or maybe what he was about to do.

He sat in front of her, hiding her body from the intruders.

She curled on her side, trying to see around him.

"Look, Duke," the first stranger said with a laugh. "Now we know why little brother didn't show up yesterday. Bradford's got him a woman. It's about time. Me and the boys were beginning to think you were a monk."

"I'm busy right now." The cowboy leaned back against her body and dug his fingers through her hair. "I'm in the middle of something. I didn't have time to try to keep you from getting yourself killed this time."

The man he'd called Sol laughed. "I can see you've got your hands full. The way her cheeks are fired up, I'd say she's ready for a good ride, but you were told to go in ahead of us in case there was any trouble, and we didn't see hide nor hair of you. Hanover won't like that, if he gets wind of it."

"I don't work for Hanover. I was just going along to watch your back. Was there trouble?" the cowboy asked while he slid his other hand over Bonnie's bottom in a familiar way no man had ever dared touch her.

She opened her mouth to speak just as she recognized the men before her.

They were two of the robbers from the gaming house. She'd only seen them for a second when they'd stormed Shelley's office, but she'd taken a good look before stepping backward into the shadows.

She froze. This cabin with the cowboy might be better than going with these two. They both had a hardness about them. She doubted they'd even care about her problem.

Sol swore and tugged off his hat. "No. There was no trouble. We got what we went after. That red-headed devil, Charlie, got the money from the safe. Hanover got that damn paper he'd been hunting down for a year." He warmed by the fire. "Charlie killed a few, even when he swore he wouldn't, but you couldn't have stopped that, even if you'd been there. Besides, we agreed, the less witnesses the better. He just made sure there were even less."

Bonnie was fighting down hysteria. She was in the nest of thieves and killers. And one of them was caressing her throat with his fingers. She felt sure the purpose was so he could snap her neck if she tried to speak.

The cowboy eased his grip. "You all want to stay for a meal? I got some stew left over." His hand now patted her hip, telling her to stay calm. "I could put off our little fun for a few minutes. After all, we've been going pretty much straight for two days."

Sol barked a laugh. "I knew once you got back into it, you'd take to it. You wouldn't want to introduce your gal, would you?"

"No." The cowboy's body shadowed her face.

"All I'm offering is food. The woman is mine." His fingers dug lightly into her flesh as if he meant his words.

"No food. Charlie and the others are already ahead of us. We'll have to ride hard to catch up with them before they go into that strip of canyon called Skull Alley. We just wanted to check on you. They're taking a surprise to Hanover. I think he'll be real tickled when he sees her, and I'd like to be there." Sol looked back at the bed. "You wouldn't want to get dressed and go along for the ride? I'm sure your gal will wait. She probably could use the rest."

"No," the cowboy answered. "I plan to be busy for a few more hours." He patted her hip once more. "Maybe longer, if she's up for it."

The older man didn't look like he expected more conversation out of his little brother. "Fine. See you in a few days when I circle back through." He lifted the last piece of corn bread from the pan still on the table and walked out eating.

The other man followed, closing the door on his way out.

Bonnie expected the ravishing to begin again, but the cowboy stood and bolted the door. It occurred to her that he could have done that earlier and avoided the scene.

She studied him as he began washing the dishes. "Your name really Bradford?"

"Brad," he answered. "No one but my brother

calls me Bradford. He's ten years older than me and was wild and gone from home before I remembered him. A few years back I came back to Texas to find him, since he's my only relative. I decided I'd better stay. God knows he needs someone to watch over him."

As she pieced together the conversation with the men, it occurred to her that he might have saved her life. She definitely would fall in the witness category, and Sol had said some guy named Charlie had killed all the witnesses.

A chill moved across her heart. Sage was there. Had she been in the body count? Bonnie had to get back and find out. If anyone survived besides her, it would be the doc. Bonnie had to believe it, because she couldn't accept anything less right now.

Brad picked up a knife off the table and walked toward her. Before she could get more than a squeak of a scream out, he slashed through the rope that bound her to his bed.

She jumped free of him and huddled in the far corner of the bed. "You're letting me go?"

"No, but there's no need to make you uncomfortable." He walked back to his work with the dishes. "The storm's getting worse. We couldn't leave now, even if we were of a mind to."

"What are you going to do with me?"

He didn't answer.

She scooted off the bed and took a few steps toward

him. "I said, what are you going to do with me?"

He straightened and turned. "I'm going to get to know you, then I'll take you back, safe and sound. I haven't had a woman close enough to even talk to in a long time. I figure you owe me that. Company is all I'm asking, lady, just company."

No one had ever said they wanted to know her. She was always the woman at the dance who never got asked, the one who sat alone. That's why she'd thrown herself into nursing. She'd wanted her world too busy for those awkward times when people looked right through her, or worse, made fun of her.

"Maybe you'd better sit down, lady," she heard him say. Then she was on the stool close to the fire. He handed her a comb and watched as she began to untangle her long, unruly hair.

He poured himself a cup of coffee and watched her as if fascinated.

"All my pins are gone," she said, thinking how improper it was to have hair about her shoulders. Her mother used to say the curly mass looked like a bush when it wasn't tied up.

"It looks fine." He pulled the rocker so close their knees touched. "When I saw you that day on the street, I thought about how I'd like to get acquainted, but a pretty lady like you would never look at the likes of me."

The man must be blind, she thought. An insane blind man.

"Then when I saw you at Shelley's place, all I thought about was getting you somewhere safe. When we got here and you started talking about me ravishing you, I thought you were teasing. Let's face it, we're both of the age to know what a roll in the hay is all about."

He took one of her hands and looked like he had no idea what to do with it. "Then, when I kissed you, I realized you didn't know. It doesn't seem possible that a lady like you wouldn't have been kissed a few thousand times by now, but that's the feeling I got."

She wanted to laugh and cry at the same time. He thought her a lady, probably because of the hand-tailored traveling suit Sage had bought her. It made no sense that he thought a man, any man, had wanted to kiss her. Not once in her adult life.

When all else failed her, Bonnie used humor to answer. "Most men can't reach my lips," she said and then straightened. "And the others wouldn't dare try."

He laughed and leaned closer. "They don't know what they are missing."

Then, as easily as if they were old lovers, he leaned closer and kissed her lightly. "Tell me about the first time you were kissed."

Bonnie stared at the fire. She'd never told anyone about that first time, but her nerves were rattled, her defenses down. It seemed as good a time as any to be honest. "My parents were old.

They had me in their late forties and weren't too happy about it. I was always too tall, too awkward. When we went to church socials, I was usually told to help in the kitchen, which was fine with me. One evening I was taking the garbage out, and a boy about four years older grabbed me and pulled me into the dark. His kiss, if you can call it that, split my lip. He slapped me hard for getting blood on his shirt. When I got home, I got three licks with a strap for being clumsy. If I'd told the truth, my father would have beat me far worse."

"Come here," Brad said as he tugged her off her stool and into his arms.

Bonnie never cried, not even when she was small. It had always been her own private little defiance. She rested her head on his shoulder and let one tear fall.

"I'm sorry," he said. "I didn't mean to be so rough with you back there. I only wanted you to look like you were hot with passion. If my brother had guessed the truth, he might not have shot you, but the man with him would have. He'd have probably killed us both."

"So, you just kissed me for show." Bonnie felt like a fool for even thinking it had been passion.

"The first time." He moved his hand along her arm. "And maybe the second, but the third kiss had nothing to do with the danger we were in."

She laughed. "Thanks for that, I guess. You know, once I heard a woman say that she had a lover that moved over her like a warm summer storm. She said it only lasted a night, but the memory was burned into her thoughts forever. I never understood what she meant until you moved over me."

He was silent for so long, she wished she could take her foolish words back. They weren't friends. They never would be. He had saved her life, back at the gambling house and again here, but in turn, she'd given him probably the only alibi this gang would have accepted.

"You know, lady, I've never been anyone's storm before. That lover of your friend must have been mighty proud to know that just once he'd had such an effect on a woman."

He moved his hand up her bare arm as if cherishing the feel of her. "I'll take you back when the rain stops."

Rocking back in his chair, he crossed his leg over one knee to make room for her in his lap. "If you don't mind, I'd like to hold you for a while. I've never held anything so fine."

"All right," she managed to say calmly as if the request were nothing out of the ordinary. Not once had her father touched her except to discipline her, and her mother saw any affection as weak. For a few minutes she could let him hold her. No one would ever know.

"Tell me about your first kiss?" she asked.

He brushed her arm gently as he laughed. "I

met a gal when I was barely grown at a barn raising in Tennessee. Prettiest little thing you've ever seen. We were married that night. I kissed her for the first time when I brought her back to a place I was farming. I was so big, more than a foot taller than her. I was afraid I'd hurt her, and in the end, I guess I killed her. She died less than a year later trying to deliver a stillborn baby. A few months later, I married her older sister. I didn't love her. Wasn't even attracted to her, but I was young and all alone, so I figured I needed a wife."

"What was wrong with her?"

"Nothing, really, except maybe she thought everything was wrong with me. I couldn't do anything right. She was taller than her sister and probably carried fifty or more pounds. I thought if I ever got up the nerve to get her pregnant, she'd be able to carry a child, and that was all that mattered to me.

"Her father said if he hadn't married her off to me, he'd be stuck with her for life." Brad laughed. "Her moods could sour milk still in the cow. He lied about her not ever finding anyone, though. A few months after we married, she ran off with a railroad worker. Last I heard, they were living up North somewhere and had a dozen kids. After the sisters, I knew I wasn't meant for the married life, so I started drifting."

Bonnie rose up and giggled. She wanted to tell him that she'd never talked with a man like this, all honest and natural. Only how do you tell someone who called you pretty that he's the only one in the world who sees you that way?

"Lady." He looked into her eyes. "Mind if I kiss you again?"

She sat very still. "No. I've no objection."

He moved his lips to her throat and began burning a trail to her mouth.

Bonnie sighed and leaned her head back, loving the feel of him. Her mouth was open slightly when he finally reached her lips. The kiss took her breath away.

Vaguely she was aware of him shifting her body in his lap so that her head rested in the crook of his arm. His kiss made her feel warm all over, and she was lost to all but feeling.

When he finally left her lips, he didn't stop kissing her. His mouth moved back down her throat as his chin brushed her head back so that he could taste her skin. His hands moved over her leg, feeling her through the layers of cotton until he reached the hem of her petticoat and began his journey back up her leg without the hindrance of the cotton between them.

"You taste so good," he whispered against her ear. "Mind if I kiss you again and again?" When she laughed, he added, "And again?"

She made one sound of invitation before his mouth closed over hers.

He finished one long kiss before moving to her

ear and whispering, "Do you like that, Pretty Lady?"

She made a sigh, and his hand moved up to her thigh as he continued to kiss her.

Now he was teaching her how he wanted to be kissed, guiding her mouth open. "More," he mumbled against her lips. "Deeper. Draw me into your mouth."

She followed his suggestions.

"Mind if we do this a while longer?" he insisted when he finally took time to breathe. "I can't seem to get enough of you."

"Please," she answered and arched her back so he could move down her throat. She was floating with pleasure and growing hungry for his mouth on hers.

"Yes," she whispered against his lips when he finally returned.

His kiss turned deep with longing, making her aware of nothing but him and the fire building inside her.

His hand moved higher, where he gripped her soft flesh and pulled her legs apart slightly. "I need to touch you. You're so soft. I want to feel all of you."

She felt his heavy breathing against her throat and knew he was waiting for her to say yes.

A tiny part of her mind told her she wasn't young, she was an old maid. Foolish passion was for girls, not women of her age.

His grip was so tight, she knew he'd already left a bruise, but she didn't care. He wasn't hurting her, he was wanting her.

She straightened, pushing him a few inches away. He fought her action for a moment, then straightened back, giving her room. His eyes were on fire as he stared at her, but his hand moved back down her leg and slowly replaced the petticoat.

Her breath came so fast, she couldn't speak. She'd never felt like this before, not for one minute. Not for one second.

He closed his eyes and rested his head on the back of the rocker. "If you're waiting for me to say I'm sorry," he finally said, "you'll wait a hell of a long time."

"Open your eyes," she ordered.

He did. She could still see the fire blended with a sorrow, a longing, a pain she knew well.

Her hands trembled as she lifted them to the front of her camisole and began to unbutton the first button. "I've never been a selfish person," she said as she pulled the first button free. "I've always thought of myself as a woman of simple needs." The second button fell and then the third.

He didn't move, but his eyes were no longer on hers.

She smiled as she tugged the next button free and felt the camisole fall open so that all but the tips of her breasts showed. "Tonight, I'd like to ask you for something, and before you answer,

I'll have you know that I'll not settle for less. I want my one time, my one memory. Then I want your word you'll take me back." She had her life planned, organized. This would be her one step off the sidewalk.

His fingertips brushed the swell of one of her breasts. As he explored in slight movements, the fabric fell away, revealing her. He looked into her eyes so she could see his pleasure as his hand spread over her flesh.

She saw what she'd longed for in his gaze. She saw herself as beautiful.

"Name it," he whispered. His eyes didn't leave hers, but his hand closed around her. As he measured the width and weight of her in his palm, she drew in a quick breath at the shock of pleasure sparking through her body.

"Name it, I said." His voice was raw with need and demanding.

She closed her eyes and answered, "Be my storm tonight. Be the one night I'll never forget. Be the memory I'll carry with me forever, and then promise at dawn we'll part."

His hand tightened, and she swayed with the sensation. She never dreamed a touch could spark her body so.

He dug his free hand through her hair and pulled her mouth to his. Now his kiss was free and wild with need, and his fingers moved over her breasts, branding them forever with his caress.

"Swear," she said when he let her breathe. "Swear that you'll keep your word. One night. One storm."

He tugged her hair back, until she arched her body toward his, and sucked hard on one of her breasts. "I swear," he whispered. "But you'll be mine, all mine, tonight."

"Yes," she sealed the bargain with one word.

He picked her up and carried her to the bed, but he didn't lie on top of her as she thought he would. He stretched beside her so that he could kiss her while he undressed her completely. One hand circled in her hair so that she'd remain still while he finished his task. She knew without asking that he was a man learning tenderness for the first time.

When she tried to reach for the blanket, she heard a low growl from him. "No," he ordered. "There'll be nothing between us. Not tonight."

Then he kissed her so tenderly, she settled against him, letting him touch her wherever he liked. When he knew she'd calmed and grown used to his nearness, he pulled away long enough to undress. When he returned, he was above her, gently settling over her.

She jerked at the feel of skin against skin.

He took his time once again, allowing her to grow used to the feel of his body against hers. His rough hands moved over her as though he'd never touched anything so dear, and he wanted to savor the feel of her.

When she relaxed once more, he explored, slowly examining, kissing, tasting every part of her. There was a hunger to his actions that left her skin sensitive and aching for him to return.

"I'm going to go slow," he whispered when he returned to her mouth for a deep, open kiss. Then he added, "I don't want to hurt you."

"You won't," she answered, hoping she spoke the truth.

She felt his words as he kissed the corners of her mouth. His hand had spread over her below her belly button. While he tasted her throat, his fingers started back to her breasts, where she knew he'd take his time learning every inch of her.

"I'm going to love you, Pretty Lady, and when we're finished, I'm going to start all over again."

And that's exactly what he did.

CHAPTER 15

DEEP IN THE SHADOWS OF THE NIGHT, Bonnie slept soundly in the arms of her stranger. Mixing with her dreams, she felt him tug her legs open and move above her.

"No," she mumbled, remembering how it had hurt when he'd entered her. Everything about the loving had been so perfect except the moment he'd shoved into her. "No," she said, trying to push him away so she could return to sleep.

"Hush, love," he whispered. His hands were

moving over her most private places as if her body belonged to him. "You're ready for me now. Go back to sleep. I'm just going to take my pleasure one more time. You're mine tonight, remember."

She couldn't seem to pull fully awake. Hours without sleep and then hours of having her blood rushing through her body as he pleased her again and again had left her too weak to shake from dreams.

He pulled her arms above her head and moved his warm hands down the length of her. He knew her body well by now and proved it. "Dream, love. Just dream while I take you, for I have to have you again."

Before she could answer, she felt him slide into her without pain, then he was moving above her, pushing harder and harder. The familiar fire she'd felt in her belly kindled, and she rocked with him, taking him deeper, loving the way her blood warmed and spread out into her limbs.

His hands came up her sides and gripped her tender breasts as he cried out with pleasure just as she felt like she rolled off the end of the earth. He jerked and pushed into her one last time as she took flight.

For a while she floated as his warm body blanketed her. She floated between heaven and earth, unable to move or speak.

He didn't rise and wash her flesh as he had the

first time. He simply rolled with her until she lay across him, too spent to move.

He cupped her bottom with one hand and moved his chin against her cheek. "Go back to sleep," he ordered. "You're mine tonight. All mine. I plan to touch you while you sleep, if you've no objection."

She made a little sound, agreeing to his request, and he kissed her lips, now swollen from being kissed.

"I like the feel of you," he said as he patted her bottom.

"Thank you," she whispered.

"Did you feel the storm?" he asked.

"Yes," she answered and felt his arms tighten. "And it was a thousand times more than I thought it would be."

She felt his laughter against her chest.

"The night is not over yet." His mouth explored her throat. "Sleep. I'll wake you again before dawn."

She didn't answer; she was already asleep.

CHAPTER 16

SAGE WAS STARTING TO LOSE TRACK OF TIME. She thought it was the fourth day when they camped at the edge of a canyon, but it might have been five. The air felt dry here, and the wind whistled as if whining along canyon walls. As the outlaws had every night, they tied her to whatever they could find that would hold her secure.

But tonight was different. She could hear the man building a fire, establishing a regular camp for the first time. She guessed they thought it safe.

The man who brought her food was one who'd never spoken to her before. She thought he was one of the two men who'd been with them when they left Shelley's, then they'd disappeared for a day and rejoined the gang. The two newcomers kept their distance and usually brought up the tail, but tonight they'd decided to move in closer, probably because of the fire.

He didn't seem as hard as the others, but his eyes were still cold and uncaring. There was a wildness about him, as if a thrill to him was worth any price. He untied her hands but left the rope around her waist holding her to a stump. The noose now hung permanently around her neck so any one of them could pull her along without having to get so close she might kick. The rough rope was loose enough for her to breathe but too tight for her to tug it off.

"Thought you might want a real meal. Got rabbit and beans." She smelled whiskey on the man's breath, but that was better than the smell of Frog.

She nodded, trying to see anything around her that would give her a hint of where she was.

He handed her a tin bowl and a cup half-full of boiled coffee. "These men ain't going to hurt you none," the stranger said. "They told me so. They're just taking you to the leader, then you'll be let go, I figure." He didn't look like he believed his own words.

She would argue with that statement, but it would do her no good. Every bone in her body hurt from riding all day tied in a saddle and then sleeping at night tied up. If she didn't walk fast enough when they stopped, the big man liked to jerk the rope hard enough to make her stumble. She doubted any one of the other men had noticed. For the most part, she wasn't their problem.

When she finished eating, she thanked the man.

He hesitated. "Anything else I can do?" he whispered, then looked like he was sorry he'd offered.

"Could I have a comb before you tie my hands?" She needed one, but mainly she wanted to keep the man close enough to talk to.

He moved a few feet away and pulled a comb from his gear and handed it to her. "It ain't very clean, but then neither is your hair."

"Thank you," she managed.

Sage worked through the rats in her hair. Finally, she parted it down the middle and braided it on either side.

She handed him back the comb.

"You look like an Indian," he said as he tied her hands.

"Maybe I am," she whispered.

He shook his head. "Charlie says you're a doctor."

"Who is Charlie?"

He moved his head slightly toward the red-headed giant she called Big Hands: the leader of the band, the cruel one.

Sage fought down a smile. She had a name. "I am a doctor," she said to the only one of the men who'd spoken to her other than in orders. "Who are you?"

He stood, realizing he'd stayed too long. "Nobody. I'm nobody to you."

She didn't want to lose the one contact she'd made. This man was hard, but he seemed at least human. "What is the leader going to do with me?" She wondered if they knew about her family. The McMurrays were not rich, but compared to most ranches, they must look it. Maybe these outlaws thought they could get a ransom.

The stranger shrugged. "I don't know. I only hooked up with this lot for one piece of paper in that safe. Tomorrow morning they say they'll hand it over to me, and I'll be on my way. I'm not close enough to the gang to be allowed to enter the hideout they'll be heading to. Not sure I want to be. They say a man named Hanover rules the place like he was king."

"What paper's worth your life?"

The stranger shrugged. "The deed to my father's land. I'm not much for ranching, but my brother is. He'll make use of the land." He hesitated, just wanting to talk. "That gambler, Shelley Lander, said I was drunk and lost my land at poker, but I only took one drink that night, and I've never been a poker player. I went in the place seeing if he'd keep the deed in his safe until the title office opened. He kept it, all right."

Sage wasn't surprised that Shelley had swindled the man. He probably would have tried to claim anything she'd been fool enough to leave in his safe also. "If you're caught, Mr. Nobody, you'll hang with them just the same. Men were killed back there."

He grinned at what she'd called him and answered, "I know. There wasn't supposed to be any killing, just robbing. At dawn tomorrow I plan to wash my hands of this gang and never set eyes on them again. My brother says we can ranch, and I reckon I'm old enough to finally settle somewhere."

"You'll be hunted down." Sage thought it was worth a try, so she said, "Your only chance might be to take me with you tomorrow. We could ride back to town. I'd tell the Rangers that you saved me. Then you'd have your freedom and your land."

He shook his head. "These men would never give you to me. They say they're taking you to Hanover. They're pretty closemouthed about it, but I think their leader, a fellow who claims to be some kind of count from England, is hurt or sick. I think they need a doctor."

"But—"

He stopped her. "Look, miss, if you ain't a doc, I sure wouldn't mention it, because that's all that's keeping you alive right now. Otherwise, you're just a witness, and all the other witnesses are dead back there on the floor of the gambling house."

Sage stared at the stranger, trying to make out his features in the darkness. "How'd you get mixed up with these men?"

"There ain't that many men in this country. I suspect I either know or have heard of most of them. These guys don't usually go into settlements. They tend to pester trading posts and freighters. I'd be willing to bet this is the biggest haul they ever made." When she didn't say anything, he added, "I figure many men in Texas have walked on both sides of the law from time to time. I've never seen the line all that clear myself."

Sage tried to think. She didn't trust this man enough to tell him who she was or to try to bribe him. All she had of value was her wedding band, and she doubted he'd risk his life for ten dollars in gold.

But if she could get a message out with him when he left, there was a chance it could help someone find her.

The stranger picked up her cup and bowl. No one else in the camp was close to them. Sage knew this might be her only chance.

"Do you know someone named Drummond Roak?"

The stranger hesitated. "I heard of him. Word is, he's fast as lightning with a gun. Never met him though. For all I know, he's a damn legend."

Sage hid her surprise. "If you see him, I swear he'd count it a favor if you tell him you saw me."

The man studied her. "I'll do that," he whispered. "Having a man like Roak owe me one might be worth the risk. But, miss, I ain't likely to see him. I plan to stay out of any town for a while."

"Just promise you will if your paths cross."

"I will." He walked away without looking back.

She sat in the dark and watched the men moving about. This was the farthest they'd ever bedded down away from her, but tonight they all seemed to want the fire's warmth, and her tree stump wasn't close.

If she could work her ropes loose, tonight would be her best chance to escape. Maybe she could hide and follow Mr. Nobody out when he left in the morning. Maybe they'd be so occupied with dividing up the take, they wouldn't notice her gone. Mr. Nobody probably wouldn't help her, but he was bound to be headed away from the rest of them.

She'd fought with the ropes for an hour when she saw Frog coming toward her. She could have smelled him, even if she hadn't looked up.

He dropped some kind of animal skin a few feet from her and lay down.

"What are you doing?" she snapped.

"I'm sleeping here to make sure you don't get any ideas of wandering off." He tugged the end of her noose leash so hard, she tumbled over toward him. His hands fumbled with the noose, pushing it tight against her throat, then he shoved her back where she'd been. His hand raked across her chest a bit too freely.

"Touch me again, and I swear I'll kill you," she threatened.

He snickered. "I ain't gonna touch you. You're too small for me. I got a woman waiting for me back at the camp. She'd make two of you."

Sage almost lost her dinner thinking of the kind of woman who would welcome a man who smelled as bad as Frog.

She heard the one called Charlie laugh somewhere in the darkness and realized he must be on guard. There would be no escape tonight, and tomorrow she'd be riding into an outlaw camp.

At dawn, she woke to the sound of a single shot. Straightening, she stared at the scene before her. The men were up, the horses saddled, the fire out.

For a moment she couldn't see what they were all staring at on the ground, then she made out the body of Mr. Nobody. Part of his head must have exploded with the shot fired at such close range. Blood spread across the dirt, dark in the pale sun. He'd fallen straight back, his arms and legs extended. A folded piece of paper was still clenched in his right hand.

The men didn't touch him as they mounted. Charlie walked her horse over and untied her from the tree. He used the rope tied around her throat to tug her to the horse as if she were a dog. Then he put his big hands around her waist and tossed her into the saddle.

"Aren't you going to bury him?" She didn't dare ask about the shooting.

"No." Charlie tied her hands to the horn and belted her legs to the saddle. "Let the wild animals feed on him. He's nothing to us, never was."

He climbed on his horse and tugged hers along. She looked back once at the dead man who wouldn't tell her his name. The piece of paper he'd risked his life for was still in his hand.

CHAPTER 17

As THE SUN CLIMBED, THEY RODE INTO A narrow canyon. The walls grew higher by the hour. At noon, when Charlie stopped long enough to give her water, the passage was so narrow that no more than two horses could stand abreast. A wagon could have passed if it moved carefully, but no more.

Sage felt the cold more than usual. The passage was almost always in shade, and the wind whipped down it as if trying to escape. She knew it wasn't the temperature that iced her spine but the knowledge that she'd be impossible to find.

The going was slow. Twice, the men had to stop and clear the trail of landslides. Sage tried to memorize every turn. When she escaped, she might be doing so at night, and she didn't want to get lost in what looked like a maze of canyons.

Mid-afternoon, the redheaded leader called a halt in a wide spot where there was plenty of room and grass to make a camp. Charlie left her on her horse while he talked to his men. Apparently two of the men would ride on to the hideout, while the others stayed behind. It appeared to be a rule of the outlaws. One or two riders wouldn't be seen as a threat; six horses might, even if one was obviously a woman. The two riders would get close enough to the guards to talk, but they wouldn't have enough time to come back until morning.

Sage was thankful when Charlie told the one she called Frog to ride on in. If they untied her tonight, she'd reach for her tiny pistol. This camp had to be easier to escape from than the hideout would be tomorrow.

Charlie finally noticed her and lifted her down. She paced around pretty much free to go wherever she liked in the barn-size opening. Charlie had tied the other end of her leash to his saddle horn when he'd unsaddled the horses. With her hands still bound, if she wanted to go anywhere beyond the length of rope, she'd have to drag his saddle with her. She'd been among the men so long none of them paid her any attention, but she had a feeling that if she tried to bolt, four bullets would be in her back before she could get out of range.

She hated this place more than anywhere they'd stopped. It reminded her of an open grave. Anyone above could kill them all with a good rifle or a few well-thrown rocks. The little man who'd threatened to kill her if she sneezed fell in beside her. He wasn't old, maybe not even twenty, and as near as she could tell, he must have been born nervous. Most of the time Charlie sent him ahead to scout or told him to take drag to make sure they weren't being followed. Maybe the boss couldn't stand his jerky manner any better than she could.

"We'll be home by noon tomorrow." Sneezy's words echoed off the canyon walls. "I'm going to ask Hanover if I can kill you if you turn out to be worthless. I've never killed a woman before." He laughed, excited at the possibility. "I've heard it's more fun to do it with a knife."

Sage frowned at him. She had one bullet and so many she wanted to kill. Right now, he was moving to the top of the list. "Why would you think that?" she asked, just to pester him.

" 'Cause women whine and beg, but they don't fight. All they try to do is get away." He studied her. "I'll have to make the first cut deep enough to slow you down but not so deep that you die before I have time to make you feel several more cuts." For some odd reason, he thought she was interested in his plan. "I think I'll have to tie you up real good, at least for the first few, or maybe I'll cut your leg so you can't walk. That way I wouldn't have to mess with bloody ropes, and I could watch you try to get away."

"Is that how you killed your mother?" She swore she saw a spark of anger in his eyes as if she'd guessed at the truth.

Charlie yelled for someone to shut the woman up.

Sneezy grinned, raised his rifle, and hit her on the side of the head with the butt.

She crumpled but didn't pass out, though she knew enough to stay down.

He hooked his hands beneath her arms and dragged her over near the saddle. Then, as if practicing, he tied her up so she could barely move. Pulling his knife, he slit her skirt open to bare her calf and felt around for the muscle.

Sage remained perfectly still, guessing that he'd get more pleasure out of his examination if she fought. By the time he moved away, he'd made the top of her list.

There was no fire tonight, and no one offered her a blanket. The only thing that kept her warm was her hatred of these men.

When she woke the next morning, she almost wished for death. Her entire body hurt from being crumpled in the dirt all night. The ropes had cut into her wrists until they bled. She couldn't remember the last time any of the men had thought to give her a swallow of water.

Charlie cut her ropes and pulled her up. "Can you stand?" he said.

She nodded, wiping the blood away from her wrist with the last scrap of her handkerchief and dropping it as Charlie grabbed her chin and jerked her face to the light.

He swore at the wiry little man for hurting her. Not that he cared about her; he just wanted his gift to Hanover to look better. He tugged on the leash and led her to her horse. Before putting her up, he tilted her head back and made her drink, then he splashed water over her bruised and bloody forehead where she'd been hit.

When he strapped her into the saddle, he put her medical bag at her side. It was the first time she'd seen the bag since Shelley's office.

He tugged the noose off her neck. "There is nowhere to run and no reason to scream, girl. You behave yourself, and you just might be alive come sundown."

They rode away from the camp. The cliffs grew lower as they rode, and by the time the sun was high, she could make out the glint of rifles above them. The canyon walls lowered still more and finally opened out into a valley big enough to be a small ranch. She saw a pond and rows of what looked like a late summer garden. There were corrals for horses and a pasture with a few cattle grazing. Built along the far canyon wall were a cluster of buildings that looked like the beginning of a town. Three two-story buildings dominated the area, with a dozen more circling them. One looked like a boardinghouse with a second-story balcony. From the second floor a few men could easily defend the entire valley. Another big building looked like a saloon. As they rode by, she noticed several women watching them pass. They had the dull eyes of opium users.

The last big building was set back from the others, at the end of the small town. It could have easily passed for a Virginia plantation house with a wide porch and high columns. Trees, a story high, had been transplanted from somewhere and now stood dead at the corners of the house.

"That's the count's place," Charlie said. "Henry Harrison Hanover, a real member of the royalty, owns everything in this town. Every man and woman who lives here works for him. In exchange we get food and board along with enough pay to frequent the saloon and whorehouse. If we don't follow the rules he sets, he pays for our burial."

Sage knew Charlie well enough to know he wasn't just talking to her. He'd probably been given orders to give the same speech to anyone riding in. No wonder Mr. Nobody didn't want to come with the rest of the gang.

Charlie pulled her off her horse and almost dragged her up the steps to the house. A guard at the door looked her over as she moved past him but didn't say a word.

Once inside, she waited in the foyer with the wiry man while Charlie made his report. The English accent she heard had to be the count. He seemed pleased with the haul from Shelley's place and asked twice if they left the gambler alive. It was obvious that the gang planned to bleed him again. Sage almost felt sorry for Shelley. Almost.

"One more thing," Charlie said as he backed through the door and grabbed her arm. "We brought you a doctor."

One second later she stood before a man dressed in an elaborate red bathrobe with a family crest embroidered on the pocket. He had flowing white hair that seemed to slide off the back of his head, and he wore a ring on every finger of his left hand.

She met his eyes and saw easily that he was ill, far more ill than he was allowing the others to see.

The strange man stared at her. "You're a doctor?" He raised an eyebrow.

"Yes," she answered. "I am. I've just arrived from Boston."

He touched her cheek with a soft hand. "Who damaged you?"

"No one," Charlie said. "She fell a few times."

The count stared at her. "Never lie to me, Doctor. I hate it. How did you get this cut?" He touched her bruised forehead.

Sage glanced at Sneezy to make sure he wasn't about to hit her again. "My head fell against the butt of a rifle."

Hanover looked like he was trying to decide whether to be angry, then suddenly, he smiled. "I'm in need of a doctor. We deal with my problem first."

Sage thought she saw a flicker of insanity in his gaze. "If you'll allow me to clean up, I'll try to help you." She flavored her words with the Boston accent she'd practiced.

He smiled and waved at a squatty little man standing behind him. "Take her somewhere she can wash, Myron. Don't let her out of your sight, but don't harm her."

The man, who looked like a proper butler, nodded and motioned for Sage to follow him.

She turned to Charlie. "I'll have my hands free first." She glared at the man who'd treated her like an animal for a week.

He pulled out his knife and slit the last of her ropes.

As soon as she was alone with the butler, she whispered, "I was brought here against my will. Kidnapped."

He didn't look interested. "Half of the people here are in the same boat. Including me. I'm a third-generation butler. Do you think I picked this residence for employment? I've got the seat next to you in misery, dearie."

"Isn't there a way out of here?"

"Only if you're bound for heaven or hell. No one leaves this place alive unless you're one of the count's trusted men." He made a face. "And never, never, trust one of those men." He held up his hand to show her that his little finger was missing.

She didn't ask more.

They went into a kitchen at the back of the house, and he handed her a towel and soap. She washed as she asked, "What's wrong with the count?"

"He's got a bullet stuck in his shoulder blade. It's poisoning his blood, but he's accused everyone who's tried to get it out of trying to kill him. Most of us have been waiting around praying he'd die, but Charlie, the snake, seems to have a fondness for the man. No one else suggested bringing in a doctor." Myron held her bag.

Sage took the time to doctor the cuts on her hands and the small cut on her forehead, not because she was worried they might get infected or leave scars, but so she could have time to form a plan.

Myron stayed in the room with her but didn't hover. He made her tea with honey. She drank the tea slowly as she thought.

"Are you ready, Doctor?" Myron finally said.

"Yes, but I may need boiling water to treat Hanover. Would you put kettles on?"

"Of course."

"Is he really royalty?"

Myron shrugged. "Who knows. He says he's twenty-third in line, but his father fell out of favor with the court of Queen Victoria. Something about bodies of servant girls turning up in the pond, he said. I try not to ask too many questions. If he wants to be a count, what do I care?"

"Twenty-three seems pretty far away from the throne."

"So does Texas, but I hear him mumbling that he'll be moving up soon." He led her back to the downstairs room that looked like it had been an office and now served as a sickroom.

Hanover lay on his stomach on top of a bed by the window. Sage guessed he wasn't asleep. She walked to the edge of the bed.

"What do I call you?" she asked.

"Everyone calls me Count Hanover," he answered without opening his eyes. "If you're a doctor, then get to it. My pain is in my back."

Sage lifted the robe back almost to his waist. The pus-filled wound almost made her gag. Dark veins grew from a core of scabs and open wounds as if something had taken root in the center of his back.

"I was shot," he said. "Several have tried to get the bullet out."

Sage didn't miss the signs that he'd been bled as well in an effort to get the poison out. "They've done more harm than good."

He looked at her then. "I agree. The question is, will you be yet another waste of time?"

Sage looked steadily back at him. "I can help you, Count Hanover, but you'll have to do what I say. It will not be painless, and I cannot make the healing fast."

He nodded. "I've endured much already." He motioned for the guard at the door. "Move closer, Luther. If she does anything to shorten my life, kill her."

The guard didn't look at her; he just nodded and pulled his knife. Apparently, he didn't plan to waste a bullet.

She turned to Myron, who was still standing near the door. "I'll need boiling water and lots of towels. I'll also need the fireplace lit and kept burning. As soon as it's afire, I'd like you to move him close to it."

Myron looked at the count, then hurried to do as she said. Within the hour, she'd begun. The temperature in the room had to be eighty. The guard Hanover had called Luther was sweating, but he never moved from watching her hands.

She'd stripped the count to his waist and placed a cold cloth over his head as she began to clean the wounds with water so hot it almost burned the pus away. The crude attempts to remove the bullet had left infections, and each had to be almost as painful as the embedded lead.

She made a tea out of the last of the willow tree bark her brothers mailed her from her Apache grandfather each year, and added a touch of opium from her bag. The tea helped him sweat, the willow bark eased fever, and the opium dulled the pain. Nothing stopped his complaining. He called her every name she thought women had been called since time began, but he never told her to stop.

Finally, sometime long after dark, he slept. Sage laced clean bandages over the wounds she'd packed with a poultice of powdered paper and tobacco to draw out the infections. She stood and told Myron to let the fire die down. She knew the count would sleep the night, and tomorrow they'd operate to remove the bullet.

Myron brought her what looked like a table-cloth and draped it around her like a shawl. "No one, not even me, sleeps in the count's house, but I've told the guard to take you somewhere safe." He patted her shoulder. "I'd never hurt you, dearie, and Luther won't either, unless he has to. He's not cruel for no reason like some of them are."

She nodded and followed the guard down the dark street to the building that looked like a boardinghouse. They went in a side door. He lit a lantern and motioned her forward. Sometime during the day he'd stopped bullying her and started treating her with a small degree of respect. After Charlie and his gang, even a small allow-ance was appreciated.

"Thank you," she said when he opened the third door they passed.

There, on the first floor was a line of rooms that looked like cells, boarded in on the sides, but barred at the door and window. Inside her cell was a bed with blankets, a tray of food, and a small bathtub surrounded with all she'd need.

"Myron set this up for you. He said after what you did today, you deserved a little peace." The guard backed away. "I'm the only one who has a key to this cell and the door beyond, so you can sleep until I come get you."

When she heard the door lock behind her, she knew she was being locked in for her safety. She tossed the shawl over the window and took a bath. Then she ate everything on the tray and crawled into bed, loving the luxury of covers. For the first time in a week she slept soundly.

CHAPTER 18

IT WAS ALMOST MIDNIGHT WHEN BONNIE Faye felt her cowboy pull the reins on his horse and stop. She'd been sleeping in his arms as they'd traveled, loving the blended sounds of the night and his heartbeat. Even though they might not have enough in common to carry on much of a conversation, his nearness made her feel safe, truly safe.

He hadn't said much to her all day, but his touch was gentle. They both knew what was expected. She'd agreed to be his lover until dawn, and he'd promised to give her a night she'd remember.

They'd made love for the last time at dawn, a

sweet kind of love that made her cry as a gentle rain tapped against the cabin windows. Neither talked afterward, but he'd held her to him until she'd drifted to sleep.

When she woke, he had the horses ready. The cold, gray morning reflected her mood as she stepped outside. The plainness of his land, now brown with fall and dead all around, made her feel sorry for him. A lonely man on a lonely spread. She fought not to show how she felt, but he probably read it in her eyes. This isolation would be a dull kind of hell for her.

She tried to ride the horse he'd saddled for her, but after a few minutes, it was obvious she knew nothing about handling a mount, so he climbed up behind her, and they'd ridden double, switching horses every time they stopped.

Neither had wanted to eat, and he made no attempt to kiss her when they stopped. It was as if the storm had passed, and they were once again two strangers. He'd left his land holding her tight, but now there was a formalness about his touch.

"Galveston's just up ahead," he said when she raised her head off his chest. "Do you want me to take you to the Ranger station or the hotel?"

For one wild moment she considered telling him to take her back to the cabin. One wonderful night could never be enough. She realized they didn't even know each other. The shyness she'd always had around men blanketed her. She couldn't talk about what they'd done, couldn't even think about it without blushing.

"The station," she whispered. "They'll know about Sage and the Smith boys."

She didn't say anything about how she'd explain the time she'd been gone. She couldn't tell him what it had meant to her. She could have told him their night was her first and probably her only time to be loved, but he knew. He understood what it had meant to her, just as she knew how it had changed him.

She smiled. He'd called her Pretty Lady and touched her as if she were a treasure.

He nudged her head with his chin. "Look at me," he said.

She looked up; the flickering lights of town sparkled in his eyes.

"I want to give you something." He reached in his pocket. "So you'll remember me and our one night."

"Oh, no. It's not necessary." She'd never forget him.

He smiled as if reading her mind, then tugged her hand up and slid a thin ring on her finger. "This was my mother's. It ain't much, but I want you to have it. I've been married twice, but tonight was the first time I felt like . . ."

He didn't finish. He couldn't find the words.

She looked down at the tiny bands of gold

that had been laced together. It wasn't a wedding ring, but it almost could have been.

"Thank you," she managed, knowing he'd be insulted if she even tried to give it back. "I wish I had something for you."

"You gave me enough. I've never been worth much, but for one night I was all you needed."

She wrapped her arms around him, and he urged the horse toward the lights. When they reached the Ranger station, he climbed down and slowly lowered her beside him. For a moment he hugged her as if he couldn't let her go, then he turned her toward the door and pushed her forward.

She took two steps and glanced back.

He was gone. Vanished into the night.

Bonnie fought back tears and touched the ring. He'd saved her; that's all the Rangers needed to know. The rest was hers to hold in her heart.

She'd had her storm to remember.

Walking into the station, she saw the Rangers stand in surprise. When she stepped into the light, they all rushed toward her with questions. Where had she been? How had she managed to stay alive? Was she with Sage?

Bonnie asked her own questions between answering theirs. After almost an hour, the captain woke the Smith boys. They ran to her and hugged her. Bonnie fought back tears, because she was exhausted. She'd never lived so much in such a short time.

"Don't cry." Will put his arm on her shoulder. "We're all right. We was just waiting here until you and the doctor came for us." He pressed close to her ear. "We been taking good care of the mutt and your cat. You'll be proud of us."

"I already am," she whispered back. "Thanks."

Harmon asked if she'd like someone to see her and the boys back to the hotel.

Bonnie shook her head.

He knelt and held Will and Andy by the shoulder. "When you're full grown, come find me," he said. "I'd be honored to have you ride with the Rangers."

Will straightened with pride. Andy leaned against her skirts, looking tired.

Harmon asked again if she wanted someone to walk her back to the hotel.

Bonnie looked around at the faces of the Rangers and saw it then. The look men had always given her. That invisible look that told her she was a woman to be polite to but never to flatter or flirt with or even talk to more than necessary.

"No, thank you, Captain, I'll be fine." She took the boys' hands. "I've got these two to watch over me."

He saw her out the door and as far as the lights of the hotel before he turned back to go to work on all he'd learned.

Bonnie walked, her head high, knowing somewhere in the night was a man who'd wanted her, who'd loved her, who'd thought of her as beautiful.

She touched the ring, knowing he'd always be with her. Her father often said she was a woman meant to be useful, but for one night she'd been cherished. She'd been a woman to be loved.

CHAPTER 19

DRUMMOND ROAK FOUND A MAN'S BODY lying beside a cold campfire just before sundown. He'd seen a buzzard circling up ahead and feared he'd find Sage dead. He'd been trailing the gang for days, watching for every sign.

Sage's small footprint had given him hope. She was with them, surviving.

He grinned. Knowing her, she was torturing the men as much as possible.

When he'd found the campsite, he wanted to rush in, but he took his time moving up. He stared down at the body of the outlaw. The man of about forty had been shot in the head, but judging from the look of him, it couldn't have been more than eight, maybe ten hours since he'd died. If he'd spent a night out here, animals would have already begun to pull him apart. As it was, only one lone buzzard had dinner plans.

Drum tugged a paper from his hand and read it. A deed, made out to Solomon and Bradford Summerfield, for a piece of land back two days' ride in the direction of Galveston. If this man had died because of this paper, he'd been the only one who thought it valuable.

Drum tucked it in his saddlebag, figuring one of the names on the deed was probably staring at him right now with dead eyes.

He studied the rest of the camp, reading it easily, thanks to the damp earth. Five men rode out. Spotting Sage's shoe print, he let out a long breath. She was still with them, still alive.

Kneeling, he picked up a slice of her handkerchief spotted with blood, and he swore. All five men who rode out with Sage would be dead soon. He'd see to it.

He turned to the mouth of a canyon called Skull Alley. Every outlaw in the state had heard of the place. It had been around for ten, maybe fifteen years. Only the lowest of the low lived there, men so worthless any organized gang wouldn't bother with them. Somewhere inside Skull Alley lay the rough makings of a town that was run by an insane Englishman who thought of himself as royalty. The only reason the army or the Rangers hadn't gone in to clean it out years ago was that the opening was a natural protection better than any fort.

Drum folded the lace handkerchief and slipped it into his pocket. He'd been a boy when his mother brought him here for one winter. She'd heard the whoring was good, and he guessed it had been. She'd stayed busy most of the time, and he'd roamed the land. He'd found a way out without going through the passage that was guarded by three layers of riflemen. The count's orders to the guards were simple: shoot anyone they didn't recognize on sight, and question the rest.

Drum figured he could bribe his way through the first guard, maybe even the second, but the third line of defense was said to be men who had been with the count for years. Their families lived in the camp, and the men knew their wives and children would be killed if the wrong man managed to get through.

Pacing, he weighed his options. If he went straight in, he'd be spotted, questioned, and probably shot. If he tried to find the path he'd used to climb out unnoticed years ago, they'd know he was sneaking in and shoot him on sight. He'd been a kid then, half the size he was now. It wouldn't be easy slipping past the guards and, if he didn't make it, they wouldn't bother asking questions. Either way, he'd be of no use to Sage.

Knowing it was too late today for either action, Drum spent the rest of the daylight burying the stranger. He tied his horse in the trees a few hundred yards from the entrance to the canyon and tried to get some sleep. He felt like he hadn't slept in days, but tonight, knowing that he was close, helped him to rest easy.

Late into the night he woke to the even sound of a low growl. Drum didn't move. The sound came again. He rolled onto his side and cocked his gun as he searched the darkness with eyes honed to the night.

The low sound came again, more like a snore than a growl. Could a wild animal be sleeping three feet away? Maybe the animal didn't notice him and bedded down in the trees as he had. No, that would be impossible, and what was even more impossible was the possibility that Drum hadn't heard anything.

His eyes adjusted enough for him to see the long form wrapped in a blanket about five feet away. The snore came again, muffled by a tan hat. Drum thought of shooting whoever it was just to teach the fellow a lesson. Then he noticed the spotted pony staked out not far from Satan.

"Daniel Torry," Drum bellowed. "What in the hell are you doing here?"

The young Ranger woke and stretched. "I figured if I bedded down close, you'd notice me before leaving in the morning."

"How'd you find me?"

"You were so busy following the outlaw trail, a duck could have tagged along behind you. Only problem I had was trying to stay awake to keep up. Didn't anyone ever tell you a man has to sleep now and then? If you hadn't stopped tonight, I would have fallen out of my saddle, and I doubt hitting the ground would have woke me."

"You didn't answer my question. What are you doing here?"

Daniel stretched and lay back down. "I thought I'd help. I didn't want to say anything back at the station, but like you, I've been to Skull Alley and lived to tell about it."

"You have?"

"My dad used to run a liquor wagon in there every month. They probably could have made their own rotgut, but the count wanted the good stuff. Soon as I was big enough to look like a man riding shotgun, my pa would take me along."

"I heard no one comes out." Drum believed Daniel, but he still asked. "I thought you said your pa was a preacher?"

"My pa would drive the whiskey wagon and preach to me at the same time." He laughed. "Too bad I took to the drink and not the preaching."

Roak leaned back, knowing Daniel would get around to telling him the facts directly.

"From what I remember," Daniel said, "only two groups do manage to ride out. My pa, who brings whiskey, and the last few years the count lets a group of gamblers ride in about the same time.

"I figure Shelley Lander must have been one of them at some point. They come in, hold a big poker tournament while the liquor is running, let one of the men from the camp take the main prize, and fleece the others. My pa said that way the count makes sure his men don't squirrel up enough money to leave. I figured the gamblers gave the count a cut, so I put the facts together and decided that maybe that's why the men came after Shelley. Maybe he left without donating his share to the boss, so the count sent his men to take it. They left him alive so they could drop by and visit him regular."

"Your pa still making the runs?"

"Far as I know. We had a fight a few years back, and I left home, if you can call the back room of a saloon home. Haven't seen him since. He'd be real unhappy to know I became a Ranger. If he's still delivering, he should be here in a day or two. It's getting close to the end of the month."

"Have any idea what day it is?" Roak asked.

"Nope. I lose count when I'm not in town to be reminded."

"Me too," Roak answered. "But I think it's the twenty-ninth. You think your pa would take me in?" Drum asked.

"He might, but if you're thinking of hiding in the wagon, how are you planning to get out? Going in among the boxes might work, but the guards are bound to notice three of us in the wagon coming out."

"I think I can find how to get out. I found a back tunnel when I was a kid. I slid down the side of one of the walls north of here. Problem I have is that I don't think I could climb that ledge and, if I did and managed to get Sage out and back down, they'd spot my horse from above. There's no cover for a mile. We'd be sitting ducks." He thought about it for a while, then said, "We ask your pa when he comes by. It'll be the quickest and safest way to get in; then I'll worry about getting out."

"My old man will probably let you ride if you got money and we convince him you're not the law. He hates lawmen, says they're a plague to business. Claims he can smell them. For half my life he was a preacher, then when Ma died, he set the Lord aside and decided he'd campaign for the devil selling whiskey. In a way, I guess he's still recruiting, just for a different location."

"I got money," Drum answered. "And I'll take a bath first light to wash any smell away."

Daniel laughed. "Mind if I go back to sleep? I'm out of whiskey, so all I got to do is dream of my next drink. My pa told me once that whiskey don't make nothing better. I agree, but it sure blurs the eyes so that the problems don't seem so bad."

"You going to talk all night?" Drum liked the young Ranger, but he could see trouble coming his way one day if he kept drinking.

Daniel put his hat over his head and within minutes he was back to snoring. Drum didn't go back to sleep; he had plans to make.

CHAPTER 20

THE GUARD NAMED LUTHER MARCHED SAGE back to Count Hanover's house the next morning without a word. She tried talking to him, but he didn't answer.

She found the count sitting up in his bed, eating a breakfast of toast and tea.

His eyes were more alert. He watched her as she walked into the room. "You look better today," he said. "Myron tells me the bullet is still embedded, so your work is not done. I do feel better, however. I suppose I have you to thank for that."

"You look better," she answered truthfully. He had a bit of color in his cheeks. They'd made a little progress yesterday.

He waved his tray aside. "The bullet still hurts like hell, but the poultice you put on and the lancing of the festering wounds has eased the pain some." He nodded, offering her a seat beside his bed. "Today you'll operate."

"Yes," she said. "And then you'll let me go, correct?"

He frowned. "Of course. As soon as I'm well."

It wasn't much of a promise, but Sage knew better than to push the point. She waited until early afternoon when she had the sun's light in the windows. The count, despite all his talk of wanting the surgery, grew more and more hard to talk to as the day aged. She was glad when she started the opium. If he'd had to wait another hour, he probably would have had to kill something or someone.

There was a good chance she could heal the wounds on his back, but the poison in his mind would still be there. He saw himself as ruler of his tiny kingdom, and he allowed no one to question him.

Myron acted as her assistant, and Luther watched her every move. If she cut too deep and left the count paralyzed, she had a feeling she wouldn't have to worry about getting home.

She wasn't aware of time passing until Myron lit the lamps. Sage forced her hand steady as she worked as fast as she could.

Finally, the bullet pulled free of bone and tumbled out. Next she had to clean the wound and stitch him up. When she finished, they didn't offer to take her back to her cell; the guards assumed she'd stay beside the count's bed all night. Myron offered her supper and a blanket.

Sage slept in a chair between checking the wound and giving more opium. By daybreak, fever had set in, and her next round of fighting began.

Myron did what he could, but he was not a nurse. He made sure she had fresh water, clean towels, and left trays of food, which she never had time to touch.

It took two days for the fever to break, and when it did, the count was weak, almost helpless. She fed him soup, changed his bandages, and listened to his ramblings. Once, he grabbed her hand and kissed it as formally as if they'd been introduced in court.

Finally, he slept soundly.

Sage crawled into the overstuffed chair and did the same.

When she woke the next morning, the count was staring at her. "You saved my life."

"Then I can go?"

He smiled as if catching her in a lie. "No. I've decided I have need of your services." He closed his eyes and sighed. "I don't lower myself to mix with the whores very often, so you'll get no diseases from me. You'll have the run of the house in daylight, and when you're not in my bed, I'll lock you in a fine room at night. You'll have new clothes and whatever you need within reason. It'll be my gift to you for saving my life."

Sage had been half-asleep when he'd started and couldn't believe what she was hearing. "I'm not interested in marriage."

He laughed. "I'm not offering marriage. At least not like you think. We do have a kind of marriage here. If a man claims a woman, no other man can take her. It's a strict rule, or we'd have fights over females all the time. You'd be mine. No other man would bother you."

"I'm still not interested." She stood. "I'll check your bandage, make sure you're not bleeding, then I'll be on my way. I can buy my own dresses."

He didn't move, but she saw the change in his eyes, the kind of insanity that comes when someone believes he has complete power.

He tapped his cane on the floor, and the guard appeared. "Lock her up," he said simply.

Luther looked confused but took Sage's arm.

The count glared at her. "I'll ask you again tonight, but let me warn you, if you don't agree, you'll be very, very sorry. No one, man or woman, refuses me."

She wanted to say she already was sorry. She should have let him die. But he was like a wounded animal. She couldn't be sure what he'd do. Maybe if she went away for a few hours, he'd come to his senses and realize she'd saved his life.

Luther didn't say a word as he took her back to the cell. He'd seen what she'd done for the count, but his job was to follow orders.

No bath or food awaited her when she stepped into her prison. Sage curled on the bed and felt along the hem of her petticoat for her little gun. She'd shoot him tonight if she had to, but she'd not live with him.

She almost laughed. She'd just spent three days fighting to save a man she was now planning to kill. There was no downhill from here. Her life had to get better.

Just to prove herself wrong, Sneezy's thin face appeared at the barred window of her cell. After his verbal torturing on the trail, she'd hoped never to see the man again.

He giggled as he stared at her. "I've been thinking about it. I think I should burn you before

I kill you. Burns hurt real bad when they bubble the skin, and I've heard tell the screams echo for days in this canyon."

"What happened to your face?" she asked, noticing the dark bruise along his forehead.

"Luther hit me with a rifle butt for no reason." He touched the spot as if he'd forgotten about it. "It didn't hurt all that much. Not near as bad as the burns are going to hurt you. There's a big party tonight. The whiskey wagon is here. Once Hanover and that pet dog of his, Luther, down a few, they'll forget all about you. When the gambling starts, I'll get a key and come pay you a visit. I owe you. You won't be so high and mighty when you smell your own skin burning."

"I'll be waiting," she answered, outlining the gun in her skirts.

He disappeared.

Sage turned her face to the wall, wishing she could sleep. Even a nightmare would be better than the hell she was trapped in.

CHAPTER 21

DRUMMOND ROAK LOWERED THE BRIM OF his new black hat until his face was in shadow, then he walked into the saloon. Because he looked every ounce a gunfighter, he found himself moving like one, slow and cautious.

On the long ride through Skull Alley, Daniel

and he had decided it would be safer for Drum to be one of the gamblers than to try to hide out in a whiskey wagon. They agreed he could pull off gunfighter far easier, and the two occupations ran hand in hand. If a traveling gambler couldn't defend himself in the street, he wouldn't last long. Daniel had seen him in action. He claimed Roak was not only the fastest gun he'd ever seen but also the most accurate.

Three days ago, Drum had scrubbed in the stream while they waited at the opening of Skull Alley for the whiskey wagon and the gamblers. When he'd stepped out in his new black clothes and fine tooled vest, Daniel almost hadn't recognized him. Drum shaved his two-week-old beard with a clean razor line across his cheek, making his jaw look even squarer than it already was. The dark beard made him look older. His bullet-gray eyes looked deadly serious beneath the brim of his black hat.

Daniel looked relieved to see his pa pull up with the gamblers about nightfall that first day. He claimed he couldn't have held Drummond at the opening for another day. By dawn on the second day, Drum was ready to ride and didn't like it much when they camped for the night halfway through the canyon. He wanted to get to Sage.

He'd lost enough money the first night on the journey with the gamblers that they not only allowed but insisted he come along the rest of the way. They saw the money they won from Drum as all theirs and not money they'd have to split with the count.

Daniel held back, acting like he didn't know Roak. They'd planned it that way. Just in case Roak was caught, Daniel would still have a chance of getting Sage out.

"Don't worry what happens to me if I'm caught," Drum had said several times. "Just get Sage to safety."

Now, after talking and planning for three days, they were in the hideout, and Drum walked toward the bar as if he had no plans other than to gamble the night away. Several heads looked his way when he stepped into the smoke-filled room. He was new, untried, but from the way he wore his gun, they guessed he was fast, and none of the outlaws seemed in any hurry to try his luck.

Drum took a place along the thirty-foot bar two men down from Daniel Torry. They didn't speak, but as the customers between them refilled their mugs and moved on, Drum closed the distance until he stood next to the Ranger.

Once the music started, Daniel whispered, "The big game starts at midnight. If I were guessing, it's set that late so the locals will be drunk before they play." He tipped his glass to Drum. "That's when you might want to have an exit plan, unless you're a lot better at cards than I think you are. The way you look, no one in the place would question you're a gunfighter, but trust me, they'll know you're not a gambler ten minutes after you sit down."

Roak didn't know how to take Daniel's teasing, so he changed the subject. "What have you heard about Sage?"

"Not much, just that the count had an operation three days ago and is recovering. Before that, there were bets on what day he'd die." Daniel took a long drink. "We might be able to look around in about an hour. They're having a virgin auction before the game, so every man in the camp will be in here watching."

Drum smiled at Daniel Torry. They'd both been around these hideouts long enough to know the scheme. Some prostitute, not known in the area, would claim to be a virgin. She'd go for several times what the normal rate was. Sometimes they'd auction her again the next night as almost a virgin.

"You ever try to save one?" Drummond asked. In all his years at the camps, he'd only been fooled once by what he thought was a woman in distress.

Daniel nodded. "The first time I heard about one being sold to the highest bidder, I was delivering whiskey with my pa down by the border. I broke into her room and tried to help her escape."

"What'd she do?"

Daniel shook his head. "I thought that woman was going to beat me to death. In fact, I blame her for being half afraid of every woman I meet.

You never know when one that looks like a virgin will turn into a fire-breathing whore. She left so many knots on my head, I couldn't wear a hat for months."

Drum laughed.

"How about you, Roak? Did you ever save a girl?"

"Nope," Drum lied. He had stepped in once and gotten a girl out. She couldn't have been more than sixteen. She'd run off with an outlaw, thinking she'd reform him. He put her up for auction for drinking money after they'd been together for about a month. Drum had stepped in, gotten her away, and took her back to within a few miles of her home.

He'd patted himself on the back for the fine job he'd done until he heard later that her father beat her so badly for running away that she'd be crippled up for the rest of her life. Folks said he treated her worse than a slave around the place, knowing that no man would ever take her off again.

Drum downed his whiskey, washing away the memory. Why did life always have to be so hard? Even telling right from wrong was hard to keep straight. The only marker he had was Teagen McMurray. Sometimes, when he couldn't tell which way to go, he'd think about what the head of the McMurrays would do. Teagen, Sage's oldest brother, was one man who saw the world in black and white. For Drum, the world was gray. He knew killing was wrong, but like Captain Harmon said, there were a few who needed to be hurried to meet their maker.

Tonight, however, he knew what was right. He had to find Sage, and if he had to tear every board of this town apart, he would. He couldn't stand the thought of her in a place like this. He knew towns like this. A good day was when the smell of a rotting body didn't pollute the air.

As it turned out, Drum didn't have to search all that far for Sage, because she stepped into the bar just as he ordered another drink.

She was angry and kicking at the guard who tried to pull her forward with the ropes that bound her. Her clothes were worn and dirty, her hair wild, her mouth gagged, but she was still all fight and fire.

Drum lowered his black hat, guessing that even if she had the time to glance in his direction, she wouldn't recognize him. The last thing he wanted in a saloon with fifty outlaws watching was for her to shout out his name. His gut tightened at the sight of her, and rage boiled through his blood.

Daniel Torry's glass hit the bar, but he recovered quickly and turned his back to the procession leading Sage to the center of the room. He let out a string of swear words in a low breath and then said simply, "They're going to auction off the doctor. Hellfire. She's the virgin for tonight."

Drummond never took his eyes off her. "And she doesn't look too happy about it."

Men all around were hooting and calling out what they planned to do with the little lady when they won the bid. The big guard lifted her up on a table in the center of the room and looped the rope around her neck to a rafter. If she struggled now, she'd choke herself.

One of the bartenders stood on a chair and shoved her hair out of her face.

Drummond saw the bruises on her forehead and cheek and almost lost control. If he drew his gun, six men would be dead before anyone could return fire. The only thing that stopped him was that he might not kill the one who had hurt her.

"These are the rules, men!" the bartender yelled. "Anyone can bid, but the man who wins gets the little lady for the night. There's a room upstairs that's included in the price. He can keep her there all night or sell her if he wants to get some of his money back. If he opens the door wide, the line forms on the right of the stairs for seconds. If he doesn't offer the invitation, no one goes in that room, no matter what we hear. Come morning, assuming she's still alive, she becomes an employee of the saloon. Is that clear to everyone?"

Several shouted for him to get on with the auction.

Drummond leaned close to Daniel. "I'll get her. You have horses ready and waiting."

Daniel nodded so slightly no one near would have noticed.

The bidding started. Several men leaned across,

trying to touch her, but the guard wasn't allowing any free samples. In an odd way, he seemed to be protecting her.

When the bidding slowed at fifty dollars, the bartender ordered the guard to release a foot of the rope. The bartender pulled her to him and ripped the front of her blouse open almost to the waist. Now her cleavage clearly revealed a young woman. Cheers rounded the room, and the bidding continued.

When it slowed again at near a hundred, the guard reached for her again, but Drummond's sudden bid stopped him.

"What was that bid from the back?" the bartender shouted.

"Two hundred dollars, and I unwrap her myself." Drummond kept his voice sharp, angry.

The bartender smiled. "Two hundred going once, twice, sold to the man in black. The little lady's all yours, and you get to unwrap her yourself."

CHAPTER 22

Sage closed her eyes and tried to breathe. She'd just had the worst day of her life, and now she'd have to fight off some crude man who thought he could buy her for two hundred dollars.

His footsteps sounded like the hammer of death nails on a coffin as he neared. She didn't want to look at him. She didn't want to remember the face of the outlaw she'd use her one bullet on as soon as they were alone.

She'd gone without food or water all day, and she couldn't remember eating for two days before that. When the guard, Luther, came after her, he didn't look happy about having to bind her hands, but he did. They walked to the count's house, and he left her standing in the dining room for an hour while the count finished his bath. She could see and smell the food on the table, but with her hands behind her, she couldn't even pinch a taste. There were two place settings as though Hanover planned to ask her to join him.

When he walked into the room, Sage almost didn't recognize the man she'd first seen. He'd been withered in pain and fever when she arrived. Now, though he still leaned on a cane, she saw a confidence and air of superiority in his manner. He wore a loose shirt, trousers, and riding boots as if he'd just been out.

He didn't offer her a chair as he sat down and began eating. After a few bites, he said, "I want you to answer very carefully this time. I would like you here with me, but I'll only ask once more. If you say no, there will be no going back after tonight. You will have your punishment without further discussion." He smiled as if he thought she'd been teasing him earlier. "Now, would you like to stay here with me and have a meal before we retire?"

"I want to go home," she answered. "I came here against my will, and I'll not stay. You will let me go right now, or I swear you will be the one who regrets this day."

She'd thought about what she would say, and her voice never shook.

He took a sip of wine. "I admire your courage, dear. So much so, I've chosen to kill you." He grinned. "But I will promise you that before this night ends, you will regret your decision. Whether you're in my house or somewhere else in our little town, you will stay. No one leaves this place without my permission." He smiled. "I imagine your answer will be quite different when you recover from your evening out."

He tapped his cane, and Luther walked in with the noose she'd grown to hate. He slipped it around her neck and tugged it tight.

The count went back to his meal, waving them away. "Take her to the auction. I never want to see or hear what happens tonight. If she's alive tomorrow, take her to her cell and leave her there without food or water until I decide if I want to see her again."

"She saved your life," Myron said from the doorway to the kitchen.

The count blustered. "Yes, and if you value yours, you'll stay out of this. Women must often be taught lessons."

The guard tugged on the rope, and Sage followed

him out, glad to be away from the horrible man. She thought she heard a hard slap and a body hitting the floor. Myron was being punished. The little butler would never be brave enough to fight for his life.

On the walk out into the night, she didn't ask any questions until they passed the boardinghouse where her cell was. Then she demanded to know what was going on.

The guard tried tugging the rope tighter to shut her up, but she still fought.

Finally, he grabbed her from behind and held her against him, so her kicks couldn't hurt. "Stop, miss. There ain't nothing you can do to change anything. I don't want to hurt you, but I will, if I have to."

"Let me go," she demanded. "Just let me go."

"If I did, he'd kill my family. I saw him do it a few years back just because one of the men lied to him. I got a wife and a boy in camp. I ain't doing nothing but following orders. He wants you to go up for auction tonight. I'm just taking you to the saloon."

"You saw what I did for him." She tried again. Luther had watched the surgery and all the hours of care that had followed.

"I did, but you were thinking he was human just because he bleeds. I'm not so sure he is."

"You could let me escape. Untie my hands. I'd run, and you could tell him I died."

He shook his head. "No."

She began to fight again. "You're no better than him."

The guard didn't answer. He just gagged her, then half carried, half dragged her into the saloon. By the time he tied her to the rafter, Sage was battling fainting from lack of air. She forced herself to stand still and breathe as deeply as the noose would allow. The world was foggy as if thick, black spiderwebs were everywhere. Men around her were shouting, but she couldn't get her mind around what they were saying. She concentrated on not passing out, but with no food or water and now no air, she was losing the battle.

Then all she heard were footsteps, and the rope went slack. She crumpled and was caught before she hit the table. A man in black picked her up and tossed her over his shoulder.

Her head jerked as the guard pulled the noose from around her neck. Then the stranger moved away from the crowd with people shouting and cheering.

Halfway up the stairs, she opened her eyes and looked down at the saloon. Everyone glared at her. They had the look of hungry dogs staring at a dying calf.

She wiggled, trying to get free.

The man in black popped her hard on the bottom, and all the crowd cheered. She stayed still from then on, not wanting to be part of their fun.

Then they were upstairs in a room, and all the noise seemed far away. The man set her on her feet and stepped away.

The room was dark except for pale moonlight melting through thin curtains and a low-burning lamp. It had the smell of a cheap hotel, dust and neglect blended with the faint smell of a chamber pot that hadn't been cleaned. Though her hair was hanging in her eyes, she could make out a bed, a washstand, and a wardrobe with one door missing. The room had two windows. One would be her escape route.

The man pulled his knife from his boot and stepped toward her.

Sage turned to run, but he grabbed her tied arms and began slitting the ropes. First her hands, then the gag. It took her a moment to realize she wasn't bound.

She took deep breaths, knowing what she had to do. Her heart felt like it had moved to her ears and was pounding wildly. For the past four years she'd sworn to help people live, and now she was going to have to kill someone.

He was saying something about how they were married now, outlaw style, but she wasn't listening as she tugged her gun from its hiding place and slipped it into her hand. The metal was cold, and her grip shook a little as she fought off fainting.

He turned his back and locked the door. Sage whirled and fired.

The man crumpled to the floor.

In a few heartbeats, she waited to see if someone would storm the door, but no one did. Still holding her gun as if it would help her, she moved to the man's side, praying he was dead. She didn't want him to be in pain. If he still lived, he might call for help.

Bile rose in her throat as she realized what she might have to do. She might have to kill him again. Her only chance of getting away would depend on her ensuring that he couldn't come after her or yell out.

Her heart was pounding so hard she feared it might break a rib. She'd done what she had to do. There was no going back. As her Apache grandfather would say, her course was set; she had to go with the current.

Lifting his gun from its holster, she prepared to fire again as she rolled him on his back.

He coughed and swore as she raised his weapon. "Hell, Sage, how many times are you going to shoot me for saving your life?"

"Drum?"

Dropping the gun on the bed, she scrambled for the light. The realization that she'd truly shot Drummond Roak didn't register until the candlelight flooded over blood dripping from his arm.

He sat up, his jaw tightened, even though he tried to smile. "I just bought this shirt. Now it's already got a bullet hole in it."

"Shut up," she ordered, helping him stand. "Strip off that shirt and lie down on the bed."

"I'm not that easy." He leaned on her. "It's good to see you, even if you do look horrible, honey."

"Shut up," she ordered again, not believing that he was talking to her as if they just happened to have met. She pushed him onto the bed and cringed when he groaned in pain.

She'd shot Drum. With all the evil around her, she'd shot the one man who would try to save her. So much for following the current.

When he caught his breath, he whispered between clenched teeth, "Great bedside manner, Doc."

She pulled his shirt open and off his shoulder. "Stop talking, and let me have a look at what damage the bullet did."

"Don't you mean what damage you did?"

She didn't want to think about what she'd done; she only wanted to fix it. "How long do we have in here before they come?"

He stilled as her hands moved over him. "We got all night," he finally answered. "This is kind of our wedding night, honey."

"Stop calling me honey."

"I heard the captain call you that once." He smiled, his eyes moving down her body. "Somehow, it kind of fits you. Your skin's got that warm glow, like you've been kissed by the sun all over." He bit back pain before adding, "Sometime when I'm not bleeding, I wouldn't mind finding out if you're honey-colored all over."

Sage pretended not to listen. She had work to do. Blood dripped from a wound on his left arm just below the shoulder. It wasn't as bad as she'd thought; the bullet had gone through without hitting a bone. She crossed to the washstand and found fresh water and a towel that looked to be almost clean. She went back to his side and began doing what she'd been trained to do.

"Maybe as your husband, I'll have time to make sure the sun didn't miss a spot."

He groaned when she rubbed the towel across the bullet wound.

"I'm not married to you, Drummond. Not even if that was an outlaw wedding downstairs." She felt him flinch as she patted the wound, but he didn't make a sound. She gentled her care and leaned close for a better look.

After she'd stopped most of the bleeding, he whispered close to her ear, "But I paid two hundred dollars for you, honey."

She straightened suddenly, aware of how near he was and, even wounded, his eyes told her he was very much aware of her. Pulling one of the pillowcases off, she began to make bandages. "I'll give you the money back when we get out of here. Then you can consider us divorced."

"I'd rather have you."

"We're not having this discussion. Turn over on

your stomach so I can have a look where the bullet exited."

He pulled off the rest of his vest, and then his shirt, and then did as she ordered. The sight of his muscular back surprised her, as did the scars that ran across it. Sage put her hand out, almost touching the marks of a long-ago cruelty.

She gently began. "How'd you find me?" If he talked, he might not think about the pain she knew she was causing him.

"I trailed you, and I'm guessing you took care to leave me a sign now and then. A shoe print, a scrap of handkerchief. Each clue told me you were still alive. I could have moved in earlier, but I knew I'd take the chance of them killing you if I fired."

"They wanted me here as a doctor, not as a woman. They treated me with less care than one might a stolen horse."

"So, how'd you end up on the auction table tonight?"

She shrugged. "I kept waiting for the perfect time to escape. Then I saw a hurting man and had to help. He turned out to be Hanover, the ruler of this little slice of hell. I didn't know how rotted his brain was until I saved his worthless life. When he got better, he objected to me not agreeing to live with him."

"You're a hard woman to talk into anything. I almost feel sorry for the fool."

She smiled and began to bandage his wound.

"Thanks for coming for me. It would have been days, maybe weeks, before my brothers could get to me, but I knew you'd come."

He twisted as she worked. "You're welcome." He smiled up at her. "How about we stay awhile and make use of the bed?"

She smiled back. "Excuse me for a minute while I reload."

CHAPTER 23

SAGE PACED AS DRUM STOOD LOOKING OUT the window. They'd talked it over and decided to wait until the gambling was well under way before trying to sneak out. Fifty-to-two odds didn't sound all that good, but the later it got, the more men would be asleep or passed out.

Sage stopped and put her fist on her hips. "I can't believe you came in here to rescue me without having any kind of plan to get away. I was in enough trouble, and now you're here. I'm not better off than I was on my own."

Drummond was starting to wonder why he'd come at all. Every time she was out of his sight, he forgot how irritating and bossy the woman could be. *And she'd shot him!* His arm ached, and the wound hurt like hell, and all she'd done was complain. He sat down on the corner of the bed and checked his gun one more time.

He glanced at her blouse, still open enough for

him to see the swell of her breasts rise each time she breathed. He could listen to anything as long as he had that view, he decided: honey-colored skin framed in white lace.

"Stop looking at my breasts," Sage demanded without trying to pull her blouse together again.

"I wasn't," he lied and forced his gaze to her face. She moved closer. "Yes you were."

He fought to keep from looking down. They were at eye level to him, the two most beautiful breasts now almost bare right in front of him. She was torturing him. That was it. Shooting him hadn't worked, so now she'd try torturing him to death.

Since the day he'd met her, he'd thought of how she'd feel beneath him when she became his woman. He'd thought of how her breasts would look, and damn if they didn't appear to be living up to his dreams. Her frame might be small, but her breasts were definitely a handful.

A tap at the door saved him from sure ruin.

"Get in bed under the covers," he whispered as he moved to the door.

She scrambled to follow his order.

"Who is it!" Drum sounded angry, bothered, just like a man who'd been taking his pleasure.

"A fellow at the bar told me he lost a bet to you tonight and said he had to send you up a meal if you won the bid so you'd have enough strength to go all night." The female voice sounded tired and a bit out of breath. "Do you want it or not?"

Drum glanced back to make sure Sage was covered and pulled his gun. "Leave the tray beside the door."

"All right." Dishes clattered.

He waited several seconds, then opened the door an inch. The tray was there. The hallway looked empty. Kneeling down, he kept the gun ready and tugged the food in.

Then he locked the bolt back in place and walked to the edge of the bed. He pulled away the covers enough to see Sage's face. "It's all right. Only a food delivery." Before she could protest, he leaned down and touched his lips to hers.

"Food," she said without reacting to his kiss. "We've got food."

He laughed when she ran for the tray. She put it in the center of the bed and began eating. He watched her trying not to act like she was starving, trying to offer him half, then helping him eat his portion.

They didn't find the note until they were almost finished. One slip of paper had been tucked beneath the last of the bread.

He handed it to her, and she read the quick scribble. " 'Wait one hour or more for my sign, then go through the door at the end of the hall. I'll clear the way.' "

Sage looked up, confused. "You didn't come alone?"

"I was followed by the Ranger Daniel Torry. If

he stays sober downstairs, he'll keep his word."

Sage looked down at her clothes as she finished off the last bite of bread. "I'll get ready."

While the hour passed, she combed her hair and braided it into a single thick braid down her back and put on an old shirt she found in one of the drawers. Drum laced his vest over it, offering some warmth.

They waited by the door, ready to move for a long while before they heard shouts roll up from below. Someone had won a big pot. Men yelped, and one round was fired that just happened to hit the light halfway up the stairs.

Drum knew it was what they'd been waiting for. He grabbed Sage's hand, and they ran down the hallway. At the end, they found the stairs and a guard that looked like he'd been clubbed from behind. Sage would have taken time to check the man, but Drum pulled her on.

In a few steps they were outside in the blackness behind the saloon. He stopped, getting his bearings, then tightened his grip on her hand, signaling her to wait.

A moment later they heard a low whistling to the right. By the time they felt their way along the side of the building, his eyes had adjusted enough to see two horses: Satan and a bay that barely looked broke.

Drum took the reins of Satan. "Are you going with us?" he whispered to Daniel.

The Ranger shook his head. "If I leave, it'll cause trouble for my pa. I came in with him. I'll leave tomorrow with the wagon. If I don't catch up to you, I'll see you in Galveston."

He touched his hat when he handed the reins of the other horse to Sage. "Sorry about this bay. It was the only one I could find that didn't look like it might be missed tonight. Drum told me you could ride any horse, but this one may challenge your skill." He turned back to Drum. "You just get the doc back safe. I'll cause enough trouble here that maybe they won't miss you too soon. As soon as I know you're through the pasture, I'll knock one of the fence posts down and let out all the horses. It'll wipe out your trail and add headache to hangover for the men in the morning."

He took off his hat and placed it on Sage's head. "You take care now, miss."

"Thank you." Sage kissed his cheek, knowing full well the danger he was putting himself in for them. "Get back to Galveston as quick as you can."

Daniel walked into the saloon without another word.

Drummond led the way around the buildings toward the wall of canyon that lay beyond the fields and corrals. Years ago he'd found a slit in the rock wide enough for one horse. If it wasn't still there, they'd have to ride through Skull Alley. If he could find the slit, they'd be in for quite a ride to get out.

When they were well away from the buildings, he said, "You know that secret path that leads over the mountains behind your ranch?"

"Of course. No one knows about that way out but my brothers and me."

"And me." He smiled. "Though all three of your brothers swore they'd hunt me down if I ever told anyone. But that path is kind of like the one we're taking out, only it doesn't go over hills, it crosses canyons. It's also dangerous."

She seemed to know what he was asking. "I'm right behind you. I don't mind the ride. I can handle the bay." She leaned forward, talking gently to the horse.

"I know. I've watched you. I have a feeling that if one of us takes a tumble, it'll be me, not you."

They climbed out of the pasture and onto rocks. All light from the homes had disappeared, but the moon offered enough glow to help them pick a path. By dawn they'd slipped into what looked like a cave with open spots in the roof. The air was cool and damp and smelled of bat guano. Drum heard Sage whispering to her horse, calming him with each step.

Satan had been with Drum so long, he followed with the slightest tug of the reins.

About noon they reached the mouth of the cave on the other side and decided to rest in the shadows, just in case men above were looking for them.

Drum unsaddled the horses and brushed them down, then sat where he could see out without being seen. Both the rifles were within easy reach. If anyone came within a hundred feet, he'd know it, and no one could spot the opening from the top of the cliffs.

Sage spread her blanket down so that she faced him. Her feet bumped against the side of his leg as she wiggled, building her nest.

He didn't say anything to her. They'd been silent for hours.

She bumped his leg again. He didn't react.

Finally, after ten minutes of silence, she asked, "What is it? What is the matter with you?"

"Besides the fact that fifty men are tracking us right now planning to kill us on sight?"

"Yes," she whispered. "Besides that. You haven't said a handful of words to me since we left town."

"It's nothing."

"No," she corrected. "It's something. I didn't grow up with three brothers without learning that when a man is silent, something is bothering him."

He felt like a fool for ever thinking about the way she'd kissed Daniel for bringing her a horse. "All right. You asked. Daniel handed you a horse, and you kissed him. I saved your life, and you shot me." Drum was sorry he said anything before the words were out. She'd probably give him a lecture on being childish, or worse, tell him she fancied Daniel Torry. He never knew what she'd do.

Maybe that was what fascinated him about Sage McMurray. She was like watching a tornado.

"I'm worried about that shot," she whispered, as if her worry made up for all his pain.

"It's all right. You can tend to it again when we're somewhere safe."

"No, it's not that." She laughed. "But now you mention the wound, I would like to check it as soon as we have both the time and some light."

"Then what *are* you worried about?"

She fretted for a minute before answering. "Maybe I've been away from home too long. Four years ago I wouldn't have missed your heart. What if I'm losing my skills with a gun? That's not good, Drum."

He groaned. "So you're worried about not killing me?"

She realized what she'd said and smiled. "Of course I am." Her tone turned teasing. "What if you'd been some crazed man determined to bed me?"

Now it was his turn to grin. "I am some crazed man determined to bed you, Sage. I've made no secret of it for years."

She laughed as if she thought he was teasing. "I'm too tired to think anymore. Can't we argue about this later?"

He tossed her his blanket. "Sleep. I'll wake you when it's dark enough to travel."

He stared out into the valley, watching for any

movement as he listened to her wiggling behind him. Every now and then her leg brushed his.

Finally, he ordered, "Sage, go to sleep."

"I can't," she answered. "I'm cold and so home-sick I can't think. Would you mind if I curl up beside you?"

She didn't wait for an answer. She tugged her bedroll to his side and spread his blanket over them both. When she nestled down again, her bottom pushed against his hip.

Drum swore to himself. He had to stop thinking about her body parts, but she wasn't making it easy.

He put his arm over her, and she stilled. She felt warm against his side, and he knew when she fell asleep by the long breaths. "Sage," he said. "Sage?"

Nothing. The woman hadn't changed. When she went to sleep, the end of the world wouldn't wake her.

He tugged on her long braid. When she leaned her head back, he kissed her. She felt so good next to him, but kissing her while she slept wasn't what he wanted. He wanted her wild and awake in his arms. He wanted her wanting him.

Clouds moved in over the valley, and a drizzling rain began to fall. Drum knew they were safe now. The outlaws couldn't track them, and the rain made it unlikely they'd hear the horses, even if they were close.

He rested his chin on the top of Sage's head and closed his eyes. She was in his arms; that was enough for now.

Drum slept.

CHAPTER 24

Bonnie made sure the boys were asleep before she went back to the parlor to talk to Sage's brother-in-law, Shelley Lander. He'd insisted on coming to see her as soon as his doctor had said he could move from his bed.

She looked at him now, grateful that he hadn't come to her to be doctored. It was hard enough seeing the man. The last thing she wanted to do was touch him. In the days she'd been back, she'd learned that he'd let the robbers take Sage, and that fact alone made her hate him.

Bullet lay on the settee. Shelley tried to shoo the cat off without touching her. "I hate cats," he said. "Can't you do something about this animal?"

Bonnie picked the cat up and took a seat on one of the chairs. She didn't try to make small talk, she wasn't sure she could. After a full minute of silence, she lifted her new glasses and picked up her sewing. Shelley Lander could stay if he liked, but he'd not waste any more of her time.

Finally, he found something to say. "What kind of name is Bullet, anyway? The cat's fat, slow, and looks blind in one eye."

Bonnie petted her cat. "She's the color of a bullet."

Shelley brushed one of the cushions off and took his place on the settee, ignoring her explanation. "I've come to see if there is anything I can do," he began as if he'd been waiting for the curtain to rise so he could start his act. "We need to face the fact that there is a possibility that Sage might not be coming back, and as her nearest, if not next of kin, I may need to make some arrangements."

Bonnie had already faced that. She'd sent a telegraph to Sage's brother in Austin. She'd also dipped into Sage's money belt, kept locked away in the hotel safe, for enough money to continue to pay the bill at the hotel and buy her and the boys' meals. With each withdrawal, she'd replaced the bill with a detailed note accounting her expenditures.

"Sage will be back," Bonnie said without doubt showing in her tone. "As long as Drummond Roak is hunting for her, it's only a matter of time." She stood and moved to the door, but he didn't get up. "Good night, Mr. Lander. It's late and not proper for you to be in this room any longer."

"I'm not leaving until I know where my dear brother's wife's valuables are . . ."

Bonnie opened the door, and a young Ranger stepped inside. He didn't look a day over eighteen, but he seemed to know his job. She didn't have to say a word; he'd probably been listening through the thin door.

"Mr. Lander." He smiled politely, but his hand rested on the butt of his gun. "I thought I'd help you down the stairs. A man with the use of only one arm could easily fall and break his neck."

Shelley looked like he'd been threatened, but he didn't say anything. He gathered his cane and hat. "I'll be back," he said as he stood.

The Ranger continued to smile. "We'll be waiting to help you up and down when you return."

Shelley glared at the man. "I don't understand the Rangers' interest in my brother's wife. There must be far more important things to guard than a nurse and two wild children."

"No, sir," the young man said without explaining. He turned to Bonnie. "You let me know if you need anything, Miss Pierce. I'll be right down at the foot of the stairs or on the landing if someone comes up."

"Thank you. I'm glad to know I'm safe." She glanced at Shelley. "I don't expect any more visitors."

He nodded once in understanding.

She heard Shelley huff from the hallway in indignation.

Bonnie closed the door. She'd noticed a Ranger in the lobby every time she'd gone downstairs. The man usually only tipped his hat and fell into step behind her and the boys. This was the first time she'd seen one outside her door, but then, this was the first time anyone had climbed the stairs to their rooms.

Ruffling Bullet's hair, she whispered, "He doesn't like cats. That's as good a reason as any to keep you around."

When she checked on the boys, Bullet jumped up and took his place on Andy's bed.

Crossing the hallway, Bonnie washed her face and pulled on her long cotton gown. In the mirror, she studied her reflection. She was plain. Not homely, not ugly, but plain. Turning away, she remembered the way her cowboy had looked at her. To him, she'd been beautiful. She knew his name had been Bradford, but she simply thought of him as her cowboy.

Each night she lay awake as long as she could and tried to remember every detail of what had happened. Then she'd read her Bible and confess the sin she'd committed. She didn't ask for forgiveness. She didn't want it.

In the mornings as she dressed, she'd try to list all the ways they were different. He hadn't had a book in his cabin, not even a Bible. Guns hung on the walls, not pictures. His life was outdoors, working the land, living in a place still wild. His brother was an outlaw, and maybe he was too. But at night, she remembered the way they were the same. They both wanted one taste of love, and they wanted it so badly they'd give away any future happiness for the one night.

Sometime during the third day after he'd dropped her at the Ranger station, Bonnie made up her mind. If Sage didn't make it back, she'd ask one of Sage's brothers to help her find employment at a hospital in Austin. If there was no work available, she'd go back to Boston where she belonged. She'd even talk to the captain about letting the boys go back with her. Both boys had told her that they wanted to stay with her. Will even said she could have all the money from the sale of their land if she'd let them stay with her until they were old enough to join the Rangers.

Bonnie wasn't sure what she'd do if Sage didn't return. Maybe she'd stay. Maybe she'd go home.

It didn't matter where she was; her memories would be with her. Her life had been forever changed.

CHAPTER 25

SAGE TRIED TO IGNORE DRUM AND KEEP sleeping, but when he said they had to get back to Will and little Andy, everything, including the danger they were in, registered.

"Where are the boys?" she asked as she sat up and pushed back loose strands of hair. She'd spent the last week so worried about herself, she hadn't thought of the boys. She assumed Bonnie would look after them.

"They're safe with the Rangers."

"Bonnie? Isn't she with them?" It seemed like a lifetime ago that she'd called for the nurse's help in Shelley's office, and Bonnie hadn't answered. Drum hesitated too long. She knew something was wrong. "What has happened to Bonnie?"

He didn't try to sugarcoat the news. "She's missing." He hurried to add, "She wasn't among the body count, but someone said he thought he saw a man dragging her out of Shelley's place and dropping off the dock into the shallow water below."

"Did anyone go after her?"

"There were no tracks to follow. We don't even know who could have taken her. Six men rowed in. Six men and you rowed away. Whoever took Bonnie wasn't one of them, so maybe he was saving her. She's probably fine back at the hotel by now and wondering where you are."

Sage collected her things. "I hope so. She's not like me. She was raised in a city by parents who never allowed her to do anything. She puts on a good act, but this whole country frightens her."

"Maybe she ran off with a fellow. Maybe some man looked at her and saw six feet of love at first sight."

"No, not Bonnie. Even if someone did fancy her, she'd never go along. She'll never marry. She believes her mission as a nurse is as great a calling as a nun's to the church."

Drum handed Sage the reins to her bay. "Well, if

she jumped off that dock with a man, you might want to reconsider your measure of her."

"No. Trust me, Bonnie would die of fright before she'd ever let a man touch her hand."

He offered Sage a step up into the saddle, then brushed her leg as he made sure her boot was solid in the stirrup. "How about you? You ever going to let another man touch you?"

"No," she answered. "And do me a favor; don't ask me again."

They didn't speak for an hour. She followed close behind him as he picked a path through the rocks, heading northeast. Since Skull Alley was to the south, she guessed most of the men chasing them would be searching in that direction. The few who came north, if any did, had the rain to slow them down. There was also a good chance none of them knew about the passage. Only a boy climbing around on rocks would have found it.

Drum pulled up and climbed off his mount. When he reached her, he whispered, "We'll have to walk for a while. The ground slopes off in a long slide from here on. If we make it down, we're home free, but it's too dangerous to risk riding."

She understood. A horse tumbling with a rider could very easily crush the rider in a fall.

They led the mounts. The slope was steep, but the rain had softened the earth. Sage dug her heels in with each step, knowing that if she tumbled, it would be more than a hundred feet before she stopped.

The moon seemed to follow them down the incline. She kept her distance from Drum. If she fell, she didn't want to take him with her. Halfway down, they both froze at the sound of a coyote howling in the distance. The black, sleeping earth spread for miles before her. She felt so alone and couldn't help wondering if the coyote felt the same. She'd never been afraid of the dark, but being alone was another matter. Her vision of hell wasn't fire and brimstone but isolation.

Drum started down once more, leading Satan. As they neared the bottom, shadows crossed one another over uneven ground, making it impossible to see the solid footing clearly. The coyote howled again, causing both horses to grow uneasy and jerk against the reins.

Drum fought to control Satan with his one good arm while holding the injured one against his side. About the time he gained control of the huge beast, Drum's foot slid on a loose rock, and he tumbled. Satan pulled free and whirled, almost hitting Sage.

She grabbed the flying reins and spoke to the horse in a language she'd learned as a child, calming nonsense words that settled Satan. With both horses in tow, she carefully continued down.

"Drum?" She moved into the blackness of a ravine. "Drum, where are you?"

Satan pulled at his reins, determined to move to the left. When Sage followed, she found Drummond. Dried brush had stopped his roll a few feet from a shallow creek bed. She tied the horses to the brush and felt along his body, trying to see if he'd broken any bones.

Warm blood dripped from a cut on his forehead, and he moaned when she touched the bandaged wound on his arm. Other than that, he seemed alive and intact.

"Come on, Drum," she whispered. "Get up."

He didn't cooperate.

"Come on." She pulled on him. "We made it out of the canyons. We're almost to safety. Come on! We can't be here come dawn, or they'll be able to pick us off."

He moaned and tried to stand.

Sage slid her arm around him and walked him to Satan. He was heavier than she thought he'd be. The horse was well trained and didn't shy as she helped Drum up.

"Can you stay in the saddle?"

He nodded.

"Then we ride."

Sage headed north, having no idea where she was going. The land leveled out, and Drum managed to stay in the saddle, but he leaned forward as if fighting to stay conscious. She pushed as hard as she dared in the darkness, and by first light they were into a wooded area. Sage turned southeast and began following a stream, hoping it would lead her toward Galveston.

Drum hadn't said a word. When it was light

enough to see his face, she wasn't surprised to find the head wound still bleeding. He'd nodded that he was fine every time she'd offered to look at the wound. Now, from his eyes, she could tell that he'd lied. Even before the fall he must have been in trouble. He hadn't allowed her to doctor him. Getting her away was far more important.

She found a cove well covered on three sides. The one side that faced the water was open, but unless someone rode in the stream, they wouldn't spot them camped. The morning was cool and the sky busy with clouds so low they almost touched the treetops.

Sage built a fire and took care of the horses. When she returned to the water's edge, she found that Drum had stripped to the waist and waded into the stream. He was using his shirt to wash away blood from both his face and arm.

Smiling, Sage kicked off her boots and walked into the cool water until she stood in front of him. "You remind me of a wounded bear."

He looked at her. She saw the fever in his gray eyes once more.

"Drum, let me help." He looked like he might push her away, but she moved closer. "We need to get you out of here and to the fire as soon as possible. You're in no shape to be standing in a stream." She tugged the wet shirt and bar of lye soap from his hand and began washing the infected wound.

He didn't argue or make a sound, but she knew the lye would burn against the wound.

She cleaned away the blood and then pulled him out of the water. By then he was shaking from fever and cold. After helping him strip off his remaining clothes, she insisted he lie on one open bedroll by the fire, and she covered him with the only blanket.

Near panic, she rushed to do everything that needed to be done. Without her bag of medicines, Sage drew on what she'd learned from her grandfather years ago. The Apache knew natural treatments, if only she could remember them.

She bound the cut on his forehead with a strip of cloth from her shirttail. Then she packed the infected bullet wound with a mixture of dried willow leaves and the soft interlining of elm bark. She found another shirt in his bags and helped him put it on, then she hung the rest of their clothes over branches to dry. Her underwear dried quickly on her body as she moved close to the fire.

She couldn't tell if he was sleeping or had passed out, but she made a soup from the last of his supply of jerky and wild turnip roots she found growing near the water. He had coffee and beans in his saddlebags as well, but she'd save them for later. The horse she felt sure Daniel Torry had stolen for her had nothing of use in the saddlebags. One broken gun, a pile of old clothes, and several cheap knives. The clothes were too dirty to use for bandages.

She finally decided to use the rags as a pillow for Drum. By nightfall she'd eaten half the soup and had even gotten him to eat a few bites. His fever still raged.

Sage built the fire as big as she dared and then curled beside him. He was so warm she had no need for the blanket but kept it wrapped tightly around him. She'd been so busy she hadn't had time to think about the men chasing them, but in the stillness, she worried. If they did find them, she needed to be prepared for that as well.

She moved the guns within easy reach and listened. The lone coyote reminded them that he was still trailing them. Logic told her he wouldn't go near the fire, and coyotes never attacked humans.

Sometime in the night Drum's fever broke, and he slept soundly. She was furious that he hadn't told her the wound on his arm wasn't healing. When he came to his senses, she planned to give him a piece of her mind. He was impossible to understand. He'd risked his life to save her, then he'd made her mad by telling her he wanted to bed her. The coyote probably had better courting skills than the man beside her. If her brothers knew half the things he said to her, they'd probably shoot him.

Sage smiled. She was flattered and insulted at the same time. Maybe Drum was right for her. They were both crazy. In the morning, if he was better, she'd explain one more time why she wasn't interested in him.

When she awoke with a start, her first thought was that he'd died. She moved her hands over his cool body until she spread her fingers over his heart and felt the steady beat.

"I'm all right," he whispered, turning to face her.

She rose to an elbow and looked into his wonderful clear gray eyes. "You gave me quite a fright."

"Sorry." He ran his fingers through his hair. "Yesterday was a fog. I remember falling and then riding. I remember you taking my clothes off." He lifted the blanket off his chest. "That last part I wish I could remember more clearly."

Sage smiled. "I think you'll live. How about some breakfast? We've got beans and coffee."

An hour later, they'd eaten and she'd checked his wounds before allowing him to dress. Drum wasn't shy about his body; he had no reason to be. She told herself she was a doctor and had seen hundreds of bodies, but she still caught herself admiring him. Drummond Roak was a sight to see as he walked out of the water, his nude body sparkling in the morning sun. She knew she shouldn't, but she took her time looking.

He dried off and pulled his pants on before she stepped close enough to wrap the wound on his arm. It looked much better but would still require watching.

"That cut in your hairline has stopped bleeding."

"I'm fine." He pushed her hand away.

"You were almost dead yesterday. You'll be weak today."

He nodded. "All right, we take it slow. Stop bossing me around."

She tied off the dressing around his arm, knowing that he was angry. He didn't like being hurt or bossed. Her first urge was to yell at him, but she decided to take another route. "Can we start over, Drum?"

He frowned at her.

She didn't meet his gaze. "I feel like I've been fighting with you since birth. Can we just start over and be friends from here on out? If we work together, we'll have a better chance of staying alive and making Galveston."

He was silent for so long she wasn't sure he would answer. Finally, he said, "I don't want to be your friend, Sage. I want to be a great deal more than that, but if friendship is all you're offering, I'll take it for now."

She nodded. "It's all I'm offering. Despite how I hate you and you drive me crazy sometimes, you're one of the few people in this world I trust. When I was kidnapped, I knew you'd come after me."

"Then trust me now, Sage. I'll get you home safely. I promise."

When she stepped closer, he wrapped his arm around her shoulders. "Friends?" she whispered.

"Friends," he said, kissing the top of her head.

They mounted and headed back toward Galveston, staying in the tree line so no one could spot them easily. After five hours of riding, they stopped long enough to rest the horses and let them graze on the small clumps of grass still green beneath tree branches.

"I'm so hungry I could almost eat grass," Sage complained.

Drum had spread out to rest. He didn't open his eyes when he answered, "I can't risk a shot, even if I saw a rabbit, and we don't have time to fish."

She sat down beside him. "I know. Maybe we could find the coyote and strangle him for lunch."

Drum laughed.

Sage sighed. "Tell me about Whispering Mountain. It was spring when I left. Spring of 1856."

"I know the date," he said.

"What's changed since I've been gone?" She lay beside him.

"Teagen and Jessie's three girls are growing like weeds. Emily is about ten now and proper as any lady. She even talked Teagen into ordering her one of those English riding saddles. Rose has decided she wants to be a teacher like Mrs. Dickerson. She skipped the first grade after a week of school and went right to the second. Bethie is five, with the most beautiful mess of auburn hair you've ever seen. She thinks she wants to grow up to be Apache. All the girls ride well, but Teagen says his Bethie rides like you did when you were her age, free and wild."

Sage laughed. These were details her brothers left out of their letters.

"Travis and Rainey live in Austin most of the time, but they still stay at their place on the ranch in the summers. Duck's as wild as ever. Last I heard, he was building a fort in the trees as a hideout from the girls. Rainey had another baby this past spring, but I forgot what they said it was. I haven't seen your family for months."

She smiled, remembering the little boy they all called Duck. Travis had saved him from men who'd killed his family and planned to sell him. Duck wouldn't talk when he came to them, but he followed Travis around like a baby duckling follows his mother.

"Tobin is still trying to keep up with his busy wife. They spend time up near the capital every winter, but come spring, he has to be with his horses. I can't remember how many kids they got. In fact, when I'm around all the McMurrays, it's hard to tell whose kids are whose. There's a whole batch of little ones. Teagen says when they all hit school age, they'll have to build a second room onto the schoolhouse.

"The main house has doubled in size, and there still doesn't seem like enough room. Martha is retired but comes over almost every day to help out. Last time I stopped by, she filled my saddle-bags with ginger cookies."

Sage leaned back next to him and said simply, "Thanks."

"Anytime," he answered as he closed his hand over hers. "You'll be there soon."

A half hour later they were riding again, but something had changed. There was a truce between them. She knew it wouldn't last, but she was thankful for it now. They did have something in common, she realized: They both loved Whispering Mountain.

An hour before nightfall, she spotted the thin curl of smoke a few miles ahead of them. She pulled her horse beside Drum and pointed.

"I know," he whispered. "I've been watching it."

"What do we do?"

"It's not the raiders, unless it's some kind of trap. Which is not likely. My guess is it's just a traveler like us."

She agreed. "Do we ride around, or do we go closer?"

Drum grinned. "We ride in. They might have food they're willing to share."

She let him take the lead as they approached the campfire. If there was trouble, she was far enough behind in the shadows not to be seen.

"Hello the camp," he called.

The distinct *click* of a round being chambered echoed in the silent air. "Ride in slow and unarmed," came a call no one would mistake as friendly.

Drum kept his hands clearly visible as he walked his horse in. "I mean no harm, stranger, just wondering if I could share your fire."

Sage remained in the shadows, but she could see both men clearly in the firelight.

The tall cowboy lowered his rifle. "You and your woman hiding there in the trees are welcome. I've got food to spare, and I'll welcome the company."

Drum offered his hand. "Thanks. Name's Roak."

The cowboy smiled. "I seen you before in Galveston. I saw you sweep a little lady out of harm's way when she stepped in the street to save a dog." He glanced toward the shadows. "That her with you?"

Drum motioned Sage in. "That's her. I'm still saving her life every chance I get."

The cowboy laughed. "I sure wouldn't have thought you two would end up together the way she was yelling at you that day." He nodded. "Evening, miss."

Sage walked slowly to the fire. "I remember you. We saw you on the boardwalk and again in Shelley's place just before the robbery." She might not have noticed him in the bar, but Bonnie had pointed him out.

Drum straightened slightly.

The cowboy laughed nervously. "I don't remember seeing you in the gambling hole by the water. All I know is I heard the bell that signals trouble in the place, and I hightailed it out of there as fast as I could." He turned to meat cooking on green sticks. "As I was running, I heard shots. Hope you weren't hurt none if you were still in there."

Sage told him about her trouble as they ate. Drum sat back, silent as ever. She got the feeling he didn't trust the cowboy, but the man seemed to be going out of his way to be friendly. He even made coffee and shared a bag of biscuits he said he'd made himself.

"Was the woman you were with that morning on the walkway also with you in Shelley's place? I remember her being tall."

"Yes." Sage fought back tears. "But I don't know where she is. I hope she's somewhere safe."

"I'm sure she is," he said. "She's probably waiting for you right now in Galveston."

"I hope so," Sage said as she curled up on the bedroll Drum had laid by the fire.

"Sage?" Drum said after a few minutes.

No answer.

"She's asleep," he said as he turned toward the cowboy. "I don't believe I caught your name."

"Brad," the cowboy said, "Bradford Summerfield."

Drum met his gaze across the campfire. "You know more than you're saying about that robbery back at Shelley's place, but I reckon you weren't part of the gang, or you'd have stayed around long enough to know that Sage had been kidnapped."

Brad didn't say a word, and he wasn't fool enough to reach for his rifle.

"Mind if I ask you what you're doing out here in the middle of nowhere?" Drum kept his tone low.

"I'm waiting for my brother. He was supposed to drop by my place a few days ago."

Drum studied the man. He looked too poor to be one of the robbers. From his gear and clothes, Drum would guess this man worked hard for his living. "Your brother named Solomon Summerfield?"

"Maybe, but if you're the law, I don't know where he is, and wouldn't tell you if I did know."

Drum shook his head. "I'm not the law." He pulled the blanket over Sage's shoulder. "When I heard she was kidnapped, I came after her."

"She your woman?"

"Yes, but she don't know it yet."

Brad smiled as if he understood. "How do you know my brother?"

"I don't." Drum pulled the paper from his saddlebag. "I found a dead man a half mile from the opening of Skull Alley. He had this in his hand." He passed the note to the cowboy. "He'd been shot at close range in the face. I buried him there."

Brad took the note and stared at it for a while before he said, "I can't read. Could you tell me what it says?"

Drum took the paper. "It's a deed to a square of land west of Galveston called Cedar Hills Ranch."

The big man crumpled to his knee, holding his middle as if he'd been kicked by a horse. He fought to draw a breath.

Drum gave the man time to get a handle on his breathing before he added, "It's made out in both your names. The land is yours now."

One gulping sob came from the cowboy. "I told him not to try to get it back, but he wouldn't listen. He hooked up with a gang for one job. He didn't even want any share of the money; he only wanted the deed from Shelley's safe."

Drum understood. "Problem was, the gang didn't want any witnesses. My guess is they planned to kill him the minute he signed on. They waited until the last day in case a posse caught up to them, and they needed an extra gun. That morning, just outside Skull Alley, they figured they were safe enough."

Drum handed him back the deed. "Just so you know, I would have killed your brother myself for kidnapping Sage if I'd caught up with the gang."

Brad nodded. "I thought I could help him. I'm the one who talked him into filing for the land, but ranch life was too hard a way of life for him. He couldn't have had it more than a year before he lost it gambling at Shelley's place. He claimed he was drugged. I think he was madder about that than about losing the land. I went in that day planning to pull him out if firing started. I wanted no part of the robbery."

"He probably was drugged. I've heard a few complaints about Shelley's place. If a man has anything valuable in his pockets when he walks in, he'd better keep it to himself." Drum pulled a flask of whiskey from his saddlebags. He'd refused to drink it when he'd been shot because he wanted his head clear if trouble found them. He offered it to the cowboy.

They sat in the night and drank. Brad agreed to stay put for a day just in case Drum and Sage were being tracked. The men didn't become friends, but they respected each other.

Finally, after midnight, Drum lay down beside Sage, but he never went to sleep. He guessed Bradford was on the other side of the fire doing the same.

Drum liked the feel of her all warm and soft next to him. She was his. When she stopped fighting the idea, he planned to make love to her slow and easy. She'd never been handled right by a man, he could tell. She wouldn't take to being bossed or bullied, but once she took to him, he intended to hold her every night for the rest of her life, and when they died, they'd be buried side by side. He might not be her first lover, but he'd be her last.

An hour before dawn, while fog still hung low to the ground, Brad lifted a sleeping Sage up into

Drum's arms as he straddled Satan. They rode off, leaving the cowboy alone at the camp.

After dawn, Drum looked back and noticed the smoke. Brad must have built the fire high so that anyone riding within miles would notice it.

If he wasn't careful, he'd suffer the same fate as his brother.

CHAPTER 26

THEY RODE FOR FOUR MORE DAYS, STOP- ping an hour before dark each night so that they could cook the game they'd killed along the way. Sage slept in Drum's arms at night. He was awake when she fell asleep and awake when she woke. He didn't want to sleep. He hated missing one hour, one minute, of their time together.

Though he could think of little to talk about, she trusted him more each day, and the silence between them never seemed awkward. They made a good team, both skilled at surviving.

He enjoyed the way she teased him, claiming he was the worst cook she'd ever encountered. She seemed to be growing younger, shedding a little of the responsibility she'd worn for months. Or maybe he was growing older, Drum thought, from worrying about getting her back safely.

They fought over chores, took turns com- plaining about how dirty they were, and shared everything.

Though the nights were not cold, they slept side by side. He accused her of fluffing him like a pillow every night until she had him turned just the way she wanted him, and she swore he petted her in his sleep, running his hand along her leg or arm several times a night.

Drum was smart enough to deny it, but he didn't stop. His favorite pastime after she slept was to move his hand along her spine until she bowed against him, and he felt her soft intake of breath against his throat. There were other places he wanted to touch her, but he wanted her awake.

To his surprise, he slept more hours beside her than he usually slept. When he did wake in the darkness, he'd listen to make sure all was quiet around him, then he'd relax, enjoying the feel of her close. She liked to put her hand over his heart when she slept. He liked to turn her in her sleep while he whispered against her ear.

"Roll over, honey," he'd say. "Your back is getting cold."

She'd moan in protest, but she'd turn on her side and cuddle into his arms.

He also loved when she woke. She'd stretch against him, then pull away as if embarrassed at her boldness. He'd keep his eyes closed long enough to let her think she had to wake him.

When they reached Galveston in mid-afternoon, Drum had to fight the urge to pull the horses and turn around. He didn't want their time to end. He couldn't stand the thought of her not being in his arms when the sun went down.

Every time he groaned, she laughed, promising him everything would be grand as soon as they had a bath and food.

Sage insisted on going to the Ranger station before they took time to clean up. She was worried about Bonnie and the boys. When Drum lifted her down in front of the station, he noticed a tear running down her dirty cheek.

"They're all right," he whispered, reading her unspoken worry.

She pressed her forehead against his shoulder. "Promise me if they're missing . . ."

"We'll go after them. I promise."

She smiled up at him and squared her shoulders. Even trail dirty and exhausted, she was still the most beautiful woman he'd ever seen, and someday he'd be brave enough to tell her.

Captain Harmon met them at the door and welcomed them with coffee and questions. He wanted every detail and, as soon as he convinced her Bonnie and the boys were safe, Sage talked.

Drum had to admire her intelligence. Most women would have been scared senseless after being kidnapped, but Sage remembered details. She told about the way the men talked, pegging what part of the country they came from, and made a guess at each one's age and height. She knew their eye and hair color and that one had a scar on his arm, another rode a horse with a brand she'd never seen. She related every detail she'd seen and heard, down to what direction the houses in town faced.

Drum made notes on which men had to die. The one she called Frog would be killed right after the wiry one who wanted to use a knife, and the leader, Charlie, who she said had big hands and red hair. He took a deep breath. Sometimes he thought he was part animal, hungry for a kill, even though he knew the captain would talk him into bringing them in to stand trial. Maybe he was part animal despite all his struggle to look civilized, but if someone threatened his mate, they needed to pay.

"There are people in the camp who were kidnapped and brought there," she finally said. "You can't go in firing without killing some of them. Knowing Hanover, I wouldn't put it past him to use them as shields."

Harmon nodded. "We'll find a way. It'll take some planning." He looked at Drum. "Can you be ready to ride tomorrow? I'd like to get a look at the lay of the land so we can know what we're getting into. It'll take me all night to round up enough Rangers. This ride may just be scouting, but I want to be well-manned and well-armed, just in case we run into some of them."

Drum nodded, knowing what he'd be asked to do. "I'd planned to take Sage back to Whispering Mountain first."

Harmon smiled. "No need to worry about that, her brother is here. He'll see her home."

Drum groaned. "Which one?" Not that it mattered. All of them would be thankful that he saved Sage, and not one of them would be happy that he'd spent more than a minute alone with her.

The captain winked as if he could read Drum's mind. "Travis, the meanest one. The ex-Ranger. He'll be wanting to talk to you both."

Sage stood, ready to leave. "Where is he?"

"Over at the hotel. He's got everything ready for your trip." He glanced at Drum. "McMurray was just waiting for you to bring her back. The good news is not for one second did he doubt you would; the bad news is he's fit to be tied at you taking so long. It was all I could do to keep him from going after you both."

Drum shrugged. "I'd have made it faster, but I got shot."

"Shot!" Harmon shouted. "When did that happen? How'd you manage to leave that part out of the report?" He looked Drum up and down, finally noticing the bulge of a bandage around his arm. "How are you, son?"

"I'm fine. I had a good doctor." He winked at Sage. "It happened right after we got married," Drum added, looking no happier about being married than being shot.

"We're not married," Sage snapped. "He bought me. That doesn't count."

"Well, until you pay me back, the divorce isn't happening. You're my wife, like it or not."

Harmon fought down a laugh. "I'd like to hear all about this, but I'd better get you over to Travis. I wouldn't tell him too soon about this marriage that doesn't count. He's never had much of a sense of humor like me." He opened the door.

"We know the way." Drum stood and followed Sage out, yelling, "And in an outlaw camp, we're married."

They were still arguing when they reached the hotel steps.

Travis, the tallest of the big McMurray men, met them on the porch. He grabbed his little sister and swung her around in a bear hug that looked to all like he might crush her.

Drum watched, knowing that he'd lost her all over again. She wouldn't sleep in his arms tonight or any other night in the future. He was an outsider in their world; he always would be. For a while, on the trail, they'd been in a world all their own. Now she was back to being Sage McMurray, quarter owner in the most profitable horse ranch in Texas.

He turned to walk away, but Travis's voice stopped him. "Roak, thanks for bringing her back."

He didn't want thanks. In truth, he wanted to keep her, but he couldn't very well say that to her big brother. "You're welcome," he managed. He looked back and noticed Sage was now hugging the homely nurse. "I need to see to the horses." It was all he could think of to say. He wanted to get away. He'd never been a part of a family reunion, and he wasn't a part of this one.

Travis stormed down the steps and offered his hand. "The captain said that place was impossible to get into. I knew you'd manage it. Come to supper in a few hours and tell me all about it."

Drum tried to think of an excuse. Travis had been a Ranger. He knew all about outlaws and, though he now lived the life of a powerful lawyer in Austin, he still loved to know what was going on. Drum owed Travis a great deal. If he hadn't spoken for him, the Rangers might never have trusted Drum enough to work with him.

"I'll be back at sundown," Drum offered.

"I have a room in your name waiting here at the hotel," Travis said.

"I'll make my own plans," Drum answered too quickly.

Travis nodded, taking no offense. He might have ordered Drum around when he was a boy, but now that he was a man, the McMurrays knew to give him space. "Fair enough."

Drum walked away. He wished he was back on the trail eating squirrel for supper with Sage. Fancy places, like the hotel dining room, always made him feel uncomfortable. He took the horses to the stable and told the owner that the bay Sage had been riding for a week belonged to the Rangers. Then he brushed Satan down himself and mixed a rich blend of oats and hay seasoned with carrots cut lengthwise.

When he hung the gear by Satan's stall, he checked the secret pouch he'd had made years ago between the leather. He'd spent almost all his traveling money buying Sage. He would have to make a trip to the bank before long. Most of his pay from the Rangers went into the bank. He had accounts in Galveston, San Antonio, and Austin. Drum wasn't even sure how much he had. It didn't really matter. Money wasn't worth that much to him.

He pulled a twenty-dollar gold piece out and headed for a tailor. He'd buy clothes for the road and a hat, but he needed a proper coat for tonight. Tonight, he didn't want to look like a gunfighter. He wanted to look like he belonged with Sage.

Two hours later, when he looked in the mirror, he hardly recognized himself. He'd rented a room down the block from the Grand, had a shave and a haircut. He'd taken care in his bath to soak off the last of the bloody dressing on his arm and tried to rewrap it neatly so that the bandage wouldn't show beneath his shirt. The suit delivered was black, well-fitting in the shoulders, with a white shirt.

"I look like a preacher." He swore at himself and tugged off the string tie. This wasn't him. He couldn't pretend.

After tugging off his jacket, he went down to the hotel desk and asked one of the runners to deliver a message to Sage that he wouldn't be joining them for dinner, then he ordered a bottle of whiskey for his supper. He knew he should be grateful they were back safe, but part of him needed time to mourn the loss of Sage by his side. They'd had a few peaceful days where there was no one else to see them or comment on how the fine doctor didn't fit with the gunslinger.

Drum opened the windows to the night air and lay on the hotel bed. It felt soft and uncomfortable after so many nights sleeping on the ground. He drank half the bottle and couldn't drown the ache for Sage. He didn't bother to light the lamp; he could see everything he needed to see in the darkness. The noises in the street sounded off-key after listening to nights in the open country. Hell, he thought, he even missed the coyote.

He was almost asleep when he heard a tap on the door.

"Go away," he said, not caring who it was. He'd make it up in time to meet Captain Harmon at dawn. Until then, his time was his own.

The knob turned, and he reached for his gun, realizing he hadn't thought to lock the door.

He blinked, not trusting his sight, as Sage walked into the room. She had her medical bag in one hand and a basket of what smelled like hot bread in the other. Without saying a word to him, she moved to the table by the window and lit the lamp.

When she turned, her eyes danced with anger. "I knew you wouldn't come to dinner. I knew you wouldn't take care of yourself. I knew you'd probably drink the night away."

He shoved his hair back and sat up. "Well, if you know me so well, why haven't you figured out that I want to be alone?"

"Because you don't," she said as she turned and opened her bag. "Take off that shirt. I'm going to check your wound one more time and put some proper medicine on it."

"I'm fine."

She faced him. "Strip off that shirt or—"

"Or you'll what? Strip it off for me?"

"Or I'll go get my brother."

"Threats of your big brothers don't scare me anymore. They haven't for years."

"Then why didn't you come to dinner?"

He tugged off his shirt, knowing she wouldn't leave until she'd done her duty as a doctor. "I'm not afraid of your brothers, Sage," he said as she cut the bandage he'd tried to tie. "I'm afraid of being with you."

He could see that her concentration was on her work. The wound was healing nicely, but it would leave a scar.

She spread salve over the scab. "Why would you be afraid of being with me, Drum? We've been together all week."

"Then, you needed me to keep you safe, and I did. Now, who will keep you safe from me?"

She laughed as she wrapped the bandage. "I don't

need to be protected from you. We agreed, we're friends. I'm not afraid of you, Drummond, so stop trying to convince me of how tough you are."

He tugged her onto the bed as she knotted the bandage. "Then lie beside me for a while just like you did on the road, if you're not afraid."

"But—"

"Tomorrow I go after the outlaws, and you head west to Whispering Mountain. It may be months before our paths cross again. Stay beside me an hour, Sage."

To his surprise, she seemed to understand.

She brushed his jaw. "Funny thing, out there on the road, I was afraid. The only time I felt safe was with you. Now that we're in town, I feel safe, and I think you might be just a little afraid."

"No," he lied. "I just want to feel you near."

"All right. I'll stay a few minutes, but no more." She placed her hand on his chest and pushed him against the pillows. Then she twisted so that she fit against his side just as she had every night for a week.

He took a deep breath of her hair, clean and smelling of honeysuckle. "How'd you find me?"

"It wasn't hard. I asked the boy you sent with the message that said you weren't coming."

He rested his arm across her waist.

"Try to sleep," she whispered. "I don't think you slept more than a few hours a night for the entire trip."

"I had to watch over you."

She rolled to face him. "Sleep now," she ordered and watched him close his eyes. "I'll watch over you."

He was almost asleep when he felt her kiss his cheek and whisper, "Sweet dreams, my hero."

CHAPTER 27

SHE'D MEANT TO SLIP FROM HIS BED AS SOON as he fell asleep. From the half-empty bottle, she guessed it wouldn't be long. But he felt so good beside her, Sage drifted off in the warmth of his arms.

She awoke to him shaking her shoulder. "Sage, honey, you've got to wake up."

Stretching, she felt the cold from the open window for the first time and tried to remember where they were. Drum's room. She'd come to a man's room.

"It's late, long past midnight. Too late for a respectable lady to be walking through two hotel lobbies." Worry lines crossed his forehead, making him look older.

She sat up. "I'm starving."

He laughed. "I figured you'd worry more about your stomach than your reputation."

She spotted the basket she'd brought. "Can I eat before I'm condemned as a fallen woman?"

He climbed off the bed long enough to grab

the basket and two glasses. "Who knows you're here?" he asked as he handed her the food and poured them each a drink.

"No one, yet. When I found you weren't at dinner, I told Teagen I was exhausted after we had soup and said I planned to call it a night. He said he wanted to go over to the Ranger station and make sure the boys were having fun. Will and Andy wanted to spend their last night in town with the Rangers. It's all arranged for us to leave tomorrow. Travis will take us as far as Austin and then pick up his family, and we'll all go to Whispering Mountain." She laughed. "We'll look like a band of gypsies on the road."

She saw the sadness in his gaze a moment before he turned away, and she decided it was safer to talk about her reputation than her leaving. "I waited until Bonnie went in her room, then closed my bedroom door, picked up my bag, and slipped out. Teagen's room is across the hall, but I'd be very surprised if he came into Bonnie's and my suite tonight. It wouldn't be proper."

She handed Drum a roll with meat inside. "I had the restaurant make these up. I said they were for the boys, but I thought you might not have eaten. I didn't realize how slim you are until I hugged my brother. You're almost the same height, but I swear he's twice your width."

Drum took a bite and smiled. "He gets regular meals, I guess. What else is in the basket?"

"Fruit pies." She giggled, thinking of how little either of them had eaten for a week. "It's a regular feast." She fed him a bite of the first pie.

They sat cross-legged in the middle of the bed and ate as they talked of their adventure. Sometime in the past few years, she'd forgotten how much she loved adventure. When she was about eight, she and her brothers would go up to their grandfather's winter camp. They'd hunt and fish and live among the Apache for weeks. She'd throw a fit if she wasn't allowed to do everything her brothers got to do, and because she was the chief's granddaughter, it was allowed.

"I feared you were dead," she said as she finished her second glass of whiskey and water.

"Which time? When you shot me, or when I tumbled down the hill?"

She laughed. "When you tumbled. I knew my aim was off in the upstairs room. Of course, if you'd been fatter, I would have hit your chest and not your arm, and you'd be dead. I guess that would make me an outlaw widow."

"In outlaw camps there are no widows. If your man is killed, you're simply thought of as eligible."

They talked and laughed for an hour before she said, "I have to go." She dusted crumbs off her very proper navy blue suit with its slightly wrinkled white blouse beneath. "You don't happen to have a disguise I could wear to make it past the front desk?"

He grinned. "I'm afraid there's nothing that would hide that body."

She frowned, looking around the room for something that would work. She reached for his new coat and pulled it on, then added the hat. "This might work, and it's warm."

He stood and tugged the hat off. "It'd never work, but you can have the coat. At least you'll be less easy to see in the dark, but in the hotel, even a drunk will see a beautiful woman wearing a man's coat."

She sighed. "Then I guess I'm ruined. Not that it matters. I'm long dead to even wanting to court much less marry again."

He tugged on his boots. "Here's the plan to save you. I'll lower you down out the window, then I'll walk you through the alleys to the back of the Grand. You should be able to get up the back stairs this time of night without running into anyone. I'll be with you, so you should have no trouble from the usual alley rats who roam at night."

She smiled and followed him to the window. A few minutes later, they were crossing through the night hand in hand. She loved knowing that she was safe but feeling as if she were on an adventure.

When they reached the back of her hotel, she stopped to catch her breath. The whole world seemed to be sleeping. Deep into the shadows she could hear tiny feet scurrying. Alley rats, she thought.

"I'll say good night here," he whispered close to her ear. "I ride out with the captain tomorrow to see if we can find a way for men to cross into the camp without having to go through Skull Alley."

She sobered, realizing he was going into real danger again. "What will you have, six or maybe ten Rangers? They'll be easily picked off in that country. One gunman could do it from any one of a dozen cliffs."

He brushed her shoulder. "The captain's not going to get us killed. Maybe we can find a point where we can watch them coming out. The next time they leave for a raid, we could get a few at a time."

"It's not much of a plan. You could get hurt, and I wouldn't be there to patch you up."

"You could come along," he teased.

"You could not go."

"That's what I do, Sage. I'm good enough with a gun to move in close. If the captain didn't want to go with me, I'd go alone. It pays well, and this time it's personal. They took you."

She pushed her head against his chest. "You're not doing it for the money, and I don't want you getting killed for me."

"It's more than that. I do it so in a few years when this state gets settled, there'll be less men like the count out there to worry about. Maybe one day folks can sleep safe in their beds without worrying that their family could be killed by raiders."

"You're making sense. In fact, you sound a lot like my brothers, but I don't like the idea of you dying." She laced her hand in his. "I don't have that many friends."

"I'm guessing I probably have the life span of a mosquito, but at least there won't be anyone around to mourn me when I'm gone."

He'd meant it as a joke, but she felt a chill pass through her. She gripped his shirt and whispered the truth, "I will, Drum. I'd mourn you." It shocked her how much.

He was so still she wouldn't have known he was there, if they hadn't been standing so close.

Finally he moved. She could feel him leaning down, brushing his chin against her cheek, touching her lips lightly with his. "Thanks, Sage, but I swear I'll come back. I plan on pestering you until we're both gray."

For once she didn't push away. She wrapped her arms around his neck and hugged him to her. She'd had all the death she wanted for a long while. He'd become a friend; he'd saved her life. "Promise."

He laughed against her ear. "Sage, you're choking me."

"Good. Then remember to take care of yourself."

"I will." He straightened an inch away. "And you remember you're not dead." He pushed his hand inside the coat and touched her waist. "You're still very much alive inside, no matter what that brain of yours thinks."

She shook her head. He didn't know what she'd gone through. She'd buried her first love, she'd run off her second, she'd worn black for a third. It was time to stop fooling herself into believing that somewhere there was a man out there who could be the great love of her life like her parents had found. Like each of her brothers had found. The odds were not with her. Everyone in the world can't be so lucky.

Drum tilted her chin up. "As a friend, do you mind if I prove it?"

She knew her own heart. He was wasting his time. "How?" she asked as his mouth came down on hers ever so lightly.

"This will not work," she mumbled against his lips.

"Come on, honey, give it a chance."

She let him kiss her without feeling anything, already knowing that she wouldn't.

After a minute, he pulled back and shook her. "Stop it, Sage."

His anger surprised her and sparked her own. "Just because your kisses don't buckle my knees, don't fire up at me. I told you I don't feel anything."

"You don't want to feel."

"Maybe I don't, but you just can't make it happen with a kiss."

A drunk stumbled down the alley. When he passed them, he tipped his hat and said, "Good evening, people. Nice weather we're having today," as if they were standing in the street. A few steps later, they heard him throwing up near the privy.

Drum pulled her through the back door of the hotel and into the tiny hallway at the base of the staff stairs. When he closed the door, they were in total darkness. When she laughed, he did too, relaxing the tension between them.

He tugged her to the steps, and they sat down. "Sage," he whispered. "Just pretend for one minute that I'm someone you could love. Pretend."

She felt his arms moving around her in the blackness. She wasn't afraid; she'd never been afraid of him. And here in the dark, what did it matter if she did pretend for just a moment? It wouldn't change anything. The only one she'd be fooling was herself.

His arm braced her, and he leaned her back against the stairs.

She didn't move. There was adventure in the air, and she decided to play along.

He began near her ear, whispering words she wasn't listening to as his mouth moved down her throat and up to her lips. In the blackness she was sixteen, being kissed for the first time by a young Ranger she met in Austin. He promised forever. Then she was on her porch, kissing a preacher who refused to carry a gun. He wouldn't get killed; she could live with him forever. Then she was holding Barret, and he was holding her the way she always wished he would. His body wasn't weak but strong and hard against hers.

When Drum reached her open mouth, she was ready for the feel of his kiss. She kissed him back, trying not to think about the Ranger dying, or the preacher running away, or Barret not loving her. She kissed him like a woman kisses a man who cares deeply.

He moved her arms up so that they circled his neck. "That's it, honey. That's the way. Pretend."

She arched toward him, pressing her breasts against his chest, feeling the familiar warmth of him. His kiss deepened, and she followed, feeling as if she were riding free across a midnight sky.

His hand moved from her waist to her breast. He touched her so gently she almost cried at the tenderness of it. Before she noticed, he'd unbuttoned her jacket and pushed it aside so that his fingers now slid over her silk blouse.

He kissed her until her head spun, then she lay still on his arm while he unbuttoned the blouse and pushed his hand in so that only one thin layer of satin stopped his touch. Then he kissed her deeper than anyone ever had. He kissed her as if he were taking a part of her and giving a part of himself back.

When he pulled away, she sighed and welcomed his touch as she tried to catch her breath and return her heart to a normal beat. She knew this was just pretend, but it felt so good to feel alive.

He let her head lean back as he lifted her and kissed his way down her throat and lower between her breasts. His warm breath moved over her damp skin as his thumb crossed the peak of one breast and made her moan.

She felt his smile. "That's the way. Just enjoy."

He continued the sweet torture for a while, laughing against her when he drove her to moan or cry out softly in pleasure. Each time, before thoughts could form, he'd return to her mouth and kiss her so tenderly she'd open and let him taste all he wanted.

She'd felt his touch for days, when they slept close beside one another, when he lifted her on the horse, when he brushed against her. She'd thought she had grown used to him and his nearness, but this was something different. Something quite different. This felt like a man holding someone he cherished. This was a lover's touch, not just a friend's.

He pulled her back against him and circled his arms around her, then moved his hands back so that he could hold each breast. She shook with how much control he'd taken of her body and started to move away.

"Easy, honey. I'm not going to hurt you. I just wanted to know if you could possibly feel as good as you looked." He kissed the side of her neck then tugged her hair until she twisted enough so that he could reach her lips.

There was such a hunger in him that it made her feel desired.

She'd expected him to kiss her again when she turned in his arms, but he drew her bottom lip into his mouth and tasted. When he finally kissed her again, she was ready and begging. He bruised her lip with his craving, but she didn't care.

She felt alive.

"More," she whispered without realizing she was asking aloud.

"More?" he answered, letting his hand close firmly over her breast.

"Please," she said as her breath came fast.

"You'll never have to ask me twice, Sage."

He covered her mouth with his, and all thought was shoved from her mind by feeling.

CHAPTER 28

A DOOR OPENED ON THE LANDING ABOVE, and light flooded the stairway below.

Drum pulled her beneath the stairs as they both fought for control. By the time one of the maids passed, Sage had buttoned her blouse, though any fool could see she'd been well-kissed and properly handled.

"I have to go." She started up the steps.

"I'll find you," he said. "This isn't finished between us." Not by a long shot, he thought. Not by a thousand nights.

"Be safe, Drum, but don't look for me."

He thought of trying to catch her, but he let her go. He'd meant to kiss her and give her something to think about. Instead, she'd changed him. She'd given him a taste of heaven.

Walking back to his hotel, he tried to remember every word they'd said to each other. He knew he'd never forget the feel of her. Even now, walking in the cold, he could still feel the warmth of her breast in his hand.

She was his woman, he reminded himself. It didn't matter how different their families were, they fit together perfectly. He'd known it the first time he'd stolen a kiss five years ago.

"You're up early." A voice surprised him from the hotel porch. "Or is it out late?"

Drum smiled. "None of your damn business, Daniel Torry." His words were harsh, but his smile wide. "Glad you made it out."

Daniel shrugged as if it hadn't been hard. "When they figured out you and Miss Sage were gone, it caused quite a stir. I even seen the count come out of his big house and offer a thousand to the man who brought back your body. Seems he had plans for Sage after you broke her. I was tempted myself to go after you, except us being friends and all, it didn't seem polite."

Drum laughed. All of a sudden he seemed to have more friends than he could handle. "How about a drink before we saddle up?"

"Sounds good to me. I reported in a few hours ago. Cap said you were shot."

"I'll tell you all about it later. You riding out with us at dawn?"

"Sure. I figure if I sleep in a bed, it'll just make me soft. One night a month seems often enough."

They walked into the small bar off to the side of the lobby and woke the bartender up.

"A round of whiskey and then a pot of coffee," Drum ordered.

By the time the bartender brought the coffee along with plates of eggs and beans, the two men were talking about the mission. Daniel didn't believe for one minute that they'd be able to ride into the camp, but at least they'd know where it was.

He also had a wild idea that somehow the murders of Will and Andy's parents were connected to the count's men. He had enough men to make both raids.

"How'd you come up with this idea?" Drum asked.

"Somebody had to shoot the count. What if he was hit in the raid on the Smith place and left before seeing everyone dead?"

Drum shook his head. "The raiders wouldn't have had enough time to ride back to the hideout with the count and then ride to Shelley's place."

"No, but they might have had time to go from the Smith place to Galveston. Or at least six of them might have." When Drum didn't look convinced, Daniel added, "I heard in camp that this Charlie guy was new. Appears he came up the ranks fast, because two of the men ahead of him were killed."

"So you're saying that all we captured at the Smith place was the cleanup crew? Charlie and his men had ridden east to Galveston, and Hanover and his bodyguards had gone west toward the hideout?"

"You saw the number of men in the camp. He had plenty to pull both jobs and still leave the camp well protected."

Drum swore as he shoved his empty plate aside. "If this is true, we're not dealing with a gang of raiders, we're dealing with an army."

They both sat silent, taking in the possibility, then they paid and walked into the cool night.

Daniel changed the subject as if needing to talk about something besides the trouble they might be riding into. "I heard Miss Sage's nurse disappeared for a few days after the robbery. One of the Rangers said she just fell off the earth, and that couldn't be easy for a woman her size. Then she showed back up about the time they'd all crossed her off as dead. She claimed a stranger got her out of Shelley's place when the shooting started and took her to his farm for safety. She swore he was kind to her and brought her back when he thought the trouble was over."

"That was mighty nice of him," Drum said, waiting for the rest of the story.

Daniel shook his head. "Strange thing is, she don't remember what he looked like or what direction his farm was, or how far they rode. Said she was too frightened to think. Some of the boys and I were talking, and we think she probably got hit on the head, lay under the dock for a few days, then came to and made up the whole story."

"Did she look frightened or hurt?"

"No." Daniel thought about it. "If anything, she looked sad, but that was probably from worry over Miss Sage. The woman is always at the doctor's side. She couldn't be ten years older, but she's a mother hen to the doc."

They walked through a deserted street to the livery. Several of the other Rangers were there already saddling up. Drum noticed a difference in the way he was treated. A few of the men took the time to congratulate him for bringing McMurray's little sister back safe. A few more asked questions about how he did it.

Drum left out a few personal details, like that he bought Sage, and she shot him before they escaped.

When the captain showed up, he stepped right in front of Drummond. "Roak, you sure you're ready to ride?"

"I'm ready." The only place he'd rather be was with Sage, but on the trail with her and her brother and Bonnie and the boys, he'd have no privacy, and that would eat at him worse than missing her. He wanted her alone. All alone. "The sooner we get started, the sooner we can develop a plan to clean out this nest of snakes."

Harmon grinned. "I thought that's what you'd say, but this trip, I want you wearing this." He held out a badge: one star inside a circle, the mark of the Lone Star State. "I want you riding as a full Ranger not just as a hired gun."

Drum looked around the circle of men. Not one frowned in disapproval.

He took the badge.

Daniel slapped him on the back. "Welcome to the brotherhood. I've thought you should be one of us for a long time. So did some of the others."

They saddled up and headed southwest. Drum looked back once, wishing he could see the wagons he'd loaded for Sage moving out. Knowing Travis, they were already miles down the road.

Sage and he were going in opposite directions: He was looking for a fight; she was planning to save lives. He had no idea how long it would be before he saw her again, but when he did, there would be no talk of pretending between them. He'd shown her she was still alive, and she'd wanted his touch as dearly as he'd needed the feel of her. As far as he was concerned, the solution was simple. The hard part would be convincing her.

CHAPTER 29

SAGE DIDN'T BOTHER TO SLEEP. SHE PACKED and was ready when Travis banged on the door before dawn. Her brother had hired two men to ride along as guards. They planned to go as far as Austin, then Travis would pick up his family, another two wagons filled with furniture for Sage's new office, and drivers for the rest of the trip.

Travis wasn't too happy about taking a stray dog and an old cat along on the ride, but he'd been married long enough to know better than to waste time arguing with determined women.

As the sun came up, they took a barge, leaving Galveston far behind for the mainland of Texas. Sage watched the water and thought about how Drum used to swim the river to visit her.

The man who'd touched her last night was nothing like the boy from years ago. She knew they were just pretending in the stairwell. He'd made that clear, just as she'd made it plain that all they would ever be was friends. Only for a short while in the total darkness, she hadn't wanted to pretend. She'd wanted a lover. Not Drum, but a real lover. He was too wild to ever be the man she needed.

Only when he'd been kissing her she hadn't thought about him being younger. She'd forgotten how wild he was. She'd forgotten that he made

253

his living with a gun. All she had thought about was how he made her feel. In his arms, she'd been alive.

She'd promised herself when she was eighteen that she'd study and help people. She had also sworn she'd never care for a man who would die by a gun. Somehow Sage believed that promise would keep her heart safe. Only Barret never handled a gun in his life that she knew of, and he'd still died.

"You all right, Doc?" Bonnie said as she knelt beside Sage. "Don't tell me you're sorry to leave Galveston."

"No. I'm not sorry. I'm ready to get home." Sage looked up at the nurse, thinking about how frightened she must have been during the robbery. "How about you? Are you all right?"

"I'm fine. Good, actually. Mostly back there I was worried about you. I'm sure glad Mr. Roak brought you back safe and sound."

"Why do you call him Mr. Roak? He's not much more than a kid really."

Bonnie shook her head. "I don't think of him as a kid and, judging from the looks other people turn his way, I'd say most people agree with me." She sat down beside Sage and added, "When I was no more than five or six, my parents took me to see a man speaking at our church. My father said he had greatness about him. He said some men are born to it, and there's nothing they can do but step into the shoes already made for them. I feel like Mr. Roak is that kind of man. It wouldn't be proper to call him by his first name."

Sage didn't see it, but Bonnie had her way about her, and she wasn't a woman to change. For the hundredth time, Sage tried to picture how bad things were for Bonnie in Boston. It must have been intolerable for her to agree to come to Texas.

They talked of their mission to open a doctor's office and a small clinic. Sage felt her world coming back in balance. She tucked away the time on the stairs and promised herself not to think about it again.

But that night when they camped, she lay on her bedroll and wished Drum's arm was around her for warmth. She ached for the feel of him against her, and all reasoning wouldn't make it go away.

Will sat beside her after breakfast the next morning. He had the old family Bible, wrapped in what looked like a deer hide, in his lap. His serious gaze watched her, and she knew he was waiting to say something.

"I need to ask you a question," he whispered.

"Of course."

"The captain said you're a real smart woman. He says you'd have to be, to be a doctor."

The boy looked like he was drowning in worry. "How can I help you?" she asked.

"My father told me if Andy and I ever found ourselves alone, that we were to talk to a judge we could trust, but I don't know how to find one. Your brother is a lawyer. Do you think he'd do? The Rangers talk about him as a great man and said he knows the laws."

Sage smiled. "Travis knows the law. He'll help you if he can. You can trust him."

Will nodded, thanked her for her advice, and stood. "I need to show him something before we go any farther. He might decide we're too much trouble to take along."

"I doubt that."

The thin little boy walked over to her big brother. Travis knelt to Will's level just as he always did when he talked to his son, Duck.

Sage watched them walk over by a pile of rocks while she began to break camp. She couldn't hear what they said, but Travis was obviously giving the boy his full attention.

When they came back to the wagons, neither made any comment about what they'd discussed, but Will had the hint of a smile and looked like he'd had a weight removed from his little shoulders.

Just before she climbed in the wagon, she kissed Travis on the cheek.

"What was that for?" he grumbled.

"For being my big brother," she said.

"I'm the best one," he teased, reminding her of years ago when her brothers always tried to get her to name the best among them. They hadn't been much older than Will and Andy when they'd taken on the job of raising her.

Travis lifted his arm, and the little caravan began to move.

It was late October when they reached Austin. Travis came home to a world of trouble. The capital seemed to be boiling over, with tempers flaring over the issue of slavery.

Like most Texans, Sage and her family didn't own slaves, but there was talk of Texas pulling out of the Union if the states split over the issue. Since Texas had entered as a sovereign country and not a territory, it had the right, at least to the minds of most Texans, to pull out. Texas had flown its own flag before, and it could again. But most people had come from other states, southern mostly. If the South fought, their loyalties would be there.

Travis was called away to the state capitol before he'd had time to change clothes.

Sage felt the turmoil moving in like a great storm and could hardly wait to leave, but Travis was torn. He wanted to go to Whispering Mountain with his family, but he knew his duty was at the capital. Travis stood with Sam Houston in wanting to keep the country together.

After three days trying to decide, he sent Sage and Bonnie and the Smith boys on alone with guards for safety. His wife, Rainey, refused to leave if he stayed, even though she cried when she said good-bye to Sage.

"We'll try to be there for Thanksgiving. If not, tell Jessie we'll make Christmas. Tobin and Liberty have promised then also," Rainey said.

Sage didn't feel like it would be home without two of her brothers there. In her heart she always thought they'd all live on Whispering Mountain and raise families. But they'd moved on to form families of their own, something she'd never have.

"Ready?" Bonnie whispered.

"Ready." Sage tried to smile. It was time to move on, she thought, in more ways than one.

The road between their home and Austin had been safe for years, but Sage still remembered the time she'd been on a stage and they'd been attacked. She left Austin well-armed and silently wishing Drummond were by her side.

The third morning out of Austin, Bonnie Faye Pierce sat in the buggy alone. Over the miles she'd learned to drive the small, one-horse contraption that carried her, the luggage, and sometimes little Andy when he decided he needed a nap mid-afternoon.

Sage usually sat beside Will in the front wagon. The seven-year-old was good with the reins and could have handled the team alone, but Sage thought it safer to ride beside him. They were the lead wagon, setting the pace on the trail. Then came Bonnie in what everyone called "her" buggy. Next, a tough old man drove the four-horse team that pulled a wagonload of supplies for the clinic. Bringing up the rear were two wagons Travis's wife Rainey had packed with household supplies she thought they'd need to set up the apartment where they'd live in back of the clinic.

Bonnie couldn't believe this crazy dream of the doctor's was happening. Months ago in Boston right after they'd buried Dr. Barret Lander, Sage had told Bonnie of her plan. She'd even shown her a letter to her brothers back in Texas describing exactly what she needed to set up an office in a little town that didn't seem to have a name.

Apparently the McMurray family had been working on the clinic while Sage and Bonnie traveled.

The McMurray family was the opposite of her family, she thought. She'd stopped by to see her brother before leaving Boston. He'd told her not to wire for money if she hated Texas, because it wouldn't be coming. Then he'd asked her to sign the house over to him. When she'd refused, he'd told her to leave, because as far as he was concerned, he had no living relatives.

Bonnie smiled to herself. She'd left his house and walked to the bank. There, she asked the banker to handle the sale of her parents' old home, should a buyer come along. He'd promised to check into selling the place but didn't give her much hope.

It didn't matter, she told herself. In a few days

the traveling would be over, and she would step into her new life as the nurse in charge of probably the world's smallest clinic. They'd planned it all and talked about every detail so often, she could see every square foot of it in her mind. She'd have her own apartment, a new place with walls that held out the wind and a roof that didn't leak.

Three mornings later, as they moved out once more, thunder rattled in the distance, promising rain, but no one slowed. They were within a day of reaching a small town located an hour from Sage's family ranch. Rain or shine, Sage planned to make it there by nightfall, and Bonnie, as always, followed along.

Only today, bright sunshine couldn't have changed her mood. The doctor might be almost dancing with excitement, but Bonnie felt the clouds press all the way to her heart.

A tear started down her cheek. Bonnie shoved it aside. She wouldn't cry. She'd act happy, even if she knew deep down she was going to destroy Sage's dream.

Bile rose in her throat, but she fought to keep from throwing up again. If she stopped the caravan one more time this morning, someone was sure to notice. Bonnie chewed down another piece of dry bread and prayed her stomach would settle.

It had been more than a month since the night with her cowboy, and even if she wanted to forget it, she knew she couldn't. She never would. For the proof of it already grew in her belly. The very proper Bonnie Faye Pierce was pregnant.

She'd thought there was no label worse than old maid. Now she realized there was one: the label of fallen woman.

CHAPTER 30

DRUM SPENT TWO WEEKS ROAMING AROUND with the Rangers, trying to find a way into the outlaw hideout. They even attempted to lead their horses up the incline that he'd rolled down, but the slope was too steep. The horses wouldn't climb, and the risk of breaking one of the animals' legs seemed too great. All the men agreed that they wouldn't want to go into the hideout on foot, so they regrouped several miles east and sent out scouts, hoping to find another way in.

Daniel Torry had Drum draw out a map of the back way in. He claimed if he ever went in again with his old man, he wanted an exit if things turned bad.

Drum found it strange that the Rangers talked to him now. He wasn't used to being included, and for the most part, he found it bothersome. The only peace he seemed to have was at night after everyone turned in. He'd slip from his bedroll and move far beyond the firelight. In the stillness, he'd take a deep breath and try to remember the exact way Sage's hair smelled or how she'd tasted

261

when he'd kissed her. He'd never missed anyone in his life, but he missed her all the way to his soul. She was a part of him; she had been since the first time he saw her.

The world had always been dark and dangerous for him. Even staying alive before he grew to be a man seemed sometimes a waste of effort. She didn't just offer light, she made him want to be a better man. He thought of all the things in his life that he'd done because of her, and she wouldn't ever know about most of them.

Drum smiled in the darkness. He'd even talked Mrs. Dickerson into teaching him to read one winter, and he'd spent a day in a fancy hotel dining room watching people eat so he wouldn't embarrass her if the McMurrays did ever invite him to Sunday dinner. He bought his clothes tailor made and his boots were custom. It seemed like everything he did, he wondered what she'd think about it or if she'd even care.

He'd wait until almost dawn, then go back to bed.

One night, Daniel rolled over when he returned. "I figure you must be part wolf or coyote, Roak. You hunt at night while the rest of us sleep."

"You're drunk," Roak mumbled. "Go back to sleep."

Daniel didn't argue with the diagnosis. "Not drunk enough," he said as he took another long draw on a flask. "I still remember where I am."

"Where are you?" Drum asked, just to pester his friend.

"I'm wandering around trying to get myself killed. That's where I am." He grinned. "It's my absolute favorite thing in the whole world to do."

Drum laughed. "I don't know which one of us is crazy, you for trying to get yourself killed so you'll die a hero or me for going along with you just so I can spoil your plan."

"I'll drink to that," Daniel answered. "At least I'm not mooning over a woman."

"What makes you say that?"

Daniel snorted. "You're crazy about that little doc. I seen it the first day. But you're going about it all wrong."

"I am."

"Sure. If you want a woman to like you, you got to act like you're not interested in her. The minute you turn away, they run toward you."

Drum knew that would be impossible. "You have experience at this?"

"Sure. I'm always acting like I don't much like the girls I meet. My problem is they all return the favor and act like they don't like me. If I ever find one willing to come after me, I'll toss the whiskey and run just long enough for her to catch me." He was silent for a while, then he asked, "Did you ever wonder what it'd be like to live with a woman, day after day? Sleeping with her every night through the seasons? Talking to her about important stuff and about nothing at all? Having a woman worry if you ate enough and dust you off like she was proud to be with you?"

Drum knew without asking that Daniel was like him; he'd never had a woman care about him. "I've wondered," he said.

Daniel laughed. "I'm wild as a mustang, but I tell you, if a woman ever roped me, I don't think I'd mind being corralled." He took another drink, and neither of them said anything else. They were both lost in their own thoughts.

Drum offered Daniel no sympathy the next morning when he had to dunk his head in the stream to clear it enough to ride. Daniel was one of the best Rangers, levelheaded and dependable in a fight, but like half the troop, he medicated his fear with whiskey from time to time. Drum never asked him about his past, but he'd heard the captain tell someone once that he'd lost his mother and sister in a fire over near Victoria when he'd been about four or five. His old man hadn't slept beneath a roof since. By the time Daniel was old enough to join the Rangers, he'd rattled around most of the state with his father selling whiskey on weekdays and preaching on Sundays. For him, being out on the land was the only home he could probably remember.

Drum offered Daniel a towel when he walked from the stream with his brown hair dripping.

"You might want to think about drinking a little less at night," he said.

Daniel nodded, then moaned. "I think about it every morning. Trouble is, once I start drinking, I stop thinking."

Drum laughed as he watched two Rangers riding in hard from the direction of the opening to Skull Alley. One led a horse with the rider bound and blindfolded.

The lead man pulled ahead and yelled, "Cap, we caught one of Hanover's guards riding out alone."

All the men in camp gathered round as the Ranger swung off his horse. "He gave up without too much of a fight."

Everyone watched the other Ranger pull the prisoner off his horse and remove the blindfold. In a heartbeat Drum recognized the outlaw as the one who'd brought Sage into the saloon and looped the rope, tied around her neck, over a beam so she'd choke if she didn't stand up straight and still for the auction.

Anger boiled in every part of his body as Roak moved blindly toward his guns hanging over his saddle.

Daniel slapped a hand against his chest and warned him to stop.

"You know who he is," Drum hissed.

"I know, and I want to kill him only slightly less than you do right now."

Daniel held him back while Drum swore. He

knew Daniel was right, but that didn't make standing still any easier.

"Roak, calm down. Let the captain have his say; then I'll help you string the bastard up."

Captain Harmon walked past Drum as if he didn't hear his newest Ranger threatening to kill the prisoner slowly and painfully. "I'll have your name," he shouted over Roak's swearing.

"Luther Waddell." The big man stood up straight, chest out, like a prisoner expecting a bullet any moment and refusing to beg for his life.

The captain studied him. "Want to tell me what your business is? And don't try to lie. I got two men here who saw you in the count's hideout, and one of them is mighty anxious to kill you." He glanced in Drum's direction. There were two Rangers holding him back now.

Luther measured Drum. "If I tell you what I'm doing, I want your word that you won't let that fellow decide my fate. I don't much mind dying, but he's promising I'll beg for death before he's through, and I can see in his eyes he's not bluffing."

Captain Harmon nodded. "Agreed, but only if you're honest. I can smell a lie."

Luther turned to Drum and yelled, "I figured she might be your lady that night in the saloon. Ain't never seen a man pay two hundred dollars for a night. Except she didn't look too happy to be climbing the stairs with you. I still thought she'd be safer with you than with most of the other men wanting her."

Drum stopped swearing and began listening.

"I know you don't believe it, but I tried to help the little doctor. I locked her in a cell at night so none of the men could get to her. I clubbed the man who bruised her face, just for the hell of it. But you should know she weren't hurt none while she was in camp. I saw to that. The night of the auction, if I hadn't tied her up to the rafter, the men would have pawed her and passed her around. I've seen it before."

Drum didn't buy a word the outlaw said. "You're a talking dead man," he whispered loud enough that the stranger heard.

Captain Harmon paced restlessly. "So, if you're one of the count's personal guards, what are you doing outside the hideout?"

"Hanover trusts me. He's got my wife and son to ensure I come back."

Drum stilled. Daniel removed his grip as they both listened. Neither of them liked the idea of a child being in the camp. They both knew first-hand what he'd face.

"The count's got a fever. He thinks he's dying. He's so weak he's messing himself like a baby. He's got it in his head that the only one who can help him is the little doctor. I'm on my way to get her. If you kill me, he'll just send someone else until he gets her back. To him, she's his property."

The captain raised an eyebrow. "Why are you telling us this?" The man was writing his own obituary.

Luther looked directly at Roak. "Your woman asked me to help her escape, and I didn't. I was worried about my family first, and second, I didn't think he'd mistreat her. I figured the worst he'd do was keep her in camp as the doctor, but I underestimated his hatred of women. She'd be dead today if you hadn't come for her, and my wife's not safe, even if I do what he tells me."

"But you were heading to find Sage and drag her back," Drum shouted.

"No." Luther shook his head. "I was going to warn her to get as far away as she could. Then I planned to go back and tell the count I couldn't find her. If I'm lucky, he'll be dead or feeling better and deciding he doesn't need the doctor. At worst, he'd still be crazy with pain and have me killed." He looked straight at Drum. "I don't care anymore. The only reason I've gone on as long as I have is for my wife and boy, but my boy is sickly, and my wife cries all the time."

Drum almost felt sorry for the man. Almost.

Captain Harmon motioned for them to untie Luther, then he offered him a cup of coffee. The man would have been a fool to reach for a gun; a dozen bullets would hit him before he could clear leather.

"Do you know of a way into the hideout besides the slow ride through Skull Alley?"

Luther held the cup with both hands. "No. If I did, I'd bring my family out. That narrow canyon keeps everyone in line. I've seen a few men try to run it on horseback. They started at night and made it past the first checkpoint, but by daylight the second guard picked them off as easy as shooting fish in a bucket. One man who tried to make it traveling only on foot got lost and ended up coming right back to camp, where Hanover had him hanged."

He looked up at Drum. "I'd given up any hope till you got out. You got the doctor out too, and neither of you crossed through Skull Alley." He took a drink of coffee. "I know, 'cause I sat up there for three days waiting to shoot anything that moved in that canyon."

Captain Harmon drew his attention back. "How'd you know the doc was back in Galveston?"

"We got a man there who sends word on anything he thinks the count might like to know. He sent a note that he'd keep her occupied until we got there."

"How'd he know who Sage was?"

Luther shrugged. "He was at the robbery when Charlie and his men took her. He says he's an almost relative, whatever the hell that is."

The captain kept questioning Luther, but Drum

had listened to enough. Bonnie had told him there was only one man who was in the room with Sage when the robbery happened: Shelley Lander.

When the captain took a break from questioning, Drum moved beside him. "Cap, I know who the spy in Galveston is."

"So do I, a scum of a gambler named Lander." He put his hand on Drum's shoulder. "I also know what you're thinking. Someone needs to warn Sage. When he sent the note, he must have not known that she'd be leaving with her brother. But if she told Shelley where she was headed, this count is just crazy enough to go after her."

"I'm on my way," Drum said.

Captain Harmon nodded, then added, "Take Daniel Torry with you. A hard ride with a hangover will do him good."

Drum motioned to Daniel. "Saddle up. I'll explain on the way."

Daniel looked confused. "What about killing Luther? I don't want to miss out on that."

As much as he'd like to stay around and beat Luther to death, Drum knew he had to get to Sage before Shelley had time to send word of where she had gone. He'd find out they'd left for Austin, and from there someone would have probably noticed what direction they took. Drum doubted Travis would speak to Shelley, even if he rode all the way to Austin. Travis wasn't friendly with his relatives on most days, much less someone else's, but there were those who knew where the wagons were heading, and Shelley might luck out and talk to one of them.

Captain Harmon waved them off. "We'll try to hold him long enough so he'll be waiting when you get back. If I have any luck, he'll be in the cell next to Lander."

Like two wild kids dismissed from school, Roak and Daniel took off at a full gallop.

CHAPTER 31

A NOVEMBER ICE STORM, WHICH HAD melted into miles of mud, slowed Drum's progress.

He'd talked Daniel into riding north of Galveston in hopes of saving a few days, but they were almost three weeks behind Sage. The shortcut helped little.

Drum missed her in Austin by two weeks, as he figured he would. Travis talked them into staying one night. He wanted details about Luther. Drum could see it in his eyes; Travis was making his own list. He might wear a suit and look to all the world like a respected lawyer, but part of him was wild and always would be. Drum wouldn't be surprised if Travis McMurray went after the man. He was probably thinking the same thing Drum was. One lone man could get in and out of the camp, leaving no sign behind, only one dead count.

After everyone went to bed, Drum walked the streets of the capital city. He couldn't sleep without knowing Sage was safe, so he tried to picture asking her to live here with him. Austin was exciting, but he couldn't see either of them being happy to ride their horses around a park. The stores were fun to look into, and there were more places to eat than he could name. He'd never thought about where they'd live or what he'd do to make a living; he'd just wanted to be with her.

When Drum turned Satan toward Elmo's Trading Post the next morning, he was on familiar ground. He'd made the trip many times and knew where all the best roads were and where to stop for the night. Daniel stayed up with him at every turn. He even stopped drinking, claiming it was a waste of time to try to swallow at the speed they rode.

The winds blew from the north, and mud slowed them more than rain. Both had good mounts, but Drum knew not to push them too hard. Satan was a McMurray horse, one of the finest in the state. If he rode Satan to ground getting to Sage, she'd never forgive him. The woman was almost born on a horse and probably loved them far more than she'd ever care about any man.

When they stopped to rest the horses, Daniel slept, and Roak paced.

One afternoon, Daniel leaned up from his nap and said, "What's bothering you? You know Sage is safe. They couldn't have gotten to her yet.

Even if the count sent another man after Luther, he couldn't be traveling faster than we are. Something else is festering like a burr under your saddle."

Drum squatted down beside Daniel. "It's that boy of Luther Waddell's. I can't stop thinking about him there in the camp."

Daniel sat up. "I didn't see any kids while I was there. My guess is the women who have them keep them out of harm's way. As many years as the hideout has been there, you know a few kids are there somewhere. I saw clothes on the lines near the little houses along the pasture line. Maybe that's where the wives stay. There wouldn't be many. The kind of man who lives that life picks his mates by the hour."

Drum agreed, then added, "Do you think if I showed Luther the back way, he could go in and get them all out before the firing starts?"

"There's a chance he'd turn on you and warn Hanover we were coming. Or, just as likely, one of the wives would tell her man and blow the plan."

Drum nodded. "Maybe, but I don't think so. He looked real sad when he talked about his family. Surely he'd know who to trust."

Daniel stood. "We could ask the captain when we get back. I'm kind of hoping the count dies of the fever before then, but in camps like that, there is always someone else to take the big snake's place."

"Time to ride."

Daniel stepped into the saddle. "I was afraid you were going to say that."

They crossed through open country and reached Elmo's Trading Post by mid-afternoon the next day.

Daniel pulled his horse. "Holy smokes, Roak, I thought we'd be riding into a little cluster of buildings around a trading post, not a town."

Roak stared. "I don't know what happened. The place looks like it's doubled." There was a regular main street with stores and a church next to the bank. A block away was a dance hall and a couple of saloons as well as homes lined up in rows.

They walked their horses down the dirt street, noticing construction happening all around them.

"Folks are moving to Texas faster than sugar ants move into a molasses pantry." Daniel pointed at a café. "You think we could stop for some food? I've been eating your cooking for so long, my teeth are thinking about falling out in protest."

Drum shook his head. "Between you and Sage I'm starting to question my skills as a cook."

"What skills?" Daniel grumbled.

He made no move to turn in at the café. "Come on. I want to see Sage before we eat. Then I'll buy you the biggest steak we can find."

Daniel took a deep draw on the air as they passed a bakery. "I figured that. How about we take her some hot rolls? Women like it if you bring them something."

"Rolls?"

Daniel grinned. "Works better than flowers, I'm told. It would on me anyway."

Roak pointed to an old building with a crooked porch wrapped around it. "I'll check with Elmo, the old trading post owner. He'll know if Sage is staying in town. I'll meet you back here in five minutes. You get the rolls."

Roak walked across the street as Daniel hurried into the bakery.

The trading post looked about the same as it always had. The area where Elmo stored mail was gone, replaced with shelves of dry goods. Roak stood in the doorway and watched an old man, withered on one side, move toward him.

"Can I help you, mister?" Elmo Anderson said with gravel in his voice.

"I hope so. I'm looking for Sage McMurray."

Elmo glanced up and smiled. "Drummond Roak." He let the name roll around in his mouth a little before he got it out. "It's good to see you again. I hear some mighty fine things about you, son."

Elmo had always been nice to Roak. He'd given him small hauling jobs when he was a kid.

"It's good to see you too, old man. How'd you let this town get so big?"

"You sound just like Teagen McMurray." Elmo shook his head. "I don't know how it happened. Let a few people in, and before you know it, things get out of hand." He laughed. "They want to name it after me. Can you imagine?"

"No offense, but Elmo don't sound like much of a name for a town."

He agreed. "And Anderson don't sound like nothing special, so I'm thinking they should name it Anderson's Glen."

Drum frowned. "There's no glen."

"I know," Elmo snickered, "but my mother was Irish, and I think she'd like the sound of it."

"I agree. Now about Sage?" He asked before Elmo got started on something else.

"They're settling in at a house north of town. It's off by itself. I heard Teagen say he wanted Sage to be able to see the hills so she'd know she wasn't that far from home. It's a pretty whitewash with trim on it as dainty as lace. Teagen got the place built for her just like she told him, but I don't think they're open for business yet. You'd better hurry if you want to catch her. She rides home ever' night to the ranch." He laughed. "And you know Sage; if she'd riding, no one's going to catch her."

Roak said a hurried good-bye and rushed out the door just as a tribe of school-aged boys bombarded the place.

Daniel was waiting by the horses when Drum crossed the street. "I thought you were going to buy some rolls?"

"I did, a dozen, but I ate them while I was waiting."

Drum frowned. "Why didn't you go in and buy some more?"

"I tried, but the lady in there told me to get out of her store before the yeast rose again and I exploded." He rubbed his stomach. "She said if I was still alive tomorrow, she'd sell me another dozen."

They climbed on their horses and headed north. Daniel continued talking as if Roak were listening. "That baker was a sweet little round kind of girl, but I don't think she thought much of me. She made me stop one foot in the door and tell her what I wanted."

Drum laughed. "You might want to think about taking a bath."

Daniel lifted his arm, took a deep breath, and crossed his eyes. "I will before I go in there tomorrow. She had cheeks as round as apples and skin as smooth as a peach."

"I think you're still hungry. Next thing you'll be telling me is her legs were green beans and her fingers as round as carrots."

"I was so hungry, my stomach's been gnawing on my backbone for two days. If we stay here awhile, I plan to eat five or six times a day to catch up."

Drum saw the white house with the trim a few hundred yards beyond where the rest of the settlement ended. The door was open, and Bonnie, wrapped in a white apron, was sweeping the long porch. Her worthless cat was sitting on the porch railing.

He urged Satan into a trot and was out front before Daniel stopped talking about food and thought to join him.

Bonnie squealed and ran down the steps. "Mr. Roak! Daniel Torry! It's good to see you."

Drum grinned. "You're looking fine and healthy, Miss Pierce." He was surprised how much he meant it. In the month since he'd seen her, the tall nurse looked like she'd put on a few pounds.

She ran right past Drum and hugged Daniel then pulled back quickly. "Wow, you do smell of the trail."

Daniel shrugged. "I've been told that a lot lately."

"Miss Bonnie," Drum drew her attention. "Where's Sage?" The need to see her had become a physical ache within him.

The nurse laughed. "She went up to her grand-father's winter camp a few days ago. Teagen told her the old man is sick when he came by to get the boys to spend some time at the ranch with him." She held a finger in the air. "No, I think his exact words were, Grandfather claims he's sick but said to tell you not to come.

"Sage said the old man would never admit to wanting to see her, but she'd ride up while we're waiting for the last of the work to be done on the clinic. We decided to turn the attic into rooms for the boys and Sage when she stays over."

"We're not heading into Apache territory tonight, are we?" Daniel asked.

"No," Drum answered. "We're getting rooms at the hotel, having a long bath, and then coming back to take Miss Pierce out to dinner if she'll consider letting us both escort her."

Bonnie blushed. "I'd be honored. I haven't been out to eat. It wouldn't be proper for me to go alone, and Sage has been too busy."

They left her still blushing on the porch and circled back to the hotel.

"I think this may be the first time Miss Bonnie has been asked out," Daniel said as they walked up the steps. "She's plain, but I think she might have gotten married if she hadn't been so tall. Aren't many men who want to look up to a wife."

"Probably so," Drum agreed. "She's past the marrying age now."

He walked to the desk, noticing the hotel owner who'd run him off a few times four years ago.

"Welcome, Rangers," the owner said with a smile. "We're always glad to see you." He turned the book around. "If you'll sign in, I'll have baths sent up to your rooms immediately."

Roak smiled. The owner didn't recognize him. Daniel ordered a bottle, then they parted with a nod to their rooms.

Two hours later, both Rangers ordered two meals at the café. Bonnie sat between them, as proper as ever. The old maid might be ten or more years older than them, but she was still flattered to be asked to dinner.

"You young men sure do clean up nice," she said. "Sage will hardly recognize you when she gets back."

"I'm riding on up to the camp tomorrow," Drum said. "I thought Daniel might stay here for a few days. If you need him, he'll be close."

"You think the boys may still be in danger?" she asked.

He shook his head. "I don't see how the raiders who killed their parents could find the boys here, but it pays to be safe." He didn't dare tell her Daniel's theory of the raiders and the outlaw being links of the same gang. "I think Sage may still be in danger. The man she treated at the outlaw camp seems to want another house call made. I'm here to make sure that doesn't happen."

Bonnie's hand shook. "There's so much trouble in this country." Tears bubbled in her eyes. "I swear I'm frightened most all the time."

Her show of emotion surprised Drum, but he had to admit for a woman who'd said she'd never gone more than a few miles from her home before she left Boston, this must be a terrifying place.

Daniel tried next. "Don't you worry, Miss Pierce, you're far enough from the saloons that even when there is gunfire, it'll never reach you."

Both men frowned when tears continued to roll down her cheeks.

"I don't think you're helping," Drum said.

Bonnie excused herself and almost ran from the room.

Daniel pointed at Roak. "Well, at least I was trying. Which is more than you were doing. What do you suggest next?"

"Pie," Drum said and waved down the waitress.

When Bonnie returned, she smiled at three pieces of pie sitting in front of her. It seemed to work; her mood did improve as she nibbled on a slice.

She filled them in on everything that happened on the trail up from Galveston. She also talked about Will and Andy. It was obvious she'd grown to love them both. During the weekdays, they'd stay with her at the clinic so they could go to school. On Friday, one of the McMurrays would take them to the ranch for the weekend, where they would run free.

"They invite me to go along," Bonnie said, "but I like my time alone here in town. There's too much going on at the ranch. I have my knitting and my books to keep me company, and of course when the clinic opens, we may have patients from time to time who are in recovery."

When she talked about the details of the clinic, both men listened politely as they ate.

Drum walked her back to the clinic while Daniel excused himself, claiming that a poker game was calling him. Drum strolled through the streets alone after he said good night to her on the porch. He took in the feel of the town and decided he liked it. Anderson's Glen seemed a safe place and, in a strange way, it felt almost like home. He knew people here, even if some of them didn't remember him.

Something else had changed. Men tipped their hats to him and women smiled. They'd say things like, "Evening, Ranger" and "Nice night." It seemed the badge he wore didn't just frighten outlaws, it was a welcome sight to those on the right side of the law.

He closed the door to his room and stripped his clothes off without turning up the lamp. Then he lay on the bed and relaxed. There was nothing he could do until dawn, when he planned to saddle up and go to the Apache camp to see Sage. After warning her, he thought he'd ride back with her to town. Maybe somewhere along the way he'd have enough time alone with her to remind her that she was still alive.

As he passed into dreams, he rolled to his side and reached for her as he had every night since they'd been together.

CHAPTER 32

SAGE TURNED HER HORSE TOWARD THE water and splashed across the stream, not caring that it was midnight and her actions would wake up half the camp. Her grandfather had been his usual impossible self, refusing to take any medicine that wasn't made the Apache way. He had a bad chest infection that could easily move into pneumonia. To make matters worse, he'd decided to sleep out beneath the stars, since it was the first clear night in a week.

When she'd objected, he'd ignored her plea and told her that a man on a black horse waited for her on the other side of the stream. She knew it had to be Drummond. Her grandfather wouldn't have let anyone else near the camp.

Sage decided she might as well go see what Roak wanted, because between worrying about her grandfather and worry over what bad news Drummond brought, she'd get no sleep.

When she reached his campsite, he stood and offered to help her down. She ignored his hands and jumped to the ground. "Why didn't you just ride into the winter camp? Grandfather knows you're a friend of the family. I told him all about how you saved me."

Drum smiled. "Your grandfather may have welcomed me, but a few of the braves still remember years ago when I used to pilfer their game. I figured he'd tell you I was here. The old man keeps up with everything that happens around him."

She moved to the campfire for warmth, and he offered her coffee. They sat across from one another. He told her all that Luther had given the Rangers about Count Hanover's condition, and she told him about her grandfather's health. They talked easily, sometimes finishing each other's thoughts. The days of traveling together had changed them, she thought. They'd become friends. True friends.

"So," she said when her coffee was finished. "What's the plan? You just going to hang around to see if anyone comes for me?"

"Something like that."

She shook her head. "I got a better one. I can take care of myself. Go back to the Rangers. Hanover will never find me here and, if he does, I'll be ready for him."

"I—"

She didn't let him finish. "I'm not your worry, Drummond. I never have been. We're friends. That's all. If I ever need you, I'll send word, just like if you need me, you let me know." She stood and moved to her horse. She had her life planned out here, and she didn't need a body-guard following her around.

"I need you," he said so low he wasn't sure she heard him. "God, how I need you, Sage."

She froze. How could she tell him? That night in the stairwell had been a mistake. She'd just been pretending, living out a fantasy with the ghosts in her life. It hadn't been him she was kissing. She thought he'd understood that.

He moved behind her. She didn't have to turn around. She could feel the warmth of his body.

His nearness had always attracted her like a magnet, but her mind knew there could never be anything between them.

"If you were older, you'd know it's not that simple. You can't just say you need me and expect me to react."

"I'm old enough," he brushed his hand over her shoulder. "And it is that simple."

She shook her head. "No, it's not."

"Stay with me tonight. Just sleep beside me like we did on the trail. I need to hold you." He hated himself for asking, but he had to try.

"No." She couldn't turn around. She knew she was hurting him. She should have stopped this the first time he'd kissed her when he was still more boy than man.

She expected him to argue, to ask again, but he moved away.

She waited until she'd climbed on her horse before looking back, knowing that her refusal may have ended the friendship they'd built. Why couldn't he understand that this wasn't about him, but her? She wasn't brave enough to take the loss of another love. Her love for adventure didn't cross to her heart. The pain was too great. For once in her life, she had to play it safe, and getting involved with a wild gunfighter was definitely not playing it safe.

The campfire cast a low glow all the way to the trees. There was no sign of Drum. He'd disappeared just as he always had as a kid. Only, he was a man now. A man who'd asked to hold her, and she'd turned him down without even facing him.

Sage felt like a coward as she rode back across the stream. Turning him down had hurt deep inside her, and she suddenly didn't like herself. How much would it have cost her just to let him hold her for a few minutes? She doubted anyone had ever held him, and when he'd asked to hold her, she'd turned him down.

Drum had been alone all his life, and tonight, she'd managed to make him feel even more so.

She'd thought she couldn't feel worse, but she was wrong. Her grandfather waited at the edge of the Apache camp for her return. The anger and disappointment in his eyes shocked her.

"I was just—"

He answered in Apache. "I know where you were."

She felt like a teenager caught behind the barn with a boy. "We were just—"

He shook his head. "I don't care what you were doing. Go back and tell Roak that he is welcome to our fire. A man who saves my granddaughter's life should not sleep on the other side of the water."

"I can't—"

"You can and you will. Teagen tells me he is very brave, and he carries you in his heart. Are you afraid of him?"

"No." The conversation had taken a turn she

hadn't expected. Her grandfather lived by a strict code. She'd insulted him by not asking Roak to come into camp. She had no idea what the comment meant about his heart, other than that Drum was constantly worried about her. "He would never hurt me, Grandfather. Teagen is right; we are friends, and he is a very brave man."

"Then go back and invite him to share our camp-fires. If he does not cross the water, you do not."

Sage had a headache. On a good day her grand-father could easily drive her to drink, and today hadn't been a good day. She wasn't surprised he thought more of Roak than he seemed to of her. To Grandfather, a brave man was highly valued, whereas women, including his four wives, were mostly a bother. When she'd been little, he'd thought she was cute and spoiled her, but now he seemed to think she was a great embarrassment to the family by not being able to keep a man alive long enough to get her pregnant.

"All right, I'll go back and invite him." She turned to the stream. "If he doesn't want to come, I'll drag him over here at gunpoint and tie him to a pole."

Her grandfather grunted. "Good. I will watch."

Sage splashed back across the water, trying to think about what she could say to Drum to get him to come with her. She'd just insulted him, probably hurt him, and now she wanted to invite him over. Men!

She wasn't surprised to find Drummond's camp empty. He'd be out walking off his anger. She sat down on his bedroll and leaned against his saddle. Maybe if he didn't come back, she could wait half an hour and sneak across the water to her bed. Surely her grandfather wouldn't stay up waiting for her. He was at least seventy years old, she thought. What does a man that age do with four wives?

Sage groaned, closing her eyes. She knew what he did. She'd heard the wives giggling about it.

She heard firewood tumbling to the ground a few feet from her and looked up. Drum stood above her, frowning. He was tall and handsome in his lean, dark way. Dressed in black with his gun worn low and his hat tilted to shade all but his strong jaw from the firelight, he reminded her of what a highwayman of old must have looked like.

"What do you want?" No welcome flavored his words.

"I came back to tell you that you are invited into my grandfather's camp."

He knelt and added more wood to the fire. "No thanks."

"If I said I'm sorry, I didn't intend to hurt you, would you come with me?"

"No," he answered, still looking at the flames. "And you didn't hurt me."

She knew he was lying. Part of her wanted to

reach out and touch him, but she had a feeling he wouldn't welcome sympathy. "What do you want from me?" she finally whispered.

"Nothing," he lied again. "I don't want or need anything from you. I never have. I've been alone all my life. What makes you think I need anyone? Go back to your grandfather."

"No."

"That seems to be your favorite word tonight, Sage. Go away."

She stood and faced him.

His gray eyes were cold as he looked down at her. "Tell me, do you turn down every man in your life? Is that why they die on you, from neglect?"

Before she thought, she slapped him so hard she wouldn't have been surprised if her grandfather heard it. She hated Drummond Roak at that moment more than she'd ever hated anyone. How dare he say such a thing to her!

When she raised her hand again wishing more than planning to hit him, he grabbed her wrist with lightning speed.

The sudden thunder of horses startled them both, leaving them frozen in place as Apache surrounded them.

Her grandfather slid from his pony and stormed toward them. For all his complaining of being sick and old this morning, he looked to be in full warrior glory tonight.

"I've heard enough." His words seemed even

more powerful in Apache. "If you two plan to argue like you are married, let you be bound."

He twisted a rawhide band around the place where Drum's fist clamped over her wrist. "It is done." He looked at Drum. "She is yours."

"What?" Sage yelled as her grandfather turned around and signaled for his men to leave. As fast as they were surrounded, she stood alone again with Drum.

"No!" she screamed, but all she heard back was the splashing of water as the Apache returned to camp.

"What was that all about?" Drum tugged on the rawhide, trying to get free.

Sage turned on him. "This is all your fault."

"What is?" He tugged again, causing her to stumble into him.

"My grandfather just married us."

"What?" he yelled.

Sage smiled without humor. "There seems to be an echo in this clearing."

He tugged again.

"Stop hurting me, and cut us free."

He stopped pulling and smiled. "Why, so you can slap me again, wife?"

"Stop calling me that."

He pulled a knife from his boot and sent it flying high into the bark of a nearby tree. "I've changed my mind. I think we'll stay bound."

She kicked him as hard as she could and would

have tumbled if he hadn't caught her around the waist with his free arm. Furious couldn't begin to measure her anger, and he was smiling suddenly.

"How about we get some sleep?" he said almost conversationally as he dodged another kick.

She laughed suddenly at the insanity around her. "My crazy grandfather hates me, and I'm tied to a madman who throws away the only knife. This has definitely not been my day. Maybe if I go to sleep, I'll wake up and find this has all been a bad dream."

He shoved his hand until his fingers locked with hers. Now the leather at their wrists no longer dug into their skin. "Daniel was right." He laughed. "He said if I'd stop chasing you, you'd come right to me. Truce?"

She was too tired to argue. "Truce."

They knelt together, keeping their hands locked. When she would have slipped farther against the saddle, he stopped.

"I can't lie on my side with my holster still belted."

She glared at him.

He tried to pull the buckle with one hand, but it didn't give. "Help me out?"

Frowning, she followed instructions, and the holster swung from his waist. They lowered, facing each other, and he placed his weapon right behind her so that it would be in easy reach if he needed it.

"Afraid I'll kill you in your sleep?"

"Maybe." He smiled. "Last time we were married, you shot me."

She almost laughed. "That wasn't a marriage; that was an auction. Besides, if I killed you, my grandfather would probably make me drag your body around until it rotted."

He placed his hand on her hip. "That's one reason for keeping me alive."

She shoved his hand away. "Don't touch me."

"But you're my wife. I married you twice."

"The first one doesn't count, and you know it, and this one is my grandfather's idea of a joke. I'll talk to him in the morning and get him to change his mind."

Drum put his hand back where he obviously thought it belonged. "He gave you to me, but you're right, nothing is going to happen tonight. I want both hands free when I make love to you." He tugged, suddenly pulling her against him.

"What do you think you're doing?"

"I'm going to kiss you, honey, just the way you like it."

She opened her mouth to object, and his lips moved over hers. When she struggled, their bodies only seemed to press closer together. His kiss was warm and hungry and wild. And, she realized, he was right. It was just the way she'd always wanted to be kissed.

Something deep inside her shattered, like a wall

she'd stored all her emotions and feelings behind. It crumbled. She shook as she lost hold of all her control. He held her to him as if he knew what was happening to her. His body moved over her, holding her to the earth as his kiss demanded she respond.

And she did. She kissed him back.

He raised his head, wanting to see her face as she gulped for air after the kiss. Her breasts were pushing against him with every breath, and her eyes were on fire with need.

He smiled and lowered slowly back over her. This time his kiss was long and meant to drive her beyond all thought.

When he pulled away once more, she lay panting beside him and made no protest as he moved his hand beneath her jacket and over her breasts.

"No one has ever kissed me like that," she said, feeling his fingers grip her breast each time she breathed. "No one—"

"Hush now," he whispered against her ear. "I'm just getting started. Think of this as your first lesson in being alive."

When his lips moved over her again, the kiss was gentle. She sighed with the tenderness of it and let him continue for a while before her hand moved into his hair and pulled hard, demanding the kiss turn once more to fire.

The campfire burned low before they both grew too exhausted to continue. He'd kissed her thoroughly, and his free hand roamed over her body now, feeling wherever he wanted without her protest. But he hadn't undressed her, not even opening her blouse as he had in the stairwell.

She wouldn't have stopped him; in fact, she would have welcomed his hands moving across her flesh, but he'd only kissed her.

He covered her shoulder with his arm. "Go to sleep, now, wife."

"I'm not . . ." She was too tired to argue.

"Yes you are, Sage." His lips moved from her ear to her cheek. "You're my woman. You always have been."

She was too much into sleep to answer, but she felt his mouth cover hers once more in a feather-light kiss. Then he reached and slit the rawhide binding their hands and twisted her so that she could sleep with him holding her as she cuddled against his side.

CHAPTER 33

DRUM HEARD A TWIG SNAP A MOMENT before he felt someone grab him from behind and toss him in the air as if he were no more than a bale of hay.

"What in the hell do you think you're doing!" Teagen roared as he stormed toward Drum with his fists ready for combat. "I should have beaten you to death when I caught you stealing horses."

Drum scrambled to his feet and managed to dodge Teagen's first two punches.

"I wasn't stealing horses," he yelled, knowing Teagen wouldn't listen. Ears were a waste of flesh on the whole McMurray family. "And I'll not fight you."

The man was a charging bear. "You had your hands all over my sister. You're going to pay in blood for that."

Drum backed away, trying to stay out of the way of two hundred pounds of fury. He saw Sage out of the corner of his eye. She looked so beautiful stretching and rubbing sleep from her eyes. Her brother's yelling evidently wasn't something she found alarming.

"Morning, Teagen," she said as if her brother wasn't on the warpath. "Leave Drum alone." She stood and straightened her clothes. "Any chance you brought some of Martha's muffins for breakfast?"

Teagen paid her no mind. "I'm going to kill Roak. Maybe we can fry him up for breakfast. I saw how he was touching you." He made another swing and caught Drum on the jaw, sending him rolling.

Drum got back to his feet. "I'm not going to fight you, Teagen, so stop hitting me."

"Why not? Are you a coward as well as a thief? If so, I'll make you eat that badge you're dishonoring." He charged again, but Drum was fifteen years younger. He might not be as big, but he was much faster on his feet. "Stand still and fight me, damn it, Roak."

Sage finally woke up enough to realize that her big brother might truly be trying to hurt Drum. "Stop trying to kill your new brother-in-law."

Just as Teagen's head turned toward his sister, Drum's fist connected with Teagen's middle, and the giant folded, dropping to one knee as he let out a low groan.

"Stop it, Drum. Don't you dare hit my brother."

"He called me a coward," Drum said, still standing ready to fight. "There are some things a man can't take, even from his wife's brother."

As Teagen rose, his fist swung at Drum's face, knocking him back a few feet.

Sage rolled her eyes and stepped between the two men. "I've had enough of this. Both of you stop!"

They now both looked ready to fight, but neither would push her out of the way in order to get on with it.

"I didn't start this fight," Drum said almost calmly, "but I might finish it."

"You started it by handling my sister, and you won't be conscious at the finish."

She knew better than to even suggest that either of them say they were sorry. "Teagen, Grandfather went crazy last night and married us. He bound us together. We had to sleep side by side."

Teagen drew a long breath. He still glared at Drum, but at least his fists were no longer raised. "What binding?"

Sage looked down as if she'd just figured out that they were no longer tied together.

"I cut the rawhide last night so she could sleep easier," Drum offered in explanation, but she didn't look pleased.

Before she asked, he answered, "I carry two knives. I just forgot about the other until you were asleep."

Now she stormed at him. "You're a liar." She turned to her brother. "Go ahead and kill him. I don't care. I'd rather be a widow again than married to a liar."

Teagen was too confused to fight. "Is he or is he not my brother-in-law?"

"If you kill him, he'll be your ex-brother-in-law."

Drum shrugged. "She's right. Go ahead and kill me, Teagen. I deserve to die for thinking I might want to sleep next to my wife without being tied."

Teagen looked at them both. Being mad enough to kill Roak and being told to were two different things. The fact that they were both telling him to fight made him certain he'd be doing the wrong thing. "I'm going over to talk to Grandfather, and I plan on telling him that the next time he binds you two together, he gags you both as well."

He climbed on his horse. "I expect you both at

the family table for Thanksgiving, and you'd better not be fighting. With all the kids, there's enough noise already."

Teagen rode off.

Sage glared at Drum.

He smiled. "I guess a good morning kiss is out of the question."

She shook her head. "I recognize that last night wasn't your fault, Drummond. My grandfather got the wrong impression when he saw us." She stomped over to her horse. "Come to think of it, this whole thing is probably my fault for ever going out to the barn and speaking to you five years ago." She reached for her bag strapped on her horse's saddle. "Come here. Your lip is bleeding."

Drum rubbed the drop of blood away from the corner of his mouth with his knuckles. "Don't worry about it."

"That's what I do." She moved closer. "I worry about you. I was bound to become a doctor because I've been doctoring you for years." She shoved his hand away. "Let me have a look at it."

While she doctored his cut, he put his hand on her waist.

"I had a good time last night," he whispered against her hair as she put up the medicine.

"I can't lie to you." She didn't look at him. "I did also. Where'd you learn to kiss like that? I didn't know a kiss could make me feel so warm inside."

"I took lessons," he said, moving his head lower so that his lips brushed her cheek. "Then I paid attention to what you liked."

She tried to push away, still pouting that he hadn't mentioned the second knife. "Since when does a man worry about what a woman likes when he's busy kissing?"

Drum tried again. "You like it soft at first, like you're just making up your mind whether you want to be kissed, then you like it wild until you have to stop to breathe. You like me to brush the outside of your breast as I push my tongue deeper. And you like to decide when each kiss ends, which I don't mind at all, because you like them long."

"Stop it, Drummond."

Her face was red with embarrassment, and he made a note that she liked doing things she didn't like talking about. That was just fine with him. The doing was far better anyway.

She started to get on her horse, then paused. "Will you go with me to the winter camp? My grandfather said I couldn't come back across the water without you."

"If I do, will you stand beside me? My Apache isn't that good. I'll need to know what's being said."

"All right."

He moved up behind her as if to lift her into the saddle. "We're double married now, honey. It's time we spent a little more time together."

She wanted to argue, to tell him they were not right for each other, but he'd cracked through the barrier she'd built around her heart. She didn't feel quite as grounded on her rock-hard determination.

"Kiss me good morning, Sage," he whispered against her hair. "Then we'll go over and straighten this out."

She turned, letting his mouth find her. His kiss was so soft, so tender, it made her want to cry. Why couldn't he have said he loved her just once? Why was it just need and want with him and never love?

The kiss turned deep, and she opened her mouth. As he pushed in for a taste, his hand slid gently along the side of her breast, and she shook with pleasure.

He was right. He did know how she liked to be kissed, and that knowledge frightened her. One thought whispered in her mind, frightening her even more. What if he *had* said he loved her? Not just needed or wanted, but loved. Would that have mattered?

When he raised his head, he smiled down at her. "Any chance you'll help me put my gun belt back on?"

She shoved him away, more playfully than with any anger. He was a man born to drive her crazy.

A man to make her question her own will.

A man. Not a boy.

CHAPTER 34

No matter how much Teagen talked or Sage complained, Grandfather had made up his mind that Drummond Roak and Sage should be married. He explained that Sage hadn't grown up big enough to take care of herself, even if she did think she was a medicine woman, and Drummond, being a brave warrior, would keep her belly full of babies. It was very important, he explained, for him to see many great-grandchildren.

Sage jabbed Drum in the ribs every time he got within a foot of her. All he did was smile and agree with her grandfather. She thought of murdering him the next time they were alone.

Finally Grandfather noticed her jabs and asked Drum if he wanted to break this bond. After all, his little wife seemed about as friendly toward him as a porcupine.

"I'd like to give it a try," he said, bowing his head in respect to the chief. "I think she might warm up to me in time."

She swung at him again, and he ducked, mumbling, "Twenty or thirty years might be enough."

Grandfather cleared his throat and glared at them.

They both straightened back into adults.

Sage listened to her grandfather, then translated as closely as she could. "He says I'm a little long in the tooth for you, and I've been married without bearing children, so there is a good chance I'm broke."

Drum thought about it and asked, "Do you think I might get a discount?"

She hit him again with everyone watching.

Drum laughed. "All right, I'm sorry. Tell him I want you anyway. I can't do anything about you being older. I'd age faster if I could." Drum winked. "Add that I promise to work real hard on the children part. I'll even give up sleep if I have to."

"I'm not telling him that," Sage said. "You're not helping, Drummond. If you'd say you didn't want me, he'd call off this whole thing."

"I can't lie about that, Sage." He faced her, and she saw steel in his gray eyes. "I can't. Not even to make you and Teagen happy."

When she swung again, he grabbed her hand and circled her under his arm. Before she could protest, he kissed her soundly.

Grandfather laughed and shooed them away. "Come back in two full moons," he said in Apache as Teagen translated. "She will kill you, or you will convince her to lie still. Either way, the problem will be solved."

The chief then pointed at Sage. "Do not kill this man before you know his heart."

Sage tried to pull free of Drum. "I'm not making any such promise."

He spoke to Drum, but Teagen's words followed. "You are a very brave man. I hear of your works spoken in hushed tones of respect. One thing I ask. You will not"—Teagen hesitated as if finding the right word—"bed her"—he finally managed as the chief continued talking—"unless she comes to you. If you do, I'll murder you in your sleep, for even the brave must sleep."

Drum raised an eyebrow. "Did the chief say he'd murder me, or did you add on a few words, Teagen?"

Teagen glanced at his grandfather. "We both feel the same."

"Tell the old man I'll wait for her to come to me before I bed her, but she will come, and I promise she'll be well bedded."

He let Sage go, and they watched the old chief walk away. Teagen reached for his horse. "I need to get back. The women have already started cooking for the feast. I'll expect both of you next week. Sage, I'll see that your room is ready, and Drum, you're sleeping in the barn." The big man turned his horse toward Whispering Mountain.

Drum wasn't surprised by his last words. If Teagen had the time, he'd probably stand guard night and day. He helped Sage onto her horse, and they headed back to town. For the first few hours, she didn't talk to him at all, and in truth, he enjoyed the silence.

He couldn't figure her out. She melted to molten

fire in his arms. The way she kissed him, he knew their lovemaking would be great, but she couldn't settle on the idea that they belonged together. She had to know that he'd give his life for her, but something inside her wouldn't accept him as her man. He decided that she had this ideal of the perfect man, and he didn't measure up. Maybe no one ever would.

Knowing Sage, he wouldn't have long to guess what was wrong with him. She'd had no trouble telling him in the past.

They stopped at noon at the edge of the hills, where they could look out on a wide valley below. Ten more miles, and they'd be back to town. He unwrapped food he'd stocked for the trip: breads from the bakery and cheese from Elmo's place. He sat watching the sky while she walked around, checking her horse and washing her hands in a nearby stream.

Finally, she settled down beside him. "I think we need to set a few rules."

"Like no hitting." He rubbed his ribs. "Your elbow is sharp."

She shrugged. "All right. I have to admit I didn't act properly back there, but all of you were trying to decide my fate, and I don't want anyone doing that. Most of my life I've been screaming and fighting to hold on to free will."

Drum studied her. "All right. The first rule is: Sage decides what Sage wants." He grinned when she looked up at him. "I don't want to own you, Sage, I just want to be your man."

"What does that mean?"

"It means I'll be the one you turn to when trouble comes. I'll be there if you need to fall apart, or cry, or even beat on someone. I'll be the one who holds you all night."

She shook her head. "For the first eighteen years of my life, I had three brothers riding herd over me, plus Martha always telling me how I should act. I think that's why I took off to Boston. I wanted to follow my own dreams and make my own mistakes without brothers around to tell me how to live my life. I wanted to make something more of myself than to just be some man's house-keeper and cook. I wanted to set my own rules. You may want to be my man, but I'm not inter-ested in being anyone's woman."

He leaned back in the grass and said, "All right, Sage, you set the rules. You would anyway."

She thought about it a minute and decided to ignore the edge in his tone and take him at his word. "Rule number one: You don't try to tell me what to do. I know you've been assigned to watch over me, and Captain Harmon would probably be the one I'd answer to if I refused to let you do your job. So you can stay on guard from sunup to sundown, but I go and do as I please. And, I promise you, I'll be sleeping alone."

"Okay," he said without opening his eyes. "If that's your rule, I'll follow it."

"Rule two: You will not touch me at any time, and in turn, I'll try to keep my hands off of you."

"That might be harder for you than you think, honey," he said.

She ignored the comment and moved on.

"Rule three: Stop calling me honey." She hesitated and added, "And don't tell anyone about what my grandfather did. I don't want everyone thinking we're really married, because then in two months they'll think we're divorced. I just want to be the new doctor in town, not the subject of every sewing-circle discussion."

"Fair enough."

She waited a half second, then asked, "You have any rules you want to throw into the pot?"

"I've got one rule. Only one."

"All right."

"At dusk, the few minutes between light and dark, you have to kiss me every night we're married, and you have to do it like you mean it, no pecks on the cheek. I'll hold you, but I'll not force you. You can step away after one kiss if you want, but until you step away, you're mine."

"Fair enough," she echoed his comment to her rules. She could kiss him good night every night. She might even enjoy it, but that didn't mean that she'd go to his bed.

He stood, dusted off his trousers, and offered a

hand to help her up. Just as she reached for it, he dropped the offer and walked away. He didn't have to say it; she knew he was following rule number two.

She climbed on her horse, and they rode out. It was almost sunset when she saw her place and the lights of town just beyond.

When they reached the porch, Drum swung down to the ground and moved to her side as she climbed down. "Good night," he said. "I'll take care of the horses."

He waited.

She stood on her toes and kissed his mouth. "Good night," she said.

He touched her hair, and returned her kiss with more politeness than passion.

She moved away. "I need to get some sleep. If Bonnie got everything put away, we may open tomorrow."

"My room's the last door at the back of the hotel. When you're ready to come, I'll be waiting." He touched the brim of his hat with two fingers and left her without another word.

CHAPTER 35

THE NEXT FEW DAYS PASSED IN A BLUR FOR Sage. They opened the clinic, and everyone in town who had a boil, ingrown toenail, or infected sore dropped by.

Four women showed up in the last stage of pregnancy. They didn't want to be examined, just wanted to leave directions to their houses and to ask if the doc took trade as payment for delivery.

A dozen children were brought in, one with a broken arm, one with an infected gash on his foot, and the rest with aches and pains. Sage kept the one with the infection, because she feared he wouldn't keep it clean if she sent him home.

Will and Andy went to school during the day and helped with chores at night. They'd serve meals to the folks staying in the clinic and help Bonnie clean up. When the weekend rolled around, the boys offered to stay, but Bonnie and Sage insisted they go to Whispering Mountain and enjoy a few days off. Andy was fitting in well to his new life, but Will's eyes were filled with sorrow, and even when he tried to smile, Sage saw worry on his face.

Bonnie had her quarters next to the clinic, and Sage stayed upstairs in a tiny room next to the boys' loft room. By the third day, the kitchen filled with payment in trade. They now had three chickens in a cage out on the back porch, two quarts of milk, a meat pie, more firewood then they'd use for the winter, and someone had oiled up Bonnie's buggy so that it no longer squeaked down the street. They were taking care of the community, and the community was returning the favor.

Drummond and Daniel Torry took turns standing guard on the porch. Sage often had to call them in to help move a patient. Drum liked to stand at the door and watch her work, but Daniel swore the smell of blood bothered him. Both men reported in to the area marshal staying in town. If Anderson's Glen was ever going to become a real town, a great deal of work had to be done. So the marshal ruled over the organization and did his best to clean up crime. Almost every day, he'd drop by and ask Daniel or Drummond to help him. The town needed a sheriff, the marshal complained, but he couldn't find anyone to take the job.

Through her study window, Sage had heard him talking to Drum a few times. The marshal spoke to him with respect, as if Drum were older and wiser, not ten years his junior. Sage also noticed the marshal talked to Daniel Torry as if he were a deputy, telling, not asking.

Each evening Daniel left in time to have supper in town with men that he'd later spend hours gambling with. Every night Drum would let Bonnie talk him into joining them for a meal. He'd talk to the boys and help them with their homework, then as Bonnie lit the lamps, he'd stand and say good night.

Sage knew that was her cue to walk him to the door. In the shadows of the hallway, she'd follow his one rule and kiss him good night. The first few nights it was done awkwardly at best, but as the days passed, she began to look forward to the ritual he'd insisted on.

He'd wait until she touched his arm, then he'd turn and kiss her soundly with his hand on the wall above her head. When she pushed on his chest, he'd step back without complaint. But each night he repeated his invitation for her to visit his room.

Sage decided to ignore it rather than argue. She liked the odd peace they'd worked out and didn't want to upset it for once. He had a passion for her, but in all else, Drum was levelheaded, calming the folks in the waiting area as easily as Bonnie did.

On the fifth night, Sage had had a hard day and needed to feel alive. She wrapped her arms around his neck and wanted the kiss to last longer.

He was happy to oblige. When she spread her hand over the wall of his chest, she whispered, "More, please."

He gave her what she wanted, long warm kisses that buckled her knees.

The next night when it was time for them to say good night, she drew him into her study and locked the door. The last light of the sun flooded into the silent room.

He didn't wait for her to touch him; he guided her to the nearest chair. When she sat, he knelt in front of her so that she was almost at eye level with him. Without a word, he unbuttoned her blouse.

Sage laughed. "This is not part of the twilight kiss."

"Oh yes it is." He smiled. "You'll see."

He pulled her blouse open, then brushed his fingers gently over the soft material covering her breasts. The sensation was so sweet, she couldn't move. Her body seemed to come alive beneath his touch.

"Where'd you learn that?" she whispered against his ear.

"Lessons," he answered as he covered her mouth once more with his.

His tender, loving touch continued as he kissed her. He wasn't holding or gripping but lightly brushing over the satin. The caress warmed her far more than if he'd pressed harder. She found herself moving into his hand when he passed over the tips of her breasts, gently demanding more of his attention.

He laughed against her lips and continued the sweet torture, while his kiss drank her in completely.

Finally, when the room had grown completely dark, she touched his shoulder and pushed him away.

He smiled at her as he buttoned her top. "When you're ready, I'll be waiting. Feel free to come any night."

"And if I'm never ready?" she asked as she stood and moved toward the door.

He leaned down and touched her lips. "Then I'll wait a lifetime."

When he walked away, Sage felt an ache deep inside. What kind of man would let her set the rules? Would wait forever?

The answer rattled her heart. The kind of man who truly loved her.

• • •

She didn't sleep well, and the morning brought more patients than she could handle. Apparently there had been a saloon fight just before dawn, leaving several men with broken noses and cuts that needed stitching. By nine the second wave of trouble came. The fight moved into homes. Drunken warriors and sober wives were an even match. She treated as many men as women. A few couples came through her door still slinging fists and blood.

Daniel and Drum helped get the injured in for treatment and arrested all the men involved in the fight as they left. By noon the new jail was packed.

When Sage finally had a minute, she went to the kitchen for a cup of coffee and found Drummond alone. He insisted she sit down while he served her a cup.

"Where's Daniel Torry?" she asked in passing. "I'm surprised he wasn't part of the fight at the saloon. Isn't that where he plays cards every night?"

Drum took a seat across from her. "I asked him. He said he went to bed early. He seems to be cutting down on the drinking as well." Drum winked. "Maybe you're working him too hard around here."

"I couldn't have done it without the two of you this morning." She realized the truth of her statement as she said it. "What's the marshal planning to do with all the drunks?"

"He says after the husbands sober up, he'll release them to their wives with a warning. The men will promise anything just to get released. The whole jail is packed with men throwing up, urinating, and swearing. Those with no wives to claim them will probably be the cleanup crew once they sober. It'll take a week to get the smell out of that cell."

Sage laughed. "I'm just thankful no one was shot."

Drum pushed a strand of her hair behind her ear. "In case I forget to tell you, Doc, you were wonderful in the chaos this morning."

She looked down. "I've been doing it for a while."

"You do it well. I'm proud of you."

He tilted her head with his fingers and leaned across the table.

"It's not dusk," she said without moving.

"Close your eyes and pretend," he whispered.

And she did.

CHAPTER 36

BONNIE FAYE WATCHED THEM ALL LEAVE FOR Whispering Mountain: Sage, Drummond Roak, the boys, and even Daniel Torry. She'd been invited, but she said no. She needed time alone. It had been two months since the night with her cowboy, and she no longer had any doubt that she was pregnant. She knew there would be problems around the corner, but she never thought she'd have a child, and she wanted to treasure every moment. A baby grew inside of her. Her baby. His baby.

She needed time to remember that one night. He'd said so few words. She knew so little about him, but she had a feeling the night had been as rare an encounter for him as for her. Neither of them had spoken of the future. Both knew they'd share only a night.

Smiling to herself, she realized that he'd left her a gift. From now on she'd have to be strong. She'd have to be brave. Not for herself but for her child.

Putting out the Closed sign, Bonnie locked the front door. Unless there was an emergency, everyone in town would be having Thanksgiving dinner tomorrow.

Except her, of course. She planned to spend her day dreaming and planning.

Bonnie picked up the clinic waiting room and walked to the kitchen. She had plenty of food; at least she wouldn't be hungry.

She ate her meal in silence, then went to the back of the house where her rooms were. Sage had insisted she have both a bedroom and a small sitting area. Bonnie had protested that she didn't need the extra space, but she loved the little room.

Just before she turned in for the night, she walked the darkened rooms, checking the back and front doors to make sure everything was locked up tight. At the back door, she stared out the long panes and saw the black hills beyond. Will and Andy were just beyond that first hill, sleeping at Whispering Mountain Ranch tonight. They'd talked about it all afternoon.

Bonnie laughed, remembering how the boys said they loved the horses at the ranch but hated Teagen's girls. When she'd asked why, Will claimed it was because the girls thought they could ride better than he could. Andy admitted pretty much everyone on the ranch could ride better than he could.

As she turned to go back to her room, Bonnie caught a movement out of the corner of her eye: a shadow crossing between the moon and the house, nothing more.

Fear gripped her body in panic. She stood frozen, watching. There was no reason for anyone to be between her and the hills. All of town lay behind her. The small barn and corral stood to the left. Whatever the shadow was, it hadn't been a horse.

"I should have gone with Sage and the boys," she whispered as the cat rubbed against her nightgown.

But it was too late now.

Bonnie backed away from the door. Nothing else moved. The night lay cold and silent around her.

Step by step, she made it to her room and locked both her doors.

CHAPTER 37

DRUM WAITED UNTIL THE KIDS WERE SET-tled into the rooms in the new wing of the house. Jessie, Teagen's wife, and Rainey, Travis's wife, returned to what everyone called the new kitchen to talk. Travis and his family had made it home for the holiday.

The two brothers moved to the old study, where they could enjoy their cigars without the wives noticing. Drum had always admired how close the brothers were. When they'd been eleven and twelve, they'd had to defend the ranch. Teagen had taken the lead, but some in town claimed that it had been Travis's skill in the fighting that had truly saved Whispering Mountain. Drum knew, to the brothers, it didn't really matter.

Drum stood in the dining room, listening to all the family around him and feeling a part of none of it.

"You going to stand there all day, Drum?" Martha asked as she pulled off her apron, "Or are you going to walk me to my place by the pond?"

He smiled at the old housekeeper. The rest of the McMurrays might ignore him from time to time, but Martha always saw him. "I'd be honored." He offered his arm.

They walked in silence across the yard. Martha

didn't care for most men, so he felt lucky she talked to him now and then. He didn't want to push his luck.

When they reached her place, he said, "I sure do like your ginger cookies, Martha."

She grinned. "I know. That's why I make them."

He pushed his luck. "I guess you know I'm crazy about Sage."

She laughed. "Everyone in Texas probably knows that."

"You wouldn't happen to know where she is?"

"Nope," Martha answered, "but if I was looking, I'd start in the last room on the second floor, where the boys used to sleep years ago." Martha turned and headed to her door, but he heard her add, "Not that I'd tell you, Drummond, even if you was to ask me."

He stepped away, fighting the need to run. If he planned to see Sage at dusk, he'd better hurry.

Teagen noticed him when Drum crossed back into the house. "Join us in the study, Roak," he said friendly enough.

"No, thanks." Drum picked up his hat as if that were the reason he'd come. "I think I'll check on my horse before turning in."

Teagen laughed. "Enjoy the loft."

"Thanks." Drum almost added that the barn seemed to be his room on this place. He'd spent more than one night there. When Teagen turned to walk back into the study, Drum added, "She's

317

my woman. You and your brothers better get used to that idea."

Teagen didn't turn around, but his back straightened. "Only if she comes willingly to you, Roak."

"I wouldn't have it any other way."

Teagen didn't turn around, but Drum knew his face would be set. The McMurrays were just going to get used to the idea, Drum decided. If he had to, he'd fight all three of them, but they wouldn't stand between him and Sage.

He circled the house, flipped up on the mud room roof, and slipped into a second-floor window.

Moving swiftly through the hallway of the old part of the house, Drum found the last room on the second floor. He guessed Teagen would have insisted Sage stay there. It was small, made for one person, leaving the larger rooms for the couples.

They should have been a couple, he thought as he walked the darkened house he knew so well. They were a couple. Each day he spent with her was torture in heaven. He loved seeing her, watching her, touching her, but she hadn't come to him. If it killed him, he'd keep his word and wait until she came to his bed.

Every evening, after kissing her, he left and spent the rest of the night longing for her. When she'd moved to Boston, if what he'd felt for her hadn't been real, he would have moved on to someone else, but for him there was no one else. She was his. Or more accurately, he was hers.

He tapped on the last door. Only a few seconds passed before she opened, and the sight of her slammed against his heart like it always did.

"You shouldn't be here," she whispered as she let him in. Giggling, she poked him in the chest with her finger. "You must have a death wish, Drummond."

"Wrong," he answered as he pulled her into his arms. "This is exactly where I should be."

He kissed her with more hunger than he'd planned and was surprised when she answered in kind. If nothing else, his one rule had allowed her to react to him without hesitation. She didn't have to decide to kiss him. She was simply following rules they'd agreed on. He knew he was building a fire inside her, a fire he'd someday satisfy.

When he finally broke the kiss, she leaned into him, their breaths and heartbeats blending.

"I never thought I'd like doing that so much," she whispered. "I look forward to dusk just because you'll make my heart race."

"You've been kissed far too little in your life," he whispered and felt her sigh in agreement.

"I think you're right," she mumbled as she pulled him closer.

They were too busy to talk for a while, then she pulled her mouth from his. "It's not just any kiss," she whispered so close he could feel her words. "I think it's your kiss. There's a drug in it that makes me want more."

He smiled, knowing exactly what she was asking for. He lifted her off the ground in his hug and captured her mouth. She liked it wild and deep. She liked the kiss to be so complete that they had to break to breathe.

When he lowered her, he moved his hand along her back, keeping her close. "Ride with me tonight?" he asked as he dug his fingers into her unbound hair. "The wind is from the north. Tomorrow it may be too cold, but tonight we could climb all the way up Whispering Mountain and see the stars."

She laughed, excited at the adventure. "If you'll have the horses saddled and at the mud room door, I'll be there in an hour."

He kissed her nose and slipped away, knowing that every second he stayed increased the danger he'd be caught. The McMurray men might be willing to welcome him at their table tomorrow as a guest, but he doubted the privileges included Sage's room.

An hour later, he watched her bolt from the back door and run to him. Neither said a word as they mounted and turned the horses toward Whispering Mountain.

When they were well away from the house, she laughed. "I feel just like a kid." With the bright moon and stars, they had no trouble seeing as they crossed the pastures and streams on the ranch. "There's a legend about Whispering Mountain, you know," she said as they moved into the trees.

He'd heard the legend, but he played along. "What legend?"

"My father believed he dreamed his future on the mountain one night right after he and my mother settled here." She looked at the hill before them that the Apache called a word that translated to Whispering Mountain. "He dreamed his death."

"How sad."

"No. I mean yes, it was sad, but because of that dream, he prepared the boys to hold the ranch. He knew my mother couldn't claim the land. Because of his dream, his sons were able to keep our land. I only wish I'd been old enough to help."

"It's a nice legend."

"It's more than that. Each of the McMurray men have climbed the mountain and slept on the summit, but none of them talk about it." She smiled. "I think they don't want to admit that the legend is true, but all came down changed."

He kicked Satan, and the horse shot into a full run. Drum shouted back, "Let's go find out."

At the base of the hills, they left their horses and began to climb. Sage felt like she was sixteen again, running wild on the huge ranch. All the worries of the world were forgotten. Drum offered her a hand when she needed it and pushed her when he thought they were moving too slowly. By the time they reached the summit, they were both breathing heavily and laughing.

He'd strapped a thick bedroll over his back when they'd left the horses, and now he spread it on the ground beneath the stars.

"Should we light a fire?" she asked, twirling around.

"I'll keep you warm," he said but he dug for his flint.

While he started the fire, she collected wood. The fire sparked and gave a low, warm glow to the clearing. While he lined the campfire with rocks, she walked the clearing, loving the magic of the night. Nothing in Boston could ever compare with the beauty of this place.

When she returned to the fire, he handed her a canteen as he pulled off his gun belt and sat down on the blanket.

Sage took one swallow and stopped. "Milk?"

"And cookies." He gave her a bag from his coat pocket.

Sage laughed. "Drum, for an evening under the stars, most men would pack wine and cheese."

He leaned back on his elbows. "I'm not most men, Sage, and cookies sounded better."

She looked in the bag. "I think we have cookie crumbs." She pulled one bite-size piece out and knelt as she fed it to him.

After the food was gone, she twisted, using his chest as her pillow, and they watched the sky. His hand gently stroked her hair. The gentleness of his touch warmed her from the inside. Sometimes when he was like this, she felt treasured. When others were around, he could be distant, even cold, but when only the two of them were together, she felt as if he let his guard down, and she saw who he really was.

"You know, Drum, I think I'm finally getting used to you being around." Much as he didn't care for being just her friend, she trusted him.

"Good," he answered as if he wasn't really listening. "It's about time."

She rose and propped her elbow on his chest. "Despite all the ways you irritate me, there are two things about you that I can't figure out. First, why you insist we're made for each other, and second why, of all the men in the world, you're the only one who knows how to make me feel so alive inside."

He circled her shoulders and tugged her down. "Let's talk about the second one first." He laughed as he lowered his mouth. "Then maybe you'll figure out the first on your own."

She felt the now-familiar bolt of pleasure and welcomed it. His kiss was soft and tender until she opened her mouth, then they both felt the fire. Tonight there was no one around to walk in or to hear them. Freedom was a drug they shared.

He pushed her on her back. His hands moved over her as his kiss made her mindless. When he unbuttoned her blouse, she struggled as if to pull away, but he didn't break the kiss, and his loving strokes continued over her, asking more than insisting that she come with him on this journey.

When she pushed again, he moved an inch away. "Come along with me tonight," he whispered. "I promise I won't hurt you. Trust me."

She relaxed, realizing she did trust him and far, far more. He might never say the words she wanted to hear, but she knew he felt them.

He finished opening her blouse and then her camisole.

As his hand crossed over her bare flesh, she jerked again, only this time in pleasure. She wanted his caress, needed it. She felt as if she'd lived through a long winter, and his touch brought the spring.

He moved down her body, exploring her every curve, tasting her skin as if she were a priceless gift he was unwrapping.

Sage stretched and moaned as he removed her clothes until his hands slid over her skin without barrier. When she thought she could go no higher, he shifted, opening her legs as his exploration and his kisses moved lower.

Sage gulped for breath. "Where did you learn to do that?" she whispered as waves of passion rolled over her.

"Lessons," he whispered, too busy to say more.

Sage was beyond forming words. All she could

do was feel. Tiny rivers tingled through her body, joining at the core to form a raging river washing all thought away and leaving only passion cutting deeply into her soul.

All she wanted to do was beg him to never stop. She'd kissed a few men, been touched by two, a tentative brush atop her clothing, but nothing like this. Drum was bold and attentive. When she moaned in pleasure, he gave her what she wanted: more.

When he brought her to climax, Sage cried out and shook with pleasure. Her heart pounded. Her breath came in rapid gulps. Her mind exploded, with every part of her body sending messages all at once. Nothing had prepared her for the joy. She was riding high across the stars.

He sat up and lifted her onto his lap, cuddling her to him as she jerked in the aftershock of a passion she never dreamed existed.

When she finally returned to sanity, he was still holding her, stroking her, loving her. His hands pushed her hair back from her face so the cool night air moved over her hot flesh.

"I never felt . . ." She wasn't sure how to put it into words.

"I know," he whispered against her ear. "I knew you'd like it. You'll feel even more next time. You'll climb higher."

She knew about sex. She'd been raised on a ranch. But she'd never guessed this kind of passion could come with it. "Any higher, and the fall will kill me." She laughed.

He nibbled on her throat. "I'll be there to catch you, honey."

He wrapped the ends of the blanket around her and lay behind her while the fire burned a few feet in front of her. When his arm circled over her, she noticed he was still fully dressed.

"Drum," she asked. "Why didn't you try to take your pleasure?" She knew she wouldn't have stopped him if he had.

"Believe me, Sage, feeling you was very pleasant, but I promised I'd only bed you when you came to me. Once you come to me without being coached by even one kiss, you'll be mine forever, and I swear I'll never let you go."

She could feel his erection pressing against her hips and knew there was nothing physically wrong with the man who held her. He wanted her, he'd always wanted her, but he wanted all of her, and she wasn't willing to give herself into another's trust so completely. She'd fought too long and hard for her independence.

"Drum, I don't want to love—"

"Hush," he whispered. "Don't think about it. Just rest for a while. If you go to sleep, I'll wake you in an hour and ask what you dreamed."

CHAPTER 38

Thanksgiving morning, Bonnie went about her work like it was a regular day. There had been no holidays in her life for years. She made sure all the rooms were ready if needed, then she sat at her desk by the window and wrote out a list of supplies she planned to order from Austin.

She told herself if she acted as if nothing were amiss, then nothing would be. Yet no matter how hard she tried to concentrate, she couldn't shake the feeling that she was being watched. Most of the time she forced herself not to look out the window, but when she did, she saw nothing, only winter-dry pasture, a half-finished barn still in need of doors, and an empty corral.

If it was a man from the outlaw camp come to fetch Sage for Count Hanover, she'd die before she told him where Sage was, which would mean, of course, that they'd kill her. If it hadn't been for her cowboy, they would have already finished the job at Shelley's gambling house, so Bonnie figured she was on borrowed time already.

There was also the slim possibility that someone could be out in the trees watching the house, hoping to get a shot at the boys. After all, raiders had already tried to kill them once. Will still talked about the bad men who killed his father, and Andy had nightmares he wouldn't talk about.

If those men found the boys, they'd shoot her if she tried to stop them.

Bullet the cat wrapped around her leg, and Bonnie voiced her worries. "It's little comfort knowing no one is out to murder me."

She picked up her teacup and went to the kitchen. The feeling of being watched went with her. Sage had ordered tall windows in every room. She wanted the light, but today the windows only made Bonnie feel exposed and alone. Though she spoke to several people in town, none had become friends. No one would visit her today.

By noon the wind blew in strong from the north, howling and rattling the house almost as if someone were trying to break in. Bonnie checked all the locks but felt no safer. As the day aged, clouds moved in, dark and brooding. She picked up the rifle Sage mounted over the fireplace in the kitchen and walked onto the front porch.

The cold wind fought to push her back, but she stood her ground. She could see smoke coming out of several chimneys in town. It wasn't all that far, she told herself. She could run for help if trouble came or fire a warning shot. But the only trouble was a sense of being watched, and she'd feel like a fool for throwing a fit over that.

She marched inside, locked the door, and stormed down the hallway to the back of the house. Once outside, she sat on the rocking chair Daniel or Drummond sometimes used and laid the rifle over her lap. She'd deal with this fear as she'd always dealt with fear . . . alone.

Brooding clouds almost blocked the view of the hills, but she stared out, ready to face whatever trouble came. When her parents died, she'd been afraid to go more than a few blocks from her house. They'd always told her such stories of the evil that would find her unless she stayed inside. After they died, she realized what a cripple they tried to make her, and she forced herself to walk out into the world.

Bonnie closed her eyes and fought the panic. Her parents had also said her older brother would take care of her. That was why they left him all the money and her the house. He hadn't been home but a few times in years. He claimed the drafty old place made him sick. Her father grew too feeble to fix anything, and her mother wouldn't spend the money. By the time they died, nothing worked in the house, and mold grew over the basement walls. Her brother was angry that the deed to the house was in her name and swore he wouldn't give her a dime until she signed it over. What good was the house without any money to run it?

Bonnie straightened, not allowing one tear to fall. She'd been so afraid, but she'd walked to the hospital where her parents had often been treated. The nurses had always been kind to her, and they were again. She'd thought if she worked as a nurse, she'd be able to make enough money to keep the house. And she had. The worthless property was still in her name.

Staring into the stormy sky, she took a deep breath and told herself that she would survive. Whatever was out there, whoever threatened, she would survive. She'd save her salary until the day came that she was too old to work, then she'd go back to Boston and rebuild a cottage on the land where her house now stood.

The last bit of sunlight played off a movement coming from the trees. For a moment she thought it no more than a trick of the light, then she saw him coming toward the house: a tall man, leading his horse. A cowboy.

His head was down to the wind. She couldn't see his face. He wore a gun strapped to his leg, but so did many of the men she'd seen. She stood and waited, the rifle at the ready, even though she wasn't sure she'd remember how to fire it.

When he reached the steps of the porch, he looked up at her.

Bonnie stared at *her* cowboy. A beard an inch long covered his jaw and chin, and he looked like he'd aged since she'd seen him, but he was her cowboy. His brother had called him Bradford.

"Evening, Pretty Lady," he said in a low tone without moving closer or smiling. "It's good to rest my eyes on you again."

Bonnie couldn't have answered if her life depended on it. In the nights she'd spent thinking of their time together, he'd become more dream than real.

He pulled off his worn hat and stared at her. "I had quite a time finding you. The Rangers down in Galveston considered jailing me for even asking about you."

She still couldn't think of anything to say.

He twisted his hat in his big hands. After several seconds, he frowned. "You got a right to shoot me. I don't know much about women, but I know I was your first, and I did kidnap you. So, if you're planning to use that rifle, go ahead, 'cause I'm not leaving till I have my say."

"Why?" She finally found one word.

Bonnie saw the hurt in his eyes. "You know, I had this crazy feeling you might be glad to see me. That one night was the best of my life, but I guess you'd see it from different eyes. I just wanted to see you again and to say I'm sorry if I caused you any trouble."

"You've been watching me."

He nodded. "I wouldn't have bothered you if I thought you were involved with someone. I even thought the boys might be your responsibility, and you wouldn't want me showing up in front of them. Then I worried over you being sweet on one of them young Rangers who hang around here."

He finally looked straight at her and didn't turn away. "When everyone left yesterday, I knew you were like me . . . alone."

Bonnie didn't know what to do. She'd never had a man come to the house, or flirt with her, or even talk to her. Bradford wasn't flirting with her now. It appeared that he traveled halfway across Texas just to look at her.

He wasn't any more skilled than she at conversation. He beat his leg a few times with his hat and didn't seem to notice the cold. She had a feeling he'd stand out here all night if she didn't do or say something.

She lowered the rifle. "You want to come in for a cup of coffee?"

"I'd like that." He nodded once as if they'd settled on the makings of a plan. "Mind if I put my horse in the barn? It looks like bad weather is coming in."

"All right." She backed to the door. "I'll put a fresh pot on to boil."

When he turned toward the barn, she went inside. For a time, she just leaned against the door and tried to think, then she crossed to the fireplace, replaced the rifle, and started a fire. By the time she heard him scraping his boots on the scraper by the kitchen door, she'd lit the lamps and had the coffee ready.

Without knocking, he stepped inside and removed his hat.

He stood watching her as if he wasn't sure what to do now that he was inside.

Trying not to stare at him, she kept busy moving

food to the table. A hundred questions came to mind, but she couldn't seem to get any out. He seemed bigger somehow in the little kitchen, and he smelled of leather and trail dust. She caught a glimpse of gray at his temples and wondered if it had been there the night they'd made love.

The silence in the room widened the space between them. She had to think of something to say.

She settled on a simple statement. "My name's . . ."

"Bonnie," he finished. "I like that. It fits you somehow."

No one had ever told her such a thing, but she didn't want to talk about her name. Not with this man who knew her so well in other ways. "Have you eaten supper?"

"No."

She'd guess he hadn't had breakfast or dinner either, but she wouldn't comment on that. "I've plenty here. It's not Thanksgiving, but it's filling. You're welcome to join me."

He never took his eyes off of her when he answered, "It'll do just fine. Thank you, miss."

Bonnie didn't look at him as she grinned. "Don't you think we should call each other by our Christian names, Bradford?"

"Yes"—he hesitated—"Bonnie, I do."

She couldn't face him and wondered if he was across the room not looking at her as well.

Finally, when everything was ready, she collected enough nerve to face him. "Take off your coat, Bradford," she ordered, noticing he was still standing just inside the door. "Supper's ready."

Removing his coat, Bradford hung it on one of the hooks. His movements were slow, as if he'd ridden for days without sleep. "The barn door needs hanging. I could do that for you."

"You can wash up at the sink if you like." She held herself so stiffly, he probably thought she was made of board. She was being bossy, but she knew of no other way to act. She wanted to be the woman she saw herself to be in his eyes, but she didn't know how to start.

She didn't move as he crossed the room and rolled his sleeves up, revealing powerful fore-arms, tanned by years in the sun. The memory of his arm resting just below her breasts as they slept returned to her in great detail.

As he washed, she reached over and lightly touched his arm.

He stilled.

She pulled away, embarrassed by her boldness.

He went back to washing.

She reached for a towel and held it for him. When he took it from her, they were only a few feet apart.

With cheeks burning, she looked up at him. When she saw the longing in his eyes, she knew he'd relived their time together a million times as well.

"Mind if I kiss you?" he said simply.

"I don't mind," she answered. She stepped closer, not knowing how to play at being coy or shy.

He leaned over and touched his lips to hers, and as naturally as if they'd kissed for years, she moved into his arms and welcomed him home.

When she pulled away, he held her chair, then took his seat across from her. His hand had brushed across her shoulder as he'd moved behind her, and his knee bumped against hers beneath the table.

She handed him a plate, smiling as she met his stare. Their fingers touched for only a second, but he smiled back.

She looked down, took a deep breath, and said, "You can hang the barn door in the morning."

"All right, Bonnie," he answered. "I'll do that."

CHAPTER 39

SAGE WOKE A WHILE BEFORE DAWN. HER first thought was that she didn't want to move. She was warm inside the cocoon of Drum's arms and a trail blanket that smelled of campfires.

Her second thought was that she was nude. Totally nude.

As carefully as she could, she pulled away from him and began searching for her clothes in the smoky glow of the dying fire. Half-dressed, she glanced over at Drum to make sure he was asleep.

He was wide awake and watching her every move.

"Turn around," she demanded.

"Not a chance," he answered.

Pulling her blouse on, she swore. "That's it, Drummond. That's why you drive me crazy." She fought with the material. "How can you be so loving one minute and so pestering the next? If you had the sense God gave a rabbit, you'd know a lady doesn't like to be watched."

He stood and helped her with a sleeve she had twisted backward. "You're one beautiful creature when you wake up mad." He laughed. "I'll have to remember that."

"You were going to wake me in an hour so I could see what I dreamed."

"I meant to, but I fell asleep. It seems the only time I really sleep is when I'm with you. It's probably because the rest of the time, I'm worried about where you are and what you're up to." He studied her as she finished dressing. "Any chance you want to tell me how you could be married to some guy back East and not know about what we did last night? Seems to me he would have brought you to—"

"We are not talking about that." She turned her back to him.

"Another thing you like to do but not talk about. I don't mind. Talking about it isn't near as much fun. But I got to tell you, when you shook in my arms, you—"

She glared at him. "We are *not* having this discussion."

"Right," he agreed. "Maybe we'll *not* talk about it again tonight."

Sage tugged on her boots. "I've more things to worry about than talking to you. I didn't dream," she said. "What good is the legend if I didn't dream?"

"I did. But it didn't make much sense," he said as he strapped on his gun belt, all playfulness gone from his tone. "It started with two carriages storming the bridge."

"Our bridge?"

Drum nodded slowly, as if piecing together a puzzle with a picture he didn't like. "I got a bad feeling about this. Something Daniel said once about how the raiders who killed the Smith boys' parents and the robbers at Shelley's place being part of the same gang. Maybe my mind just put them together in my sleep."

"Or maybe your dream put the pieces together for you," Sage answered. "Pieces that belonged together."

"We'd better get back." Drum kicked dirt over the fire. "I just remembered the last detail of the dream."

She helped him roll up the blanket. "What was it?" she whispered, knowing that it had to be something terrible by the frown on his face.

"I'll tell you later. The sooner we get back, the better."

She trusted him enough to know he wasn't lying. They moved down the mountain as fast as they could, and by daylight they were riding full-out toward home.

Sage knew something was wrong when she walked into the kitchen. Martha and Jessie were cooking. Teagen and Jessie's three girls and the two little Smith boys were playing games in the dining room, but she could feel something in the air.

"Where is my brother?"

Jessie rushed toward her. "Thank goodness you two are back. Daniel said you went for a morning ride. It may be nothing, but we all agree it feels like trouble. Guests traveling on Thanksgiving? Men surrounded by guards are demanding to come onto the ranch. They claim they know you."

Daniel walked through the door with an armload of wood. Sage glanced at him and swore she saw him wink at Drummond.

"Where are my brothers?" she asked again, trying to make sense of what Jessie had said.

This time it was Martha who answered. "Teagen is handling the trouble at the bridge. Travis and Rainey haven't come up from their place yet." She pointed toward the window that faced the bridge. "The ranch hand on guard wouldn't let anyone pass and sent up a round to signal a warning.

Teagen rode down. The other three hands on the place rode out to the back pasture a little after dawn to check on a horse after breakfast. If they heard the shot, they should be riding in soon."

Drummond stepped forward, his voice a low command. "Jessie, I need you to collect the girls and get to somewhere safe as fast as possible. If there is trouble, you need to be somewhere safe."

He looked at Sage.

"Don't even ask," she said. "I'm here to help. If there is trouble, I stand." Teagen's wife, Jessie, was six months' pregnant and not raised to fight, but Sage was a McMurray. She saw no reason she couldn't stand.

"Tell the old hand in the barn to saddle three horses, would you Daniel? Have him bring them around to the side of the house so they can't be seen from the bridge," he said without taking his eyes off Sage.

The young Ranger left as Drum whispered, "Can you take Will and Andy through the hills? They have to be away from here. If my dream is coming true, the men at the bridge have some kind of papers. They'll be demanding custody of both boys."

Sage didn't like the idea of leaving when trouble might be riding in, but she and Drum were the only two at the house who knew the back passage. She also knew Teagen might try to stall, but he'd follow the law. He'd think it his duty to hand the boys over if the proper authorities demanded it. Right now, Drummond's suggestion made a great deal more sense.

As everyone around her hurried to follow orders, Sage stared at him. "Tell me your dream."

"Two closed carriages, surrounded by guards, at the bridge. The first holds a judge who Teagen knows and trusts, and a man claiming to be a relative of the boys. The second carriage holds Shelley Lander and a big guy with red hair. He fits the description of the outlaw you called Charlie, who kidnapped you. In my dream Charlie was swearing to Shelley that you and the boys will be tied up and on your way back to the count before nightfall. He laughed and said he'd be paid a thousand for bringing you back alive and ten thousand for each of the boys' heads. It seems, unlike you, the boys are no good to him alive."

Sage felt a chill go all the way to her heart. Even if Drum told the judge his fears, he wouldn't be believed. After all, the only evidence he had was a dream. Teagen would believe him, but would he stand against the judge?

She ran to the porch and lifted a spyglass Teagen kept hidden on a windowsill. Two carriages waited along with a dozen men on horseback. Teagen was on horseback, barring the entrance.

She didn't want to believe it, but the scene was exactly as Drum had described. She had to get the boys away. If she took the pass, she could be in town an hour before the carriages could go by road. She could collect Bonnie and disappear. Charlie was chasing her and the boys; he wouldn't waste time pestering the McMurrays if she were gone.

"I have to stand with Teagen," Drum swore as he pulled a rifle from just inside the door, "much as I want to go with you, I can't leave him alone if that outlaw you called Charlie is with them and decides to cause trouble. From what you told me, he'd kill anyone and everyone to get to them."

She knew what he wasn't telling her. She could get the boys to safety without him, but her brother might not survive without more firepower. He was outnumbered twelve to one right now at the bridge. The old, broken-down cowhand in the barn might fire a few rounds, but he would be little help in a fight. The other men who worked on the ranch were probably too far away. Travis would help, but his cabin was too far in the woods to have heard the alarm round fired.

Drum looked down at her, and she saw the conflict in his eyes. She was his world, but other things mattered, others demanded his help, and honor drove his actions now.

"Find me," she whispered. "When you put an end to this, find me."

"I will," he answered as he stepped off the porch.

He motioned for Daniel to take the horse Sage had ridden in on.

"Drum," she whispered.

He heard and turned as he shoved his rifle into its sheath.

"I love you." Her words, raw and honest, shocked her as much as they did him.

"Go!" he demanded. "I'll come after you."

She watched them ride toward the bridge, knowing Drum would buy her as much time as he could, even if it cost him his life.

CHAPTER 40

THE LITTLE BOYS AND SAGE MADE IT TO THE beginning of the pass before they heard gunfire. When it came, it sounded like thunder rolling off the hills.

Will looked up at her with his sad eyes. "Jessie's girls? Are they safe?"

"Yes," she answered, loving that he worried about others more than himself. "They know where to hide. They'll be safer when we are away."

"It's the men who want our blood," Andy said. "I was afraid they'd come again."

"Your blood?" Sage asked.

Will nodded. "Our father said there were bad men who wanted to wipe our blood off the earth."

"Why?" Sage didn't think the boys were making much sense, but they both seemed to agree.

"I don't know," Will said, "I just heard Father

say to Mother that we had to keep moving, keep running, or they'd come."

The talk of blood gave her a chill, and she kicked her horse.

"Stay up with me, boys," she said, watching Andy closely. Will handled horses well, but Andy was still learning. She slowed her pace slightly. "We have to go get Miss Bonnie." If the men were looking for her and the boys, the second place they'd go would be the clinic.

As they climbed, she tried not to listen for shots being fired. Drum and her brother were back there, and all she could do was outrun trouble.

Part of her wanted to ride back and make sure Drum and Teagen weren't hurt, but she couldn't risk it. Not now. If one of them had been shot or captured and she rode back, their sacrifice would have all been for nothing.

She led the boys down the pass and along the creek. Teagen had chosen the location of her clinic well; she could ride in now without anyone from town knowing she and the boys were there.

When she neared, she saw a man working on the door to the barn. He was tall, very tall, and lean, but he didn't stop his work when she rode in.

As the boys slid down from their mounts, Sage said, "Go pack what you can. A change of clothes, extra socks. I need to talk to Miss Bonnie."

The boys hurried into the house.

Sage walked from room to room until she found Bonnie in the kitchen.

The nurse looked shocked to see her. "Back already? I thought you were staying for Thanksgiving." Bonnie didn't give her time to answer. "What's wrong?"

Sage noticed the table was set for two. "Drum thinks the men who kidnapped me and the raiders who killed Will and Andy's folks were part of the same band. They're at the ranch now, looking for us."

Bonnie paled.

"We have to disappear, at least for a while." Sage kept her voice low and calm so she wouldn't frighten the nurse. "How fast can you be ready to ride up to my grandfather's camp? The Apache will take us in."

Bonnie shook her head. "Doc, I can't ride. You know that. I'd only slow you down. Go without me."

"No." Sage could not leave her here. "We'll go slow. You'll make it fine. I can't leave you here alone."

"No," Bonnie said as she spread her hand across her middle. "I can't risk a fall."

"I'll watch over her." A man's voice came from the doorway. "She'll be safer here with me."

Sage turned. The tall cowboy who'd been fixing the barn door filled the entrance. It took her a minute to place him. The man who'd bumped into them the first day in Galveston, the cowboy in the saloon at Shelley's place, the man Drum had talked to on the road one night who'd lost his brother. It made no sense that he'd now be here in her kitchen. His words were meant for her, but his eyes were on Bonnie.

He crossed the room to stand in front of the nurse.

Sage started to ask what was going on, when she noticed neither of them was paying any attention to her.

The stranger spread his hand over Bonnie's just below her waist. "Why didn't you tell me?" he demanded.

"I planned to," Bonnie answered. "I wasn't sure how you'd react."

They stared at one another. Sage shook her head, trying to get the picture before her to make sense. "Tell him what? Who is this man? What's he doing here? What's he doing touching you?"

Apparently everyone in the kitchen had gone deaf except Sage, who could still hear her questions echoing off the wall.

Finally, the stranger turned toward her. "I'm Bradford Summerfield, the father of this child"— he moved his hand over Bonnie's middle—"and you're not taking my family anywhere, Doc. They'll be safe. I'll give my life to keep them so."

There are times in life when the earth tilts too far on its axis for just a second, and everyone in the world is in danger of falling. Sage felt one of those moments. A dozen questions came to mind, like how did Bonnie, who never even talked to men, manage to find a family? Sage wanted to yell for her to stop allowing that man to put his hand on her, but about the time she opened her mouth, Sage saw the tears on Bonnie's smiling face.

The cowboy saw them too, and he pulled her into his hug. And there they stood, totally forgetting Sage was in the room all over again.

She didn't try to interrupt them again. She just stared at the pair, wondering why love couldn't come that easily for her. Bonnie couldn't have been with this cowboy more than a matter of hours. Neither of them looked like great talkers, but somehow they'd found one another, fallen in love, and started a baby.

He whispered something to Bonnie, then pulled away. "I'll water your horses, Doc, then you can be on your way."

While Bonnie packed them food, Sage drilled the cowboy on all she thought he should do. Tell the marshal Bonnie was in danger. Stand guard. Make sure she eats right.

Finally, they were ready to leave. Sage turned to Bradford and added, "If you hurt her, I'll shoot you."

"If I hurt her," he answered. "I'll load the gun."

"Fair enough." Sage took the reins and motioned

for the boys to climb up. Bradford helped Andy, making sure his feet were in the stirrups.

Sage glanced back as they rode away. The cowboy had his arm around Bonnie. They looked like a settled couple. The only thing that worried her was that they seemed to have settled faster than water in a shallow well. She made a promise to herself to keep an eye on the cowboy.

Sage smiled. Both of them were old enough to know their own minds. If Bonnie wanted the cowboy, and he obviously wanted her, who was she to stand in their way?

She glanced back one last time. At the rate they were moving in the relationship, they'd have a half dozen tall, thin kids by the time she got back from the winter camp.

CHAPTER 41

DRUMMOND AND DANIEL TORRY MADE IT to Teagen's side about the time the arguing started between Sage's big brother and the judge. Teagen was a man of logic, and his tolerance of fools was a gnat's worth of time. To him, the judge stopped being rational when he insisted that the boys needed to leave immediately and suggested his sister, the doctor, come along.

When Drum caught Teagen's glance, he turned his gaze to the hills, silently passing the message that Sage and the boys were gone.

Teagen nodded slightly in understanding and took a breath as if reconsidering the judge's threat. "All right, Judge Calvert. I'm trying to see your logic. If that man is the boy's guardian, I should hand them over, but it's really pointless to argue, since the boys are not on my ranch."

"What?" shouted a thin man dressed up like a man of wealth. He'd only opened the carriage door to listen before, but now he stepped out.

The judge frowned at the thin man and shook his head at Teagen as if he wouldn't be fooled with a lie.

"If you don't want to take my word that the boys are not on my ranch, I'll let you in to look. But just you. No one else."

"As a gentleman and the boys' only relative, I object." The man with the judge looked about as much like a gentleman relative from England as sock puppets look like real farm animals. In fact, Drum decided, sock puppet was a good parallel. Someone had dressed him up in clothes that almost fit but still controlled the strings to his every action.

Judge Calvert stared at Teagen. "The man's got a right to say who comes on his land, and I've never known a McMurray to lie."

The relative huffed. "There's always a first time."

If looks could kill, the stranger's body would be splattered from the bridge to the border. Teagen was not a man anyone would dare call a liar.

The judge lifted his hand. "He doesn't know you, Teagen, or he wouldn't be so foolish."

"Who are you calling a fool, sir?" the relative shouted.

Drum swore he could see Teagen building steam. "Mister"—Drum looked directly at the stranger—"your being a fool is the only thing keeping you alive right now. Teagen is an honorable man. He wouldn't shoot a man in cold blood, but as for me, I get paid for it. About two bits would be my price if McMurray wanted to hire me. You'd be dead before a scream would have time to crawl up your throat."

The fool had enough sense to back away, sputtering an apology.

Daniel loaned the judge his horse and stood guard while Drum and Teagen took Calvert back to the house.

When they stepped on the porch, Calvert turned to Teagen. "I've no need to look around if I have your word that your sister and the boys are not here."

"You have my word," Teagen answered.

"And if you knew where they've gone, would you tell me?"

"No," Teagen answered honestly.

The judge considered his answer. "That English fellow's got all the right papers and enough money to hire a gang of hard men to see he gets what he wants, but I can't say as I blame you. There's something about the man I don't trust. With or without the boys, when I get back to Austin, I plan to do some research." He took out his pipe. "They keep saying that the boys are with your sister. If they are, she's in danger. These men plan to get what they came after with or without me. I wouldn't want to think of her getting in their way and, if she was my sister, I sure wouldn't want her going along with this crew to wherever the relative suggests."

"I'll tell her that if I see her," Teagen answered. "But my sister is a woman with her own mind. She doesn't take much to being told."

Drum almost swore in agreement.

As they turned to head back to the horses, gunfire rang out from the direction of the bridge.

Drum was in the saddle and riding full out before Teagen could calm his horse enough to mount. They both reached the bridge with their guns out and ready.

Shelley Lander had climbed out of the second coach and was waving his arms wildly. "Hold on, Roak," he shouted. "Hold on; the men are just letting off a little steam. Don't start firing at them. We've come a long way to get the boys, and now they feel like they've been tricked."

Drum disliked Shelley and wouldn't have minded killing the man, even if he was the brother to Sage's first husband. He held his gun level and glared at the gambler.

If the man named Charlie, whom Sage had described as the outlaw who'd been so cruel to her, stepped from the carriage, Drum wasn't sure he could stop his gun from accidentally going off three or four times. But if anyone else rode with Shelley, he didn't show himself.

Teagen and the judge caught up. Both demanded to know what was going on, but the riders were already turning about, heading toward town.

Shelley yelled for the judge and Smith boys' relative to get in the carriage. If Sage wasn't at the ranch, she was bound to be in town. "Hurry," Shelley shouted. "We're close. I can feel it. When we catch up to her, I'll convince her to come along for the safety of the boys, and we can all be on our way."

"I doubt it," Drum whispered and didn't lower his weapon until they were almost out of sight.

Teagen drew his attention. "Where's the Ranger?"

Drum twisted in the saddle. Daniel Torry was nowhere in sight. The judge had left Daniel's horse standing a few feet behind them.

Gunfire sounded from the direction the men had gone as if they were firing off rounds to celebrate.

Both Teagen and Drum slid from their horses and looked around.

"He couldn't have walked back to the house so fast," Teagen commented.

"He sure as hell didn't go with that gang of

worthless flesh." Drum didn't like the only other possibility. "Either he climbed into one of the coaches, or . . ."

Drum didn't finish. He saw the answer floating near the riverbank: Daniel's body, facedown.

Both men dropped their weapons and dove in from the bridge. They hit the water swimming. Both moved to the rocky side and began tugging his body out. As soon as they were at the bank, Teagen drew the lifeless Ranger over his knee and pounded hard on his back.

Drum stood, helpless. Daniel thought he was so tough. He would have fought the entire gang of men if they'd tried to cross the bridge. But Daniel couldn't swim. They must have tossed him over, then fired their guns to cover up his shouts for help. They'd claim he drowned if questioned, and Drum couldn't prove different.

Teagen kept pounding. Daniel's body bowed with each blow, and his arms and legs flapped.

Drummond hadn't protected his one friend, and Daniel didn't get to die a hero.

"Breathe!" Teagen ordered. "Breathe or I'll break your back."

Drum raised his hand to stop the next blow just as water poured from Daniel's mouth and he began spitting and cussing.

Teagen held Daniel's head down until it seemed he'd spat up half the river. When he let him up, the Ranger was as gray as a tombstone.

"Are you trying to kill me?" he sputtered. He gave Teagen a look that said he'd take a swing at the man if he had the energy.

Drum grabbed Daniel and pulled him up by his shirt. "Damn it, you scared a year off my life."

Daniel made no attempt to fight. "Well, pardon me. I was busy dying. I had two choices, stay underwater or be hit by the bullets slicing through the river just above my head."

All three men laughed. For men who didn't laugh easily, they roared. Daniel sat down and put his head on his knees. Drummond dropped by his side and fell backward. They were all three wet and cold and very much alive.

Teagen stood and helped both young Rangers to their feet. They rode back to the house and drank, while Martha put Thanksgiving dinner on the table.

"First warm day," Drum promised, "I'm going to teach you to swim. I don't know if my heart could take dragging my only friend out of the river again."

Daniel shook his head. "When I was a kid traveling around with my pa, he'd stop now and then and go back to his preaching ways. I was washed in the water every time we'd draw a crowd. Left me with a real fear of water over my head."

Daniel raised his glass. "I'm in both your debt."

Teagen drank then said, "That you are. As soon as you have a good meal, I want you and Drum riding toward town. Daniel, you stay close to the clinic to make sure everything is all right there. Drum, you know where Sage is headed. With luck, you'll catch up to her before nightfall. You stay with her until we come for you."

"Agreed," Drum answered.

"But if we go toward town, we'll be headed right into that gang again. I'm not looking forward to having to die again to keep from drowning."

"Take him through the pass," Teagen ordered.

Drum raised an eyebrow.

"Blindfolded," Teagen added.

Drum nodded. "Only one change in the plan. We leave now."

Daniel Torry stood. "I was afraid you were going to say that. Hanging around you is going to make a skeleton of me. I swear I'm going to find me a fat wife who loves to cook and quit this life before I'm nothing more than bone."

By the time the men had changed into dry clothes, Martha had packed them both food. Daniel was so grateful, he kissed her.

Drum hardly noticed the food. His mind was on reaching Sage before anyone else did.

CHAPTER 42

BONNIE WATCHED SAGE AND THE BOYS RIDE back toward the hills, turning northwest as they entered the tree line.

She hugged Bradford's side. "I've never had anyone to take care of me."

He pulled away. "You should have told me you were pregnant last night." His voice was rough with worry.

She smiled, remembering the sweet hours they'd spent together last night. "Why? Would you not have made love to me?"

He stared at her a minute then answered, "I might have only done it once."

"But I was the one who wanted it the second time."

He laughed as he kissed the top of her head. "You're going to be a hard woman to say no to."

She tugged him to the corner of the porch, and they talked for a while. Bradford would never be a man of many words. She guessed that they'd eat most of their meals together in silence, but she didn't mind. He was a hard man, worn by life, she imagined, but he had a kindness in his eyes when he looked at her, and that somehow was enough.

"Will you stay around to see this child into the world?" she asked, needing to know how long they had.

"If it's a girl, I'll be around for her wedding and more," he answered. "If you've no objection?"

She laid her hand over his in answer.

"I sold my land to the rancher next to my place a few days after I took you back to Galveston. I'd planned to go have a talk with you, but worries over my brother kept me out longer than I'd planned. When I reached town, no one knew or wanted to tell me where you were."

"How'd you find out?"

"I didn't. I just knew you were with the little doctor, and I'd seen her with the gunfighter, Drummond Roak. When I started asking where he was, the Rangers didn't mind telling me. I guess they figured I wasn't any kind of trouble Roak couldn't handle."

"But what will you do? You sold your home."

"It was just land. I can buy more. One thing this state's got plenty of is cheap land. If you're settling here, I could look for a place nearby." He studied her as if trying to find words she'd understand. "You could move in with me, if you'd be willing."

"That would not be proper."

He touched her belly. "We're a little late for proper. I'd marry you today, but I'd bet there's not a preacher within a hundred miles."

Bonnie looked up and noticed Daniel Torry riding toward her. She smiled. "I wouldn't be too sure."

She waited until Daniel reached the house and

listened while he explained that Drum saw Sage and the boys riding off, so he joined them.

When the Ranger climbed down from his horse, she introduced him to Bradford.

As the men shook hands, Bonnie said, "Get your Bible, Preacher Daniel, I've work for you to do." Marching into the house, she added, "I'll be ready in ten minutes."

Daniel shoved his hat back. "Who died?"

Bradford grinned. "I did." He laughed. "If I don't marry that pretty lady, she'll probably kill me. Either way, you'll make your dollar for the ceremony."

CHAPTER 43

DRUM CAUGHT UP TO SAGE AS SHE BEGAN TO climb the first hill. She didn't seem surprised to see him. He knew the boys had slowed her down coming through the secret passage.

He pulled his mount close to hers without a word. He could protect her and the boys now. He could breathe.

"How are things at the ranch?" she asked as if trying to make her words as casual as possible. "Is the company gone?"

"Yes," Drum answered, wishing she'd look at him. "As I was leaving, I saw the ranch hands riding in from the far pasture. The bridge will be well-guarded from now on, and I doubt one of the men we saw could swim the river."

Sage smiled. "I've only known one man who could do that besides my brothers."

He was glad she said *man* and not *boy*. "Teagen told me to make sure you and the boys stay with your grandfather until Travis can check into these 'legal rights' the stranger with the judge claims to have over the boys."

"You don't think he really could be related to them?"

Drum shook his head. "Even if I hadn't had the dream, I still wouldn't believe it possible. If he were the real thing, why would he bring what looks like every gunslinger from the gutters of Galveston to ride guard?"

They rode in silence for a while, then he finally said what had been bothering him for hours. "You know back there what you said about loving me?"

"I know," she answered without looking at him, but he didn't miss the blush on her cheek.

"Well." He had to speak his mind. "I don't want to hear you talking like that again."

"What?" Sage fired like he knew she would.

He was trying to have a conversation about something she said, and she looked like he'd slapped her. How could he explain how much he hated the word *love?* He could never admit to her how many times he'd heard his mother tell a man she loved him when half the time she didn't even know his name. And the drunks would always answer something back like, "You bet you will" or

"For three dollars, you'd better." What they'd done was in no way loving.

He wouldn't explain it to her. It was a world she'd never seen and probably couldn't understand. He grew up in places where love was a commodity to be bought and sold but never given.

So he did the only thing he could think of, he fired back. "Are you getting hard of hearing in your old age? I said I don't want to hear you say those words to me. It seems a simple enough request."

She kicked her horse, pulling away from him. "Order, you mean, and I don't take orders. But don't worry, you'll never hear them again. I must have gone mad for a moment to even have thought of saying them in the first place."

"Fine," he yelled back, letting her ride ahead.

He glanced back to see if the boys had heard anything he and Sage had talked about, but both Will and Andy looked like they were half asleep in their saddles.

When he turned to watch Sage, he heard Will whisper, "He was probably kicked in the head by a milk cow when he was a kid."

Andy answered, "That would explain it."

Drum rubbed his forehead. They were right. He'd handled Sage all wrong. Why couldn't she just be his woman and forget about foolish things like love? From what he'd seen outside the outlaw camps, love was no more than a cheap trick men and women used to manipulate one another.

He spent the rest of the afternoon looking at her back, and when they reached the camp, she seemed to get even less friendly. Once she walked by him and stomped on his foot. While he fought down a few swear words, he heard Grandfather laugh.

The boys saw the camp as a grand adventure after they got over their fears. Within an hour, they were running with boys their own age, learning the language one word at a time, and examining everything they came across.

Sage talked with her grandfather. She spoke the Apache language so fast, Drum didn't even try to keep up. He took care of the horses, watched the boys play, and wished he were anywhere but here. She might feel right at home among her mother's people, but they'd never been very friendly to him.

The women were building the cook fires by the time Sage stepped away from her grandfather. She walked toward Drum but stopped before she got within stomping distance. "We're welcome here. Grandfather says you can sleep down by the water. The boys can choose to sleep with me in an empty tent or with you outside." She stared at him with cold eyes. "They are welcome and protected either place, but you are not to enter the tent."

"I wasn't planning on it," he lied. "If the boys are safe, I plan to leave before dawn to hunt. The least I can do is bring game in for the meals."

"All right." She turned to leave.

"Sage," he stopped her with one word. "I didn't mean to make you so mad back there. I just don't like those words."

"I understand." It was her turn to lie.

"Good," he said, knowing she didn't. "Can we go back to being like we were and forget about it?"

She didn't answer. She just walked away, and he had a feeling the answer was no.

For the next three days, they walked around one another. He hunted, brought in meat, and she visited with the women while she watched the boys. As always, she learned of cures they used and doctored those who would let her help. Each day more herbs dried on poles beside her tent.

The only ones enjoying themselves were Will and Andy. Will was a natural diplomat. His easygoing manner and willingness to accept others served him well. Andy's ready smile made him friends, even if he did have trouble with the language. By the fourth day, he'd given up trying and began teaching English to the Apache.

Each evening, Drum sat across from Sage, watching her in the firelight. Here, among her mother's people, he could see the trace of Apache in her. With her hair in braids, she looked just as beautiful as she had the day he met her when she'd been all dressed up like a proper lady.

She never said good night to him, but Will and Andy always went down to the water with him to wash up before turning in. Drum got in the habit of telling them stories from books he'd read, but he never let them stay too late. Sage might need some time alone, but he didn't want her to worry about them.

They'd been in camp more than a week before he finally found himself alone with her. He'd returned to his campsite by the water to find her washing out the boys' clothes. For a while he stood watching her, wishing he could touch her. He needed her near as dearly as he needed air, but he wasn't about to tell her.

Finally, he walked to the water and squatted down five feet from her. "Talk to me, Sage. I miss you."

"I don't have anything to say and, if I did, I'd probably use the wrong words, and you'd bite my head off."

"I didn't bite your head off."

"Yes you did." She kept working, beating the clothes as he was sure she would have liked to beat on him.

He moved a few more feet away for safety and changed the subject. "God, how I've missed touching you. Sometimes at night I can almost feel your skin. You've got the softest skin in a few places. Like just under your breasts. I—"

"Stop it," she snapped. "You said you wouldn't speak of such things."

"Me? You're the one who didn't keep your word. You forgot about my one rule."

"I didn't forget. I decided you wouldn't be interested."

He frowned. "Doing my thinking for me now, Doc?"

"Well, somebody needs to. You obviously don't waste time doing any."

He took a step toward her and noticed the braves standing behind her at the tree line. Four men, all with arms folded. All watching. They might not hear or understand what he was saying, but he had no doubt that if he laid one hand on Sage, they had orders what to do.

Drum backed away. "You know, Sage, lately, I'm starting to believe in reincarnation."

She looked up at him as if he'd lost his mind.

"I figure I must have had an earlier life and done something terrible. That's why I've got to go through this life attracted to only one woman in the world and she determined to either kill me or drive me insane. No matter how I look at it, wanting you is terminal."

She didn't look like she cared.

He fought down his irritation. "But we made an agreement by your grandfather's time clock, and I've lived up to my half. You don't have to even talk to me, but I want you to meet me at the stand of oaks between here and the camp at dusk and live up to your word."

She stood and walked away without even looking back.

So much for being forceful, he thought. She'd come or stay in the camp, whichever she liked. He had a feeling his demands had very little to do with it.

How could he tell her that he didn't want to own her, or boss her around, or control her? He just wanted to be with her as an equal. But part of Sage was still the princess of Whispering Mountain, and part of him was still the outlaw kid. Until she saw him as her man, nothing would really change between them, even if he did kiss her.

Drum stayed away from the camp most of the afternoon. If his mood got any blacker, it would block the sun. He rode in and tied Satan to one of the oaks just as the sun was touching the horizon. Turning, he watched the sunset, not allowing himself to stare at the camp to see if she was coming.

He didn't wait long before he heard her steps, but he didn't move until she touched his arm. He turned and kissed her with all the longing he'd felt for days.

She was cold in his arms for a few seconds, then she warmed little by little. She wasn't kissing him back, but she wasn't protesting. He kissed her as tenderly as he could, even though every muscle in his body wanted to crush her against him.

When she pulled away, he fought for a moment before letting her go. She didn't say a word. They turned and walked toward the campfire. They weren't touching, but he no longer felt the cold.

As usual, they hadn't made peace, they'd only drawn a truce. It wasn't what either one of them wanted, but it would have to do.

As they ate, he said a few words to her, and she nodded. She passed him a slice of meat, and he thanked her. Drum spent the night alone, in thought. There were so many things about her he admired. He even found her temper fascinating to watch. The fact that she didn't like him most of the time didn't bother him; that fact hadn't changed in years. The fact that she wouldn't sleep with him did. He knew she wanted to. Maybe she was waiting for him to say the right words, but he wouldn't draw her in with fancy talk. If she came to him, she'd come for one reason: she couldn't stay away.

The next night she met him again. When he kissed her, he felt her warming in his arms. The kiss lasted a long time before she pulled away. As before, she turned without speaking to him.

"Good night," he whispered.

She didn't answer.

The following evening, she came to him wrapped in a blanket for warmth. Fog had moved in, making them seem even more isolated in the stand of trees. He gently pushed her against the trunk of the oak and opened the blanket. Then, leaning, he pressed his body hard against hers as he began the kiss.

She lifted her arms, enclosing them both with the blanket. He deepened the kiss as his hands brushed along her ribs. She reacted, pulling him to her and returning his kiss with passion. He laughed at the slight moan she whispered into his ear as his hand moved over her breast.

She was hungry for his touch. His wild Sage of fire could not stay ice for long.

As the sun's gray light faded and the oak branches shaded them completely, he slowly drove her mad with his caress. One thought crept in with all the feelings raging in his mind and body: He wondered if they could go a lifetime without talking and live each night like this. She was liquid fire in his arms, playful, loving, and demanding, and he was her mate.

When she pushed away, he let her go, even though every part of him wanted her to stay. She staggered, still out of breath.

"I'll walk you back," he whispered, pressing a kiss on her forehead.

"No," she said. "I'm all right."

He put his arm around her shoulders. "I'll see you to your door."

Thanks to the fog, they moved through the camp without seeing anyone, even though the sounds of people moving and talking drifted around them. Tonight the meal would be taken in tepees.

As they rounded her tent, he pulled her between the thick racks of leaves and plants she was drying. "I have to kiss you again. I'm not ready to say good night." He cupped her face. "Do you mind?"

"No," she answered, opening her blanket once more. "I'm also in the mood for more."

He'd sworn when he was ten that he'd never say he was sorry for anything he said or did, but as he unbuttoned her blouse, he found himself whispering, "Forgive me," even though, for the life of him, he couldn't remember doing anything wrong.

"I always do." She laughed as he shoved his hand beneath the material and gripped her breast still warm from his touch.

She leaned her head back as he lowered his mouth and tasted her flesh. "Yes," she whispered. "Yes."

His arm braced her back as he feasted on the softest spot he'd found. When he covered her wet breast with his hand and returned to her mouth, she melted against him in welcome.

She was his, warm and ready. She was his, he thought as he kissed her. She just didn't know it yet.

She was out of breath when he finally set her gently away from him.

"Come to me tonight, Sage. We're not finished."

She let him hold her for a while before she answered, "I'll think about it."

"Don't think. Come," he said as he let her go.

That night, around the small evening fire in Grandfather's tepee, neither said a word, but her gaze often rested on him, and he saw the passion building in her eyes.

The fog remained when he returned to his camp-site. Tonight he couldn't see the Apache tents, and he felt totally alone. He lit a small fire so she could find him if she came, then he lay down and waited.

It was after midnight when he heard her cross through the trees. The swish of her skirt against the tall grass made him smile. Without a word, he lifted the blanket and let her slip in beside him.

Her body was cold against his. For a while, he just held her, warming her.

"Are you sure?" he whispered into her hair.

"I'm sure," she answered. "To my great surprise, it seems you're the one man I can't live without. I don't want to live without."

He waited until her heart slowed, then he began making love to her. She was ready, welcoming him against her, moving as he moved, answering every touch with one of her own.

When he started to unbutton her blouse, she stopped him. "I can do it," she whispered.

"No. I'd like to, if you've no objection."

She moved her hand away. "All right. If it pleases you, go ahead."

"It pleases me greatly." He kissed her temple. "You made me very happy by coming tonight. Now it's my turn."

He leaned close and whispered of her beauty as his hands worked the buttons and ribbons free. She tried to unbutton his shirt, but her hands trembled, and he ended up rolling away to tug off his own clothes. When he returned and pulled her against him, she laughed nervously.

He brought her slowly to passion, taking time to caress every part of her. He pulled her hair free of the braids and wrapped it in his fist as he kissed her full and deep. When she was warm and shaking with need, he pressed his body over her, loving the way her soft curves molded against him in invitation.

When he pushed into her, she cried out softly, and he froze. Reason sliced through the desire, and he forced himself to lift his weight so that he was no longer crushing her, even though he didn't pull away.

"Am I hurting you?" he whispered in a voice raw with passion.

"No, not so much." She took a deep breath and relaxed against him. "I knew it would be uncomfortable; I was a virgin." Her voice was low as her body moved, begging him to continue.

He didn't know how that was possible. He didn't care as he brushed away a tear on her cheek. All he cared about was that she was his, all his, only his. He kissed her deeply as he began to move inside her, easing away the pain as passion built once more.

Hesitantly she moved with him, and he laughed at the pure joy of feeling her beneath him. It seemed he'd dreamed of this night all his life, and the magic of it was so much more than he'd thought it would be.

Swearing, he finished before he'd pleased her. She didn't seem to understand or mind.

He rolled to his side and whispered, "It'll be better next time."

"It was perfect," she whispered. "Very nice."

"No. It wasn't perfect, but it will be." He had to ask, "Are you sorry?"

"No," she answered, "and if it gets much better, I'll die from the joy of it." She cuddled beside him and fell asleep. He covered them both with the thick blanket and slept for the first time in weeks. Sage was with him.

At dawn, he came awake all at once as a shadow passed between him and the first beams of sunlight.

Drum pulled the blanket over her as he reached for his gun.

"No need for that gun." Daniel's familiar voice cracked the silence. "I best be getting my Bible out, though." He rifled through his saddlebag. "I swear I'm using the book more lately than the bottle. Something must be in the air."

"What do you think you're doing?" Drum smoothed her hair off Sage's face as he tucked the blanket tightly about her shoulders.

"I don't want to be around when her brothers find out what you have been doing up here. I figure the only way to save your life is to marry you two right and proper."

"We're already married," Drum insisted as Sage continued to sleep.

"Sure you are," Daniel said as if he didn't believe a word. He read a few lines, then said, "Do you take . . ."

"I do," Drum humored his friend.

"And do you, Doctor . . ."

"She does," Drum answered for her. "She already has." He shook her shoulder gently. "Wake up, wife. We've got unwanted company for breakfast."

Sage opened sleepy eyes and stared up at Daniel just as he said, "Then, I pronounce you man and wife."

She opened her mouth to object.

Daniel added, "If I were you two, I'd get dressed. I rode in with your brother Travis, and as soon as he says hello to the chief, he'll be looking for you."

Daniel swung back up on his horse. "I think I'd be wise to vanish until the gunfire settles. Travis being an old Ranger won't take to talking before he starts shooting."

Sage pulled the blanket over her head. "I think I'll lie right here and sleep."

"Oh, no, you don't." Drum stood, picking up his trousers. "You might sleep, but if they find you like this, I'm the one who'll die. Get dressed, wife."

She picked up her clothes and tried to put them on beneath the blanket. "Don't talk to me. I'm still not speaking to you, and don't call me wife."

"That's fine with me. How about we only com-municate in moans after midnight? As long as you're here all warm and willing at night, I'll become mute all day."

She tried to wiggle into her skirt. "Don't talk about it."

He grabbed his shirt. "Fine. While we're not talking, why don't you explain to me how it could be possible that you're a virgin?"

"Was a virgin," she corrected. "And I don't have to explain anything to you."

"But—"

"Oh, figure it out, Drummond."

He stopped dressing and watched her trying to button up her clothes without seeing them. "First"—he smiled—"why are you hiding while you dress? There isn't a freckle on you I haven't seen, touched, and probably kissed."

She saw his logic and tossed the blanket as she pulled her camisole over perfect breasts brushed by the sun.

"What's the second thing?" she asked as she laced up the silk with a ribbon.

Drum had forgotten. He was too busy staring. Finally when he was able to form words, he said, "Maybe we should both get back under the blanket."

She glanced up at him then and smiled, almost knocking the air from his lungs. "Not a chance," she said. "You told me to get dressed."

She was torturing him again, he thought, but about now he'd gladly die on the rack.

"Second," he managed to say, "your first husband must have been dead when you married him not to have touched you." The memories of their first kisses came back. "He didn't even kiss you, did he?"

Sage held her head high. "He was very involved in his work, and toward the end, he was very ill." She turned away, offering him a quick view of her backside as she slipped into her skirt.

Drum thought of saying they could be tossing dirt in his grave, and he'd still have touched her, but suddenly it hit him. He was her first. There was no first husband whom she'd slept with. He was her first. Just as she was his. That's why she hadn't said anything about their lovemaking not being right. She didn't know that there was more.

He frowned. That's also why he didn't do it right the first time. If he'd practiced, he would have been able to please her more, but practicing on another woman never seemed right.

He didn't see her tears until she turned around. He wondered if she was thinking of him or if she was sorry she'd given him such a precious gift. He knew she wanted him to say something to her. She probably wanted to hear the words of love that she'd said to him back at the ranch. But he couldn't say them. They rang too hollow in his mind. Couldn't she understand that he wanted her, needed her, every day of his life? Wasn't that enough?

"Are you sorry?" he had to ask one more time.

She looked up at him with unshed tears sparkling in her beautiful eyes. "No," she said. "I'll never be sorry." She hesitated, then added, "Thank you for waiting until I came to you, Drum. By doing so you told me a great deal about the measure of you as a man."

He was about to ask more when he heard a horse thundering toward them. "In-laws," he whispered, making her laugh.

CHAPTER 44

SAGE STEPPED INTO HER BOOTS JUST BEFORE her brother Travis rode into their small campsite by the water.

He lowered himself slowly as he always did, nursing an old injury. The big man was dressed today like he had when he'd been a Ranger, in buckskin. He walked right past her and offered his hand to Drum.

"Roak," Travis said in his voice that could out-shout an entire courtroom. "Grandfather tells me you are married to my sister."

Drum took his hand. "I'm probably the most married man you'll ever meet."

Travis laughed. "See that you remember that."

Drum shook his head. "Don't start threatening me, Travis."

"I don't have to. I know my sister. I'm guessing

she'd make herself a widow again before she'd put up with her man running around on her."

"I'm right here," Sage commented, but neither of them looked her direction.

"I'm sorry I took so long to come in from Austin, but Will hired me to do some legal work."

"Will?" Sage and Drum said at once.

Travis pointed at the coffeepot, and everyone knew the talking wouldn't start again until he had a cup in his hand. She filled the pot with water and coffee, while Drum built up the fire. While the water boiled, she braided her hair and looked very proper by the time Drum passed her a cup.

Travis took a drink and began. "Will's father told him to always keep the family Bible with him, no matter what, and if trouble came to give it to a judge worth trusting. I guess he figured I was close enough, so he put it in my care. Since then, I've been piecing together facts and guesses, and this is what I've come up with."

Sage held her breath. She knew she'd still be in danger, but maybe Travis had found a way to make the boys safe so they wouldn't worry about raiders returning to murder them.

Travis leaned in close. "The boys' father has a bit of royal blood in him. Seems he was sixth in line to the throne of some small European country. When he was about five, his father died under questionable circumstances. His mother watched her oldest boy take the throne and die within the year. Her next son took over, but she had three other sons who were still children. She sent them to live in Virginia for safety. Everything was fine for years. The second boy king married and had children, so everyone forgot about the royals growing up in Virginia as they moved farther and farther away from being in line for the throne."

"This sounds like some kind of fairy tale," Sage said.

"It gets better," Travis added, "or worse. The three boys must have grown up as Americans and probably had no reason to want to go back to an aging country in turmoil. That was fine with everyone until the king, their older brother, died in a fire.

"Here's where I start guessing. It seems one of the three American brothers was killed soon after his brother died in the fire. Another, the oldest of the three, left for parts unknown more than ten years ago. He's thought to be dead. The third, and youngest, was Will and Andy's father. He must have feared being killed, or he wouldn't have kept moving west."

"How can you know this?" Sage asked.

"Will's father kept a record along with the family tree of births and deaths. He also kept correspondence with a few family friends who helped him from time to time. One apparently bought the ranch for them. Too bad he didn't pick a safer place.

"A letter their father started but hadn't finished was tucked into the fold. In it he worries for the dead king's children and for his own. He said he felt there was a traitor among the American friends he trusted."

Sage looked up and saw Will standing quietly just behind Travis. "Will," she whispered.

He stepped forward like a little soldier. "I'm not going back to my father's country. Never. My father never wanted to have anything to do with them, and neither do I."

Travis put his arm around the boy. "You don't have to," he said. "I don't know who those men were at the bridge last week trying to take you, but I went all the way to the governor. I've applied to have Drummond here named your and Andy's legal guardian, if you have no objection."

Will fought back tears. "That would be all right with me and Andy."

"When you're an adult," Drum said, "if you want, I'll go with you back to where your father is from."

"No. I'll never ask. Andy and me belong here." He leaned his arm on Drum's shoulder. "Mr. Roak will protect us."

"You bet he will." Travis smiled. "Now you're married, you might as well have a family."

Drum smiled at Will. "Go get your brother. If we're going to be a family, we might as well start by having breakfast together."

As soon as the boy was far enough away that he couldn't hear them, Drum turned on Travis. "I'm not so sure I like you planning my life for me."

"Would you turn them away?"

"No," Drum admitted, "but my wife only likes me a few hours a night. What makes you think we'd be a good home for them?"

Travis stood and tossed the coffee. "You're a good man, Roak, and you know what it's like not to have anyone in the world to turn to. They'll be grown and out of the house before Sage and you have enough kids to fill the dinner table." He stared at the cup. "And by the way, you sure didn't marry my sister for her cooking skills. That's the worst coffee I've had in years."

Sage had heard enough. She turned to Travis. "I agree with Drum. Stop planning our life for us. What if the carriages and the hired guns come back?"

"They won't. They stayed around town looking for you for a few days, then headed south. I've got two men following them. My trackers sent two messages, saying they're still heading toward the coast."

"But they might return, and Drum can't promise he'll always be near," Sage said, thinking of what his next assignment might be. "He's a Ranger. You remember what that was like. You were away two years once."

Travis gave up. "All right. You win. I'll take them back to Austin with me."

"No," Drum said. "They are safer here. If they're my responsibility, I'll make the plans. For the time being, we'll keep them with us at Whispering Mountain, but not in Teagen's house. I'd be more comfortable in the barn. Anytime they leave the ranch, Daniel or I will be riding guard."

"You can have our place. Rainey's ready to get home to Austin, and I've got work piling up." He thought about it a minute and added, "Come spring, you and Sage might want to build your own place. I checked on that investment you made with that drunken sailor."

Sage felt lost again. "What investment? You loaned money to a drunk?"

Drum shrugged. "It seemed like a good idea at the time. I had money in the bank I wasn't using, so I signed papers so he could draw on it as needed." Before Sage could question, he asked Travis, "Is there enough money in my account to buy a house in town?"

Travis smiled. "There's enough to buy half the town."

Sage sat down on the blankets and gave up. Too much information, too fast.

Travis kept talking. "Mind my asking why you loaned a man you met in a saloon your savings?"

"I didn't need it." Drum shrugged. "And I saw the dream in his eyes."

Travis nodded as if Drum made sense and walked back toward camp. "See you back at the ranch," he said without turning around.

An hour later, the boys waved good-bye to Sage and Drum as they headed back to the ranch with Travis. They'd made friends in the camp. Will missed little. If trouble came, he knew he could get back to the ranch.

Drum had insisted he and Sage ride into town and spend a night or two at the hotel. He claimed he wasn't ready to face the entire McMurray clan just yet, and Sage needed to check on the clinic.

She had a feeling what he really wanted was a night with her in a real bed. In all the times she'd slept in his arms, they'd never once been in bed.

CHAPTER 45

SAGE AND DRUMMOND CHECKED INTO THE hotel and ordered dinner and baths delivered to the room. The desk clerk thought it strange they didn't use the same tub. After all, a tub full of water should be good for half a dozen scrubbings, but for an extra two dollars, he sent two tubs up with hot water for both.

With the food and wine waiting on the table, Sage stripped down and stepped into the tub. Drum did the same, making no pretense to follow her order not to look. He turned, watching her.

"Stop staring at me," she finally ordered.

"I can't. I spent years dreaming about what you'd look like without clothes and, I got to tell you, you look far better than I could imagine. I'm crazy about the way your—"

"Stop right there."

"Mind if I stare as long as I keep my mouth shut?"

She stepped out of the tub and reached for a towel. "I doubt if I can stop you."

He grinned, noticing she took her time drying off and letting him see slices of her body not completely covered by the towel. "You're so beautiful, Sage. I look forward to spending the rest of my life watching you."

She stopped and faced him, the towel dangerously low over her breasts. "We're truly married, I guess. I'm even bathing in front of you. Something I thought I'd never do, but I guess married couples make a habit of it."

He grinned, not surprised the idea was just registering. "You've always been my woman, Sage. From the first time I met you. It doesn't matter to me how many times we marry or don't marry; nothing changes that."

"But we've never talked of the things people plan, like children and where we'll live. There are so many things I don't know about you."

He stepped from the water and wrapped a towel around his waist. "You know I'd die to keep you safe." He crossed to stand in front of her. "You know you matter to me more than anyone ever has or ever will." He gently wrapped her in his arms. "And no matter how many fights we have, I'll still be dying to do this at the end of the day."

His mouth closed over hers before she could ask any more questions. Without breaking the kiss, he lifted her up and carried her to the bed. He tugged his towel off before he joined her. "I'm dying to hear those little moans you make." He shoved her towel down and gripped her breasts with the assurance of a man who knows his advance is welcomed.

When she moaned, he smiled down at her. "Like that," he whispered against her ear as his hand moved over her damp body. "How about we plan tonight and worry about the rest of our lives in the morning?"

She agreed as he moved over her. He kissed her long and deep as his body brushed hers. He smiled when she tried to pull him closer, her body begging for attention.

"All right, honey," he whispered against her ear as he gripped her thigh and eased her legs open. "I agree, it's time."

When he entered her, there was no resistance this time, and her body arched to meet his. He moved slowly at first, making sure she was climbing into passion with him. Her body was hot beneath him. When he felt her tighten and begin to shake, he pushed deep inside her and sent her over the edge of all control.

She clung to him, making little sounds of pleasure as he moved above her, then he tumbled out of control also, and they held each other, becoming one completely.

When he could form a thought, he rolled, pulling her against his side. He could feel her heart pounding against his. He pulled the covers over them both, but his hands still stroked her bare body. He'd discovered the round softness of her hips and decided that was now his favorite part of her to touch. His hand moved back to her breast, then her hip. He couldn't make up his mind. They were both wonderful. Maybe if he tasted them, it would help make up his mind.

"Drummond?" she whispered. "What are you thinking?"

"Nothing." He decided being brain dead was preferable to answering.

"Did you know it would be like that?"

"No, but I prayed it would."

She stretched, pushing her breasts against his side. He gripped her leg and pulled it over him, enjoying the feel of her inner thigh against his skin. God, he loved the feel of her, all soft and damp from their lovemaking. About the time he was considering kissing the inside of her thigh, she asked another question.

"Will it always be like that? Can we do it again?"

God bless her, he was crazy about every inch of this woman. "We can, and we will, but I'll need a little rest first." He had to think of some-thing, or she'd be the death of him tonight. "How about we eat before we start again? We've got all night."

She stretched again. He'd never thought of him-self being a man who'd die in bed, but the woman was definitely going to be the death of him. Drum smiled. He'd go without a single complaint.

Watching her stand, he almost forgot about the food. She slipped into his shirt. It hung almost to her knees, and she looked adorable. He stood and pulled on his trousers, already thinking about the next time between the sheets while she uncovered the dinner.

He moved behind her and lifted her hair so he could kiss her neck. She sighed and leaned against him.

He felt her shiver and knew this time it was from the cold. "I'll light the fire," he said, thinking he'd much rather have a fire than have her put on any more clothes.

As he lit the logs, he watched her.

"I love you, Drummond," she said calmly with her back to him.

"Don't say that." He fought to keep anger from his voice. What they'd just done was nothing like what his mother did for a living. "I don't want to hear it."

Sage faced him. She knew he'd never been loved. Maybe he couldn't accept it, but she would.

She'd tell him until he understood that she meant the words. "I love you," she said again, direct, without emotion in her voice. More slowly, she repeated, "I love you."

He stormed, "I said I didn't want to hear you say that. Never you."

Sage calmed enough to consider he might be completely mad. "Why?" she asked simply.

He stared out the window, knowing he had to be honest. No matter how ugly, there could be no secrets between them. "When I was little, I'd hide under my mother's bed at night. I heard her say those words to every man who came in. She didn't say them to me, only to them. Most of the time she'd be too drunk to remember their names so she'd just say, 'Course, I love you, mister. Leave the money on the table before we start, would you.' " He turned to her. "I don't want to ever hear you say those words. What we have . . . what we feel . . . what we do is nothing like her."

"I agree," Sage answered, looking down at the food. "But that doesn't stop me from loving you. No matter what you think, it's not a dirty word."

"Just don't—"

"Did she drink all the time?" Sage asked before he could finish the order.

He didn't look at her. "Yeah. From the time she got up."

Sage picked up the bottle of wine and hurled it at him.

Drum ducked a second before it hit his head.

"Then I shouldn't drink, because I'm nothing like her."

Drum raised an eyebrow. The woman who'd melted in his arms minutes ago was now fighting mad because he didn't see things her way. He smiled. That was his wife.

"Did she eat beef?" Sage asked as she picked up the plate of steak.

"Of course," he answered as the plate flew toward him. He ducked, but the corner caught him just above the eye.

"Did she eat vegetables?"

"Stop it, Sage!" Drum yelled as peas and corn slammed against the wall behind him.

"No." Sage stormed toward him. "I don't want to be anything like her. That's what you want, right? So I can't even tell you I love you."

"Stop." He shoved blood out of his eye, knowing the cut was more bothersome than bad.

"Love is just a word to you. A dirty word. Well, it's far more than that to me. It's not just a feeling, it's a commitment. I'm saying I want to spend the rest of my life with you, you idiot. I want to wake up every morning with you, fight over everything and nothing with you, and make mad love to you every night." She picked up the apple pie. "And I want to tell you every day that I love you without you comparing me to your mother."

He took the pie from her hand and set it back

on the table before he grinned at her. "Every day, Sage?"

"And night." She dabbed at his tiny cut with the napkin.

"So you want to be my woman. Only mine until we die. Is that what 'I love you' means to you when you say it?"

She understood what he'd been asking. "Yes." In his mind, that was how he asked her to marry him. It was his way of saying he loved her, and he'd been saying those words since he was a kid.

He pulled her roughly to him. "I am your man, Sage. I always have been."

She squealed and pulled away. "Not until we agree. I'll not have a marriage where you always get your way. If I can admit I'm your woman, you can sure as hell say you love me."

"I doubt we're in danger of you ever not getting your way." He knocked the chair over to reach her. "You're a spoiled brat."

She squealed again and darted away.

"Come here, wife!" he yelled. "When I catch you, I'll make you pay." He took one more step, slipped on peas, and hit the floor hard.

Sage crumpled, holding her sides, trying not to laugh.

The door to their room crashed to the floor. Teagen stormed in with his gun drawn. He took in the scene. The room was a mess. His sister was curled on the floor in a ball. Drum was flat on his back. "I told you if you ever hurt my sister, I'd kill you."

Drum had had it. Sage's big brother had threatened for the last time. "Well, just shoot me, Teagen. I'm tired of waiting for the bullet." He stood, wiping peas off his chest. "Don't waste time, considering that I'm the one bleeding here. You've got it in your head to kill me, so go ahead. Make another pile of dirt for Sage to cry over."

Sage tried to pull the shirt she wore down at least to her knees as she stood. "We were playing, not fighting. I got mad and tossed our dinner at him, not that it's any of your business, Teagen. What are you doing here, anyway?"

"I came to talk to Drummond alone about something important, and I thought I heard him beating you near to death."

She smiled. "I'm all right." She patted her big brother's cheek.

Drum felt sorry for Teagen. He'd been her protector all her life, and now he'd lost his job. She didn't need him anymore.

"I would never hurt your sister," Drum said. "I love her."

"What?" Sage stared at Drum as if she didn't believe what she'd heard.

He grinned. "I love you."

Sage turned her back to him. "Teagen, put that door back on its hinges and go home to your family. I'm fine. I'm with my man."

Teagen holstered his gun and backed out of the

room, still glaring at Drum. "I'll tell the clerk that you need another meal delivered, just in case you need something to throw at him." He picked up the door and set it in place. "What I came to say to you, Roak, can wait till morning. I'll meet you for coffee at dawn."

They heard Teagen storming down the stairs, probably waking anyone who might have slept through the fight.

"We've got to get us a place shouting distance away from my family," she mumbled to herself as she faced Drum. "Sit down so I can have a look at that cut."

"It's nothing," he said, but he turned the chair over and sat.

While she examined his cut, he slipped his hand beneath the shirt and brushed his fingers over her bottom.

She kissed the spot where the plate had hit him and whispered, "We're going to make love again tonight, aren't we?"

He breathed her in, loving the way she responded to his touch. "After we eat and the door gets locked solid. Not before. I don't want to be interrupted when I'm satisfying my wife."

He kept his promise. Once they'd had dinner, he made slow, passionate love to her. When she cuddled next to him and slipped into sleep, he whispered, "I love you, honey."

"I love you too," she answered.

CHAPTER 46

Long after dawn, Sage awoke alone. The night of lovemaking filled her thoughts. She no longer had any doubt about how much he cared for her. He'd spent most of the night showing her. She remembered the way he held her, the way he kissed her, the way he made her explode inside. Just thinking about it made her long for the night.

Slowly, she climbed out of bed. Her body was sore, her lips slightly swollen. She smiled. She'd been well-loved.

She washed and dressed, then went down to the café, where she guessed Drum must be still talking to Teagen. Knowing her brother, he'd sat on the porch all night, just in case they had another fight.

The desk clerk nodded politely when she passed. "Good morning, Mrs. Roak."

The name seemed strange, but like she had with Drummond, she'd get used to it. He couldn't have been more different than her first husband. With Barret, she'd felt needed. With Drum, she felt wanted. No, more than wanted . . . cherished.

Teagen was the only one in the café. Sage hid her disappointment. She wanted to see Drum. "Where is my husband?" she asked as she kissed Teagen on the cheek and took the seat next to him.

He frowned. "Now, don't get upset, Sage, but he's gone."

She felt like screaming, but she waited.

"We talked this morning, and he had to leave on a mission," Teagen rushed on. "I told him to go up and wake you, but he said if he saw you, he wasn't sure he could leave. We both knew no one else but him could do this job."

Her mind had been so full of the night and of loving Drum, it took her a minute for Teagen's words to register. The waitress gave her coffee and offered to bring a breakfast plate, but she shook her head.

Glancing out the window, she noticed Daniel Torry bounding up the steps. When he made it to the café, he came right to the table.

"Want to join us for breakfast, Daniel?" Teagen offered. "We're talking about Drum's mission."

"No, thanks. I eat my breakfast every morning at the bakery. I've put on a few pounds. That little baker tells me it looks good on me." He straddled a chair. "She won't serve me if she smells whiskey on me."

"You know about this mission?" she said to Daniel, not caring about his sweet tooth.

He nodded, his smile disappearing. "I offered to go with him, but he turned me down. Said it was too dangerous, and this time he needed me here more."

"What for?" Sage hadn't had enough sleep to piece together all the parts, but neither man with her was telling her what she wanted to hear.

"To watch over you and the boys," Daniel said. "His exact words were, 'Keep my family safe, and tell Sage I swear I'll be back.'"

Sage felt as if she were made of sand and someone had poked holes in her. All emotions drained out of her. "Tell me about this mission." She stared at Teagen.

He'd never lied to her or sugarcoated anything he'd ever told her, and he didn't lie now. "Word came from the trackers we put on the carriages when they left Whispering Mountain. One went to Galveston, carrying your almost relative and the judge. The other turned west and disappeared into Skull Alley."

"So, the count was behind the attempt?" she guessed.

Daniel cut in. "I talked with Miss Bonnie's new husband a few days ago, and he filled in the blanks. He's never been to Skull Alley, but his brother used to talk about what went on there and what the count was like."

"More than that." Teagen shook his head. "Travis figured out that Hanover, who calls himself Count, wants the boys dead because he's next in line to be king after them. He'll still have several to kill to reach the crown, but we figure he decided to start with his relatives here first. We think he's their father's brother, who disappeared years ago. If someone got the land for the Smiths, it could have been Hanover himself. He wanted them close so he could destroy that line of the family tree. If so, the boys will never be safe as long as he's alive and is hoping to be king one day."

"I always had the feeling he was behind not just the robbery at Shelley's gambling house but the raid on the boys' parents' place," Daniel jumped in again, excited that he'd figured out the puzzle first.

"We came to the same conclusion last night. Travis left at dawn for Austin, and Drum was saddling up before I could finish with the details. The count is getting ready to go back to Europe. He needed to clean up the loose ends here first, like relatives he didn't need showing up, and collecting enough money to travel back to his family in style."

Sage gripped her hands together on her lap as she asked, "What's Drummond's part in this?"

Neither Teagen nor Daniel seemed in a hurry to tell her.

Finally, her brother leaned forward and said, "He's going into Skull Alley to arrest Hanover. If that's not possible, Roak will leave him dead."

"He went into the outlaw camp of over fifty men, alone?"

"Sage." Teagen made her look up before he spoke. "That's what he does. He's the best any of us have ever seen. He works alone. He goes where not even Rangers will go, and he always finishes the mission."

Daniel agreed. "He's a legend. The best among the best. Half the Rangers don't even believe the tales told about him. Now and then he's paid big bounties for those he brings in, but this time, he didn't do it for the money."

"Why'd he do it this time?"

Daniel swallowed. "He told me he didn't want a dozen Rangers dying trying to get through Skull Alley, and someone had to stop the count." Daniel didn't meet her eyes. "He said he wanted Andy to sleep without nightmares and Will to stop looking over his shoulder."

"But Count Hanover is ill. He may already be dead. We heard that guard, Luther, tell us so."

"Maybe, maybe not. Luther could have been lying to throw us off."

Sage didn't want to think about Drummond going back to that horrible place alone. If they caught him, they wouldn't just kill him, they'd take pleasure in torturing him first. She reached for her coffee cup, but her hand shook so badly she was afraid to pick it up. It crossed her mind that she might go mad, thinking of the man she'd loved so completely last night riding straight into danger.

Teagen's big, rough hand covered both hers. "This is what he does, Sage. What he's good at, and you got to believe he'll be back soon. If he didn't think you could handle it, he would have never been able to leave."

She raised her chin. "I know." She felt Teagen's

solid strength moving into her. Drum was doing what he had to do, and now she had to do what women of warriors always had to do. She had to survive.

"Doc?" a man said from the doorway of the café.

Sage recognized him as Bonnie's cowboy. "Yes?"

"Bonnie sent me to see if you were still here. She said to tell you Mrs. Monroe's time is at hand, and it looks like twins."

Sage stood. "I'm on my way." She might not be able to help Drum right now, but she could do what she'd been born to do. "Grab my bag and the sack of herbs I brought down from the mountain. They're with the saddlebags in the lobby."

Teagen stood with her, and she saw the pride in his eyes. It seemed the fact that his little sister was a doctor had just struck him.

She followed Bradford out of the hotel and climbed in the buggy. He drove with a great deal of skill and speed to a shack at the other end of the town.

As they walked in, he carried her bags. "What can I do to help?"

She looked at him, still wondering where Bonnie had managed to find him. "Keep the husband busy. This may take a while."

Bradford nodded as they stepped into a dirty two-room cabin. The place smelled of rotting food and urine. Sage fought to keep from gagging as she crossed the first room and passed by a moth-eaten curtain into the bedroom.

Bonnie was already there. She'd cleaned off a small table and shoved enough clutter aside for Sage to walk around the bed. Phoebe Monroe lay on the bed curled into a ball.

Wide-eyed, she looked up at Sage. "Doc, I hurt. I hurt real bad."

Sage sat on the dirty bedcovers and said in a calm voice, "I'm going to help you, but you've got a lot of work to do."

Phoebe nodded. "The baby's got to come out. I know that much, but it feels like it's going to split me in half."

She brushed the girl's hair back. "How old are you, Phoebe?"

"I'll be fifteen next month. Fred tells me to tell folks I'm eighteen, but you're a doctor, you'd probably know better."

"Fred is your husband?"

"He says he wants to be soon as he gets work regular."

Sage looked through the crack in the curtain. The boy in the next room with Bradford didn't look much older than Phoebe.

Bonnie stepped close. "If you think we've got time, I'd like to go after some clean sheets." She didn't say more. She didn't have to.

Sage nodded. "Tell Fred to start boiling water."

Sage began her work. With Bonnie's help, they

bathed the girl and made her as comfortable as they could as the contractions grew closer together. She was young, but Phoebe was brave.

She had to be, Sage thought, to run away with Fred.

Hours passed, and Bradford brought more lamps in for light. He didn't say anything, but Sage saw the way he looked at Bonnie. The young girl on the bed was not his problem. The woman leaning over her for hours was.

When Bonnie stepped out for more water, she returned and said, "Bradford made a potato soup and coffee. He said he'd keep it warm for whenever we have time to eat."

"He can cook?" Sage smiled. "Where did you find this man, Bonnie?"

"He kidnapped me," she answered as calmly as if she'd said she'd met him at a church social.

Phoebe's next contraction drew them back to their work. A little after dawn, Sage delivered twins, one girl and one boy, both healthy.

When she went out to tell Fred, she almost didn't recognize the main room. It had been cleaned spotless. All the trash was gone. The dirt floor had been swept, and a stack of clean dishes sat on a shelf above the pump.

"Who did this?" she asked a dozing Bradford.

"You told me to keep him busy. Cleaning was all I could think of. We did laundry and chopped wood until dark, then we started on this room."

He glanced over at Fred, sleeping with his head resting on a log. "He's a little tired."

When she touched the boy's shoulder, he bolted upright. "Phoebe," he said. "How is Phoebe?"

"She's fine. You want to see your children?"

Fred rubbed his eyes and followed her into the little room. As they marveled over their babies, Sage whispered to Bradford, "Take Bonnie home and see that she gets some sleep, would you?"

He nodded.

"I'll stay here all day helping out. When you come to get me, bring a box of groceries and whatever you think the babies will need."

Bradford whispered, "It's time these two grew up."

Sage agreed as Fred climbed in bed beside Phoebe and went to sleep. "When I leave tonight will be soon enough."

"Anything else I can do, Doc?"

She smiled. "Yes, ask Elmo at the trading post if he knows where this kid can find regular work, and tell Daniel Torry to get his Bible out."

Sage spent most of the day teaching Phoebe to hold and care for her babies while the new father slept.

That evening, Bradford returned alone with all the supplies he could fit into the buggy. Apparently, Elmo got the word out, and several mothers, no longer needing cribs, donated all the things the babies would need.

Sage gave Fred both the babies and helped bring in the supplies.

She heard Bradford say to the young father, "I brought twenty pounds of potatoes. You know how to make the soup, so make it every night when Phoebe is too busy or too tired. Before you run out of the potatoes, I'll be over to teach you how to do stew. A man, even one with a wife, needs to know how to cook a few things to survive."

Fred nodded. "Thanks, Mr. Summerfield."

"You can call me Brad. You're a man now."

Sage smiled all the way home. As they climbed out of the buggy, she had to ask, "Where did Bonnie find such a wise man?"

He tipped his hat at the compliment and answered simply, "She kidnapped me."

Sage ate a few bites, then went upstairs to her little room. Someone, probably Bradford, she guessed, had collected her things from the hotel. In among them was Drummond's shirt.

She slipped into it and crawled into bed. He'd been gone two days, and she'd survived. If she was going to love him, she had to accept what he did for a living. Closing her eyes, she slept without dreams. She'd save the dreams until she was back with her man.

CHAPTER 47

DRUM RODE AS HARD AS HE COULD PUSH Satan over land cold and dead with winter. When he did stop for a few hours' rest, he forced himself to think only of the count and the danger the boys were in. The memory of Will and Andy's mother all beaten and broken would have made him volunteer for the job, even if Hanover wasn't a threat to Sage. Knowing he was left no question of what had to be done.

When Drum reached the mission at Goliad, a Ranger, sleeping down by the Guadalupe River, was waiting for him. Captain Harmon had sent him with word that the guard, Luther Waddell, was released for lack of evidence. No witness could put him at or near either the raid on the Smith place or the robbery at Shelley's gambling house. Just being a guard for Hanover wasn't a crime.

"Cap had him followed," the Ranger reported to Roak. "He was seen walking into Shelley Lander's place. Then he disappeared. He's either still there, or he somehow slipped out after dark by boat."

"Why'd you ride so far to tell me this?" Drum asked as they walked along the outside of the mission chapel. Hundreds of men, fighting for Texas independence, had died here, shot by a firing squad. The McMurrays had told him once that their father was among the dead. His body lay in the mass grave beyond the mission walls.

Drum swore he could feel the ghosts walking beside him, even though it had been more than twenty years since the Alamo and Goliad missions fell.

"The cap thought you might stop here to spend a night or two. He wanted you to know Luther was free."

He didn't have to say more. This was a frequent relay point for Rangers, a place where they could pass messages without worry, a place where they could rest up if hurt or hide out if running from trouble. No one spoke of it, but Drum figured the Rangers considered themselves protected or at least watched over by the spirits of the brave buried here.

Pulling out a scrap of paper, Drum wrote three words on it. "Give this to no one but Captain Harmon. Tell him it's from me."

The Ranger glanced at the paper. " 'I'm going in,' " he read. "That's the message?"

Drum nodded and stepped into the shadows of the mission. The young Ranger was still asking questions when Drum crossed the yard and rode away unseen.

He rode all night and slept in places where no one would find him. As he moved, he planned. Drum hated it, but he'd have to leave Satan and go in the back way. The horse was lucky to have made it once down the steep incline without breaking a leg; he'd never make it up. On foot it would mean an extra day, but he'd risk it. He'd also have to travel light: less guns, less supplies, less prepared.

By the time he reached the foot of the incline, he'd planned every detail. He slept off and on until sundown and then began the journey up the incline and through the caves to the outskirts of the outlaw camp.

It was almost dawn when he reached the edge of the back pasture. He knew he couldn't make it across before sunup, so he climbed into a tree and found a secure place to sleep until dark.

He almost laughed, remembering how he'd fallen out of trees a few times before he perfected this sleeping method. It wasn't comfortable, but it was definitely safer. Men hunting him tended to study the ground. He made a habit of leaving footprints heading away from the tree. The dried leaves still hanging to the branches offered him some cover, but the ones on the ground offered him an alarm system if anyone walked near.

Drum slept. In his dreams he couldn't push Sage to the back of his mind. She was with him, cuddled against his side.

The wind kicked up in late afternoon, and the air turned to freezing. Drum barely noticed the cold. His mind was full of what he had to do. He slipped silently down from the tree and moved as a shadow across the pasture.

When he reached the dark side of the barn, he stood and listened as he watched the house Daniel Torry had said looked as if it could be where Luther's wife and child might be staying.

Nothing. Not a sound. If she and the boy were inside, they'd gone to bed before dark.

Drum waited until all sounds died in the village, then he walked the shadows toward the big house. The count's house.

A guard sat on the corner of the front porch railing, his gun over his leg as he smoked.

Moving around back, Drum wasn't surprised to find the second guard asleep by the back door.

Silently, he slipped to the side of the house and climbed up to the second floor. People often lock their doors and windows on the first floor but rarely on the second. The third window he tried opened easily.

He slipped into the room, which was cold and dark. Furniture was scattered about among boxes. Crossing carefully, he opened the door and saw a lamp burning low outside the last door.

He walked down the hallway and opened the last door. The smell of a sickroom floated on the stale air as he looked in. A man, thin and pale, lay in the middle of a big bed. He looked asleep, but even awake, he didn't look strong enough to fight.

Drum slipped his gun from its holster and moved inside.

Candles burned on both sides of the man, but the

rest of the room was dark. A fire crackled in the corner fireplace. A teapot, giving off the smell of burned berries, sat on the bricks of the hearth.

Drum moved to the bed, knowing what he had to do.

"If you shoot him," a voice came from the shadows, "half the men in town will be waiting for you when you step out of this place."

Drum fought the urge to fire into the darkness. "Who are you?"

"I'm Myron, the count's butler." He took a deep breath. "And I'm a prisoner here, Mr. Roak, just as you will be unless we are both very careful."

A short, chubby man moved into the light. His clothes were worn but clean, and Drum noticed bruises fading on his face. He'd been beaten recently.

Myron must have known what Drum saw, for the man raised his head slightly. "He's been too weak to beat me for a week. He's left orders that I'm to be killed when he dies as if I'm not more than a pet to him."

"How do you know who I am?" Drum remembered Sage speaking of Myron. She'd said he'd tried to help her. That fact was all that was keeping the butler alive right now.

"Luther told me you'd be coming." Myron smiled. "How is the little doctor?"

Drum wasn't here to pass the time of day. "If you know who I am, you know I've come here to

404

kill him. Arresting him and getting him out of here would be impossible."

Drum watched the man in the bed, who showed no sign of waking. "What's wrong with him?"

Myron held his hands palm up. "I've been poisoning him for weeks. Just enough to make him weak, not enough to kill him. Luther said you'd come, and when you did, we'd have to be ready to go out a secret way with you."

Drum frowned. "I don't take passengers."

"You have to. When you kill him, I have to escape, and Luther says he can get his family out in the chaos that follows."

Footsteps sounded.

"That'll be the guard change at midnight. Step into the shadows."

Drum kept his gun on the door, but he did what Myron said.

The door opened, and the guard Drum had met weeks ago stepped in. "How's the count?" Luther mumbled as he closed the door.

"Drum's here," Myron whispered.

Luther's body stiffened, but he didn't go for his gun.

"How'd you know I would come?" Drum asked.

Luther glanced around the room, trying to locate the direction the question had come from. "I knew the minute the count came up with the scheme to go after the boys. He might have been able to pull it off, but he wanted the doctor too, and I

405

knew you'd never allow that. I also figured you wouldn't want her living with the fear of the count trying to kidnap her. So your only option was to come back here and end it all."

"And the price of your silence?" Drum asked.

"You take us with you. The next guard change is at noon. We've no time to waste."

Drum looked at the count. Killing a man in a gunfight or who was about to kill someone else was one thing. Killing a man in cold blood was something he'd never done.

"We take him with us." Drum knew it wasn't smart, but it was his only choice. "He'll stand trial for what he's done." He looked at the two men. "It's the only way I'll take you with me."

Luther nodded. "My wife and son are sleeping next door in a storage room. I'll go get them and be right back. They've been packed and waiting every night for a week."

Myron went to the fireplace. "We can tie him on a stretcher. He's lost so much weight, he won't be hard to carry. I'll give him a dose of tea that will keep him sound asleep."

Drum crossed to the windows. What he was about to do was crazy. He got in, he could get out without too much trouble, but it would be near impossible with others along.

Myron produced a lantern full of oil with the wick burning low. "I thought I'd put this by the front door. When anyone opens the door, it'll spill and cause a fire. That should give us a little more time."

"Good idea." Drum doubted it would help, but the little man was trying.

Just when he thought it couldn't get worse, Luther returned. He not only had his wife but three other women and several children.

"We can't take all of them," Drum said, not wanting to hear their stories. He could see it in their faces. They'd all been abused. "We can't."

A little boy moved under Luther's arm. Frightened eyes silently stared at Drum.

None of them moved or begged. Drum shook his head. "You all have to know, if you go with me there's a good chance you die. If they get within firing distance of us, we'll all be shot."

"We're dead already here," one woman said.

Luther and Myron were strapping the count to the stretcher and covered him with a dark blanket.

Luther whispered as he worked, "I'm the back guard tonight. No one will check on me until after first light. I figured out you released the horses in the pasture when you escaped before because that's the way you went, but I can't find any way out. I've crawled over those rocks for days."

"North," Drum answered. "Straight north over the rocks and into a small tunnel to a cave."

"I've got a wagon out back. If we stay on the road, we'll leave no trail until we have to leave the wagon and start climbing."

"Good enough." Drum looked at the women. "Everyone including the children carries water."

They moved silently down the back stairs and out into the night. Once the stretcher was loaded, the women crowded into the wagon, and Myron took the bench with Luther.

"I'll meet you at the rocks," Drum said. He didn't need to explain that he didn't trust either man. He knew he could run straight across the pasture in half the time Luther could circle around. That gave him a few minutes to set up more lanterns in the house, the storage rooms, and the laundry. The buildings were so close together, there was a good chance that if one burned, others would catch as well.

Luther nodded and headed down the back alley toward the north.

Drum climbed to the roof and watched the house for a while to make sure no one saw the wagon leave, then he climbed down and ran toward the pasture.

The wagon was there when he arrived. He looked at Luther. "I'll move the women in and come back for you. Meet me up there," he pointed a hundred feet above, "after you get rid of the wagon."

Luther agreed. "I'll leave it in the barn with a lantern propped against the door."

Drum led the women as Myron and one of the older boys carried the stretcher. The climb wasn't easy, but no one complained. It took him two hours to get them into the cave and go back for Luther.

The count hadn't moved. Luck seemed with them.

Luther was waiting when Drum returned, hidden in the rocks but watching the pasture. "I didn't think we'd make it this far," he said. "Until now, I figured this was suicide. I'm thinking we might have a chance."

They hurried back to the cave. He'd taken the women deep enough so that they could light a fire. When he saw them, he froze. They weren't asleep, as he'd thought they would be, but circled around the stretcher as if in prayer.

Myron stood when he heard Drum. "The count's dead," he said. "I must have killed him with too much sleeping potion."

Drum walked closer to the body.

"No," a woman whispered. "I killed him. I stabbed him when we were in the wagon. He had my husband killed a month ago and told every-one not to feed me but to let me starve."

"No." Another woman raised her chin. "I killed him. I held his mouth and nose so he couldn't breathe just like he did my baby's."

"I poked a needle in his heart," an older woman said.

Drum frowned. "How many of you killed him?"

All the women raised their hands.

"Well, I can't take you all in. What do you think, Luther?"

The guard lifted the body and tossed it into a cavern in the floor of the cave. "He died in an accident," Luther said matter-of-factly.

Drum didn't have time or want to argue. "All right. We have to get to the other end of the cave before we stop for the night. Then we'll rest and move at dusk again."

Everyone stood.

As they moved silently through the cave, Drum planned what he would do once they got past the slope. He'd circle back and pick up Satan and disappear. Now, that wasn't going to be easy.

They slept the day away. Drum walked back far enough to see the fires. It looked like the lanterns had done their job. Half the settlement seemed ablaze.

That night, with only the moon for light, he showed the women how to move down the slope. Several tumbled and rolled, but not one complained. Drum headed them east toward Galveston with Luther in the lead, while he backtracked to get Satan. When he caught up with them, he was surprised at the progress they'd made.

Drum scouted ahead, moving them by day when there was cover and by night when they were in open country. He also rode away from them to hunt game and managed to have a deer or rabbits skinned and waiting by the time they made camp.

Luther and he took turns at guard, but Drum rarely slept. The small band was following the same path he and Sage had traveled, and that knowledge made him ache each night for her. During the days, he did his job, but he felt something he'd never felt deep in his gut. This was the last time, the last mission. When he made it back to Sage, he'd never leave again.

By the time they reached Galveston, all were too exhausted to even talk. They made quite a sight walking into town, dirty and thin. Drum turned them over to the captain's care and checked into the same hotel room he'd shared with Sage in what seemed like a lifetime ago.

He closed his eyes, remembering how they'd both slept that night and how she'd been afraid to walk through the hotel lobbies so late. He'd kissed her before dawn that night. Really kissed her for the first time.

Finally, he slept, lost in dreams of his wife.

At daybreak, he cleaned up and went to have a talk with the captain.

By noon the next day, he headed home, no longer wearing the Ranger badge on his shirt.

CHAPTER 48

Sage had worked all day patching up three men who'd been hurt while roofing the new schoolhouse. One had a broken arm, another a fractured bone in his leg, and the third had suffered a puncture wound in his side that was still bleeding. She kept all three in the clinic for the night.

Bonnie offered to stay, but Sage said she'd take the next few hours. Bradford was already waiting for his wife in the buggy. He'd been helping out at the clinic when he wasn't building a house on a piece of land a mile from town. He said he didn't plan to ranch or farm, but he wanted to make harnesses and saw a living in the work. When Sage asked why he needed to be a mile from town to do that, Bradford simply replied that he didn't like people all that much.

Sage smiled as she watched them leave for a picnic out on their land. The cowboy might not like folks much, but he was crazy about Bonnie. It had been almost two months since Drum left, and Bonnie was starting to show. The cowboy was so protective of his wife, Sage wouldn't have been surprised if he started carrying her to the buggy.

Sage touched her own middle, wishing she'd gotten pregnant that night with Drum. At least then she'd have a part of him. Now, she had nothing. No news. She didn't even know if he was alive or dead.

"Evening," Daniel Torry said as he came around the corner of the house.

"Evening." Sage smiled. Daniel stopped by two or three times a day just to check on her. He also rode along with the boys to school and back when they stayed with her in town.

"It's going to be a nice night," he said, smiling.

Sage almost laughed at his effort at conversation. "Another month, and we'll see spring."

He swung over the railing and took his chair on the porch. "I thought I'd stay here and watch over the clinic for you until Miss Bonnie gets back."

"That's nice, but I'm not going anywhere."

He grinned wider. "I thought you might want to take my horse and ride in to see the new sheriff in town."

"Not interested."

"He's due to be sworn in before dark."

"Still not interested." In this size of town she'd meet him soon enough.

Daniel kept smiling. "Not even if he sent you an invitation?"

"He did?"

"Well, kind of. He told me to go tell his woman he wanted her next to him."

Sage was off the porch and running to Daniel's horse before he finished. She was at full gallop, only half aware that Daniel was laughing.

Several men stepped aside as she rode to the newly constructed sheriff's office.

A lean man dressed in black turned in time to catch her as she jumped from the horse.

"You're home!" She hugged him, not caring that half the town was watching.

He swung her around. "I missed you, honey."

He kissed her once, then straightened. "Let's

get this over with so we can go somewhere a little less public." He glanced toward the hotel.

"Agreed," she whispered and took his arm.

As they stepped up to the marshal, Drum held her close. She listened as he took the oath and accepted a sheriff's star. Then everyone was congratulating him and hugging her.

Through it all, she felt his hand on her, holding her, touching her.

When things had settled, he whispered, "I got us the same room at the hotel. Dinner will be waiting." He laughed against her ear. "I had to pay double for him to let us in, so try not to be so much trouble."

They crossed the street and went up to their room.

She didn't want to argue or even talk, but she had to ask, "Why didn't you come to me first?"

He pulled off his coat and guns. "I knew if I did, it'd be days before I took the oath, and I wanted you to know that I'm staying put right here in Anderson's Glen. I'm never planning on leaving you again."

"But you're the best, Drum. I'd understand. I could survive."

He pulled her to him. "I don't want you to just survive. I want you safe and happy. Besides, I plan on working hard to be the best at something else."

"Really, what?" She laughed as he undressed her.

"At loving you," he whispered, "just the way you like to be loved."

Center Point Publishing

600 Brooks Road ● PO Box 1
Thorndike ME 04986-0001 USA

(207) 568-3717

US & Canada:
1 800 929-9108
www.centerpointlargeprint.com

/